BASTIAN:
THE LORDS OF SATYR

BASTIAN:
THE LORDS OF SATYR

ELIZABETH AMBER

APHRODISIA

KENSINGTON PUBLISHING CORP.
www.kensingtonbooks.com

APHRODISIA BOOKS are published by

Kensington Publishing Corp.
119 West 40th Street
New York, NY 10018

All Kensington titles, imprints, and distributed lines are available at special quantity discounts for bulk purchases for sales promotion, premiums, fund-raising, and educational or institutional use.

Special book excerpts or customized printings can also be created to fit specific needs. For details, write or phone the office of the Kensington Special Sales Manager: Kensington Publishing Corp., 119 West 40th Street, New York, NY 10018. Attn. Special Sales Department. Phone: 1-800-221-2647.

Aphrodisia and the A logo Reg. U.S. Pat. & TM Off.

ISBN-13: 978-0-7582-4130-6
ISBN-10: 0-7582-4130-5

First Kensington Trade Paperback Printing: May 2011

10 9 8 7 6 5 4 3 2 1

Printed in the United States of America

For Nancy Bristow, Tracey Anderson, Annette Stone, Dani Keith, Kimberley Sutton, Katie Seely, and the many wonderful, supportive members of my e-newsletter group at http://groups.yahoo.com/group/ElizabethAmber.

And for you. I hope you enjoy Bastian's story.

—Elizabeth Amber

The Satyr Clan in Rome
(Descended from Bacchus, the Roman God of Wine)

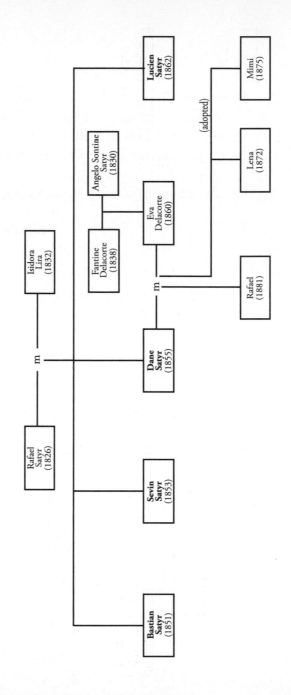

The Satyr Clan in Tuscany
(Descended from Bacchus, the Roman God of Wine)

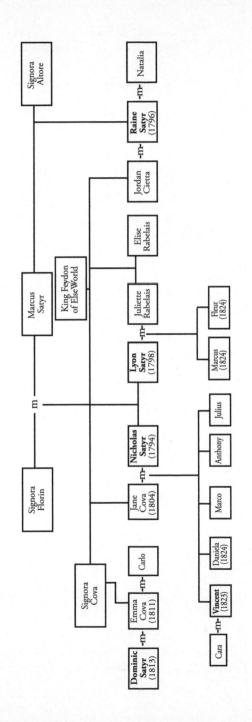

PROLOGUE

In centuries past, many of the Satyr secretly dwelled throughout Italy, working in the vineyards of the wine god, Bacchus. After a Great Sickness arose, many perished, and few remain now to protect the sacred gate between Earth and ElseWorld, a parallel realm populated by creatures of myth.

Within a corridor of lands that extends from Tuscany southward to Rome, all is so thoroughly bespelled that ElseWorld immigrants largely go unnoticed. Still, the magic that cloaks this territory is fragile, and discovery by humans is a constant threat to a small clan of Satyr lords in Rome. These four brothers—Bastian, Sevin, Dane, and Lucien—are of ancient royal blood and have been entrusted with safeguarding their ancestors' artifacts and antiquities, which are now under excavation in the Roman Forum.

Upon the coming of each new month, their blood beckons them to heed the full moon's call to mate. To deny this carnal call is to perish. To heed it, bliss.

Scena Antica I

February 2, 374 A.D.
Roman Forum

"Where are we going, Mother?" six-year-old Silvia asked, skipping excitedly. She had no inkling that her destiny was about to be decided as she walked with her parents toward the Roman Forum.

"Hush, child," came the sharp reply.

"Father?" Silvia persisted, turning her clear blue eyes his way. He sent her a pained expression. "Do as your mother says."

But Silvia knew she could always coax him from his moods. She tried to take his hand, but for once, he shook her off.

Her mother sent him a condemning look. "I see how your eyes and hands linger on her; don't think I don't."

"I love her."

Her mother snorted. "A perverted love."

Her father was rarely angry, but his voice turned tight with anger now. "She's my only daughter. I'm not going to do anything to hurt her."

"Not today maybe, but she's only six," her mother went on, her *voice accusing.* "What of when she's older?" She snatched Silvia by the wrist—careful not to touch the palm of her hand—and led her off again. Her father followed more slowly.

A crowd had gathered in the Forum near one of the temples. There were other girls there, too, all about her age, standing in a group. And in their midst stood her uncle, studying them with an intent gaze. Something about the avid, waiting quality of the on-lookers frightened Silvia, reminding her of the bloodthirsty audiences in the Coliseum during the gladiator fights. She tried to hang back.

"It's the ceremony to choose the Virgins," her mother scolded. "It's an honor to be considered."

"No! I don't want to go!" Silvia jerked from her hold and ran to wrap her arms around her father's waist.

He groaned and held her away. "Cara, you can't stay with us, do you understand? If you do, I worry that I'll—I'll hurt you. Your mother is right about that." He released her and gave her a shove toward her mother, who stood glowering at them.

"Don't you love me?" Silvia asked him in a small voice.

His gaze slid over her; then he ran a hand over his face, looking beaten. "Too much, Silvia. I love you too much. You're special. A temptation to any man. Service in the temple is what you were born for, with those hands of yours. Go. You are to do as your Uncle Pontifex instructs you. Don't ever return to us." With that, he turned his back on her and left them for home.

But Silvia ran after him again, grabbing his arm, begging him not to leave her. "If I'm good and do as Pontifex bids me, will you let me come home again?"

Her mother wrenched her away from him and pulled her by the scruff of her neck toward the Forum again. "Don't touch him with your devil's hands, child."

Silvia stared at her hands. Her wretched hands. Her own father had turned away from her because of them. She wished she could cut them off, if only it would make him look at her with affection again.

Instead, she did as her father wished and let her mother take her to the Forum and place her hand in that of her uncle, Pontifex Maximus. He felt its strange and terrible warmth, and smiled at her mother. "Yes, you were right about her. Even her hair is like fire."

He smoothed his palm over Silvia's wild, red-gold hair and lifted her pointed chin. "Come, Amata. Come join the others."

"I want to go home," she whispered.

"This is your home now, little fey," she was told. As he tugged her toward the temple, she watched her mother depart with a bag full of coins, payment for surrendering her.

And so it was that at the tender age of six, Silvia found herself inducted into the service of Vesta, Goddess of Fire.

1

Esquiline Hill, Rome, Italy
Earth World, February 1881

Lord Bastian Satyr was certainly a big one.

With an experienced eye, Silvia sized him up in a long, sweeping glance as she stood at the foot of his bed, her arm loosely wrapped around a bedpost corded with carven grapevines.

Dark, cropped hair; broad, sculpted shoulders; a pronounced indentation running the length of his spine; powerful thighs and buttocks; flesh glistening from his exertions; knees dug into the bedcovers between the smooth, stockinged thighs of his bed partner.

Michaela looked so vulnerable and feminine lying in his enormous bed, under his enormous, straining warrior's body. Her slender calves hugged his hips. Her body was open to receive each thrust of his organ. Silvia could only employ her imagination regarding how sizable that portion of his male anatomy might be. From her vantage point, all she could see was his backside. His naked backside. His naked, flexing backside.

She swallowed, her throat strangely dry. By firelight, he was magnificent—a golden god. Which just possibly made him worthy of the woman he was riding. Michaela was her closest, dearest friend in both worlds. Had been since their childhood in Vesta's temple.

Silvia had always watched over her as best she could. And when it came to hedonistic matters such as these, had lived vicariously through her. Tonight was no exception.

Michaela had been born a Companion, a courtesan with the power to please any man. Like most in her profession, she had taken hundreds, if not thousands, of lovers over the centuries. She always chose them carefully. That in itself told Silvia that this particular specimen of manhood must be something quite extraordinary.

Confident that neither of them could see her in her current form, she meandered around the perimeter of the bed, pausing at the sight of the confectioner's box on the bedside table. *Cioccolato. Mmm.* There were few things that could have drawn her attention away from the carnal display on the bed, even momentarily, but chocolate was one of them. She bent and put her nose to it, inhaling deeply, wishing she could smell the sweet delicacies hidden inside the gay wrapping. But she was an Ephemeral, and when in a noncorporeal state as she was now, her sense of smell was nonexistent. She didn't dare partake of them or do anything else that might draw the notice of the room's other two occupants. But, Gods, she was starving.

At least the room was warm. The February wind was cruel outside these walls. She'd been half frozen on her way here. She moved to the hearth and held her hands to the fire.

Behind her, Lord Satyr was taking his time, rutting with long, vigorous strokes that caused his bed to lurch and shudder, and that had Michaela sighing with pleasure. She glanced over her shoulder at them. They looked so perfect together. His incredible masculine body moving on Michaela's exquisitely feminine one. His flesh darkened by his heritage and the sun. Hers a smooth, olive perfection that was so unlike Silvia's own flawed, pale flesh. She touched her fingers to her cheek briefly, a gesture made so often she no longer knew when she did it.

Lord Satyr's big hand slid under Michaela's bottom, tilting her in a way that better accommodated him. Silvia could only assume from her friend's soft, appreciative cries that it satisfied her as well.

Although copulation was a private matter, she had no qualms about observing them. She and Michaela had no secrets. At least, not until recently, when Michaela had severed all connection after leaving Venice. After she'd been able to wind up matters there, Silvia had rushed here to Rome, worried Michaela might be in some sort of trouble. But now it appeared that any trouble was more precisely *in* her.

She'd taken a Satyr as a lover, for Gods' sakes! And not just any Satyr. The eldest scion of the four wealthy, powerful brothers who were the de facto rulers of the ElseWorld community here in Rome. He was the man in charge of excavating the Roman Forum. His celebrated archaeological finds had made him the darling of human society. And had made him her next assignment.

He was speaking now, his lips at Michaela's temple, murmuring to her in a mesmerizing blend of the ancient ElseWorld dialect, Latin, modern Italian, and if she wasn't mistaken, a hint of the Far East. At the sound of his voice, some wayward emotion began to wind tighter inside Silvia. Disturbed and restless, she went roaming in an effort to dispel it. The door to his armoire was ajar and she peeked inside. She found dark coats and trousers next to starched linen shirts, all hanging neatly in a row. Too neatly, with the same increment of space between each hanger. Lord Satyr was certainly fastidious!

She moved to his desk, an immense affair of polished olive wood. Her fingers itched to search its drawers, but he might hear. And if he turned his head, the desk was in his line of vision, which meant she dared not move anything. Drawers seemingly opening by themselves would require explanation. Until she assumed a corporeal shape, she would remain invisible to him. Even Michaela would not be able to see her until she chose to show herself.

Perching atop the desk, she lay on her side, propped her chin in one hand, and commenced reading several letters he'd left out. Two were from Italian ministers of government regarding the state of the excavations in the *Forum Romano*. It was the third that caught her eye. Written in typical long-winded Else-World Council fashion, it was addressed to Lord Satyr, and it fairly hummed with magic. She skimmed it, her attention caught by one particular passage:

> *Your recent letter was greeted with renewed hope that the fragile enchantments, which cloak and protect our Italian colonies, may soon be bolstered due to your efforts in Rome. We pray to the ancients that it will be so! I need not remind you of the grave repercussions—most particularly to your own family, but also to the health, welfare, and greatness of ElseWorld itself—should they falter. The task of safeguarding our heritage via the Forum excavations has fallen to you since the death of your father; and in view of your accomplishments over the last decade, we continue to believe them to be in excellent hands. It is with great enthusiasm that we await more news of your search for the Temple of Vesta, the adjacent House of the Vestal Virgins, and the relics themselves!*
>
> *Gods be praised,*
> *Minister Eighteen of the Artifact Recovery Bureau*
> *The Worshipful Council of ElseWorld*

So Lord Satyr was searching for the temple. Interesting! And how well suited to her own purposes. But she would make sure that any relics he found would find their way into her possession, not the Council's.

Michaela cried out, startling Silvia, and her eyes whipped Michaela's way, heart in her throat. But she quickly saw that it had only been a cry of passion, for the bodies upon the bed were moving in sensuous harmony—Bastian's giving, Michaela's receiving. Feminine palms smoothed over the well-defined musculature that was his chest, working their erotic magic.

Silvia's jaw dropped. Most men would have come instantly under Michaela's preternatural touch. Who was he that he could withstand her wiles so easily? And how much longer would this go on? The intensity of their coupling was beginning to make her distinctly uncomfortable.

She had pressing business to discuss with her longtime friend. Still, she hated to interrupt. Gods knew, Michaela deserved some fun. She'd nearly been killed by a jealous Harpie in Venice three months ago—the last time they'd been together.

Satyr's head lowered, and his lips trailed the length of Michaela's throat. She whimpered. Silvia's fingertips lifted to her own throat, tracing a similar path. Realizing what she was doing—what she was feeling—she snatched her hand away. Her face was flushed, hot. Fifty hells! She'd never known a man to take so much time chasing a single orgasm. Michaela's usual complaint was that they were too quick.

Hurry up, will you? Silvia urged him under her breath.

To her astonishment, his body ground to a halt so abrupt that it visibly jolted both his partner and the bed frame. His head snapped around in Silvia's direction, his brow knit in confusion. She pushed up to a sitting position on the desk, alarmed.

Silver eyes pierced the dimness, like stars in a twilight sky, relentlessly shining in her direction. The almost brutal, carnal expression on his masculine face made her heart trip, her breath stop. For the first time, she took in his features full on—the strong blade of his nose, his straight brows, square jutting chin. And those lips! Sensual, yet sharply cut. An uneasy attraction stirred in her breast, and she shivered; this time not from the bone-deep cold she'd weathered to get here tonight.

Unaccountably nervous, she tucked her knees to her chin, wrapping both arms around her calves. He couldn't see her. Of course not. Yet those eyes of his seemed to bore into her very soul!

"No! Don't stop. I beg you, Bastian," Michaela protested. Her palm cupped his cheek, tugging his attention back down to her. Her other hand clenched on his back, as if she feared he might leave her. *Leave her?* Leave the most accomplished Companion in the history of the Vestals? No man had ever left Michaela before she was ready for him to go. What was going on here?

With an almost imperceptible reluctance, Michaela's lover returned his full attention to her. Easing onto his back in a subtle shift of perfectly honed muscle, he brought her up to ride him. Her frilly white gown slipped low on her shoulders. Its lacy hem bunched on his thighs, like snow drifting over granite. Somewhere under the fall of her gown, his big hands cupped her bottom, moving her on him now in a powerful rolling motion. His gaze was hot on the lush upper curves of breasts that peeked from her bodice.

Michaela shrugged, baring them for him, her own expression hidden by her silken hair. As if she couldn't help herself, she bent and nuzzled her cheek along his shadowed jaw. Something about her pose suggested a deep affection. The beginnings of fear crept up Silvia's spine. Is this what had delayed her? Had she fallen in love? With this man—this *Satyr?*

Her gaze was sharp on him now, weighing his intentions. His chin was high, his throat arched. Silver eyes slitted by passion were shielded by long, dark lashes, as he hunted his pleasure within her most cherished friend. Did he even recognize how precious she was? Did he sufficiently appreciate the gift she offered him of her body and heart?

The sounds of their coupling escalated. Harsh breathing, soft moans. Flesh slapping in slick, staccato pulses. Without corporeal form, Silvia could not scent their lovemaking. But their erotic hunger hung thick in the room now like a voluptuous fog.

She'd witnessed others mating before. Had seen Michaela under a man countless times. But it had never affected her like this. Each thrum of her heart boomed in her ears and sent heat to rouge her cheeks. She was beset by faint shivers, and her eyes grew dry, for they refused to blink lest they miss something. Somehow, she'd managed to remain virginal throughout her life. Not by choice. But she'd taken vows. And the penalty for breaking them was dire. Because fornication was forbidden to her, her vicarious enjoyment of Michaela's lovers had always been a decadent delight. Tonight, it felt like something more . . . dangerous.

Silvia's hands dropped to clench on the edge of his desk on either side of her. She squeezed her thighs together; felt a gentle throb in her most private places, where tissues had engorged and flushed, wet and hot. She was horrified to realize she could almost feel his movements herself. Feel her passage yield . . . Gods! What was wrong with her? This man was Michaela's! She had no right to feel an attraction to him. It was only that they were so beautiful together, she assured herself. Anyone would be affected by the sight of them. Anyone.

Slipping lithely to the floor, she fled the room, telling herself she had better things to do. She would use the time they spent in coitus to make a systematic search of the rooms along the corridor.

But first things first. Assuming corporeal form, she went downstairs to the kitchen. Earlier this morning, she'd rushed past it on her way upstairs, anxious to be certain Michaela was all right. Now she helped herself to some wine grapes and a sandwich of thinly sliced meat, bread, and cheese. Keeping her ears open for any trouble, she gobbled the repast hastily, for she could eat only when she was visible and had to render herself so before satisfying her hunger.

Afterward, she rinsed her mouth and went invisible again. Padding across a gleaming floor tiled in black, gold-veined Portoro marble, she opened doors as she passed, glancing into various chambers. What she sought here in this city wouldn't be easy to find on her own. Had Satyr already discovered it for himself? Until she spoke to Michaela, this question must go unanswered. Still, she continued her search along the hall, and each small act of invasion calmed her; felt normal and right. Michaela's business might be entertaining men, but her own talents lay in investigating them.

His home was something of a museum, its every room lined with fascinating artifacts. She entered the most promising of them—his study. Inside, she found gilt-edged books, ancient maps, and a desk twice as large as the one in his bedchamber. Paper, pens, a letter opener, and other tools of business were neatly aligned upon it. She smiled slightly at this further evidence of Lord Satyr's obsessive neatness.

But this was a public room. If he had a firestone—or relic as he and the council termed them—in his possession, it was likely he would have hidden it in more private quarters. She took the stairs upward again.

Down the corridor from his bedchamber she found what appeared to be his library. Its perimeter was lined with costly bric-a-brac from his excavations and travels, as well as books and statuary. And not just any statuary. These were striking pieces. Familiar ones sculpted by the ancients. They were the sorts of treasures that only museums housed. How had he come by them? Had he, in fact, stolen them from the Forum? Interesting indeed.

Despite the profusion of items, everything was as orderly as a monk might keep it. She ran her fingertip over the edge of a picture frame and found no dust. The busts on the shelves all sat parallel to one another, noses turned precisely in the same direction.

Surely no one who wasn't slightly deranged kept their lodgings this tidy. Though there were no servants about, he obviously employed some. Likely hamadryads, the traditional servants of the Satyr, who worked only after midnight.

One thing was certain, if any of the firestones she'd come to find were here, they would have been cataloged, numbered, and filed. All she needed to do was locate his records. Someone as finicky as he would undoubtedly have boxes of excavation cards, documenting each and every find, no matter how minuscule. Where were they? She took one step toward the desk, then froze.

A harsh, masculine, guttural groan chased down the corridor, unerringly finding her. The unmistakable sound of a man achieving sexual fulfillment. She hunched her shoulders, as if to ward it off. But in her mind's eye, she pictured them together. Saw the sleek, powerful muscles of Satyr's back arched taut, his face contorted with his lusty coming. Saw Michaela's fingers clawing the bedclothes in ecstasy, her opulent breasts heaving with each breath as he fountained hot seed deep, so deep, inside her.

Silvia clasped both fists tight to her chest, strangely helpless to block it all out. Helpless to stop the liquid heat that pumped through her system at the vision she'd conjured of their coupling.

Moments later, she heard him moving through the hall, coming in her direction. Her eyes flew to the door in time to see it open in a smooth swish. Although well aware he could not see her, she quickly tucked herself between two of the tall statues. Standing among them as if she'd become one of them herself, she peeked at him.

Gods, he must be almost seven feet tall. And naked! Or nearly so. Unbelted, the front of his long robe swirled open as he cut through the room, coming her way in a confident, pantherish lope. His passing stirred her unbound hair and the thin fabric of her long white shift.

Her eyes dropped as he came even with her, widening at what was on display. Rooted in the dark nest at the apex of his thighs, his manhood hung long, ruddy, and thick—still semi-tumescent in spite of his recent climax. It was quite . . . extraordinary. A fleshly instrument of pleasure surely forged by Vulcan himself. No wonder her best friend was drawing this assignment out so long!

As if he felt her study, he whipped the front of his robe together and tied it closed with a hard jerk of its belt. He reached inside a corner cabinet at the far side of the room, then moved her way again. He came closer. *Wham!* She slammed back against the wall of books, cringing away from him as he leaned forward. A well-muscled arm lifted toward her. She muffled a shriek and sidestepped. When his hand merely withdrew his shaving apparatus, she realized she'd only been in the way of his reach.

Beside him now, she watched him stand before his mirror, beginning to razor away his dark, morning stubble. This masculine ritual seemed so familiar, yet strangely threatening at the same time. She wanted to shut it out. She pinched her nose against the tang of shaving cream, forgetting that she could not scent anything in her current state.

With a growing sense of unease, she found herself taken back to memories of her childhood. Then the reason for her skittishness came to her. She'd watched Pontifex do this many times, long ago when she was a girl.

"If you hurt her, I'll kill you," she blurted, then pressed trembling fingers to her lips.

He jerked, cutting himself, and swore. Then he whirled around, confronting the room as though facing off with an unseen enemy. "Who the hell's there?" His voice was velvet and black sand, low and dark. And sexy—even when he wasn't fornicating.

"Answer me," he said, a graveled warning in his tone. She folded her arms. As if she'd simply drop her deception at his command and give him her name! Despite her silence, he somehow detected her whereabouts. Abruptly turning her way, he planted his forearms on the wall on either side of her, surrounding her with masculine strength and heat.

Startled, she leaped forward. Her body passed through his toward escape. It was the way of all Ephemerals that they could move through fleshly beings and any clothing they wore or objects they held. This was not accomplished without difficulty and complications, and was therefore something she normally tried to avoid. And she wasn't unaffected by their contact. She rubbed her arms, hugging herself, feeling unsettled and jittery in her own skin.

It was as if, for a split second, she'd become part of him. And now his most recent memories swirled chaotically in her brain and flashed sensation through her body in unexpected, erotic pulses. She now knew as well as he did how it had felt to press his flesh between Michaela's thighs. Knew the pleasure he'd known as he'd moved inside her, knew the pure, sharp ecstasy of his climax. She shook her head, backing away from him, from his private memories. She didn't want them.

Standing in the center of the room, her heart thumped erratically as she surveyed him. From fear or desire? Fear, yes, of course it was fear!

He'd swung around and now stood half-crouched in a battle-ready posture, watchful eyes scanning the room. He looked . . . stunned. "What are you?" he rasped.

Fool! This wasn't a human she was dealing with. He'd sensed her presence, even when her very closest friend had not. Who knew what sensory gifts he possessed? Quickly, she flung an echo of herself as far into the distance as she could. Sent it through window glass, beyond stone steps and the shrubbery in his garden, and farther onward, into hilly fields, and deep into the lush forest on the outskirts of his land, and through the wrought-iron fencing that marked the perimeter of his holdings.

He moved to the window to survey sweeping landscape, his body a dark silhouette against the pale morning sunlight streaming in. Her ruse had worked. He assumed that she—the presence he'd felt—had departed his home.

Eyeing him as she would an unpredictable viper, she left the library and scurried down the corridor toward the bedchamber he'd recently departed.

Behind her, Lord Bastian Satyr was left reeling. He ran his fingers through his dark hair, hardly able to credit what had just occurred. When he'd felt the presence move through him, for just a moment the world had no longer appeared to him only in stark black, harsh white, and dull shades of gray.

He—a man born color-blind—had seen color.

Glorious, lush color.

For the first time in his life.

And now it was gone again.

2

Upon entering the luxurious bedchamber Lord Satyr had recently vacated, Silvia rendered herself visible. Immediately, the scent of sex hit her and she staggered back a step under its impact.

Her eyes went to the massive bed. In its center, looking fragile among rumpled covers, lay an exquisite beauty. A woman whom exalted, ancient practitioners of the Sensual Arts had trained in the giving of pleasure. One whom knights had waged tournaments over in medieval times. One to whom a Venetian prince had recently offered a priceless tiara encrusted with rare jewels for a single night in her company. A woman Pontifex had lusted after—Michaela.

Her face was turned away, her dark hair in a silken tangle across the pillow. Her arms were artlessly flung overhead, her knees still slightly raised and apart. The bunched hem of the frothy gown she wore swooped low between her stockinged thighs like some sort of exotic bunting that just barely preserved her modesty.

Quickly, Silvia shut the door behind her and locked it. "Michaela!" she whispered.

There was a rustling of sheets as Michaela came up on her elbows. "Via? Is that you?" Her violet eyes found Silvia across the room, and her lips, berry red from her lover's kisses, curved in delight. In the aftermath of lovemaking, she was quite simply stunning.

And quite simply . . . *mortal?*

Praying she was wrong, Silvia rushed forward and took Michaela's wrist in her hand. Turning it over, she saw the blood pumping there through pastel blue veins. She dropped it and stepped back, aghast. "What have you done? Made yourself fey again, and mortal?"

"As you see," said Michaela, unrepentant. "I have indeed permanently reverted to my own form. I'm no longer an Ephemeral. Can never be one again."

For the past fifteen centuries, they'd each gone from one fleshly host to another in order to survive. They could only reclaim their own corporeal forms briefly before supplanting them with new hosts, which must be shed again in favor of another upon the coming of each full moon. They'd seemed likely to remain Ephemerals forever, and their friendship had seemed destined to be an eternal one. Now, in an instant, all that had changed.

"You'll die!"

Michaela smiled, her eyes teasing. "Not right away. But someday. Mortals do. Oh, don't be cross with me, Via," she coaxed. Rolling to her knees on the mattress, she stretched out both hands toward her.

"Cross? You've thrown your immortality away for some infatuation with a Satyr. Do you expect me to congratulate you?" Distress had Silvia pacing over the thick carpet, which was patterned with a design of exotic ElseWorld beasts entwined with grapevines. Ogres, monsters, demons—she'd done battle with them all. But nothing had ever frightened her as much as the thought of losing her most cherished friend to Death.

"I fell in love. I wanted to be with Bastian in my own form, which meant becoming mortal. It's done. And cannot be undone. I won't return to Pontifex ever again. Let's speak no more of it." Michaela pushed the covers aside, making room. "Now, come sit beside me. We haven't seen each other for months."

Silvia's gaze dropped to Michaela's belly. Her eyes went wide and she put a hand to her breast, another shock striking at her like a body blow. Unless she was very much mistaken, her best friend was with child.

"Oh, no." Her appalled gaze shot to Michaela's. Read the dangerous truth.

"How could you be so foolish?" Silvia demanded. And then in the same breath, "Is it his?" She nodded toward the door to indicate the man beyond.

"No." Michaela laid a palm over her slightly rounded abdomen as if to shield it from Silvia's disapproval. Her gaze slid away. She was hiding something.

"Whose, then?" Silvia persisted. Going to sit beside her on the edge of the bed, she tried to catch her eyes.

Michaela shrugged. "It simply happened. A hazard of my profession."

"Does he know?"

"That I'm with child?" asked Michaela. "Of course. It's the reason he brought me into his home." She grinned, happy. "He's the protective sort."

"You mean you actually reside here in this museum?" Now that she thought about it, though, she hadn't seen any evidence of feminine occupation.

"Temporarily. But I will become a permanent fixture soon enough, if I have my way. For now, I'm still employed in the *Salone di Passione*, the pleasure house owned by Sevin."

"His brother," Silvia noted, having done her research.

Michaela nodded. "Officially, I still live at the salon, but I use it as nothing more than a glorified closet. I spend most of my time here. And after I miscarry—"

Silvia grabbed her arm. "What?"

Sadness twisting her features, Michaela clasped her hand. "I fell ill with the Sickness just after Venice," she admitted.

"Oh, *cara*, no." Silvia slipped both arms around her friend, grieving for her. Michaela had long dreamed of having her own family someday. When things were safer for them. When they'd freed themselves of Pontifex. But now, that family could never be. The Sickness had killed half the females in ElseWorld and had rendered the rest incapable of bringing a child to term. Did Satyr know she'd been ill? Is that why he didn't mind that his paramour carried another man's child? Because he knew it would not live?

Tears welled in Michaela's violet eyes, and she scooted lower to lay her head upon Silvia's lap. Silvia stroked her hair, comforting her. Just as she'd sometimes done when Michaela had nightmares as a girl, holding her until they'd drifted off to sleep in their shared bed in the Atrium House near the temple. There had been twelve of them residing in the house and temple complex then, centuries ago. Six Companions and six Virgins, all of them servants of the goddess of hearth and home, Vesta.

Long since, all twelve had become Ephemerals, gifted with eternal life. All changed by the goddess fifteen hundred years ago during the temple's fiery destruction, when it had seemed the only way of saving them. Of the original twelve, only she, Michaela, and another Vestal named Occia currently roamed free.

Michaela turned on her back, gazing up at her. "Remember how we used to pluck daisy petals on summer nights trying to guess who we might someday marry, after our service to Vesta ended?"

"Umm-hmm." Silvia remembered:

> *Who will I bed?*
> *Who will I wed?*
> *Merchant, Taverner, Baker,*
> *Guard, or Ribald, or Candlestick Maker?*
> *No one.*
> *You'll marry no one.*
> *It's your destiny to be alone.*

"I used to secretly change 'baker' to 'Satyr' in the rhyme, and try to trick the flower into promising me the latter as my husband," Michaela confessed with a giggle.

"I miss that time," said Silvia. Her palm smoothed over Michaela's hair, enjoying its silky texture. "Before the temple was destroyed, when we were so innocent of the worlds' evils." When they'd both sworn to protect Vesta's flame forever.

She gazed toward the fire in Lord Satyr's grate, feeling a deep sense of loss. She was glad Michaela had found love. But Bastian had taken up residence in her heart, and now there would be less room within it for a friendship with Silvia in the future. It was simply the way things went with love.

Michaela looked up at her through her lashes, her eyes knowing. "You're aroused."

Silvia straightened. "What? No."

"Don't bother fibbing. A Companion can always tell." With sensual grace, Michaela shifted aside and patted the mattress between them. "Come here," she urged gently.

Silvia's white teeth tugged at her lower lip, her blue eyes searching violet ones. Michaela's hand lifted, her fingers tangling in Silvia's long, red-gold hair. The backs of her knuckles dusted Silvia's breast, forcing her to acknowledge the need that surged at the light touch. All that Silvia had learned here tonight was staggering. She was going to lose her friend one day to Death. Had already lost a part of her to Lord Satyr. The desire to feel close to her now was acute.

Silvia glanced toward the door.

"There's time. He'll bathe, dress, and work at his desk before he returns to make his farewells for the day. Please. Lie with me." Michaela tugged lightly at one end of a lock of her hair. And Silvia gave in because she wanted to, sliding low until they lay facing one another.

For these rare few moments, Silvia would pretend they were ordinary beings without worry or care. She would forget that all the plans she and Michaela had made were suddenly crumbling. That she would soon be alone. She sighed, allowing herself to relax, and rested her cheek upon perfume-and-passion-scented sheets. Upon a feather mattress still warm from the powerful body of the man who'd just left it.

Michaela lifted the weight of Silvia's hair and pushed it back over her bare shoulder, smiling at her affectionately. "Did you watch us?" she asked softly.

Silvia shrugged, letting the truth show in her eyes.

"I'm glad, Via." Their eyes held as Michaela's palm smoothed over Silvia's throat and breast, shaping the contours of her body as it moved down the curve of her waist and then her thigh, her knee. Then it caught her hem and drew upward again, dragging the front of her shift along the seam of legs still firmly locked against invasion.

Silvia gasped as an olive-skinned hand found the pale silk triangle that shielded her privates, cupping her there. The heat of Vesta, which Michaela held in her palms, was designed to arouse. Silvia felt herself surrender to it, melt for it. Something—the pad of a fingertip—brushed her clit, once, then again. Pulling upward and gently distending it. Though the touch was light, its effect on her was profound.

Suddenly, her entire being was urgently focused on a single objective—the swift pursuit of sexual gratification. She turned into the touch, and her thighs parted in tacit assent, her calf wrapping itself over Michaela's. For this, she was rewarded by the tantalizing rub of Michaela's skilled fingers. Fingers that had entertained legions of both sexes in similar circumstances over the centuries. High between her legs, her nether flesh flushed and wept with the beginnings of pleasure.

Silvia's eyes fluttered closed, her long lashes fanning dark against ivory skin. A soft moan left her. Sex with Michaela would be—had always been—tender and calm. It was all she required; all she would accept. An occasional act born of sisterly affection, it would satisfy her need for physical comfort. It would reaffirm the bonds of a centuries-old shared history between them. It would be a welcome relief from the tension that had filled her after watching the act of copulation that had so recently occurred here in this very bed. Nothing more.

"What did you think?" Michaela whispered.

"A-about what?" Silvia managed. A slim finger pressed, parting her petaled feminine folds, stroking along them in precisely the sweet, gentle rhythm that would best excite her. Another moan escaped her.

"Lord Bastian," Michaela murmured, her lips brushing Silvia's temple. "He's something special, *sì?*" Her voice was rife with concupiscent memories of her lover.

At her words, an erotic vision of Lord Satyr laboring over Michaela in this very bed only an hour ago rose in Silvia's mind. She nurtured the carnal image, remembering, allowing thoughts of their coupling to fuel her own rising passion.

"Mmm-hmm," she said. "I noted the dimensions of his most *special* attribute when I encountered him just now in his study." Against her hair, she felt Michaela's smile.

"I don't mean *that*, Via, although I agree it's quite nice." She sighed contentedly. "Shall I tell you what I truly love best about him? Physically, I mean?"

"As you please." Her eyes fell upon Michaela's breast. Saw

the bruise-like splotches there on voluptuous olive flesh—marks made by the pull of *his* mouth. Mesmerized, she placed her own mouth where his had been, sucking gently, tasting *him* on her skin. That slender finger chose that moment to dip inside her, spiking feverish need throughout her entire body. Silvia gasped and gripped Michaela's wrist in warning. "Not too—"

"Deep. Yes, I remember. I'll take care."

Michaela shifted closer and Silvia lay back.

Damp now with Silvia's honeyed balm, slippery fingers rouged her clit and then worked inside her again, and then out, and in and out, rocking over her clit with each push and tugging with each pull. Her back arched and her own fingers curled into the bedcovers. She felt herself moving swiftly toward the precipice of release and hardly realized when she began moving her hips, riding Michaela's touch. Gods, it had been almost a year since they'd done this together. Climax would not be long in coming. And Michaela knew. Always knew.

"It's not what you think." Michaela's voice was husky as her lips traced upward along the side of Silvia's throat.

Silvia's brow knit, trying to follow what she was hearing through the sultry haze of her passion.

"It's his hands that I love best, Via. They're slow. He takes his time. Knows how to concentrate. On a statue"—a damp, lingering stroke—"on a bit of pottery"—another stroke—"on a woman."

As impending orgasm swelled, Silvia grabbed a pillow, trying to duck her face into its softness.

"No." Michaela rose on her forearm, her nimble fingers strumming Silvia's well-buttered flesh. "Please don't hide."

Silvia relented, but laid the back of her wrist across her eyes instead, unable to completely bare her tumultuous emotions, even to a treasured friend. Her pulse thrummed too loudly in her own ears, a seductive drumbeat. Need was choking her, mortifying her. She smothered another moan. "Hurry. Let's be done with it. Please. He's bound to return soon."

Michaela's red lips parted. "All right," she whispered. "Love me, Via." At this familiar signal, Silvia's eyes fluttered open and caught Michaela's. Her hand went low between them, over Michaela's rounded belly and high between her stockinged thighs. Her fingers trembled, slipping between warm folds that had so recently accommodated another lover. She found her ready, still moist with Lord Satyr's ejaculate.

"Do you feel his spend?" Michaela murmured at her ear.

Silvia swallowed. Nodded.

"Good. Oh, I wish you could know him in that way, too, Via. Could know the pleasure he can give."

Silvia's brow knit in confusion. "Wh—?"

"Shhh." Through half-closed eyes, she watched Michaela's lips come closer. A truly talented Companion could bring on an orgasm with a mere kiss. Her dearest friend was so gifted.

"I'm going to come." And then Michaela pressed her sweet mouth to Silvia's mouth, kissing her with lips Lord Bastian Satyr had kissed. The taste of him lingered on her here as well, and it acted upon Silvia like a sweet aphrodisiac. A slight pressure came on her clit, then a tug, and . . .

The climax that had been building within her since she'd first arrived to find Lord Satyr mounting Michaela in this very room now broke over her in rolling, delicate, joyous waves. Distantly, she heard Michaela come as well, for Silvia's slightest carnal touch had always quickly incited her to release. Silvia curled away from her, onto her side, as exquisite pulses rippled high between her legs, squeezing, then releasing only to squeeze again.

Michaela's body curved around hers, her arm wrapping itself at Silvia's waist, offering shelter as she'd done when they were young. "My dear, darling Silvia." A kiss brushed her hair.

Ah, this was heaven. This feeling of closeness. This tender, shared climax. They clung together as their breathing slowed, as the tumult eased. But these moments were bittersweet, for this would likely be their last such encounter.

They'd discovered this reciprocal talent for giving pleasure years after they'd been initiated as Vestals. They'd been told they were to serve the goddess for three decades—Michaela as a Vestal Companion; Silvia as one of the Vestal Virgins. And as time had passed, their bodies had ripened and their friendship had grown, and become more. Denied other outlets for their passions, they had turned to each other. The Atrium House was adjacent to the temple where Vesta's flame burned, and Silvia still remembered how the firelight had limned Michaela's body that first time they'd coupled.

Sighing inwardly, Silvia lifted the arm at her waist and pulled away. From now on, things must be different. Michaela's loyalty lay elsewhere, with Lord Satyr. Silvia had pushed her away often enough, unable to give all of herself to anyone. So be it.

Uneasy now with what had passed between them, she shoved her plain shift down and rolled to sit up, eyes averted. She had never felt the full, wild heat of passion that Michaela had often described finding with her other lovers. Wasn't sure she ever wanted to bare herself to another partner so completely. And she most definitely wished to avoid any discussion of feelings in the aftermath of coitus. Unlike Michaela, who relished such talk.

"I took a look around, while you were . . . otherwise engaged," Silvia said, anxious not to dwell on what they'd done. On what she perceived as a moment of weakness. "How far along is Lord Satyr in the Forum? He should have found the temple by now."

Michaela didn't let her off so easily. "Seeking pleasure is not a sin, Via." A strained silence passed, and she feared Michaela would press her to wallow in what they'd shared.

"You haven't even shown him where the temple is yet, have you?" Silvia accused. Provoking Michaela seemed the best way to shatter any intimacy. "I read the letter on his desk. He's still searching for it."

Unperturbed, Michaela stretched luxuriously, catlike. "I won't steal from him. No more than I would from you. And don't you wonder why Pontifex wants to recover our fire-stones so badly? He has gone to considerable trouble to obtain the six he has. I'm not sure he should have them, much less the rest."

Silvia pounced on this new topic, relieved when she let the matter of their lovemaking go. "I have no intention of giving anything to him. But if I can find them, I can use them to trick him into freeing the others. He believes he can harness our stones' power. Use them to do—"

"The work of a madman."

"That goes without saying. But exactly what he plans for them—that's the mystery I must solve. For if he can use them, so can we. But first, we have to recover them. To find out what powers they have and how they work." Silvia rose from the bed.

Michaela reached out to her. "Wait. What are you going to do?"

"What you would not. Steal from Lord Satyr."

"There's nothing to steal, Via. Not yet. The remaining six stones still lie buried. I kept him from finding them."

Silvia nodded, having guessed as much. On the night the temple had been destroyed, each Vestal had been in charge of the safekeeping of her stone. In the chaos, they'd all been lost— most in the Forum. But some had made their way into the world and were believed to be in the hands of various collectors, who had no idea what they possessed. And six had made their way into Pontifex's hands.

Going to the fire to warm herself prior to facing the elements again, she said, "Damn, Michaela. This won't be easy to explain to Pontifex. I'll have to move quickly to steer your lover toward the temple in order to have something to show for our time here."

When Michaela looked ready to protest, Silvia added, "Satyr won't guess my manipulations. And you needn't be involved. I'll gain employment at the dig in order to legitimately observe his progress there." She forced a teasing smile. "That will also afford me a chance to weigh Lord Bastian's worth, and decide if he's indeed good enough for you."

"He is." Michaela sent her an inscrutable glance. "When you go to him for employment, will you go as yourself?"

"In my own form? Don't be ridiculous. I have no wish to be made mortal."

"It's not that bad."

"I have a job to do, Kayla. And I can't do it in my own body. Not when I can only use it for twenty-four hours at a stretch without rendering myself forever mortal. I can't let him know what we are. What we want. It would be too dangerous."

Michaela rolled to lie on her belly, chin resting on both fists. Her bare legs stretched out behind her, long and shapely in a tangle of sheets. The artful display was a Companion's trick, meant to lower the defenses in a negotiation. "Well, at least say you'll try to locate a form that's more appealing than the one you assumed last time we were in Rome, will you?"

Silvia grinned. "You didn't like me in the guise of a Cloaca sewer worker?"

By way of a reply, Michaela pinched her nose between two fingers as if she'd smelled something awful.

Laughing quietly, Silvia turned to go.

Michaela leaped from the bed in a swirl of silk and perfume and scurried to stay her, her grip on her arm urgent. "It doesn't have to be this way. You could stay here. You could show yourself to Bastian when he returns in a few moments. His family is powerful. They could fight Pontifex."

Shaking her head, Silvia eased away. "Don't pity me."

"I don't!" Michaela tucked a lock of Silvia's unruly hair behind her ear, her gaze soft. "It's just that I love you. And I love him. If you and he could learn to love each other, everything would be so perfect."

"Perfect?" Silvia echoed in surprise. Searching Michaela's eyes, she realized what she had in mind. "You want me to join the two of you here, in his bed?"

"You watched us," Michaela began urgently. "You saw that his passions run high, that his male endowments are generous. He's well able to accommodate another female in his bed, at least from time to time."

An erotic image of them all locked together in a voluptuous embrace rose unbidden in Silvia's mind, and she quickly banished it. Pulling from her hold, she stepped back, smiling ruefully. "I'm not sure he'd see things as you do, dear Kayla. Rather, he might find your suggestion beyond the bounds of his *generosity*."

"I'm serious," Michaela insisted, stamping a bare foot.

But Silvia only went for the door, unlocking it. "Enjoy your new love, but don't think to include me. I'll continue our search for the missing firestones, and once I have them, I'll return to Pontifex a final time, and do what it takes to free the others. As planned. I can look no further than that for now."

At the mention of Pontifex, Michaela crossed her arms. "What will you tell him of me?"

Suddenly reminded of that awful long-ago night when Michaela had shielded her from harm at Pontifex's hands, Silvia felt a fierce surge of protectiveness toward Michaela rise within her. "Whatever lies will keep you safe," she replied simply. Rendering herself invisible, she then departed the room and the house, managing to avoid another encounter with their owner.

But shortly after she arrived at the Forum, Lord Satyr did as well. From her position atop Palatine Hill, she watched, her hungry eyes following him across the grounds until he eventually entered the large white tent that dominated the landscape. She sighed. If she were to choose a man to lie with, he was certainly an appealing specimen. But now was not the time in her life for such things.

She spent the entirety of the morning and early afternoon along the periphery of the Forum, scouting it from the adjacent hills that overlooked it. Time had changed the terrain, and it was with some difficulty that she exacted the location of the temple, which now lay buried beneath centuries of accumulated soil. Once she was certain, she made her way into the lush orchards of nearby Aventine Hill, which were on the property of Lord Dane Satyr, one of Bastian's brothers. There, in solitude, she briefly assumed her corporeal form again in order to dine on what fruit she could find that was not yet rotten.

As dusk approached, she quickly changed into the noncorporeal form she'd decided she would take for this venture. That of a child—the very same six-year-old girl she'd been fifteen centuries ago on the day she'd been chosen to serve Vesta.

And then she went calling on Michaela's lover.

3

With a dramatic flourish of white canvas, Bastian threw back the front flap of the expansive tent, which served as his office in the middle of the Roman Forum excavations. He tossed his topcoat onto the stand, where it caught at the collar and draped its length into neat folds, as if it didn't dare do otherwise in his commanding presence.

"Signor Satyr?" His foreman, Ilari, had followed him across the Forum grounds, nattering on about nothing of importance. An agent of the Parliament appointed to work under Bastian, he was loyal to the government, not to Bastian or the dig.

Bastian ignored him as he often did, his mind still dwelling on the presence he'd felt in his study that morning. On the color he'd seen. He was carefully dissecting the matter in his thoughts, turning it round and round, unshakable as a dog with a bone until he solved a puzzle. To one who'd never before witnessed a world awash in color, it had been a miraculous event.

And it had had a curious effect on him. Afterward, he'd craved another lie-in with Michaela. Although he'd fought it, bathing first and completing business in his library, he'd eventually succumbed. He'd lain with her twice more that morning, and was now late getting in. A rather unprecedented occurrence in itself. He was always eager to begin here, often appearing before dawn and driving himself harder than any of the workers.

"Signor? How shall we proceed?"

"Slowly," he replied, having no idea what Ilari was asking, but figuring it was usually the best advice in any archaeological case. "Now remove yourself from my sight. I'll join you outside when it suits me." Going straight to his great leather chair, he sat and surveyed his desktop, anxious to begin work. The well-worn chair was a comfortable fit for a man of his powerful build. His father had once sat in it himself as he lorded over the early excavations here in the *Forum Romano*. That had been eleven years ago, when he'd been alive. Before Bastian had killed him.

Shaking off the morose memories through dint of long practice, he began sorting through neatly arranged items on his expansive desk—maps, tools, various containers of yesterday's pottery shards, a stack of blank excavation cards, and another stack of cards upon which recent finds had been cataloged. His mornings were spent in study and his afternoons in the field, though there was some overlap and always many interruptions. And thus he typically passed the long, fulfilling days thoroughly entranced by the ancient past in the Forum.

It seemed only minutes had passed when he heard Sevin's voice. Another interruption in a day during which he had scarcely managed to steal a moment of time for what lay on his desk. "I trust you will not be too fatigued to participate in tonight's festivities, big brother," Sevin announced, pushing aside the canvas flap. "In view of your strenuous morning on Esquiline, I mean."

Bastian favored him with a lift of one dark brow. He saw no reason to respond. For like all blood-related Satyr, he and his siblings each shared the libidinous encounters of the others, albeit from a distance. When one of them engaged in fleshly pleasures, all experienced something akin to an echo of that pleasure. It was a certainty that his brother knew he'd bedded a female the previous night and again this morning.

"Well? Come in or get out, but choose one," said Bastian, "before that wind douses my fire."

Sevin came inside, throwing himself into the only other chair within the tent. Slight indentations that he refused to call dimples creased his cheeks, only emphasizing his masculine good looks. Although none of Bastian's brothers had ever encountered difficulty attracting female attention, Sevin was the one that women of all ages were drawn to like felines to catnip.

With the twist of one wrist high in the air, Bastian quickly bespelled the perimeter of the tent against any eavesdroppers that might choose to loiter outside the tent walls. Confident that their conversation would remain private, he asked, "What brings you here so early? Moonful isn't for hours yet."

Sevin held up a single finger. "*One* hour, brother. Singular."

"Damn. Really?" Bastian surveyed his desk, frustrated that he'd soon be useless at his work, rendered so by the coming of night. Although there was much left here to do, it would all suddenly seem unimportant when the fullness of the moon summoned him to take part in carnal rituals the Satyr had enjoyed since the dawn of time.

"But since you ask," Sevin added, picking up the thread of their conversation, "I've come to enquire after the welfare of my employee."

"Michaela?" Bastian glared at him.

Sevin's expression was all innocence, but his silver-blue eyes gleamed with humor.

Bastian gestured in an innately Italian way, a turn of his hand that brushed off any concern. "You'll see for yourself this very night that she's unharmed by my attentions."

"Ah. Your attentions. Frequent, are they?" Sevin's long legs found the footstool and he crossed booted ankles upon it. Setting his elbows on the arms of the chair, he steepled his fingers over his expansive chest, tapping them with a satisfied air.

Settling in to enjoy his teasing, Bastian assumed. "I'm sure you're well aware of their frequency. As I'm aware of the *in*frequency of females in your bed lately."

Sevin's smile only widened. "Alas, it's true. I'm surrounded by women at my establishment, but loath to bed even one lest she form an attachment to her employer. I discovered early on that favoritism is bad for morale. Business at the *Salone di Passione* is brisk and new employees are in need of lodgings. Yet, Michaela's chamber stands empty for nights on end. Shall I make it available to another who would put it to more profitable use?"

"I have no wedding plans if that's what you're angling to know," Bastian informed him. "Michaela and I are both satisfied with the current nature of our relationship and need no coaching in any direction from the likes of relatives. Let her keep her lodgings at the salon—lodgings I fund, I'll remind you—as a closet for her belongings in the manner in which she currently does. She has not taken up permanent residence with me. And will not."

Sevin chuckled, unfazed. "You're a bear this evening. Too many sleepless nights?"

"The only thing troubling my sleep is the damned Roman Parliament." Bastian perched a pair of goggles with elongated lenses on the bridge of his hawkish nose and took up the largest of the shards that had been found outside in the dig only an hour ago.

"How so?" Idly, Sevin picked up a terracotta urn from the nearest shelf, then gazed at it with distaste. It was newly unearthed and still covered with grime.

Bastian tossed a wire brush to him. "Make yourself useful and polish that into gold, will you?" He smiled to himself, knowing how his brother disliked anything to do with the digs.

"Terracotta into gold? That would be a neat trick." Grimacing, Sevin nevertheless began whisking the brush over the surface of the urn. Their archaeologist father had taught all of them the rudiments of excavation as boys, and Sevin knew the work well. But Bastian was the only one who'd followed in their father's footsteps.

Bastian adjusted the magnification of the goggles' lenses until he was finally able to read the writing he'd noted earlier on the shard: "Amata." *Beloved.* He smoothed the pad of his thumb over the word, enjoying the slightly gritty feel of it and the knowledge that he was touching something that had been created untold centuries ago.

"Every find we make here is lauded and exclaimed over, but I've hardly finished one when Parliament is clamoring for another," he went on in disgust. "The new Minister of Culture has no respect for history, only for power and gold."

"If I have the minister to thank for this lowly task, then I despise him, too," said Sevin, giving the urn a particularly hard whisk.

"He has political aspirations and seeks to ride on the back of our discoveries here in order to better his own station," said Bastian. "Between these blasted Roman politicians and the ElseWorld Council, it's enough to send a man to drink." A potent silence greeted his statement.

"A joke, brother. Only a joke," he added when the silence lengthened. "I do make them on occasion." Bastian stretched his shoulders, causing the fabric of his waistcoat to stretch over honed muscle. The coat was of Chinese design, one of many unique items he'd brought home from his travels to the Orient when he was eighteen. He didn't recall the circumstances of how he'd come by the garment. In fact, there was much he didn't remember of that time after the death of his parents. He'd been drunk. For four long years.

"What's that thing you're staring at?" Sevin asked after a moment.

"A clue to the whereabouts of the goddess Vesta's missing relics." Pushing the goggles to his forehead, Bastian went to stand before one of his bookshelves. In the lamplight, his well-muscled, six-and-a-half-foot body cast an impressive shadow against the inside walls of the white canvas. Running all along its perimeter stood sturdy shelves lined with thick reference books, bits of precious pottery, maps, and ancient artifacts, all meticulously arranged and cataloged. To him, order and schedules equated sanity and sobriety, and he was hell-bent on retaining both.

Locating Alexander Adams's best-known work, *Roman Antiquities,* he thumbed to the passage he wanted, and read aloud from it, skimming: " 'Vestal virgins were chosen . . . by Pontifex Maximus, who . . . selected from among the people twenty girls above six [years of age] . . . free from any bodily defect . . . It was determined by lot in an assembly of the people which of these twenty should be appointed. Then Pontifex Maximus went and took her on whom the lot fell, from her parents, as a captive in war, addressing her thus, "Te Amata Capio.' "

Bastian glanced up triumphantly. "There, you see?"

"No," said Sevin, polishing with more zeal than finesse.

"*Amata,*" Bastian said patiently, gesturing toward his desk. "It's there, written on that shard, which was found today near the Temple of Castor and Pollux. Not fifty feet from here. *Amata* was a generic title given to all the Vestals."

"Ah." Realization dawned on Sevin.

"Exactly!" Bastian snapped the book shut and shoved it back into precise alignment with its neighbors on the shelf.

Making his way back to his desk, he again lowered the goggles to examine the shard. Fourth century, he guessed.

"And like our father, you believe Vesta's Virgins are the key to reinforcing the magic that prevents humans from discovering that we walk among them?"

"Not the Virgins themselves, as Father maintained. No, the relics they guarded are what I'm after. They're referred to by the ancient philosophers as stones or relics, but I believe they were jewels of some sort. I think they're the keys."

Bastian broke off abruptly, as something prickled over the back of his neck. *Something ancient is stirring, somewhere deep in the earth.* He replaced the centuries-old terracotta shard carefully upon his desk, his every sense going on alert.

Directly across from him near the tent's opening, a mist appeared where before there had been nothing. He squinted, attempting to determine whether it was only the annoying Ilari come back to prattle at him or an actual phantom; then he recalled that he still wore the goggles. Intended for close work, they were thick and greatly magnified his surroundings, making objects at any distance over a foot away impossible to see clearly. He ripped them off. And saw her.

Just inside the door stood a girl of six years of age or so. Save for a shock of long, wild hair, she was pale as a wraith. And just as unreal. Excitement shot higher in him. A vision. He hadn't had one in months. He'd begun to wonder if his gift had deserted him. Every muscle drew taut as he slowly rose from the leather chair at his map-covered desk.

When he didn't respond to something Sevin said, his brother straightened from his sprawl in the opposite chair, his boots hitting the carpet that covered the dirt floor. Quickly gauging the nature of what was going on, he said, "Less than an hour till Moonful, big brother."

The vision started in surprise, as if she hadn't realized there were two men in the tent. Bastian followed her gaze to his brother, staring in an unfocused way that caused Sevin to curse. Sevin was right in his dismay, of course, he thought with detached interest. The Calling beckoned and the entire family was soon to engage in the ritual tonight on his land. His body was already beginning to quicken in anticipation of it. His skin was heating, his loins tautening, and his cock had grown hungry for the taste of a woman. Yet at the moment, all that seemed singularly unimportant.

His eyes swung back to the vision, and he took a careful step in its direction. Seeing that, the girl exploded into action, bolting off and disappearing through the solid wall of the tent in a whirl of filmy blacks, whites, and grays.

And he was right behind her, ramming his bulk through the tent door. Outside, he searched the landscape for her.

"Twenty hells! Bastian!" Sevin swore as he leaped to his feet. "Not tonight. It's damned inconvenient. Can't this—whatever it is you're chasing—wait?"

Ilari ran over, peering inside the tent at him. Keeping one eye on Bastian's rapidly disappearing figure in the distance, he asked with barely contained excitement, "What's happened? Is it a new discovery? Did he say?"

"It's nothing. Here, put this somewhere." Tossing the urn to the startled man, Sevin threw on his overcoat and snatched Bastian's from its hook. Seeing his brother atop a rise some forty feet from the tent, he took off after him.

The landscape of the Forum was eerie in twilight. Slabs of stone rose here and there like the ghosts of their ElseWorld ancestors, who'd once populated Italy. Lanterns in the hands of workmen bobbed among them like giant fireflies.

Catching up to his brother, Sevin murmured, "High time we made our way to the safety of your home on Esquiline, don't you agree?" He said carefully, "Dane and his wife are likely there already, awaiting us."

Unhearing, Bastian remained still as death, waiting for another move on the part of the wraith. She stood a mere ten feet ahead, her back to him. And of all those in the Forum, only he could see her. "What have you to show me?" he murmured under his breath. His words were caught in the wind and whisked in her direction. Did she hear? Though an impatient man, he had the patience of Saturn, the Roman God of Time, in certain matters. Such as the divining of the secrets of the ancients, or those of a female.

The object of his fascination began walking again, now and then glancing back to ensure that he followed. He did. Her dainty feet scarcely touched the ground, and made no impression on it. Behind her, his black leather work boots struck the earth soundly, crunching rocks and punching thumbnail-sized mosaic tiles deeper into the dry, volcanic soil of the Forum floor.

Sevin trailed him, silent and watchful now. As far as he could see in any direction, there was nothing unusual on view. But his brother saw something others could not, and every eye was on him. All around them, the slam of picks and scrape of whisks dwindled as minions stopped their work to follow in his wake. Excited whispers were exchanged. One workman gestured to another, who summoned others, until a veritable flock trailed him. They were anticipating a show. All waiting to see what the most celebrated archaeologist Rome had ever known would discover this time.

Sevin had seen his brother star in scenes like this one before. Bastian's gift had first made itself known at the tender age of five, when a vision had led him to discover the Sacred Petroglyphs of the Ancients in ElseWorld. It was a discovery their father had taken credit for, to protect him from the Council's scrutiny. But they'd eventually discovered the truth. And as a result, the entire family had been sent here, to this world. To mine the Forum for treasure, with the use of Bastian's talent.

The wraith halted suddenly at the northeast corner of the Temple of Castor and Pollux. Maintaining a careful distance, Bastian stopped behind her. He widened his stance, feeling the need for greater purchase with the soil and for a connection with whatever lay hidden beneath it. The past—it was what nurtured him. It fascinated him like nothing in the present ever had.

"Who are you?" he murmured. But the girl only shook her head. Raising her arms to the heavens like an angel, she began to twirl in place, in a slow, ethereal circle.

Whispers escalated among the workmen. *What did he say? What's happening?* Several men crossed themselves against evil.

But Bastian was oblivious and only waited and watched, his entire body—cells, flesh, sinew, bone, muscle, senses—all open to the past, craving to learn more of its secrets. Suddenly, more filmy apparitions appeared around the first girl, one by one like lights blinking on, until there were twelve young girls in all. Each was dressed in ancient Roman costume, their tunics with long, flowing skirts fluttering to their slim ankles.

"Why twelve?" he wondered aloud, for the philosophers had only written of six Virgins. But he expected no reply and received none.

Clustered in moody grays and gauzy whites, the girls all solemnly appeared to await the verdict of the single man who stood at the center of their group. He was a man of religion, dressed in lengthy ceremonial robes. His authoritative hand fell upon the shoulder of one girl, his first selection. Then he chose another, and another. He would ultimately divide the dozen of them into two distinct groups, each comprising six girls. His hand fell on the last girl's shoulder. The very one who'd led Bastian here.

"*Amata*," Bastian breathed, channeling the man's utterance. *Beloved.*

Her sorrow at being chosen reached out to Bastian like a living thing. She would go into service now, to the goddess Vesta. For three decades, she would tend the sacred flame. And so that nothing should turn her mind and heart from her duty, she would be forbidden to wed or enjoy fleshly pleasures.

As they were led away, a strong gust of wind blew over the vision, ruffling skirts and hair, then moving in his direction. Just as it reached him, the girl darted a glance over one thin shoulder. Eyes that were wise beyond her age found his, as if to determine how he judged what he'd seen. Eyes that were a pure, clear, cerulean blue. Color! Suddenly, she bloomed into a riot of shades—pearly skin, rosy cheeks and lips, and wild golden hair streaked with copper. His heart pounded with equal parts of joy and shock at the sight of it.

"Your name. Tell me your name!" he demanded, boldly stalking her now.

Her eyes widened and she shook her head, her long fire-gold hair lifting in the wind. Before he could reach her, the fog swirled, brushing her in mystery. In gloom and gray. The scene dissipated.

And with her departure, he became aware of the whispers. And the cold. *Hells! When had the weather turned?* He glanced around to find himself encircled by curious, fearful faces. *Damn.* He'd revealed too much. Humans already gossiped about them. Wondered about the strange goings-on that seemed to follow him and his family. And now he'd only made them more suspicious.

Sevin lounged a dozen feet away, having watched everything from his post against a pillar that had once been part of Caesar's temple.

"Where did all this fog come from?" Bastian asked blankly. He shuddered then, hard. The winter breeze came at him like icy fingers, brushing chills in their wake. "Gods, it's freezing."

"Your coat, brother," said Sevin. He tossed it to Bastian, who threw it on without questioning how he came to have it with him.

His assistant Ilari was bursting with questions. "Signor? What have you discovered?"

"It appears that some damage control is in order," Bastian told Sevin under his breath, subtly angling his chin to indicate Ilari and the onlookers.

Sevin nodded. "Your behavior tonight isn't helping in the battle to keep our kind from human detection," he observed.

"My apologies. It's difficult to be circumspect when one is interacting with an apparition."

"Understood."

"Shall we?"

They spent the next few minutes bespelling the workforce into forgetfulness. But that in itself would make them suspicious, for later some would wonder about the time they'd lost here tonight. As the crowd dispersed, Bastian called out to his now-confused foreman, announcing, "We dig here. Starting tomorrow."

"What is here?" Ilari called after him in surprise.

Beyond him on the overlook at the edge of the Forum, Bastian's eyes met those of a woman. One who'd been his consort for the past three months: Michaela. He knew her eyes were violet only because she'd told him. Knew her hair was a lustrous blue-black and her lips unusually red, only because others had informed him of this.

His desire to sink himself between a woman's thighs had compounded exponentially over the last fifteen minutes. The color he'd seen in the girl had affected him again, as it had this morning. The episodes were related somehow, but his mind would not be up to the task of sorting out the mystery over the coming hours. This was a special night for all of his kindred.

It had just gone dusk. As the moon slowly fattened overhead, his carnal need would dramatically escalate. Like his brothers, he would change physically and fornicate the ensuing night away. Would bury himself in Michaela's welcome, again and again, exhausting himself only with the coming of dawn. But unlike his brothers, he would tread all too dangerously close to the line that separated beast from man.

Fortunately, Michaela was a Companion, and therefore a suitable partner for him on these occasions. She would be unoffended by his lecherous appetites and peculiarities on this night. And she was accepting of the fact that he could not love her. With single-minded purpose, he turned in her direction.

"Wait!" Ilari pressed again. "Tomorrow—what will we dig for?"

"The House of the Vestals," Bastian called as he struck out across the grounds.

"Where are you going now, damn you?" Sevin demanded, catching up to him.

"Moonful, brother," Bastian told him, slinging a companionable arm over his shoulder. "It's time to heed our Calling, as you're so fond of reminding me. And I see Michaela there on the ridge. Let's be off."

As they made their way from the Forum, a frenzy of activity commenced behind them. Ilari shouted orders to workmen. Surveyors excitedly unrolled maps by lamplight. All of them making plans. Discussing approaches to the work ahead. They would toil far into the night.

At dawn, Ilari would take the news of Bastian's expectations of a new discovery to Minister Tuchi—the man who'd sent him to spy and to whom he surreptitiously reported. He, in turn, would spread it to the entire Parliament.

All based on Bastian's word. And with good reason. He had never yet been wrong. Not in the seven years he'd been in charge of the excavations in the Roman Forum.

* * *

Silvia morphed from a six-year-old girl back into her adult Ephemeral form. Invisible now, she perched on a low wall to watch the two brothers depart. Pontifex considered Lord Bastian Satyr a brilliant man and, therefore, a dangerous one. A threat. Yet, he was also the man who would lead her to some of the lost firestones. As of tonight, and thanks to her, he was one giant step closer to finding them. Showing him the vision of herself as a girl just now had been risky, but it was the fastest way to convince him where the Vestal Temple and House were buried without revealing her true form to him.

The two men had reached the outskirts of the Forum now. Silvia watched Bastian and Michaela meet, analyzing everything about their initial embrace. She was struck anew by how right they looked together. Both so beautifully made. So golden and perfect. Her fingers went to her pale cheek, tracing the slightly raised edge of the scar there.

She gazed up at the darkening sky. The moon would show itself soon. Its fullness affected all ElseWorld creatures, but none more so than the Satyr. Bastian and his brothers would undergo the Change, might be undergoing it even now. From tonight's dusk to tomorrow's dawn, they would glory in rites of fornication. Theirs would be a night of debauchery dedicated to Bacchus, the ancient Roman god of wine.

How would Michaela deal with all that masculine energy directed her way? she wondered. She would have to ask her about the particulars. Another time.

The trio was moving off now and entering a carriage. Where would he take Michaela? To his home perhaps or to that of his brother? Silvia watched their conveyance disappear on the horizon.

Hopping from her perch then, she headed for the canvas tent he and his brother had recently vacated. Stealthily, she ducked inside. A slight smile curved her lips and she shook her head in amusement. The shelves and his desk were meticulously organized, everything aligned just so. Scrupulously neat, as was his home.

She spied the shard on his desk and took a step in its direction. She'd seen him holding it when she arrived here as a vision earlier, and she had recognized it for what it was. Just the thing she needed to convince Pontifex that all was on a good course here.

Three steps inside, she heard someone enter behind her. Startled, she turned to see a burly, pot-bellied man. He was unremarkable and looked like any of a dozen men she regularly passed on the street here in Italy. But on closer inspection, she realized she'd seen this particular man on the grounds earlier, speaking to Bastian. He was some sort of foreman. Moving furtively to the desk, he greedily snatched up the very shard she'd come for herself and then slung himself into Bastian's chair.

"Bastard," he muttered. Sitting back with a satisfied air, he surveyed the domain he obviously coveted. "Lording your great talent over everyone. No matter. I'll be sitting in this chair soon enough." He hid the shard inside his coat and held it there under one arm as he stood to go.

How dare he try to steal it? Ignoring the fact that she was equally guilty of that intent, Silvia crouched behind the desk and quickly rendered herself visible. "Put it back or die, human!" she murmured in her best imitation of a ghostly spirit. The foreman whipped around so fast that he tripped on the carpet and fell to his knees.

"Who's there?" Wide-eyed, he searched for the source of the voice, but she was hidden and had already gone invisible again. Looking terrified, he tossed the shard back to the desk and ran.

Once she heard his footsteps moving off through the Forum grounds, she rendered herself visible, for she could not carry the shard while in wraith form. Deftly, she pocketed it. Since it was dangerous to linger in her visible form, she unlatched the back flap of the tent and departed through it without detection.

Slipping from the tent, she found harbor in a nearby bosk of olive trees. She'd been here in Rome over two hundred years earlier when these trees had been young. When they'd brought in their first crop of olives. Their flesh was gnarled now, their cores had rotted away, and their branches were twisted and half dead. It made her feel old to look upon them.

Rubbing her hands together, prayer-like, she recited an ancient spell and then blew lightly between her palms. Heat stirred and smoke coiled. Then fire rose, cupped between her palms. It was an ancient fire of hearth and home, born of the goddess Vesta. She tossed it into the air before herself and watched it burst into a vertical wall of flame. A firegate. This spontaneous flame enabled transport between worlds, by means of a gate that only she and eleven other beings in the worlds had the power to create. The Vestals. Quickly, she stepped through it and by doing so disappeared from EarthWorld. With her departure, the fire was immediately extinguished as if it had never been.

And in the next instant, Silvia found herself transported from EarthWorld . . . to ElseWorld.

Back to the one place that terrified her more than any other in either world.

The lair of Pontifex Maximus.

4

Silvia bypassed the snaking line of visitors who sought an audience with Pontifex Maximus V in his gaudy throne room. To each side of this queue were clusters of women who waited as well for a different purpose. They were the Lares, the familiars of the Vestal Virgins—now Pontifex's sexual vassals. So that none would break free from the group or be molested by his guests, they were guarded at intervals by armored soldiers of the ElseWorld Council.

Although Silvia would have preferred to escape notice here, it was impossible. Ephemerals became visible, solid entities the moment they entered this world. Fortunately, showing her true form to another ElseWorld creature would not have the effect of rendering her mortal as it would if she were to show herself to a human on the other side of the gate.

The Lares hissed at her as she passed on the central walkway that divided the nave, casting bitter accusations. *"Traditore. Schiuma."* Traitor. Scum. Their feminine barbs struck her like the stings of venomous insects. Their insults filled the great hall and then rose to bounce off stone walls, arches, and the gilding of the domed ceiling, directing everyone's attention to Silvia's arrival. The Lares who hurled these slanders at her had once been her allies. But they hated her now, and with good reason, for she was a disciple of their enemy. Or so they believed. And it would be dangerous to inform them of the true state of things. Stiffening her backbone, she gazed neither right nor left as she strode toward him whom she despised above all others. Pontifex.

He sat at the end of the carpeted walkway, draped ostentatiously in the skin of a lion. Behind him was a massive wall, covered with nine small doors that were oddly shaped and of varying sizes. After one surreptitious glance, she studiously avoided looking their way again, for it was too painful.

Having noticed her, Pontifex waved away his current visitor, and eyed her up and down as she approached. "Your old friends don't seem too fond of you," he offered snidely and by way of greeting.

His enormous throne was hideous, its high back covered with skulls he'd had gilded and incorporated into its design. Each was the head of a former rival he'd defeated over hundreds of years. A steady slaying and ingesting of them had allowed him to live far beyond the normal life expectancy of a mortal ElseWorld creature. A fresh head hung upon his throne now, blood congealed at its jaggedly sliced throat. Several young Lares sat on the carpet to either side of him. Manacles on their ankles, they looked terrified.

Before Silvia responded to Pontifex, she paused and perused the bountiful display of food set on the pedestal at the end of the carpet to one side of the walkway. She took care in making a selection, just to keep him waiting. And because she was still famished. And because she dreaded this confrontation. Though she feigned confidence, her hand shook as she plucked out a golden pear. He terrified her as much as he did everyone. The only difference between her and them was that she didn't let him know it.

Munching, she gestured to the bloody skull. "I see you've made a new friend yourself, and I doubt he's a fan of yours, either. Murder victims rarely are."

She stood twenty feet away from his throne, unable to move closer without invitation. And a bridge. For between his throne and the throng that awaited his pleasure, there was a fifteen-foot-wide moat filled with an acidic substance from which rose a putrid, chemical smell. Those who displeased him often found themselves tossed into its turbulent waters.

Pontifex reached up and petted the gristled, bloody cheekbone of his recent skeletal acquisition. "A former *augur ex quadrupedibus*. He was quite the hunter."

He stroked his other palm over the lion skin that was draped over his head and body. "This was his finest kill. It becomes me, don't you agree?" The lion he wore had been a magnificent beast, it was plain to see. But now its jaws were artificially propped open and held wide in a frightful, soundless roar, and its eyes were glass. Pontifex wore its head like a ghastly hood so that his own head was held within its mouth. Its jaws framed his face so that he appeared to be the lion's dinner. If only it were so.

"Are we to spend our time together stroking your ego?" Silvia raised her brows and leaned forward a bit, as if only just noticing the woman on all fours who knelt before him with her head bobbing over his lap. "Oh, I suppose not, for I see it's already being stroked."

Shocked gasps rippled over the crowd around her. No one else but she dared speak to him in such a manner. In a strange way, she knew he enjoyed sparring with her. He would have squashed her by now otherwise.

"Where's the other one?" Pontifex asked Silvia, watching her now with slitted eyes. "The Companion."

Silvia tensed. So he wanted to play with her tonight. "In EarthWorld. Doing her duty."

He tapped a long, yellowed fingernail on his chin. "Yes, it's the Calling there, isn't it? Day and night are largely reversed between our world and the next. The moon is high on the other side of the gate. Lord Satyr is no doubt fucking her?"

Silvia ground her teeth. "If he is, it's likely with better results than Occia is achieving here." Hoping to divert his attention from the question of why Michaela suddenly no longer required replenishment at Vesta's fire, she craned her neck toward the woman who still serviced him.

"Greetings, Occia," she cooed. Diverted, Pontifex smirked down at the woman, stroking her hair, for he enjoyed seeing her humiliated.

"I see you've been dabbling in taxidermy again," Silvia went on, referring to the lion. Once a Vestal as well, the woman was skilled in the horrific arts of preparing, stuffing, and mounting the skins of animals to a lifelike effect. "Please, don't get up on my account. I can see that you're busy."

Occia didn't dare take her mouth from Pontifex's prick to spew her usual venomous retort. But she must have faltered in her service, for he winced and gripped her hair, pulling it taut between his fingers. "Careful," he warned in a dangerous tone.

Occia nodded wordlessly and continued her suckling. She had worshipped him for hundreds of years, since they'd all been girls brought to Vesta's temple. Although he was incapable of love, Pontifex enjoyed toying with her, and she ate it up—ate him up. Silvia had seen him invite guests to lift the back of Occia's skirts and fornicate with her while he transacted business with them. On a whim, he might ask the woman to suckle one of his guards or even a dangerous beast. Occia craved humiliation and pain and sex at his hands, and she was jealous of any other creature Pontifex looked upon with favor.

She was the only one of the Vestals who'd ever serviced him . . . voluntarily.

"What have you brought me, Virgin?" he demanded of Silvia.

"I've come to Replenish myself at Vesta's altar."

"First things first. What do you offer in return?" Eager to depart this depressing place, Silvia took the shard from her pocket and hurled it toward him. It sailed high, but fell short, landing on the back of the woman who knelt at his feet.

"Wh-what?" Occia abruptly bowed up from his lap, startled. When she turned in profile to see what had struck her, her lips glistened wet in the candlelight. The shard clattered to the ground and she picked it up.

Slap! Pontifex backhanded her. "Give that to me."

Whimpering, she scrabbled over the marble floor, crablike, and brought it to him. He took the shard and examined it. Then he looked at Silvia, clearly disappointed. "It's not one of the stones."

She shrugged. "No, but it's a step closer. Be happy with it."

"You dare give me orders!" Standing, he tapped his ornate walking stick on the polished, platinum-veined floor, sending sparks of white fire in every direction and causing his audience to cringe.

Although he was elaborately dressed, her peripheral vision informed her that his naked phallus stood high, ruddy, and grotesque from his crotch for all to see. As usual.

She gestured to it and made a *tsking* sound, her voice dripping with false commiseration. "No cure yet? Pity."

Most of his considerable powers had been stolen from his rivals over the years. A decade ago, he'd become enamored with the size of Priapus's cock and had made the colossal mistake of murdering the demigod and absorbing his essence. And now, like Priapus himself, his phallus had grown freakishly large.

But there had been an unforeseen side effect. Pontifex's cock now stood eternally erect, with little hope of ejaculation. It required almost constant suckling or he sickened. These days, she rarely saw him without a mouth or some sort of orifice attached to his organ.

"Watch your tongue, Virgin," he warned. "Or put it to better use as Occia does."

He sank back onto his throne and turned the shard over and over in his fingers. "Where did you find this? And what the hells is it?"

Crunch. She finished off her pear and tossed its core into the moat, where it fizzed into oblivion. "I found it in the *Forum Romano.* On the eldest Satyr lord's desk. It bears the word *Amata* as you see. There can be no doubt it's from Vesta's temple."

This presumed betrayal of the goddess on her part brought more insults her way from the Lares. "Silence!" Pontifex thundered. Immediately, the disparaging remarks subsided.

As he studied the shard, her gaze flicked surreptitiously upward, her heart weeping at the sight of those nine doors. For beyond them, secreted deep in the wall itself, were unseen cages. Some were only a dozen inches across and others as big as three feet or so. None were large enough to house a woman. But all were big enough to jail an Ephemeral spirit.

The doors were designed in quirky, haphazard shapes, like cells in some crazy, outsized honeycomb. If she weren't careful, two more would be built there, and she and Michaela could wind up in residence against their wills, along with dear Licinia, Floronia, and so many others. She grieved most especially over the incarceration of sweet, simple Aemilia, who'd always tried so hard to please. Aemilia would never understand why she was being mistreated in this way and likely believed it was because she'd actually done something wrong.

"Has Satyr found your stone?" Pontifex asked her eagerly.

Her eyes dropped to his, hating him. "Only this shard so far. But tonight I showed him the way to the House and Temple. He'll begin digging soon."

"Soon?" Pontifex's expression soured and she felt the crowd's wariness. "How long will it take?"

She shrugged. "A month or more, I imagine."

"Too long!" he roared, striking his fist on the arm of his throne.

At his bellow, the young Lares on either side of the throne cowered. She wanted to go to them and gather them in her arms and console them. But if she did so, he would only harm them in order to hurt her. The best way to protect them was to ignore them. The day would come when she would free them all. But that day was not today.

Occia was sitting at his feet as well, gazing hungrily at his distended cock. Angry at her for not offering comfort to the Lares, when she so easily could have, Silvia sniped at her. "How can you just sit by?"

Occia blinked. "Because I love him. Something you wouldn't understand, *Virgin*."

Pontifex dipped his fingers in a small basin of oil he kept nearby and began stroking himself with one fist, making smacking sounds. "It grows painful," he snarled, as if it were Occia's fault.

Fellatio could be strenuous, and even Occia had her limits, it seemed. She snapped her fingers toward one of the Lares and indicated Pontifex's lap. But Pontifex held the new candidate away and instead leaned toward Silvia, the light of the devil in his eyes.

"Why don't you put that hot, clever mouth of yours to better use . . . *niece?*" He smiled, his voice suddenly gone silky and mesmerizing. It was a voice he'd stolen from a Siren he'd murdered. The sound of it had lured many into his unspeakable web. A bridge materialized across the moat and he curled his fingers, beckoning her to take the short walk across it to his throne. "Come, Silvia. Sit upon your uncle's lap."

Silvia's skin crawled at the very idea. And at the reminder of their blood tie. She covered her ears against the magic in his voice, but it was no use. Words of refusal formed in her mouth, but she could not make them fall from her lips while his voice filled her head. He could still render her willing as he had others before her. The thought chilled her.

Occia's brown eyes narrowed and she shot her a look of loathing as she spoke to Pontifex. "You can't want *her*. She's flawed!" She gestured toward the scar marring Silvia's otherwise smooth cheek. "Let me try again," she pleaded eagerly. "I have obtained a new potion from one of the apothecaries, who specializes in the Arts of Aphrodisia." Pontifex knocked her away, sending her to the very brink of the moat. The ends of her long brown hair fell into its waters and were singed away.

"Come, Silvia," he repeated. He leaned forward and the lion's pelt parted, revealing his bare chest beneath it. A single, large pendant in the shape of a ring pierced his left breast, in the fleshy muscular part just above his nipple. On the ring were nine small keys that could open the Wall of Doors. Free the others. If she got close enough to him, maybe . . . No! He was planting foolish ideas in her mind. If she succumbed, he would soon own her Ephemeral soul, too!

Seeing the direction of her gaze, he strummed his fingers over the keys, brushing them back and forth so they made an almost musical sound. He smiled slightly, revealing sharp, white teeth that could tear a man twice his size limb from limb before he knew what hit him.

Somehow, she managed to shake off his spells. "I have felt the effects of your avuncular love once before." Silvia brushed her fingertips along the scar, reminding him of its cause.

"I won't hurt you," he lied.

"Yet you ask me to break my vows?" she went on. "To go

the way of so many before me?" She fluttered a careless hand toward the wall of cages behind him, hoping he couldn't see how it shook with fear and revulsion. "You'll forgive me, *Uncle,* if I forgo the pleasure of taking your cock as pacifier. Thank you all the same."

He ground his jaw, angered and obviously in pain, then sat back on his throne and gestured at his prick. "Do something," he muttered to Occia, and heaved a sigh of relief when she put her tired mouth back to work.

"Go!" he told Silvia, but she didn't move.

"I brought you a tithe," she reminded him. She nodded toward the shard he still held. "Let me be Replenished."

"Do it, then, and get out! When next I see you and that other one, there had better be a Vestal firestone in both of your fists."

At his command, a ring of guards stepped away from a high marble pedestal to her left. Upon it rested a shallow golden bowl several feet in diameter. The sacred hearth of Vesta, brought here in 394 A.D. from the Roman Forum. Her eternal flame had once burned brightly within it day and night. It pained Silvia now to see the hearth so cold and empty.

She took the three steps up to it and laid her hands upon its outer rim as if holding it. There were twelve shallow depressions running around it, just inside the rim. Six contained stones.

The guards leaned in to watch her every move, lest she attempt to make off with any of them. All the other Vestals had revealed the locations of their stones to him, but only six had been located. The other six still remained at large, and those were the ones she sought in EarthWorld. Her own and Michaela's were among them. If she brought them to him, Vesta's fire would leap high again. But he would possess the goddess's fire and use it for some evil purpose. Silvia would not let that happen.

She closed her eyes, shutting out the despicable horror of her surroundings. Quietly, she murmured a benediction to her goddess. The preternatural heat of her hands intensified with each word she uttered, until the air near the surface of the bowl began to shimmer. A flame suddenly burst from the center of the bowl, scattering the guards.

Lifting her chin, she inhaled deeply of the wisps of magic that flumed upward, and gloried in the replenishing of her eternal spirit. Ephemerals were kept alive only by virtue of Vesta's fire, which she and the eleven others carried in their hands. But their fire—their very lives—must be renewed periodically by contact with the remnants of this single fire brought here from ancient Rome after the destruction of the temple.

Replete at last, Silvia opened her eyes and stepped back. The fire in the golden bowl dwindled, then quickly died.

Somewhere behind her, Pontifex spoke. "Gods, you are never more beautiful than when you do that." His voice was thick with emotion and lust. "It makes me want to come inside you. To drill myself in your heat and never leave."

Violently repulsed, she refused to glance his way as she slowly shook her head. Putting her palms together, she brought forth her own renewed inner flame, created a firegate, and promptly vanished from his domain.

The instant she rematerialized in EarthWorld, Silvia felt the near-dead summoning her. In a city as large as Rome, there were always some who found themselves hovering on the brink of their demise at any given time, just as surely as others were being newly born. It was the former that now called to her.

. . . please, let me live a while longer . . . there is so much left to do . . . my children, what will they do without me . . . my cat . . . my fortune . . . my husband . . . my wife . . . please . . .

Some in the worlds considered the work of an Ephemeral to be cruel, but in fact, those who lay dying hoped she would choose them. Begged for her to resurrect them so that they might live on, if only for a time. There was always something they'd left undone; and in exchange for the temporary use of their bodies, she would help them finish it.

The prospect of taking on a new corporeal form gave Silvia purpose and helped her shake off the lingering revulsion she felt after having visited Pontifex's realm. She could have her pick of hosts tonight and sifted through the macabre possibilities on offer. A lowborn prostitute, an elderly clergyman, a twelve-year-old Imp pickpocket, a fey fishmonger. The list went on and on. Although a dozen were caught in the clutches of the grim reaper at this very moment, these four seemed the best candidates.

She would need to don fleshly form in order to insinuate herself into the inner workings of what went on in that large white tent in the Forum. But who best to aid her in getting close to Bastian Satyr? She envisioned likely scenarios: A prostitute might woo him into illicit sex. No, that would be a betrayal of her Vestal vows and of Michaela's trust. A clergyman might marry him to her best friend. No, that didn't sit well either, and was getting ahead of things since there had been no mention of a wedding. A fishmonger? No, since she doubted Lord Satyr did his own marketing, and it wouldn't achieve her goal of inserting herself into his life.

That left the pickpocket. An Impish youth would come across as harmless. And the boy's thieving skills would be useful ones to add to her ever-growing repertoire. After all, she *was* here to steal from Lord Satyr.

Settling on her choice, she made haste toward the unfortunate victim. If he died before she arrived, it would be too late. She must be there at the very instant of death in order to claim him.

Half an hour later, Silvia reached the ruins of Aqua Claudia. Remnants of the ancient brick-faced aqueduct had been incorporated into the Aurelian Wall, which had once surrounded the Seven Hills of Rome. Its nooks and crannies were favorite hiding places of the homeless and nefarious populations of the city.

She found the boy hidden beneath one of the aqueduct's crumbling arches, where bricks had been hollowed out to form a sleeping place. He lay shivering on a makeshift pallet, his breath shallow. If she hadn't been pulled here and known where to look, she'd have missed him entirely. A dusty, white, mixed-breed dog she hadn't noticed at first rose from his side, standing stiff and cautious. Few animals could sense her in this altered state, but canines were among them. They eyed one another, sizing up their intentions. Uncertain, he barked once.

She held out her hand, letting him sniff. "It's all right. I'm here to help," she coaxed. Still unsure, the dog went back to his master, nudging him worriedly with his wet nose. Silvia moved closer and knelt beside the boy. He was very close to death. She would have to act quickly. She didn't know what had caused his illness, but once she melded with him, she would know everything there was to know about him.

All was quiet as she did what she must. Moments later, she stood and stared at the empty pallet. The dog sniffed her again, suspicious. She knew his name now. Salvatore. And her own adopted name—Rico. Rico, the twelve-year-old pickpocket, who had been bitten on his ankle by a rat two days ago, and who had been orphaned as a baby and learned the skill of thieving on the street from a variety of sources. He was quick-witted, and though unschooled, had taught himself to read. And he loved Sal above all else. He had trained and cared for him over the past year since he'd found him starving in the streets.

"Good boy, Salvatore." She extended a hand to the dog as she'd done before. Another sniff. This time with a better result. The dog's tail wagged tentatively, then more exuberantly in recognition. In the early days after a resurrection, a host's scent, memories, and emotions still thrived. Believing her to be his master, the dirty dog followed her from the aqueduct, prancing with excitement.

No one she passed paid her any mind. To all appearances, she was a ragged, homeless boy with only a dog and a small rusty knife in her pocket to call her own. She had for all intents and purposes assumed Rico's identity.

Instead of dying as he should have, his body would now live on, through her. But for no more than one month. The Dead always passed on at Moonful. Still, she would retain some of his abilities and memories after he left this world, just as had happened with every host. So in a small way, a part of him would continue on within her forever.

She called Sal to her side, and when she patted him, a puff of dust fluffed in the air from his coat. "*Phew!* I think the first order of business is a bath. For both of us. Come on, boy."

The dog whined. But fortunately, he followed. It was a matter of personal pride to her that she had never yet failed to fulfill the Deathwish of one of her hosts. Rico had worried for the future of his dog. She'd promised to find Sal a home. And she would.

"I wonder how Lord Satyr likes dogs," she mused aloud as they headed for the Forum.

Scena Antica II

February 2, 374 A.D.
Vestal House, Rome, Italy

Along with the other eleven initiates, six-year-old Silvia was taken from her parents that first morning and ushered inside the Atrium House in the Roman Forum. The girls were separated almost immediately, before they could speak to one another, and each was led by an entourage of attendants into a discrete chamber. Although she complained vociferously, Silvia nevertheless found herself poked and prodded as her teeth, ears, and eyes were examined.

Despite her struggles, her shift was subsequently removed and every inch of her skin checked for flaws. Upon passing this test, she was laid on her back upon a stone table by hard hands at her wrists and ankles, and she was gently examined high between her legs. Amid her angry shrieks, a large hand smoothed over her hair. She looked up to see Pontifex standing beside her.

"Only a virgin can serve the goddess, dear niece," he soothed. "We have to be sure."

"Sure of what?" she demanded tearfully.

Her captors smiled among themselves. "So innocent," said Pontifex, pleased.

When they were thoroughly satisfied, she was allowed to rise. Immediately, she tried to flee but was caught again and bathed. Her golden-red hair, which her father had called sunset-beautiful, was then summarily shorn until she was bald. By now she was sobbing uncontrollably.

"Your locks will be hung on the branches of the lotus capillata as a devotional offering to the Gods," she was told. As if that made everything all right.

Her own simple shift had disappeared, and she was now clothed in a soft, white, flowing one, which was clasped at her breast by a fiery opal brooch. Her smooth head was loosely draped with an infula—a scarf that fell over her shoulders. Then she was released barefoot into the center of the rectangular, column-lined atrium. Furious and humiliated, she tested the doors at either end.

"I've already tried them," said a girl from behind her. "They're locked."

Like her, the girl was now wearing a white shift and head covering. Beneath it, she was bald. Her violet eyes looked huge in her olive-skinned face and her cheeks were tear-streaked. "What do you think they are going to do to us?" she asked.

Another girl with brown hair and eyes joined them, having been released into the Atrium by their captors as well. "We're going to serve the goddess," she said.

"Why us?" asked Silvia. "Why choose us?"

The violet-eyed girl held her hands out, palms up. "They said I was chosen because of my talent." She touched Silvia's bare arm and Silvia felt the warm tingle on her skin. Surprised, she touched the girl's arm with her own palm in return. The girl started at the sensation, and they smiled at one another in wondrous recognition.

"We're alike," Silvia breathed. Despite her fear of this place, a tentative curl of joy wrapped itself around her heart. She'd always felt so different, so alone. To find another like her was something she'd prayed to the Gods for every night.

The third girl touched each of them with one of her hands and Silvia jumped as she felt the burning tingle from her as well. "Ow!" This girl's touch had stung. More girls joined them, each with her head newly shaven. When questioned, they all revealed that they, too, had been born with a strange preternatural heat in their palms.

Once all twelve girls stood in the atrium, servants brought out a feast such as Silvia had never seen before. Trenchers of melon, grapes, and olives. Platters of meat, fish, bread, and cheese. Pitchers of honeyed water and wine. The girls crowded around, eager for a taste. But then Pontifex came and they were told to wait as a large, shallow golden bowl was placed with great ceremony upon a pedestal at the center of everything.

Then he raised his arms wide and addressed them. "Initiates! You are privileged to wear the twelve jewels of Aeneas at your breasts, precious opals brought to this world from ancient Troy. Before we feast, each of you will remove the jewel from your brooch and solemnly insert it into one of these depressions within the bowl," he instructed. He ran a fingertip around the inside of the bowl, indicating the two rings of six concave cavities each. "Note that one ring is set higher than the other. Take great care in your choice."

When no one else volunteered, Silvia pried the opal from her brooch, went to the bowl, and randomly placed it in one of the upper depressions.

"Our first Virgin!" Pontifex proclaimed, setting an olive wreath on her head with great care and excitement, as if she'd accomplished something awesome. She went to the table but was disappointed to discover that it was guarded and that she must wait for all of the others to do as she had before she could feast.

The violet-eyed girl went next. Sending Silvia a smile, she inserted her jewel in the lower ring, just below hers. Instead of an olive wreath, one made of laurel was placed upon her head. "Our first

Companion!" The brown-eyed girl embedded hers in the lower ring and was given a laurel wreath as well. "Our second Companion!" Pontifex announced.

The other girls came forward one by one, and the placement of each jewel was announced by Pontifex and then echoed by a scribe who noted it on a tablet. Once the bowl finally blazed with the shine of twelve fiery opals, Silvia and the others were made to repeat words whose meaning they didn't fully comprehend: "Today I am remanded to the care and keeping of Vesta's fire. For three decades I will serve her and the flame of hearth and home."

As their chanting died away, a stunningly beautiful flame in colors of scarlet, gold, sapphire, fuchsia, and titanium erupted spontaneously from the center of the bowl. Shocked, the girls leaped back. But Pontifex only smiled beneficently. Lifting the bowl, he left the atrium with it, pompously announcing that he was removing it to the adjacent temple.

Once he departed in great state, they feasted. The violet-eyed girl came to sit with Silvia. "I'm Michaela," she whispered.

5

In her new incarnation as Rico, Silvia strode through the Forum along the ancient street, Via Sacra. It was a beautiful, crisp February day and she was half-amused to find herself bouncing as she walked. She felt an unusual energy within herself and put it down to the optimism of youth.

Her new host might be a pickpocket, but he was also a bright boy, full of curiosity. He had a youth's natural fondness for treasure hunting, and his interest was piqued by the prospect of digging up the Forum. Sharing his excitement came naturally, for she was bonded with him for the foreseeable future.

Observing the work on all sides of her, she was gratified by the frenzy of activity. Sections of earth were being measured and cordoned off in the vicinity of the complex that included Vesta's temple and the Atrium House that she'd once called home. The very spot she'd shown to Lord Satyr only last night.

"Looks like Michaela's leisurely lover can move quickly when it is warranted, eh, Sal?" The dog's ears perked at his name and she gave his head a friendly pat.

Unfortunately, the temple and house were currently buried. In fact, the entire Forum was only a scattering of weathered marble blocks, soaring columns, partially excavated arches, and broken walls. But she remembered it from ancient times as a lively place where on any given day, thousands of pedestrians had surged through a maze of stalls exchanging gossip and coin. This had once been the political, religious, and cultural center of Rome—the place to witness a sacrifice, procure a prostitute, or hear a political speech. After the fall of the empire, flooding from the Tiber River and a slow accumulation of sediment had built up year after year, obscuring everything.

"Only eighteen or so feet of earth to excavate by my estimation," she told Sal. "No doubt Lord Satyr will drag his feet over every inch. I'll have to light a fire under him." Silvia grinned at her own joke, a favorite of the flame-tending Vestals fifteen hundred years ago.

She bit into the apple she'd just stolen from a vendor's display in the nearby market. Rico's thieving skills were impressive. Using Sal as a distraction, she'd managed to lift a veritable feast of bread, cheese, and fruit, which they'd finished off between them. For the first time in days, she wasn't hungry in the least. And she was clean. She'd managed to bathe both herself and Sal in Bernini's "ugly boat" fountain at the base of the Spanish Steps before being shooed away by the *polizia*.

Ahead, between the old basilica and Caesar's temple, she spied the gargantuan white tent that served as Bastian's headquarters. There were flaps set in all four of its sides, which would be open in good weather. Today, all were shut against the cold breeze, but she saw shadows move within. It appeared that Lord Satyr already had company.

"What do you think, Sal? Shall we pay a call on Michaela's beau?" Sal barked, and she nodded to him. "*Sì*, I think so as well." She tossed the apple core a distance away and he chased it, gobbling it before it hit the ground. Then he returned to her and they continued on.

A small building of some sort was being erected not far from Bastian's tent, and the sound of paving materials and hammers echoed over the grounds. Taking care to avoid being noticed by the construction workers, she meandered circuitously around to the back of the tent. She knelt outside it, then held Sal's mouth closed for a few seconds, indicating that he was to remain quiet. He didn't protest. Rico had taught him the trick of remaining silent when *polizia* occasionally came to the aqueduct to roust out squatters. Drawing forth Rico's prized, rusty knife, she pried open a corner of one of the sealed flaps, creating a slit at eye level in the canvas. Then she put one eye to the hole and settled in to spy.

Inside, Bastian sat at an enormous desk, looking twice as large as she remembered. Of course she was now only two-thirds of her normal size. But that didn't account for the fact that he also looked twice as handsome as she recalled.

"There are those in the Ministry of Culture who grow restless with the cost," the man seated across from him was saying. "They wonder if results cannot somehow be achieved more quickly." Sizing him up, she disliked this stranger on sight. Though he was dark haired and handsome, there was a cruel twist to his lips.

Bastian tapped his fingertips on his desk blotter, slowly and precisely, as if his patience was being strained. "Systematic excavations began here just over one decade ago. Since I took charge of them seven years ago, I have located tenfold of what was found prior, with far less damage and better recordkeeping. My methods are sound. If it's haste and blundering you want, Minister Tuchi, then find someone else to lead these digs."

"No!" His companion leaned forward, his manner ingratiating now. "I didn't mean to give offense. It's just that nothing has been discovered since November."

"You call the amphorae of Bacchus nothing?" Sounding irritated, Bastian carefully unrolled a map on his desk and began studying it, giving the other man only half of his attention, apparently having grown bored with him.

"No *major* discoveries, I mean."

Silvia kept her eyes on the minister. He was slender, dressed well, and his mannerisms were effeminate. And when Bastian rose to get a book from his shelf, the man studied the contours of his well-shaped backside with ill-concealed hunger, then quickly removed his top hat and placed it to cover his lap. He was obviously attracted to Michaela's beloved as a man usually was to a woman.

"What, then, of the urns of Jupiter?" Lord Satyr murmured, sounding distracted. He shifted his attention back to the map on his desk, appearing to compare it to an illustration in the book.

"Urns? Bah! Take a dozen steps in any direction in Rome and you'll stumble upon two dozen of them. No, the Parliament wants something spectacular. They want to be titillated or made rich. Both if you can manage it. Jewels! Gold! Statues. A gilded Venus. Something the likes of which will be the envy of every museum in the world!"

Without looking up from his desk, Bastian enquired, "Will Vestals do?"

An excited gasp split the air. Then eager questions came. "Do you mean the Virgins? You've found the Virgins?"

Bastian inclined his head in a regal sort of affirmation. "A complex containing the temple and house, as well as the Regia. Or so I believe." He gestured in Silvia's direction, and she ducked, before his next words made it clear he hadn't noticed her. "In the area you no doubt saw across the way, now being cordoned off into sections."

"But are you sure? What clues have you found?"

"A shard with the single word *Amata* written upon it. It's

the name Pontifex Maximus gave each of the virginal initiates as he selected them to serve Vesta."

"May I see it?"

"No."

"But—"

"It went missing last night."

Silvia had known he would notice the loss of the shard, of course, but the spurt of guilt she felt for her part in its theft surprised her.

The minister began blustering something about lax security, but Bastian cut him off, saying, "To prevent subsequent thefts, I've authorized the construction of the more permanent structure you see being built next to us. Henceforth it will serve as locked storage for especially valuable artifacts until they can be curated."

"I see." A pause. "As you progress, will you, um, do the actual digging out of the Virgin's temple yourself?" Silvia rolled her eyes. The man was undressing Bastian with his gaze, no doubt imagining him sweating at hard labor, muscles bulging. It was a scene she wouldn't mind observing herself.

"Some." Bastian shrugged. "But archaeology is not all digging."

"When will you know for certain that you've located the Vestal complex?"

A silence. Fingertips tapped the desktop again. Lord Satyr's patience was thinning dangerously. "A month? Possibly less. But all will get done more quickly if you vacate my office now so that I may better concentrate on my work." He stood and gestured toward the door.

The minister's eyes furtively swept his impressive physique, and his Adam's apple bobbed. "You're rude, Signor." This fact seemed to excite him, for he had to re-cross his legs and readjust the position of his hat.

"Only busy, Minister." Bastian wandered out of Silvia's sight, ostensibly to usher his guest out.

She considered moving to better observe, but Sal was growing restless. She wrapped her fingers around his muzzle again and shook a finger at him, then released him, hoping he would remain silent just a few more moments. Then, without warning, the flap on her side of the tent was suddenly whipped open. A large hand came at the back of her neck, snatching her up by the collar, and yanking her into the tent.

Dangling in midair, Silvia looked up into unyielding silver eyes. She'd been discovered! By Lord Bastian Satyr. This close, he was a terrifying, indomitable giant. With the flex of one bicep, he held her high and seemingly without effort. Although Sal was barking and dancing around his legs, and the minister was demanding explanations, the sounds of all hell breaking loose around them seemed distant to her as she felt herself fall into those silver eyes. This close, she could see that they were shot with flecks of moss green and ringed with a thin band of ebony.

"You're choking me!" she protested, hooking a finger at her shirt collar. It wasn't true, and he knew it. She churned her legs, kicking at him, and pushed both hands flat against the sculpted rock that was his chest. Gods, under his fine tailoring, he was built like a gladiator! Men like this weren't often found here on this side of the gate.

"Is this your thief?" the minister demanded, hovering just behind him. "Does he have the shard?"

Bastian eyed her like she was a particularly interesting bug he'd caught on a pin. "That remains to be seen. I believe you were on your way out, Minister?"

"*Buon giorno,*" Silvia told the politician sarcastically, wiggling two fingers in farewell.

She noted the slight curve of Bastian's lips and knew him to

be amused, even as the minister's expression tightened in irritation. "You might take a more accommodating tone when next
we meet, Lord Satyr," he snipped. "I'll remind you that it is the
Italian Ministry of Culture upon which you rely for continued
access to the digs. And we vote on your reinstatement as lead
here at the next session. With the departure of my predecessor,
mine is now the deciding vote." Smacking his tall, felt hat on his
head, he departed in a decided snit.

"Bastard."

Silvia started at this utterance, realizing only then that there
had been a third, silent man in the room all along, who was
seated in the corner chair. Another silver-eyed Satyr. This one
was younger than Bastian and leaner, his skin pale as if it had
rarely seen the sun. Pontifex had schooled her well on their
family's history. This was likely Lucien, the one who'd gone
missing for years and whose reputedly fearsome talents were
shrouded in mystery. He'd known pain in his life, this one. Yet,
there was something hauntingly beautiful about that haggard,
watchful face.

She glanced back at Bastian, and saw he was still analyzing
her with those shrewd eyes of his. She shrank into her shirt up
to her nose, fearing he would somehow discover her ruse.

"Let them nag as they will, Luc," said Bastian. "In spite of
Tuchi's complaints, I've achieved more than Parliament hoped
for and in a shorter time than planned. There is no one skilled
enough to replace me, and they will continue to accede to my
way of doing things as they always have."

"And him? What will you do with your little thief?" Lucien
asked, flicking his fingers to indicate Silvia.

"Offer him a reward?" suggested Bastian, his smile broaden-
ing. "After all, it was his appearance that rescued us from the
minister."

At the sight of that masculine smile, Silvia stopped struggling for a moment, watching him with bemused fascination. He had a sense of humor? Michaela hadn't mentioned that. "The only reward I want from you is my release," she informed him. "And a job."

"I don't employ thieves," he returned. He seemed to finally register the fact that Sal was dashing about, barking wildly and nipping at his boots. Lowering her to the ground, he murmured, "Luc."

Behind her, Lucien whistled a single, clear note. Instantly, Sal went quiet, his head whipping toward Bastian's brother. As if in a trance, he trotted over to him, lay at his feet with his muzzle on his front paws, and proceeded to snore.

"Keep your spells to yourself, you blasted Satyr! What the hells did you do to him?" Silvia demanded. She lunged in the dog's direction, reaching out for him, but a large hand caught the back waistband of her trousers and slung her to sit on the edge of the desk.

"You'll have your dog back when you answer my questions, Imp," said Bastian, looming over her. "Where's the shard?"

"What's a chard?" she asked, feigning ignorance.

"Answer me!" He gave her a shake, his voice going hard. Suddenly he'd gone fierce and frightening again.

"Why do you suspect that I'm the one who took your—whatever it is?"

His lips tightened. "When I leave each night, I make sure this tent and the perimeter of the Forum grounds are webbed with unseen spells. Spells that turn human trespassers away without their knowing why. But there are some creatures they cannot repel. Aren't there, Luc?"

"That would be ElseWorld creatures," his brother affirmed. "Such as Imps."

"I didn't—" Silvia began.

Suddenly, Bastian's hands were everywhere, running over

her back, ribs, belly, the outsides of her thighs, the insides. "Stop it!" she shrieked, wriggling to escape him. Rico was apparently ticklish.

Coming up with nothing displeased her interrogator. He planted his hands on either side of her atop the desk and pressed his body threateningly close, leaning over her until she fell backward onto the surface of his desk to avoid him.

"Have you sold it?" he asked with a quiet ferocity that chilled her.

"No!" Fisting both hands, she wedged her elbows between them, but he proved impossible to shove off. Yet when her knuckles accidentally brushed against his throat, something changed in his face. Abruptly, he reared back from her as if he'd been burned. She stared at him in wary surprise.

Lucien half-rose from his seat, looking alarmed. "Bastian?"

But the eldest Satyr motioned his brother off and continued staring at her. Some deep emotion passed over his expression, like a fast-moving thundercloud in a changing, stormy sky.

Oh no! Had she—? Silvia glanced at her hands, relieved to see that both were still fisted. She was always careful not to touch others open-palmed, for she still carried Vesta's fire, no matter whom she assumed as host.

But if her palms hadn't grazed him, why was he acting so oddly?

Stunned, Bastian stared down into the Impish boy's face.

He had just seen color again! For only the third time in his life. And all three occurrences coming within two days of one another. Again this time, along with the color, he'd experienced that same rush of lust. Damnation, the urge to go looking for the first willing female he encountered surged strong in him. What the hell was happening? He rounded his desk and flung himself into his chair, giving his body time to recover. And allowing himself a moment to consider the matter.

The Imp's fist had brushed his throat. When flesh had met flesh, that's when the color had flared. It had not been vivid this time. Rather, it was as if a black and white scene had been washed with pastel shades by some invisible, unearthly paintbrush.

As soon as he had let the boy go, the color had subsided. Although he craved more of it, he found it suspect. Why, after twenty-nine years of life, was this happening to him? And how? What could the Presence he'd felt yesterday morning, the childish wraith of yesterday afternoon, and this Imp possibly have in common?

"Your name," he demanded sharply. "What's your name, Imp?"

"Rico."

He crossed his arms. "Your *real* name."

The boy looked nervous, bolstering his suspicions that some trickery was afoot. His eyes never leaving his captive, he spoke to his brother. "Imps are notorious liars and thieves, are they not, Luc?"

"That's my understanding," came the reply. The boy sent him a sour glance that for some reason made Bastian want to laugh. Schooling his features to sternness, he said, "Shall I take you to the *polizia* and see what they can pry out of you?" His brother rose, disturbing the dog and making as if to take the Imp into custody.

"Wait!" Rico backed away, then quickly asked Bastian, "How did you discover that I was outside the tent just now?"

Bastian sat back in his father's chair, hearing the discreet, familiar creak of expensive leather under him. "I know the scent of Imp when I smell it."

"Then, answer me this. Did you smell 'Imp' this morning in your tent, after the theft occurred?"

"The boy makes a good point," Lucien noted.

The brat *did* make a good point, for he hadn't detected such a scent. "Yet, you were eavesdropping just now," he accused with gentle menace. "Why come here today, if not to steal?"

Rico shrugged. "Heard you found some Virgins, so I came running to see what's what." He grinned in a boyish leer that was strangely innocent. The minute the words tumbled out, he pressed fingers to his lips in surprise, as if dismayed he'd spoken them. Visibly shaking off his discomfort, he added, "And I've come to *trade* you information, not steal it."

"What could you possibly know that would interest me?"

"Got some information about the Virgins, is what."

Bastian snorted in gentlemanly disbelief.

The boy commenced ticking facts off on his fingers, "One: Aeneas brought the eternal fire to Vesta's temple from Troy. Two: It burned there for nine hundred years. Three: Twelve Vestals kept it going. Four: In ancient times, magistrates—like that love-starved minister who just left, for instance—sacrificed to Vesta before taking office. Five . . . I can keep going. Any questions?"

Twelve Vestals, the boy had said. Not six as the philosophers mentioned. The other information he could have learned from books or teaching. But even Bastian himself hadn't suspected there were twelve, until last night's vision.

"How is it that you spew ancient history like an encyclopedia?" Bastian asked, his interest now thoroughly captured.

Rico spread his hands. "Don't know. Just do. Hire me to work for you, and I'll tell you more of what I know." Cocky now that he'd impressed them, he sauntered around the room, cursorily examining the vast collection of books and artifacts. Having come awake, his dog trailed him.

Bastian and Lucien exchanged glances. "Looking for more plunder?" Bastian enquired.

The boy lifted and dropped his shoulders carelessly. His eyes lit on the small white box of expensive chocolates on one of the shelves. Michaela had a fondness for them, and Bastian had bought them for her. Rico bent and sniffed. His stomach growled and he put a hand to it, looking a trifle embarrassed. His eyes shot toward Bastian. "For your wife?"

"None of your business."

"Ladylove, then? If you're looking for gifts, I know a bit of cly faking. Can filch you some fine handkerchiefs over in the market. Just say the word—"

Before the Imp could finish, his dog leaped up. In an instant, it snatched the box from the shelf and was now intent on ripping it apart to reach the chocolates within.

"Sal!" Rico scolded. When he tried to retrieve the torn box, the dog took it in his teeth and bounded off, running in circles around the tent. *Whap!* His tail smacked a terracotta urn, knocking it against an adjacent one in just the wrong way. It cracked, partially shattering into pieces.

With a muffled oath, Bastian took a long step in the dog's direction. It bounded around his feet growling, unwilling to give up its sweet treasure. "Ninety hells! Get that mutt out of here! Luc!"

Again, his brother summoned the dog. The half-eaten chocolates were immediately dropped and forgotten as Sal went to him. This time, however, he wasn't sent into slumber, but only sat there at Lucien's feet, watchful.

Rico picked up the mangled confectioner's box, looking unsure what to do with it. "His name is Salvatore."

"Savior?" murmured Bastian, surveying his cracked urn. "Hardly seems fitting under the circumstances."

Sidling over to the desk, Rico set the box on it and then stood there, digging one toe of his sandal to trace a pattern in the carpet. "I call him Sal. He's a good rat catcher." He glanced around as if looking for rodents. "Might be useful to have a dog around here. You interested? Only one lira."

Bending over the urn, Bastian gingerly inspected the destruction. "One lira for that flea-ridden mongrel?"

The boy glanced at the dog, who was scratching. "*Fermi quello!*" he scolded softly. Then to Bastian, he persisted. "He wouldn't have fleas if he had a good home. Maybe—"

"I don't have time for a dog. I'm here from five in the morning until ten at night."

"He could keep you company here," Rico persuaded. "He'd make a good guard dog. He could watch over your shards for you. Some of this pottery looks valuable."

Bastian held up a fractured piece of the urn. "Some of it was," he said sardonically.

"He could even keep that minister away," Rico went on.

"In that case, you might want to consider it, brother. Politicians are an annoying lot," Lucien agreed, tongue in cheek. "Since he has taken over his post, Tuchi seems to be constantly underfoot. Every time you turn around, he is here, and for no reason."

"Oh, he has a reason," Rico announced. Two sets of silver gazes swung in his direction. He pressed his fingertips to the seam of his mouth as he had the previous time, as if hoping to stop his own runaway mouth. But words burst from him nevertheless. "The minister likes men. In his bed."

"What?" Bastian blustered in astonishment.

Lucien cocked his head, consideringly. "An *omosessuale?*"

"He had a knot the size of a fist in his pants. Don't tell me neither of you noticed?" Rico insisted.

Bastian rubbed a hand over his face, unsure whether to laugh or groan. "What the hells am I going to do with you?"

"Give me a job?" suggested Rico.

"Homeless, are you?" Bastian said, eyeing him speculatively. "And looking for honest work?"

The boy straightened. "Yes!" he said, appearing hardly able to believe his fortune might be taking a lucrative turn.

"Very well. We'll try you at the dig and see how long you last."

* * *

Silvia followed Bastian out of the tent. In view of her recently reduced height, it was hardly surprising that her eyes
naturally dropped to his muscled backside. As he walked, his
hips rolled in a devilishly sexy way that drew the eye. Remembering him as he'd been the morning before, laboring over
Michaela in his bed, she blushed. *Stop it!* she told herself. She
was as bad as the minister!

She quickly found herself taken to his foreman, whom she
recognized as the sneak thief from the tent the previous night.
Interesting.

"What the devil is this?" the foreman demanded when she
was presented to him.

"Our newest employee," Bastian informed him. "Feed him
and his mutt, then put him to work. And don't let him out of
your sight."

Then to her, he said, "Do what Ilari says. We work from six
to two, then we break for lunch and siesta until four. Then
more work until dinner at seven thirty."

Then he turned to go.

Knowing he'd be suspicious if she didn't ask, she called after
him. "What's the pay?"

He tossed a figure back at her. She had no idea if his offer
was fair or not, but she nodded. Then he turned back and held
out his hand as if to shake.

Startled, she ignored it and put hers in her pocket, pretending not to understand what he wanted. But from his satisfied
expression, it seemed she'd confirmed something for him by
her reluctance.

"Steal so much as one shard of pottery and I'll see you put in
jail," he said by way of good-bye. With that, he turned on his
heel and disappeared into his tent.

Behind her, she heard Ilari muttering something about not
being a wet-nurse. She had a feeling they weren't destined to be

fast friends. A feeling that quickly gathered momentum when he assigned her the lowest scut work there was to be had.

Within a few hours, she was exhausted. When they broke for lunch, Sal gobbled up his second meal of the day as though he hadn't eaten in a month, then proceeded to nap the afternoon away in a nearby bosk, occasionally rousing himself to trail Bastian when he left his tent to supervise the dig. She, on the other hand, spent her day moving bits of rubble from one pile to another. It was mind- and body-numbing labor, and she made her feelings known to the foreman with an ongoing list of grievances regarding the dirt and cold. The fact that she was irritating him wasn't all her fault. In the first few days, the host still wielded considerable control over the body. It would fade soon, but for now it was difficult to stop Rico from having his say.

From time to time during the day, she saw Bastian standing in the doorway of his tent, eyeing her. Or out in the digs, eyeing her. Or holding maps and gesturing to workmen, and eyeing her. Or shouting orders others leaped to obey. He was obviously a man accustomed to obedience in his work. Yet he wasn't above rolling up his sleeves and joining in at the hard labor, and when a large piece of fresco was located, he was there in the fray, muscles straining as he helped to uncover it.

At the end of the day, he found her again. "You'll return tomorrow?"

Tiredly, she nodded. "Ilari won't get rid of me that easily."

He nodded. "Breakfast is at five thirty. If you want to eat, be here." He glanced around. "Where will you sleep?"

"That's my business." Exhausted, she ambled off in the direction of the most recognizable feature in the Forum: the Arch of Septimius Severus. She had a particular fondness for Emperor Septimius's wife, Julia Domna, for she'd seen to it that Vesta's temple was rebuilt after the fire in 191 A.D.

Silvia curled up in the shelter the arch provided, shivering, and when Sal joined her, she snuggled into his warmth. On her side, she stared at the lights in the large white tent where Bastian still toiled somewhere inside. Now and then she could see his shadow in the lamplight. Didn't he ever tire?

She ran a hand over Sal's fur. "It's good that he's so industrious, don't you agree, Sal? Maybe he'll manage to get a firestone or two out of the ground within the month." She turned on her back. "One can only hope. Because when next Moonful comes, I'll have to shed myself of your owner's body so that I can return to ElseWorld."

Sal whined and licked her face, as if he understood and was saddened by the knowledge. "I know, I know. You may be sure I have no desire to go back to Pontifex, but I must. And I can't return to Rico once I leave him. Still, I promised him I'd find you a good home before I go. And I will." She yawned and turned over, gazing toward the tent again. "In fact, I think I already have."

With the comforting rumble of Sal's furred belly as a pillow, she was almost instantly asleep. Sometime during the night, a blanket found its way over her and was tucked around her by powerful, masculine hands.

She snuggled into it, grateful. Half-asleep, she murmured, *"Buona notte, papa."*

Bastian stood there, looking down upon the boy and wondering at the mystery of him. And then he turned toward home.

Scena Antica III

May 15, 374 A.D.
Rome, Italy

Vestalis Maxima clapped her hands. "Remember, girls. Decorum. All of Rome waits for a glimpse of you at your work on this glorious festival day." Vestalis served the girls in the capacity of mother, and was constantly attending to their manners.

Silvia adjusted her infula, letting the ends of the headdress fall to drape around her shoulders. Her hair was growing out again, but only an inch or so thus far, and it currently curled tight to her head instead of flowing wild and free in its former, customary manner. Michaela's silky, blue-black locks had already shaped themselves into a cropped style that lent her an attractive pixie look. But Occia's thick, unfortunate hair stuck out from her head in odd dirt-colored tufts that would not be tamed. Under their headdresses, all twelve of the shorthaired girls still looked like boys.

It was a curious, privileged kind of life they'd all lived for the past three months since coming to serve Vesta. They were set apart from all of Rome and held in high esteem. Each day, they were schooled by revered scholars, who in the normal course of things only instructed highborn males. Unlike all other women in Rome, they would one day be allowed to own property. They were allotted the best seats at races and gladiator bouts in the Coliseum. And as part of their duties, they reigned at numerous public ceremonies, as they would today.

This morning, having led a procession of worshipful crowds here to the bank of the Tiber, they had then awaited Pontifex. Once he finally arrived to great adulation, he bade them throw their collection of straw figurines called Argei into the river. Over the past few weeks, Roman citizens had placed these simple dolls in the temples to absorb any evil that might be lurking about. The tainted dolls had since been collected and today were to be ritually sacrificed in an effort to purify the city. Silvia pitched a half dozen of them into the Tiber, laughing and leaning out in childish delight to watch them splash. More of the Vestals—Aemilia, Floronia, and Michaela—followed suit, making a game of it.

"Who is that man staring at you?" Occia asked, elbowing her.

Glancing up, Silvia was overjoyed to see her father. She'd had no contact with either of her parents since coming to the temple, and the sight of him sent her running in his direction. She quickly found herself pulled up short by Pontifex's hand. "Father!" she called, struggling to reach him. He stood only a few yards away, his eyes riveted to her.

"Tell her how things are, brother," Pontifex commanded from behind her.

Her father's eyes flicked from her to Pontifex and back again. Then he said softly and with crushing finality, "I am your father no longer, Silvia."

His words struck her like poisonous arrows and she drew back as if from a physical blow. What was so awful about her that her own flesh and blood could not love her? she wanted to cry out. Yet she did not plead with him. Instead, she closed her heart off, and silently vowed never to trust in love again.

Turning, she went to rejoin the others, unaware that two sets of lustful masculine eyes burned over her back.

6

Bastian entered his tent at daybreak the next morning only to find his chair occupied, a small boy-sized coat hanging on his coat rack, and the notes of a crudely made reed flute infusing the air.

"Up, brat," he said.

The music ceased midnote as his newest, youngest employee swung around, scattering the vellum sheets he'd been perusing. One fluttered to the floor and the boy bent to retrieve it before his dog could.

"What are you doing with those?" Bastian demanded.

Rico glanced down at the collection of erotic illustrations on the desktop. His brow lifted, and he absently wove the flute between his fingers one after the other, then back again, with the skill of one who'd done the maneuver often. He shot Bastian a baiting look. "Better question might be what are *you* doing with 'em?"

"They're priceless lithographs." Tossing his coat on the stand to cover the boy's, Bastian waved him up from the chair.

Rico guffawed. "Pull the other one." He tried to sidle past, but Bastian stepped in his way, holding out the flat of his hand, palm up. "I'll take that."

"Wasn't going to thieve." The Imp let go of the thick vellum sheet just above Bastian's hand and it drifted to lie on his palm.

Bastian glanced at it and found himself abruptly struck dumb. The lithograph had changed drastically since the last time he had viewed it. Or rather, his perception of it had. Before, he'd seen it only in blacks and whites. Now, however, it was brilliantly tinted with dazzling color. *Simply because this boy had held it.* Hungrily, Bastian's eyes roved the sheets of paper scattered across his desktop seeing that all appeared pigmented to him now. Leaning over the desk, he shifted them, trying to memorize colors that seemed like rare, precious jewels to a man who'd never seen them before. It was readily apparent which sheets were the ones Rico had touched more recently, for their color was the most vivid and lush. But all were quickly fading.

He studied the illustration in his hand. It was most luminous and depicted three lovers in a ménage à trois—the eternal triangle. Two of the figures were standing and one prone. The latter was female, a receptive courtesan lying on her back upon a mattress. One of her shapely ankles rested high on the shoulder of a male lover, who stood facing her between her thighs. His cock was clearly in the process of embedding itself inside her, even as the other man who stood at his back was in the process of penetrating him. All was meticulously and tastefully rendered, almost in the style of a medical or botanical drawing.

"What's wrong?" Rico demanded, his brows drawing together.

"Nothing," Bastian replied automatically. Hiding the fact that he was color-blind had required a lifetime of subterfuge on his part. But it had been necessary. An archaeologist who was unable to discern the subtleties of color was not one who could have risen to lead the prestigious Forum excavations as he had.

Only his father had known. Bastian had never told another living soul, not even his brothers. Realizing early on that this handicap would prove detrimental to the future of his eldest son's otherwise bright career, his father had schooled him to silence on the matter. He'd taught him to generally determine each color based on its value. And on his own, Bastian had learned other ways to compensate. He'd become highly skilled at tricking others into revealing the color of an object if he wished to know it.

Often, he hired artists to write detailed color descriptions of artifacts he'd found, on the pretext that he was too busy for the task of this recording himself. Over the course of his career, he'd managed to turn his lack to his advantage. Ironically, he'd become renowned for his meticulous care in the description of pigments.

A sense of grief touched him as he watched the residual color slowly fade from the drawing he held—the crimson leaching from the drape behind the woman and from the pillow at her side; the rosy flesh of the three lovers turning gray. It was like watching something die.

With a hard flick of his wrist, Bastian tossed the sheet of paper onto the desk. "They're from a series illustrated by Edouard-Henri Avril. Two years ago, I made an academic study of them and presented it before the Esteemed Society of ElseWorld Antiquarians."

Rico smirked. "Umm-hmm. I'll wager that most admirers of Avril's work weren't of the academic sort."

Bastian's lips curved. "The passage of time does tend to change one's perception of things. Utilitarian objects become artifacts. Something once considered pornographic becomes art."

"This isn't art."

"What is it, then?"

"Fucking," said Rico. Then he darted another of those strangely embarrassed glances toward him, as if startled at the words he himself had uttered. Recovering quickly, he went on, "And if you have to ask someone less than half your age about it, you're going to need more than chocolates to woo your lady-love. You'll need a lesson in what goes where and how often."

Smothering a chuckle, Bastian ordered, "Stack those up and put them back where you found them." As Rico complied, Bastian pondered him. Normally, he got straight to work himself every morning; but last night, he'd mulled the matter of this boy until the wee hours. In all of his years of study, he had never come across a single reference to a creature that could lend color to an adjacent object. Yet, he was certain that this Imp had been the conduit for the transference of color yesterday and again today in the case of the lithographs. Until he could investigate further, he wanted to keep him where he could see him.

"What're you looking at?" Rico challenged, noting his stare.

"How old are you?"

"Old enough." The boy reached across him for one of the drawings and Bastian grabbed his wrist. Immediately, the area around them—his desk, the illustrations, the coats—flashed with color again. "How old?" he demanded.

"Twelve," Rico admitted quickly, twisting away. "Old enough to be looking at the likes of these illustrations, if that's what you're wondering," he said, nodding to the stack in his hands. "In ElseWorld, twelve's plenty old enough for the rites of purification."

"What do you know of that?" Bastian mused, watching the color ebb around him.

"It's February, isn't it? The month of purification in Else-World, just as it used to be here in ancient Rome." The boy deposited the drawings on the shelf, somewhat less neatly than they'd been when he'd found them. Then, instead of going outside to work in the dig, he wandered the perimeter of the room, offering his dog a pat along the way. "If I were in ElseWorld right now, I'd get myself over to the Temple of Venus. And I'd take my turn at the basket of names and choose me a bit of papyrus painted with some female's moniker on it. Whoever I selected would become my lover for a whole year." He paused and sighed, a blissful expression on his face.

"Lucky her."

"Damned right."

Bastian smiled and shook his head, unable to help but find the boy amusing.

"Careful, your face might crack like one of them statues you dig up out there," Rico commented, seeing his amusement.

"Why aren't you out at the tell?"

Rico cocked his head. "What's a tell?

"You mean there's something you don't know? It's the Hebrew word for an archaeological dig or mound." It was rare that Bastian had difficulty concentrating on work, but the urge to continue sparring with the boy was strong. He forced himself to appear busy at his desk. "I'm sure I'm paying you for something besides loitering here."

Rico jerked his thumb toward the general area where he'd toiled yesterday. "My talent is wasted out there." He came to the opposite side of the desk and leaned in confidingly. "I got penmanship, did you know?" He picked up Bastian's pen, intent on proving it. Curling his tongue at one side of his mouth, he wrote his name.

As Bastian looked down on the boy's bent head, something shifted inside him. He well remembered his own avid interest in assisting his father in these digs in any way he could. Recalled his father teaching him to help keep the records. Recalled how eager a sponge he'd once been. Just like this boy.

Turning the paper he'd written on, Rico shoved it toward him across the desk. Bastian wasn't sure what he'd expected, but it wasn't this beautiful cursive. "See?" Rico said smugly. "I don't lie."

"No, you only thieve."

Rico shrugged. "All the more reason to keep me close if that's what you believe. Just so I don't make off with anything."

"I suppose if I ask you where the hells you learned to write like this, you'll say you don't know."

The boy's expression altered to an interesting mixture of adult craftiness and youthful innocence. "Right you are. I was just born knowing some things. All mysterious-like. I can draw, too, and never been taught." He tapped the stack of excavation cards on Bastian's desk. "When you find something in the Forum dirt, I could draw it and do the words for you. Save you some time. And some strain on your aging eyes."

Bastian's aforementioned eyes narrowed. The boy's talents were so exactly what he needed and he'd arrived in a suspicious fashion. It was too convenient. "Documentation of a find *in situ* is exacting work. Training is required."

"Give me something to draw and I'll prove myself," Rico boasted.

Since it suited his purposes to keep the boy under observation, he might as well make use of any gifts he possessed at the same time. Bastian stood, retrieved his coat, and made for the tent's opening. "Very well. Come. And bring some of those cards and a pen. We'll see if we can put your mind to more profitable use."

Once they emerged from the tent, Bastian glanced down at the fine coat Rico wore but could not afford. "Where did that come from?"

"Found it just this morning. All unexpected-like."

"I'll bet."

As they crossed the Forum grounds toward the Vestal dig, the foreman shot an evil look in the boy's direction. Rico only smiled and waved. "Your Signor Ilari looks a little disappointed to see me again."

"Can you blame him?"

"I did my work."

"Yes, I heard how you did it. Grumbling all the way."

"His methods are archaic."

"You have quite the vocabulary when it suits you," Bastian observed.

"I'm a quick study. And you have to admit he's an *idiota*. Where are we going?"

Suddenly realizing that she'd left Bastian several yards back, Silvia retraced her steps to find him poking a trowel into the earth.

Within minutes, he came up with a substantial piece of fresco, which he handed to her.

Surprised, she looked from it to him. "How did you know where to—?"

"Sketch that on your card," he ordered, cutting her off. "You have three minutes."

Dropping to sit cross-legged on the ground, she drew a careful, rudimentary sketch of the painting, then handed it up to him and stood awaiting his verdict.

He studied it a moment, then took the fragment from her and handed it to Ilari, who'd come to observe. The man nodded in grudging admiration.

"Told you I could sketch," she said to Bastian.

"Next to the drawing, we write its scale," was all he said in reply. "To indicate that the fragment itself is approximately three times the size of your drawing, we write 3:1. If the opposite were true—"

"I'd have needed a bigger card."

"And you'd have written 1:3," Bastian continued. "Now, here in the top left corner, we indicate the depth at which an artifact is found, and the approximate date of the item itself. So having found this fragment near the surface, we write Level One, and I estimate its age at 350 A.D." He scribbled the information in a neat hand.

Silvia observed this silently, shifting from one foot to the other with a desire to correct him. She could have told him enough to fill this card and ten more. The fresco had come from a wall of the Atrium House. It had been painted by an artist who smelled of garlic and had owned twelve white cats. He'd been an unimportant figure in history, but one she'd met in the flesh when she was a girl. And Bastian had gotten the date wrong. It had been done in 381 A.D.

Still, he seemed satisfied with her talent, and by the end of that day, she'd completed dozens of cards for him. Some of the artifacts had hardly seemed to warrant recording, but he was extremely meticulous in his work, which led to occasional good-natured bickering between them.

When she dropped off the cards and corresponding bits of pottery in his tent at day's end, a small smile flitted over her lips. The stack of erotic illustrations she'd placed haphazardly on the shelf that morning had been straightened, so that every corner aligned perfectly. "The man is certainly fastidious," she murmured to herself. One of the cards she held fell to the floor and she bent to pick it up.

"What are you doing in here, boy?"

She turned to see Ilari blocking the exit. His expression was suspicious, but likely no more than her own. "I might ask you the same. There's been thieving in this tent before."

Looking on the verge of apoplexy, the man lunged for her. "You dare?"

"What the hells is this?" Bastian demanded, entering to find them at a standoff.

"Nothing," Silvia said easily, putting down the book she'd been about to hurl. "Ilari and I were just bidding each other good night. I happened to mention to him that a shard had been stolen from this tent recently and he seemed to take exception to my statement. Very odd." She left them to make what they would of that.

That night, she bedded down in the lee of the Arch, under the blanket that had mysteriously appeared the night before. She reached out and stroked Sal's fur. "I begin to think Michaela has made a good choice for herself. It takes a weight off me, knowing her Satyr's a good sort."

The dog gave her hand a lick, then padded in a tight circle as if tamping down long grass as his ancestors had done in order to make a good sleeping place. Then he curled up alongside her, his back a warm comfort against her own. She drew the blanket over them both and snuggled in for the night.

Seeing the light go out in the tent, she lifted her head to watch Bastian emerge. He looked in her direction and she ducked. By the time she peered out again, he was wending his way upward toward Esquiline at the far side of the Forum valley. He would pass the night with Michaela in his bed. Press his cock inside her as she'd seen him do that first night. A turbulent emotion welled up in her and she sought to put a name to it. *Longing*, she decided after a moment. A longing to belong to someone as Michaela did to him and he to her.

Beside her, Sal whined, and she wondered if he longed to stay with her as well. She relaxed against him again, giving him a reassuring pat. Pets were the worst things about changing hosts. She'd once had to abandon a parakeet in London, and she still worried over it, though it was surely long dead by now. She sincerely hoped it had gone on to live out its natural life span, even as she'd gone on to live out her unnatural one over the centuries.

"Don't get used to this," she warned Sal, yawning. "I can't keep you. I'm too much of a wanderer. But I promised Rico I'd find a good home for you, and I swear to you I will. In fact, I grow ever more certain that Lord Bastian might suit you perfectly, for he'll stay put here in Rome."

7

One week later

At the sound of boyish laughter, Michaela paused just outside the large white tent in the Forum. A low, masculine chuckle came in response. Bastian. His amusement was followed by the boy's voice again, sounding piqued this time. There was something familiar about the timbre of that youthful voice. It bore the barest hint of an ancient accent. Unless she was very much mistaken, the owner of it would prove to be her closest female friend.

It was an unseasonably warm winter day, and a canvas flap in one wall had been anchored upward, so that the tent was left open to the outside air. She peeked inside and was instantly certain she was right in her assumption. Certain mannerisms—a turn of the head, a shrug of the shoulders—were distinctive enough so that she saw through Silvia's disguise. Delight soared in her, for the two people who were most dear to her in both the worlds had finally met. And even more promising, they seemed to be getting along famously. But damn it all, trust Silvia to obstruct her plans by taking a ragged young boy as host.

The pair sat in chairs drawn close at Bastian's desk, their heads close together as they pondered some archaeological puzzle. It appeared to be a damaged section of mosaic, with numerous pieces missing from it. It was laid out upon a flat board on the desktop, and they were reassembling loose tiles upon it, carefully recording the position of each piece.

"No, how many times do I have to tell you? Blues go there." The boyish Silvia rolled her eyes and picked up a small blue glass tile Bastian had placed incorrectly among greens.

"My mistake," Bastian said, reaching for a notebook on the far side of Silvia. "Why don't you assemble and I'll do the note taking? My old eyes aren't as keen as your young ones."

Michaela's brows arched, for she had never heard that indulgent tone from him before. Her elation increased tenfold at what it might mean. Was it possible that her plans for the three of them might come to fruition once Silvia reverted to her true form?

Silvia guffawed, every inch the boy in that moment. "A fine idea. How the hells old are you, anyway?" She reached across him, repositioning the tiles he'd mislaid.

A hint of a smile touched the corner of Bastian's mouth. "Old enough."

"Blind, though, that's for sure. Blue goes with blue. Red goes with red. Green with green. One wonders how you've gotten along in your work before I came. Where did you learn your arkeelogy, or whatever you call it, anyway?"

"It's archaeology, as you well know. And I learned it from my father." Bastian's voice had gone abruptly toneless, as it always did when he was reminded of his parents.

"What happened to him?"

Bastian didn't respond.

But a new voice spoke up from behind Michaela and she

turned to see that Sevin had arrived. "He died eleven years ago, shortly after we arrived in this world," he supplied. "Bastian and our father began the excavations here, and since our father's death, Bastian has continued the work." He nodded to Michaela, giving her the easy, dimpled smile that most female residents of the *Salone di Passione* fairly swooned over, and belatedly added, "Good afternoon, *cara*. You're looking well."

Michaela smiled prettily in return, and both Bastian and Silvia rose as she stepped into the room. Poor Silvia looked so guilty. It took her a moment to realize the reason. Why, she was *attracted* to Bastian! More so than Michaela could recall her ever having been to any other man in all the centuries that had come before. But then, what woman wouldn't be attracted to him? she thought, her eyes roving his powerful frame. Even one disguised as a boy.

Looking from one to the other of them, she was startled to sense a lack of welcome toward her. A Vestal Companion could always detect the smallest signs of a man's displeasure, and she noted the mild irritation in Bastian's glance. She'd only come here today because he had mentioned this boy to her several times over the past week, and it had made her more than a bit curious to see him for herself.

However, although she'd been with Bastian for months now and Silvia had barely known him a week, she suddenly felt like the outsider among them. The quality of their banter had suggested an easy camaraderie; a bond that sprang from interests shared. It was a closeness from which she was excluded by her lack of familiarity with Bastian's work. She had never been invited here, and had never expected to be. A man's work was a man's work, and she had little interest in excavations. Still, she didn't like feeling shut out of things.

"To what do I owe this unexpected visit?" Bastian enquired.

Michaela went to him, propelled by a sudden need to mark him as her own in front of the others. Going on tiptoe, she offered her mouth and he took it, kissing her, his warm hand steady at her back. She loved the way he held her. Even the most casual touch from him, such as this one, was a thrill in itself that she would carry with her into the ensuing hours.

"Are we interrupting?" she asked, her gloved hand stroking his nape.

When Bastian did not leap to reassure her, Sevin swept into the breach of good manners. "Not at all. My big brother and I have business. But it's always a delight to see you."

Michaela smiled into Bastian's eyes, willing him to share his brother's professed delight.

Silvia nodded to Sevin, who'd come to perch on the edge of the desk next to her and pass a few moments helping with the puzzle. Chin resting on her fist, she chatted with him easily, for they'd met numerous times by now and had formed a tentative sort of friendship. "You're better at this than your elder brother. He has no sense of color sometimes."

"Really?" said Sevin, suddenly watchful. "He's generally thought to be quite clever with pigments."

"Hmph." She made a scoffing sound, only half her attention on the mosaic as she openly observed the other two occupants of the tent. Analyzing the quality of their embrace, she realized something was off. Bastian had seemed pleased enough with Michaela that first morning when Silvia had seen them together in his bed. Yet, although Michaela was now employing all the usual tricks of her Companion trade, they appeared not to turn this man to mush as they did all other men.

Perhaps it was the fact that he didn't easily succumb to her wiles that made Michaela want him above all the other men she might have chosen. Or perhaps it was his wealth of masculine sensuality, Silvia thought as she watched him alter his stance with an easy shift of his hips. His back was to her and his every move tautened the fabric of his shirt and trousers over a splendid musculature that in Renaissance times would have rendered him a subject worthy of Michelangelo's chisel. If she'd had to design a male to stimulate the mind and delight the senses, she couldn't have forged a better one.

"Your attention is wandering, Imp," Sevin murmured, and she saw he'd been watching her watch his brother. Blushing, she was chagrined to note her mistake in the mosaic. Correcting it, she turned her back on the couple she'd been studying, belatedly concentrating on the puzzle and doing her best to afford them privacy.

Over Bastian's shoulder, Michaela noticed and smiled to herself. Same old Silvia, avoiding emotional entanglements. Her spurt of jealousy had been misguided. Of course it was. What had she been thinking? This was Silvia, her dearest friend, not some competitor for Bastian's affections.

As Bastian released her, Michaela pretended to turn her attention to the boy for the first time. "And who is this?" she enquired, smiling.

"A thieving, ill-mannered Imp come to work for me," Bastian announced casually, sprawling his big form into his chair again. His brother let out a muffled chortle as if accustomed to, and amused by, their sparring. Michaela's brows rose.

Irked, Silvia got to her feet and with all eyes upon her, executed a low bow in a manner that obviously came as a surprise to both brothers. They could have no way of knowing that she'd served as a valet in the French House of Bourbon in the 1600s and could effect perfect manners when required. Coming forward, she kissed Michaela's hand and greeted her in polished Italian accents. "*Incantato, signorina. Il mio nome è Rico.*"

"Who the hells *is* he?" Sevin asked, favoring Bastian with a bemused look.

"A courtly Imp, apparently," Bastian offered mildly, but it was plain that the mystery of her intrigued him.

Michaela touched her fingers to Silvia's cheek. "I think your manners are quite adorable, Rico. As are you."

"One wonders where you learned them," Bastian added.

Silvia shot him a mischievous glance. "From my betters."

Sal wandered over to greet Michaela. Bending to pet him, she murmured to Silvia, "Don't think this disguise will foil my plans for you."

Silvia grinned, realizing she'd been found out.

"I thought so," Michaela whispered. "And who is this?"

"Rico's dog. Whom I'm trying to get your lover to adopt." Then more loudly, she said, "Yes, Signorina, Salvatore is indeed a superlative dog as you've noticed. In fact, Signor Satyr pleads with me daily to part with him, for he has come to admire him greatly and desires to claim him for his own."

Bastian glanced up from his conversation with Sevin. "What lies is he telling?"

Michaela laughed lightly, drawing the interested attention of every workman within hearing range outside the tent. "None. I find him quite amiable. In fact, if you could spare him, I'm going to the market and he would be a help with my packages."

"Might not be a bad idea to have a scrappy, streetwise boy at your side, to act as protector." Those sensuous lips curved sardonically as Bastian added, "And I can definitely spare him." Dismissing them, he bent over the mosaic, examining her recent work.

"Don't touch it while I'm gone," Silvia commanded worriedly. "Promise."

Bastian raised both hands, palms outward to affect innocence. "Your mosaic is safe from me. Go." He waved her off.

Sal trotted after Silvia and Michaela as they left together. Once they were outside and a distance from the tent, Michaela glanced back at Bastian, who was leaving with Sevin to inspect one of the digs. Watching her, Silvia frowned at the hungry way her eyes followed him. She only allowed them to light on him with this desperate longing when he didn't see.

"Is all well between you and Lord Satyr?"

Violet eyes blinked at her. *"Scusi?"* Michaela snapped her parasol open, appearing embarrassed and anxious to change the topic of conversation. "Of course. How go the digs? Neither of you seem to be overly anxious to reach the temple."

Silvia's brows rose. "His men do the digging. He only directs it."

"Of course," said Michaela, but Silvia had an odd feeling she really didn't understand what went on here.

"And that's just as well," Silvia went on, trying to lighten the tension that had sprung up between them. "For you were right about your lover. He *is* slow. It has been just over a week since I showed him the location of the temple and his men have only dug one third of the way down to it. In spite of my continued instruction and nudging in the proper direction."

Having found a stick he'd mislaid, Sal retrieved it and begged for a game. Silvia wound up and tossed it for him.

Michaela glanced at the dog, wrinkling her nose. She'd never had a fondness for pets. "Is finding a home for this mongrel another of your wish fulfillments?"

Silvia nodded blithely. "Rico's last request." She was the only one of the Ephemerals who steadfastly insisted upon carrying out her host's deathbed wish. It was a matter of honor to her.

At the mention of Rico, Michaela shot her a stern glance. "I know you took this form on purpose, Via. So that I would not coerce you to lie with Bastian and me."

"It would be somewhat inappropriate, don't you think?" Silvia teased. "Considering that I'm an impressionable child of twelve." Sal returned with the stick. Silvia threw it even farther and he dashed off after it.

"But a boy?" Michaela *tsked,* shifting her parasol to her other shoulder so she could better glare at her.

"I rather like the freedoms masculinity offers," said Silvia. "Standing up to relieve myself. No husband or suitor bothering me for sexual favors. You have no idea how much effort it has taken to remain virginal over the centuries. I've dodged thousands of hands, make no mistake."

"Well, you won't be a child for long. Another two weeks or so, and it will be Moonful. You'll have to take another host. Make it an adult female next time, will you?"

"Why?"

"Because I want him . . ." Michaela broke off on a frustrated sound.

"To know I'm a woman? Do you truly think it would be as easy as that to persuade him?" asked Silvia. "No, forget what you're thinking, Michaela. I annoy him. And I doubt it would be any different if I wore skirts."

"*Rico* annoys him. And not as much as you think. He seemed fond of you."

Silvia brushed off her comment. "Even if he did wish me to join you in his bed on a permanent basis once I'm female again—and that's a very large 'if'—it would only bring Pontifex's wrath down upon his family."

"*If* he found out."

"He has spies everywhere. Spies that have already alerted him to the fact that you're a little too closely involved with the Satyr clan here in Rome."

Michaela gasped.

"He seemed to accept it," Silvia assured her. "He has other things on his mind. The stones. But we must tread carefully for now and avoid doing anything that might push him over the edge."

"We promised only three decades of service to Vesta," Michaela said grimly, walking faster as her irritation increased. "Pontifex made sure our service extended well beyond that time. He broke the initial agreement. It's only fair that we break our vows."

"My vows are to Vesta, not to Pontifex," said Silvia.

"Honestly, Via." Michaela twirled her parasol, eyeing her in a calculating way. "Exactly how long do you plan to remain a virgin?"

"Exactly? Hmm." She tossed the stick again for Sal, pretending to consider. "What do you want me to say, Michaela? Would you have me promise that the moment I locate the stones, I will beg the nearest male to divest me of my hymen?"

"We've been searching for the stones for hundreds of years. When will they be found? After another century has passed? Another century in which your life is barren of a man's love? When Bastian and I are dead and gone and it will be too late. Share my happiness now, while you can." She took one of Silvia's hands in her own gloved ones.

Silvia squeezed her pristine, gloved fingers, seeing how she dirtied them with her own grubby ones. Although she bathed each morning in a fountain, a day in the Forum left her dusty again. Afraid she might acquiesce, and even more afraid that her agreement might soil Michaela's happiness in the same way her fingers had soiled her gloves, she pulled back.

"I'm determined, Silvia. I want a life with him. And with you. A real one, not our eternal damned nothingness. When you've finished your work, come back to me. I can never be truly happy knowing you're out there in the worlds alone. Promise me you'll consider it."

"I'll consider it," Silvia agreed, if only to end the matter. "Although at times I do wonder if your Satyr will ever get to the temple at all. A burrowing mole could move faster." Silvia shook her head, smiling at a fond memory that illustrated her point. She began to tell the story to Michaela and walked on a short distance before realizing that Michaela hadn't kept pace.

When she glanced around, it was to see that Michaela had dropped her parasol and clutched both hands to her belly. Her face was parchment white, a feverish splotch of color concentrated high on each cheek.

Silvia hurried back to her side. "What's wrong?" But in her heart, she already knew.

"I think I'm . . . losing . . . Oh Gods—Via!" She made a wild grab at Silvia's arm before she collapsed.

"Michaela!" Silvia caught her, twisting under her weight in a tangle of legs and skirts as they fell to the ground. Michaela was hardly even showing, not more than a few months into her pregnancy. And already it was ending.

"Back away from her, *ragazzo!*" A gentleman in a tall beaver hat and morning coat rushed over to them, misconstruing the situation and beating Silvia off with his walking stick. "What have you done, cur?" She found herself summarily yanked away by another set of "helpful" male hands. She fought to reach Michaela's side. "I'm assisting her. She's my friend." But her strength was puny against the two misguided gentlemen, and they pushed her aside in an effort to render assistance. Instinctively, she leaped up and ran for Bastian, her heart pounding in terror. She tore open the tent and found it empty, then saw him a distance beyond it with his brother. She rushed their way, shouting. "Bastian! Michaela's . . . her baby!"

Bastian's face tightened with concern. "Fetch a physician!" he ordered his brother, sending Sevin in the other direction. "One of our own. Send him to Esquiline!"

Silvia's feet scarcely touched earth as she and Bastian ran to Michaela's side. He quickly took charge as she—a poor boy—hadn't been allowed to. He knelt beside Michaela, loosening her corset and bodice with hands that were experienced at such things. When he lifted her in his arms, Silvia blanched. The back of her skirt was damp with blood. His expression grim, Bastian headed across the Forum, Silvia trotting at his side.

An hour later found them all at Bastian's home on Esquiline Hill. Michaela lay in his bed, still as death, her face creased with pain. A graying pixie, who was no taller than Rico, was the physician who'd been summoned, and he was currently examining her. An ElseWorld creature himself, he would be skilled in treating creatures of their world, Silvia reminded herself as she and Sal paced the corridor.

They wouldn't allow Rico or Sal inside, but when she peeked in to see the men's backs were turned, she managed to slip in unnoticed. She touched Michaela's cheek. Held a hand to her mouth, felt her breath. She lived.

"Out of here, you filthy boy!" the doctor shooed upon seeing her. He reminded her of a busy insect, darting about the room and fussing with his instruments in quick twitches. He tried to eject her, but she jerked away, her back bumping into something warm and solid. And broad-shouldered.

An arm came around her. Bastian. She tried to fling him off, but he curled her face into his shirtfront and put a hand on her back, rubbing in a fatherly fashion. "She miscarried. It was bound to happen—she had the Sickness," he murmured. "You understand?"

She nodded against the starched linen of his shirt and hiccupped.

"Your quick thinking in coming to me likely saved her life," he told her. "She's lucky you were with us today."

"What do you know about the circumstances of conception in this case?" They glanced over to the doctor, who was tucking his instruments away, looking perplexed.

"It was rape," Bastian supplied succinctly.

Silvia looked up at him, shocked. Michaela had glossed over the manner of conception when they'd spoken of it, leaving Silvia to assume it had happened in the normal course of her occupation. Now, to learn she'd been forced!

The physician sighed, then spoke again, drawing her attention. "It's just as well she lost the child."

"What does that mean?" Silvia demanded.

The little man looked at her over his spectacles. "It was irretrievably deformed. A grotesque. It would not have survived under any circumstances."

An awful silence greeted his statements.

"Was it of ElseWorld blood?" Bastian asked after a moment elapsed. "She wouldn't name her attacker."

"Attackers," the doctor corrected. "I cannot say how many, but the child was a mix of at least two discrete creatures."

A sob of hysteria escaped Silvia. And for the first time in a life of centuries, she fainted.

Scena Antica IV

380 A.D.
Vestal House, Rome, Italy

Early one morning during Michaela's twelfth year, she shook Silvia out of a sound sleep. Their shared bed was tucked in a private sleeping alcove—one of a half dozen within the Atrium House where the girls slept.

"Our sheets are damp," Michaela whispered. "I'm bleeding."

Alarmed, Silvia came up on one elbow, blinking awake. "Why? What happened?"

"It's my woman's blood," Michaela informed her, with a significant glance.

Silvia's eyes rounded. "Oh."

When it was learned that Michaela was the first of the Vestals to be thus transformed from child to woman, a great fuss was made over her. Pontifex himself came to examine their bedsheet. It was then displayed in the public Forum, where it flapped in the breeze like a banner of victory outside the temple as the girls breakfasted in the house.

"What good does it do us to become women?" Occia groused. "The blood is for bearing children, something we'll never do."

"When we leave Vesta's service, we can marry and bear as many children as we wish," Silvia countered.

Michaela shook her head. "Occia's right. Since we're to serve here for three decades, we'll be thirty-six by then. Lucky if we're still alive."

Aemilia nodded. "My own mother bore me, her last child, at twenty. My father was angry with her when she no longer swelled with another babe every year. He took slaves into his bed thereafter. That's what husbands do."

Silvia thought back to six years ago when she'd last lived at home, and recalled her father disappearing on occasion with one of the younger female servants. Her stern mother had subsequently found reason to remove those servants he favored from the household.

"All the more reason to excel at our studies so we are useful as something other than wives and mothers when we eventually depart the temple," Silvia said decisively.

Michaela smiled fondly at her; then she rose to depart since she and Occia were scheduled to tend fire that morning. "That's my Silvia, always thinking." She leaned to offer her a kiss in parting.

"Oh!" Silvia scrubbed at her cheek with her fingers, gazing at her in consternation. The touch of her lips had sent a strange and pleasant sensation humming over her skin.

Surprised by her reaction, Michaela then pressed her lips to her own forearm, jumping when she felt the slight buzz herself. She pressed her fingertips to her mouth and her body twitched again in reaction. "My lips," she said in awe. "They have the same effect as my palms now. Try it yourselves," she urged the others. "Kiss your own arms and see if it happens to you as well."

Silvia did, then made a moue of disappointment. "Nothing happened." It was the same with the others. When none felt anything unusual, Michaela kissed each of their cheeks in turn so they could feel the strange tingling. Aemilia giggled and begged her to do it again. Although she was the darling of the other Vestals for her sweet nature, Aemilia was the despair of their teachers, for unlike the rest of them, who excelled at their studies, she had not yet been able to grasp the fundamentals of reading and writing.

"Michaela?" Vestalis swept into the dining hall. "Pontifex Maximus commands your presence in the Regia. Follow me, please. Aemilia, you will tend fire with Occia in her stead."

Occia complained loudly over this change, for it meant that, in fact, she would do all the work. Aemilia was too easily distracted and could not be counted upon to keep the temple fire going.

Silvia raised her brows at Michaela, who only shrugged in answer, having no idea why she was being sent for. She followed Vestalis from the room and wasn't seen again for the remainder of the day.

Silvia was almost asleep when Michaela finally climbed into their bed. "Where have you been?"

"With Pontifex, and then Vestalis Maxima," Michaela replied.

"Because of what happened with your—?" She gestured to Michaela's mouth.

Michaela nodded, tearing off her clothing piece by piece before snuggling under the light blanket in her shift. "They say it will happen to some of us when our blood comes."

"Some?"

"Only to the Companions. And because of it, from now on, my last hour of afternoon instruction will be separate from everyone else."

"What are they going to teach you?" Silvia asked, hearing the envy in her own voice. She soaked up their lessons like a sponge and was generally considered the brightest student among them. If there was something new to be learned, she wanted to join Michaela in her studies.

Michaela's eyes turned secretive. "Do you really want to know?"

Silvia nodded.

"I'm to be taught to observe men. To learn their interests. To anticipate their wants. Much like a wife."

"But why, if we are to remain chaste?"

Michaela yawned. "I don't know. Turn over." When Silvia obliged, she fitted herself along her back and curled an arm around her waist, as she liked to sleep.

Long after Michaela dozed, Silvia lay awake, pondering this new development and what it might mean. Pontifex was not to be trusted, and she was concerned for Michaela. With such training as she described, a woman might be able to elicit political secrets from unsuspecting Ministry officials. Or steal virtually anything from any man if it might benefit Pontifex's schemes. Her mind raced, considering the worrisome possibilities that might be in store for her friend.

As the moon rose to leach the night of color, she rose and slipped out into the Atrium courtyard. There, she knelt before the statue of her goddess, Vesta—she whom Silvia had come to love and trust above all else. The Goddess stood as always, an expression of benevolence in her eyes, her arms at her sides slightly outthrust from her body, and both palms facing forward in welcome.

In her left hand she held the sacred crest of Chastity; in her right, that of Fire.

The two symbols that defined Silvia, and every initiate in the House.

Placing her hands in those of Vesta, Silvia felt the reassuring warmth emanate from the Goddess's palms. And with all her might, she prayed that all would be well. Only when she heard the others begin to stir did she return to her bed, secure in the knowledge that Vesta would watch over them.

8

Still in the guise of Rico, Silvia poked her head in the door of Bastian's bedchamber. Michaela sat there on the bed, working with a pile of burgundy-colored silk in her lap. "What's that you're doing? I thought you were supposed to be resting."

Michaela didn't look up from her stitching. "I'm making a gift for Bastian. A dressing robe."

"By hand?"

"Mm-hmm. Handwork is so much more personal than sewing by machine." She held it out, displaying the unfinished front edge. "What stitch do you think he might prefer for the buttonholes?"

"Raised satin stitch blossoms? Or perhaps a lovely scallop?" Silvia suggested, tongue in cheek. Anything to bring a smile to Michaela's wan face.

As she'd hoped, Michaela laughed. "I'm certain he'd adore either. So masculine."

"I can whip out a few buttonhole stitches for you if you like," Silvia offered. "Just let me wash the Forum dirt off my hands and I'll be back."

When she returned ten minutes later, Michaela was gazing out the window, her expression melancholy. Silvia joined her, unsure how to cheer her up. She'd tried everything over the last few weeks, but Michaela remained introspective. Having never lost a child herself, she could only imagine how her heart must ache.

"The secret in men's tailoring is to put the purl on top instead of on the side," Silvia said, adopting a brisk attitude. "And pull the whole thing tight toward the finish so the insertion will be snug. You see?"

"It's amusing to see you stitching."

"These boy's hands do fumble at it." Silvia bent over the fabric, sewing with care. Her fingers were tired from making out excavation cards. As they dug closer to the house and temple, artifacts were thick in the soil and their hours were long.

"The full moon comes tomorrow night," Michaela announced.

Silvia nodded. "I'm aware of that."

"I'm to meet Bastian, of course." A pause. "You could join us."

Silvia's fingers trembled. "No."

Michaela sighed. "Dane spends his Callings with his new wife, but his brothers, Sevin and Lucien, will require mates. If you won't lie with Bastian and me, perhaps . . ."

After keeping herself pure for a millennium and a half, Michaela would foist her on men she barely knew? Appalled and a little hurt, Silvia shook her head. "You know I must go to Pontifex. To Replenish my magic at Vesta's fire."

"And to do that, you will have to divest yourself of Rico. You'll revert to your own form. So—"

"Michaela. Stop."

An uneasy quiet fell between them, then Michaela's voice came again, sounding sleepy. "I don't recall you ever taking a tailor as host. When was that?"

"It was only for one month, eighty years ago in Florence.

And I was a dressmaker's assistant actually. Our shop was known for the production of nightwear and lingerie. I must have sewn ten thousand miles of lace on satin and silk, day in and day out. We specialized in the risqué. There." Silvia finished the buttonholes some fifteen minutes later, having babbled the time away for Michaela's entertainment. But when she looked up, her friend was asleep. "Michaela?" she whispered, just to be sure.

"How is she?"

Silvia glanced toward the door to see Bastian. Her eyes swept over him and she raised and lowered a shoulder. "Recovering. You look tired."

"As you must be." He came to stand beside her chair. "What are you doing?"

Silvia looked down and saw the needle was still between her small, calloused boy's fingers and the dressing gown on her lap. "Helping your ladylove with her sewing. I'm a boy of many talents, as I've told you before." She peered on either side of him, searching. "No chocolate today? You're slacking off."

He smiled slightly. "Because I know who eats it. You're the one getting fat, not Michaela."

"No, not Michaela." She glanced worriedly at the slumbering woman on the bed.

"Don't look so concerned. The doctor said she's fully recovered. You should get some rest."

"I'm not tired." Immediately, she yawned, then grinned up at him.

"Brat," he said, but his lips curved with affection. She'd grown to love seeing him smile at her, or rather at Rico, in that fond way.

Raising his arms, he gave a mighty stretch of his massive chest, rolling his shoulders and then his head to work the kinks from his neck. Gods, he was handsome, and so . . . so *male*. The light dusting of twilight bristle that now shaded his strong, square jaw only increased his appeal. Her eyes slipped down the strong, corded column of his neck, the immense expanse of chest, his tapered waist, narrow hips. She looked down at her sewing, but his thighs and boots remained in her peripheral vision to tantalize her. *You're no better than Minister Tuchi, who surreptitiously studies his body at every sly chance,* she silently scolded herself.

It had been over three weeks since she'd assumed Rico as her host. His essence had faded away, day by day, and was almost completely gone now. With every new dawn, it was becoming harder and harder to remember she was supposed to be a boy. Especially when Bastian was near. Out in the Forum, they worked closely, and she'd had plenty of opportunity to memorize his every contour, his every gesture. She'd become accustomed to his laugh, his moods, his habits. He liked coffee, not tea. He did not have a sweet tooth. He could work in long stretches with tremendous energy; then his mind would just as readily turn inward, toward academic pursuits. He had incredible focus when it came to his work or to solving some puzzle. He was temperamental, annoying, pompous, slow . . . charming, brilliant, fascinating, wonderful.

She was attracted to him. How he would laugh if he knew. Rico alternately amused him and annoyed him, but their relationship was most certainly not a foundation for passion. Still, she found herself considering the suggestion Michaela had made earlier. Once she left Pontifex, she could return here in female form. Not her own, of course, for that would require becoming mortal as Michaela had. But she could take a female host. Join them in his bed. If he agreed.

Yet, she wouldn't. For it was one thing to consider accepting Michaela's invitation to partake of her lover. Quite another to want him for herself. She pushed the traitorous thought away as she did every time it surfaced. And because she wanted to keep on looking at him, she made herself rise and move around the bed on the pretext of straightening Michaela's coverlet.

An uncomfortable moment passed and she worried he'd noticed the strange tension that hovered in the air between them. A puzzled frown creased his brow and he searched her face as they gazed across the bed. "There's something different about you."

Alarmed, Silvia backed away. "A bath and new clothes is all," she said, bursting into speech. Then, "Tell me something, B—Lord Satyr. You like Sal, don't you? I mean, you'd take care of him if anything happened to me?"

"Nothing's going to happen to you, brat."

"But if something did, would you—"

"Yes, I'd take care of him."

As if he sensed he was under discussion, the dog wedged his nose in the gap Bastian had left in the doorway and made his way inside the room, his tail wagging. "Salvatore! Out! Michaela doesn't like you in here," Silvia said, shooing him off.

But he'd already woken Michaela. "You're home," she said, her eyes finding Bastian. She reached for a pillow, and Silvia rushed to needlessly arrange things for her. "Help me get her more comfortably settled," she told Bastian, knowing Michaela would enjoy his attention.

"I'm filthy," he said, spreading his hands.

"Then bathe and return to me," Michaela suggested in a flirtatious tone.

Bastian nodded and left his bedchamber, having expected as much from her. He was fastidious by nature. However, when he returned from the Forum each day, she always looked so pristine and feminine. And on occasion the urge took him to fuck her as he was, fresh from his labors, so that his body would leave its earthy, passionate mark on her. But she'd always recoiled from his attentions until he bathed.

"I heated water for you," Rico called after him as he moved down the corridor.

He returned moments later to find the boy missing and was disappointed, for he'd come to enjoy Rico's quick wit. Michaela's heart-shaped face lit up when she saw him. His lady-love, Rico had called her. Before her illness, he'd lain with her every day and night for three consecutive months. He'd made love to her hundreds of times and enjoyed the hell out of it. But he didn't love her.

He had no illusions that he would ever find a deep, enduring love—the kind that his parents had found with each other—with any woman. His life was his work, and he did not apologize for that.

It had been the same with his father, yet his father had found time for a family. But perhaps this was because his mother had trained as a surveyor. They'd worked in concert, both excited over each new excavation, over every discovery. And Bastian had been their pride and joy. Their gifted son. It was his gift that had killed them.

"Shouldn't you be lying down?" he asked.

"I'd like nothing better, if you'll join me in my bed," Michaela said, coming to stand before him.

His gaze narrowed. "Are you—"

"Knock, knock," said Silvia, tapping on the bedchamber door as she entered. "You two aren't doing anything that would shock an innocent boy of twelve, are you?"

Michaela smiled, noting that she'd changed into one of the boyish outfits they'd purchased for her a few days ago. She'd seemed content enough to wear Rico's rags, but Michaela had protested. "You're going to break some hearts one day," Michaela teased her now, "and soon I hope." Only the two of them knew the whole of what she meant.

"Likely so," Silvia replied lightly. "I'm already quite a favorite among the ladies at the *Salone di Passione.*"

Bastian frowned at her. "You've been to Sevin's salon?"

"Don't you dare say I'm too young," said Silvia, eyeing him.

Bastian's expression lightened with humor and he reached out a hand to rumple her hair. "You're too young. Save the ladies for your old age—eighteen at least, hmm?"

"Hmph. I'll wager you didn't wait so long," Silvia chided, ducking away. "Besides, Michaela's friends seemed to quite enjoy having me help them out with their . . . needs." She wiggled her eyebrows.

"No doubt fetching their cologne and bonbons and the like," Bastian said.

"Umm-hmm. The 'like' is the part they liked best," said Silvia, baiting him.

Michaela observed their sparring closely. Not listening to their words, but to the inflections in their voices. She weighed Bastian's body language as she'd been taught to do in those afternoon classes at the Vestal House. While Silvia had spent the centuries learning hundreds of skills from hundreds of hosts, Michaela had spent her time wooing men and fucking them. It was all she was good for—determining what a man desired in order to get what she wanted of him.

She'd always secretly pitied Silvia for her awkwardness with the male sex. But no more. For if she wasn't very much mistaken, Bastian liked his protégé—liked him a great deal. And it was a liking that might easily tip in a new direction—toward love, if Silvia were to present herself to him in her true form as an adult female.

Michaela's heart tripped. When she'd pictured them all together, it was always with her as the star of their amatory trio. Bastian was to be wildly in love with her, and Silvia only hovering in their orbit, coming second in both their affections. But now a real fear suddenly swamped her that Silvia might somehow supplant her in Bastian's heart. Shocked at herself, she squashed it. She was making something out of nothing. All would go as she'd planned between them.

Still, a sudden urgency gripped her to be reassured of her attractions. To reinforce the fact that Bastian was hers in front of Silvia, lest she forget it. Ignoring her friend, she put her hands on Bastian's strong shoulders and went up on tiptoe. "Lie with me," she whispered. "It's been too long."

Bastian's attention was caught, his big hand settling at the small of her back. "Are you sure?"

"I'm perfectly well." She sent him a meaningful glance, sliding her arms up to loop around his neck.

This woman's touch never failed to excite his body, and Bastian did nothing to hide his physical response from her. Feeling his hardness at her belly, her lips curved in a slow, feminine smile. It was a smile he understood perfectly. From the moment they'd entered their teens, he and his brothers had all been on the receiving end of many such come-hither glances from females. He smoothed his knuckles down her soft cheek.

Behind him, the bedroom door banged. Rico making himself scarce when they got "lovey-dovey," as he called it. Bastian smiled, thinking of the boy's sour views on such things.

Michaela returned his smile, believing it was for her. Her hand cupped him through his trousers. A part of him—the part she sought—wanted this. Wanted to toss her on the bed, come inside her, and fuck the hours away.

But as he gazed into her eyes, he wondered for the first time if he'd become more to her than he ever wanted to be to any woman. And the concern stayed his impulse. Before they'd lain together that night they'd first met at Sevin's salon, he'd informed her that he would never love her. She'd laughed at him back then, teasing him about the size of his ego. And later, in darkness, about the size of another of his assets.

Opening his trousers now, she found him and drew him high and long with her fist. The erotic heat in her palms had a predictable effect, and he hardened to granite under her stroke. His body wanted hers, yet he felt emotionally detached. His affection for this woman did not extend to love. And in truth, another body would have done just as well for him. It would hurt her to know, he realized.

He gripped her wrist, holding her off. Their eyes met and he saw panic slowly bloom in hers. "We should talk," he said, straightening his trousers.

"And while we talk, why not let me make you come?" Her violet gaze made sensual promises.

His hand went to her spine, going under the fall of her hair. "Michaela . . . if it's love you want, you should look elsewhere."

A silence, then she murmured, "You're not as incapable of love as you believe."

It was the wrong thing to say. There was a time in his youth when things had been different for him, but now he considered himself a man of logic, and any attempt to prove otherwise was met with the swift raising of a stone wall.

He stepped back, and Michaela's heart shattered. But her smile didn't falter. She could charm him. She would. She must. She'd die if he abandoned her.

Her lashes fluttered lower, and when her eyes reopened she was the consummate Companion again. Her fingers found the buttons of his shirt, unfastening the topmost from its moorings. "All I *want* from you, Bastian"—she pressed a kiss to the vee of chest she'd bared at his throat, then popped a second button. "All I *need* . . ."—a third button and another kiss—"is your cock . . ."—another button, another kiss, as she moved still lower on him—"inside me. You may keep your heart." *For now.*

He took her shoulders in his hands and pulled her up before she could sink to her knees before him. "You're certain?"

She laughed, a flirtatious, melodious sound that had first drawn him to her when he'd heard it in Sevin's salon that night several months ago. "Of course, darling," she said. "I'm a Companion, after all. We rarely remain with one patron for long. But you and I—we're good together. And tomorrow will be Moonful. I know the darkness of the beast in you that comes with the Calling. You've said yourself that not just any woman will do for you then."

Bastian tilted her chin up, his lips pausing a breath above hers. "I don't want to hurt you."

"Then don't ruin what we have based on some misconception of my feelings," she told him. "Instead, why not fuck me, Bastian, as your body urges you to? Give us both a taste of what tomorrow night's Calling will bring. It's been too long." And when she lay back upon his bed and tugged him down into her kiss, Bastian went, believing her lies.

Through the slit in the doorway, Silvia watched him kiss Michaela and cover her body with his own larger one. His hand fumbled between them, shifting clothing as he mounted her. Both were fully dressed, as if they hadn't been able to wait to have one another. Unlike the last time she'd played voyeur here, she took no enjoyment in watching them couple. But she forced herself to stay, trying to brand this image of them on her heart, so that she could recall it anytime she dared to want more than she could have.

She knew the instant his body claimed hers. Saw Michaela's eyes drift closed, the ecstasy of having him inside her plain on her face. There was no mistaking her feelings for him. It was love.

Feeling like Death, Silvia backed away. Then she ran down the hall and stairs. Out of the house. Down Bastian's sloping lawn, causing peacocks, squirrels, and doves to scatter. And still she ran on, through piazzas and on to the Forum, until her sides were heaving and she was gasping for breath.

Since Rico had become a trusted fixture at Bastian's side, the guard hardly noticed her as she passed, heading for the tool shed. Quickly, she found the implements she needed and rushed to the Atrium House dig site. And there, she picked her spot and began to hack away at the earth, heedless of any damage she was inflicting on small bits of pottery as she bored down toward the ruin. Who cared about minuscule pottery shards? She had another goal in mind.

When she sensed she was close, she worked with more care. Then, just before she reached what she sought, she crawled out of the void she'd created in the silt and slumped in exhaustion. Something warm licked her hand and she reached out blindly, looping an arm around Rico's dog. Hanging on to another living being made her feel slightly less alone in the world, something she needed just then.

"I want him, Sal," she confessed into soft, white fur. There, she'd admitted it, even if it was only to a dog.

Sal whined and his big brown eyes seemed to rebuke her. "I know, I know. I cannot have him. And I'm at a loss to explain why he has this hold over my heart. Still, horrible person that I am, I lust after Michaela's lover. I dream of lying with him." Her voice sank to a whisper. "Lying *alone* with him."

A few moments later, she sighed deeply and stroked a hand over Sal's back. "Forget I mentioned it, will you?" Straightening, she got to her feet, stretched, and then headed back to Esquiline.

"Let's go, boy," she told her companion. "Tomorrow is to be a big day. A day when Lord Satyr is going to make the discovery of his career."

9

By the time Silvia arrived at the digs the next morning, Bastian had found the statue. Or, the top of its head, at least. A crowd had gathered around him, and Silvia had to push her way through to reach him.

"What is it?" she asked, pretending she hadn't spent hours the previous night digging for it. Leaving it so he had only to dig an inch or so to uncover the first hints of white marble.

"A statue," said Bastian, and she heard the suppressed excitement in his voice.

"Of?" She peered around him, her own excitement growing.

"One of the Vestals, most likely. All of their likenesses were carved in stone. Their statues lined the atrium of the house where they resided," he informed her needlessly.

Yes, she knew. Six on each side of the atrium. Companions on the north side, Virgins on the south. But last night, she'd dug in the place she'd calculated he would find the thirteenth and most important statue of all that had graced the house. Had she chosen correctly?

All that was currently visible in the depression she'd dug

was what appeared to be an upside-down white bowl—a small mound about the size of the top of a head. Bastian was carefully smoothing away loose sediment from around it, revealing more. Beneath his fingers, white marble gleamed. Seeing that strong, capable hand of his brush over a carving she'd once passed every single day of her youth, something shifted inside Silvia. She fell to her knees beside him, and he moved his hand so that she might set her warm palm on the statue's earth-cool crown.

"Her hair," she breathed, feeling the ridges under her palm. "It's in waves. It's not one of the Vestals. It's the goddess herself, isn't it?" She was certain now that this was the statue of Vesta. The one she'd knelt before in worship each morning and each night of her girlhood, centuries ago.

She glanced up at him then, tears of joy in her eyes. Without thinking, she blindly reached out to him. His hands came at her ribs and he lifted her and swung her around, both of them for the moment oblivious to the surrounding crowd. It was as if they were alone in the Forum, their laughter a shared, wonderful bond between them as both delighted in this sublime moment of discovery.

Then she touched ground. One foot. Then the other. And then he let her go. He knelt again and began gently cleaning sediment away with a brush. Without realizing what she did, Silvia reached out her hand to smooth his hair. But before her hand fell, he began issuing orders to his workmen. She snatched back her hand and pretended she'd only been after a tool that lay beside him.

"We'll go slowly," Bastian murmured, his mind wholly focused on the upcoming task. "And with the utmost care."

Smiling through welling tears, Silvia rolled her eyes. "Of course we will."

Working round the clock, it would likely take two weeks or more to unearth the statue. Although she would watch from a distance, she knew she would not be working at his side as he *slowly* uncovered the statue. In fact, he would never see her again. She would only swoop in stealthily and steal what belonged to her once he'd accomplished its disinterment.

For tonight would be Moonful.

The night Rico must die.

The night Silvia must pay another visit to Pontifex.

The night Michaela would lie with Bastian again.

Bastian, whom they both loved.

Tonight.

It was early afternoon when Silvia slipped away from the dig. She left without a word of farewell to anyone, taking Sal with her. Her heart heavy, she trudged to Bastian's home and found it empty. Michaela had gone out.

Along with the dog's favorite stick and the collar she'd fashioned for him, she set a hastily scribbled note upon Bastian's desk.

> *Take care of him, Bastian.*
> *And yourself. And Michaela.*
> *I'm off to wander.*
> *Ciao.*
> *—Rico*

"Good-bye, Sal," she told the dog, giving him a last, fond hug. "Be a good boy for Bastian and Michaela. They may be trusted to take good care of you."

As she left the house, Rico's dog tried to follow her, but she stopped him. "No, Sal. You belong to them now." She shut the door securely, leaving him inside. Shutting him out of her life, in the same way she was closing the door on Bastian and Michaela—on this life that was not her own.

"I'll miss you," she whispered. And then she fled the house, intent on leaving her current existence behind. Putting one foot in front of the other, she set out for the aqueduct. A half hour later, she lay down in the sleeping alcove where she'd first found Rico one month ago.

And within minutes, she was standing again and straightening her Virginal shift. The tips of her golden red hair drifted to her waist. She was her Ephemeral self once again. Invisible to all in this world unless she chose to show herself.

Solemnly, she stared at the olive-skinned boy now lying in the alcove of the aqueduct. The rat bite on his ankle was fresh again, as fresh as when she'd first found him. Bastian would miss him, and she hated to pain him in this way. But Michaela would concoct some lie, for she knew Rico would not return on the morrow.

In a few hours, Moonful would come. It was time for her to move on. To say another, final farewell. She bent to Rico and touched his hand.

"I carried out your wish," she assured him. "Sal has a good home. He'll be happy. You can rest easy now." She smoothed back his dark, unruly hair and kissed his forehead. "Good-bye, Rico."

Although he'd died weeks ago, only now was his body truly lifeless. Without her occupation of it, it would begin to decay from this moment. She heaved a ragged sigh and stepped back from him. He'd been a good sort—always up to mischief. And he'd taught her something about theft. A useful ability she could now add to her growing list of half-talents. She hardened her heart against sorrow and made herself turn away. There had been a surfeit of this sort of grief over the years. Sometimes it all hurt too much.

Desperate to escape the pain of this world if only for a while, she decided to leave it. Hidden in the shelter of the aqueduct, she somberly cupped her hands and blew, creating fire out of nothingness.

She would visit Pontifex earlier than usual today, well before the moon rose in this world. Then she would return here and crawl into some hiding place to lick her unseen wounds. And have a good cry.

Within minutes of creating a firegate, Silvia once again stood before Pontifex in ElseWorld. Finger combing her unbound hair from her face, she straightened her shift and stalked toward him.

"Why so early?" he demanded suspiciously from where he sat upon his throne. "It's not yet Moonful in your adopted world. Dare I hope you're eager to see me?" His brows snapped together. "Or has something happened?"

"Lord Satyr has discovered one of the Vestal statues," Silvia announced in a voice that rang through the great hall.

Muffled cries of protest and anguish rose from the Lares.

But Pontifex was not satisfied. "Still no firestones?"

"Soon," she promised.

"Soon? *Soon?*" he snarled. He beat his fist to his breast. "Do you know how I suffer under Priapus's curse? At night I do not sleep. If I manage to nod off, I'm awakened again by a terrible need that is never fully satisfied. Sycophants must nurse at me all through the hours in shifts. Do you think I can conduct my business in this way? I can't travel to visit dignitaries in other lands. I can't go into battle. I can't even walk without a woman attached to my crotch!"

A muffled giggle sounded nearby. The offender was summarily hauled forward and tossed into the moat, where he swiftly disintegrated. It had been one of his augurs, thank the Goddess, not one of the Lares this time.

"I need those fucking stones!" Pontifex raged. "Now!"

"Is that why you want them so badly?" Silvia hazarded. "Because you think they'll cure you?"

His expression turned crafty. "My reasons are not for the

likes of you, wench." He groaned then, grabbing his phallus and squeezing it as if to relieve a desperate ache.

Occia made to kneel at his lap again, but he spurned her. "No, I weary of your fruitless efforts. Summon another."

She flicked a glance at Silvia, obviously embarrassed to be scorned in her presence. Still, she called another over, one who scurried and knelt before him and dutifully ducked her head onto his lap. Occia sat beside her, observing closely and murmuring instructions to her, as if she were the expert on such a service and no one else could provide it without her advice. Really, it wasn't brain surgery. Although, some men's brains did reside . . .

Somewhat soothed, Pontifex sent Silvia a furtive glance; then he stretched out his fingers, idly considering his manicure. "Did the child live?"

Silvia's stomach dropped. "What?"

"Michaela's child. Did it survive?"

He knew! Silvia's mind raced, wondering how much his spies had told him. Would he retaliate against Michaela in some way? "I don't know what you're—"

"Oh, spare me. You're a smart girl. You must have guessed at the father's identity."

A sudden suspicion leaped into her mind, one far too horrible to credit. "Don't expect me to believe the child was yours. You have admitted yourself that you cannot . . ."

Pontifex just stared at her, his expression knowing, and his silence grew more terrifying by the moment. "Ah, but Michaela was gifted," he offered at last.

"What the hells does that mean?" She took a step forward and the waters of the moat fizzed threateningly.

Knocking the female at his feet aside, Pontifex rose and moved close to the edge of his side of the moat, his fist slowly working at himself. "Once a month, she comes to me here. And I feed her this." He looked down at his obscene cock and watched his hand pull it high and long. Gesturing to it with his other hand, he added, "And I let her make it come."

"Liar!" Silvia shrieked. Her shrill denial echoed throughout the hall, and every living thing within it cowered, fearing his retaliation.

But Pontifex only glanced in Occia's direction. "Tell her."

Occia nodded, her expression sour with suppressed jealousy. "What he says is true."

Silvia's mind flew, thinking back to times in the recent past. Times when Michaela had mysteriously disappeared for an afternoon and offered only a flimsy explanation upon her return. Silvia hadn't pressed, assuming she'd simply been enjoying a furtive romance with some lover. But now, she wondered if Michaela had in actuality been with Pontifex on those occasions. The possibility sickened her. "And how long has this supposed liaison been going on?"

"Long enough," Pontifex teased cruelly. "I sent Michaela to Rome a few months ago to seduce her Satyr during one of their Moonful orgies. She conceived that night."

Silvia was already shaking her head before he finished. "The Satyr can control their childseed. Lord Bastian wouldn't have been so stupid as to give his to a woman he didn't know."

"Didn't say he gave her childseed. But he did spend himself in her. More than once that night. Afterward, she came directly here," Pontifex continued in his smarmy voice. "And I fucked where he'd been. I let her wrap her sweet cunt around my cock. And I managed to squeeze a bit of ejaculate out of this thing. Just for her."

Silvia felt bile rise in her throat. "In the Gods' names . . . why?"

Pontifex shrugged. "They say the spendings of the Satyr can boost the potency of another male's seed." His eyes met hers and he added softly, "They're right. My seed mixed with what he deposited and she did conceive. My child."

Silvia's hands fisted at her sides in impotent fury. "You lie. Why would Michaela do that?"

"A tithe. If she gave me a child, I promised to let the two of you go free."

It all made a horrible kind of sense. *Oh Michaela.* Agonized tears welled in Silvia's eyes, blinding her. A rumbling sound reached her ears and she dashed tears away to see a narrow slab of stone sliding toward her, quickly forming a bridge between both banks of the moat. And Pontifex awaited her at the far side of it.

Silvia stared at it, too stunned to comprehend what was happening. Behind her, guards crowded closer, forming a semicircle. Caging her with their bodies. She looked from the bridge to Pontifex.

"Your friend promised me a child," he said. "And she didn't deliver. I now consider our bargain is moot. And she must pay for her reneging."

"What bargain?"

"I want an heir." With a thunk, the bridge connected with her side. Pontifex lifted a hand toward her, beckoning her to cross it. "Dear Silvia, let us strike a new bargain, here, tonight. One between us."

She took a step backward and came up against his guards—her jailors. "No."

"Come, be reasonable. Let us see if you can manage what Michaela could not," he told her. "I've tried all the others over the years, for the Oracle at Delphi prophesied one of the Vestals would bear my child. You are the last of them to remain virginal. It must be you."

"You're delusional!" cried Silvia. Then she cursed Occia for a traitor. "Damn you! You knew what he was doing to Michaela and said nothing!"

From beside him Occia stared daggers at her. If looks could

kill, Silvia would be facedown in the moat. She would jump into it herself before she would lie down with Pontifex!

In a blind rage, Silvia swung her arms and swept the entire collection of victuals from the pedestal display into the moat. The acidic liquid within sloshed upward in a wave that lapped over the far bank of the moat, burning Pontifex's legs. He howled in pain, and during the melee that ensued, Silvia ducked between the guards and rushed to Vesta's hearth. Without taking time for benediction, she welcomed the goddess's fire in a hasty Replenishment, then threw out a firegate.

And just as hard hands reached out to take her captive, she disappeared from their grasp.

10

Back in EarthWorld, the late-afternoon skies were gray and looked ready to weep. Silvia wanted to weep as well for the suffering she now knew Michaela had undergone at Pontifex's hands. A fierce need to avenge her dearest friend fisted in her belly. But above all else, she wanted to find her, and hug her close and promise to protect her. Wanted to tell her she knew the awful truth that she'd hidden for—how long? How long had this been going on?

Silvia stilled, listening carefully to the city around her. Having given up Rico's body, she would require another host within a day's time. But at the moment the voices of the near-dead were silent. It happened sometimes, these pauses in available bodies. So, in her invisible state, she rushed to Bastian's home in hopes of finding Michaela. Instead, she found only Sal inside, who no longer recognized her scent, but sensed her presence and chased her through the halls.

"Hush!" she called to him. Though her voice was imperceptible to mortals, animals were more cognizant of it, and the dog went silent at her command, cocking his head as she moved on.

She searched through the main floor, throwing open every door she passed and calling out for Michaela. In the study, she eventually found a note from her addressed to Bastian on his desk, beside the one she'd left for him about Sal. And without qualm, she scanned it, reading aloud: "She has changed their plans. She is to meet him in the *Suburra* just prior to the Calling." She looked at Sal. "Whyever for?"

The *Suburra*, a suburb of the Monti district, was a disreputable area where one only went to gamble, secure a prostitute, or to engage in activities of a criminal sort. Though it made little sense that Michaela would venture there at night, Silvia dropped the letter and made for the door.

On her way from the room, she tripped over a decanter lying on the floor. The blood-red liquid it had contained had leaked out and stained a priceless carpet she recognized as having been woven on ElseWorld looms.

"How unlike the fastidious Lord Satyr," she mused. Lifting the finely cut crystal bottle, she sniffed, naturally expecting wine, since the Satyr were well known to be vintners. "Damn." She'd forgotten she couldn't scent anything. Quickly, she took her corporeal form and sniffed again. It was wine all right, yet its scent was like no liquor she'd ever come across before. It was bitter, more like the squeezings of unripe olives, blended with a variety of ElseWorld spices and something more indefinable. A hint of . . . Ogre? She wrinkled her nose, then realized that the latter scent was only on the surface of the crystal, not in the drink itself, which at its core was an alcoholic spirit of some kind. She shuddered. Who would drink such a concoction?

But this mystery was immediately forgotten when she heard the sounds of horses and carriage wheels; then the opening of the front door. She set the decanter back as she'd found it, and peeked from the study into the hall. Voices both male and female reached her ears. Moving stealthily to the staircase, she saw that Bastian's brothers—all three of them—and a single woman had arrived.

Sal bounded up to them. "When did Bastian get a dog?" she heard the brother she didn't recognize ask. Bending, he playfully rubbed Sal's ears. Silvia smiled to herself, knowing he'd just made a friend for life, for there were few things Sal enjoyed more. She'd never met this fourth brother, Dane, but this appeared to be he, and his wife must be this woman he held so tenderly.

Though Silvia wanted to stay and observe them, other matters pulled at her attention. Turning, she went to the back of the house, where she shut the door on them all and then proceeded toward Monti.

Her feet fairly flew past fountains, churches, storefronts, palazzos, up staircases, and over brick piazzas dotted with people scurrying to reach their destinations before the coming rain. If only she had her firestone. Occia had once let slip that with their aid, a firegate could be made to function within this world. If that were so, her travel would have been so much swifter! The moon would not rise for another hour and a half at least. Plenty of time to find Michaela before she became engaged with her lover for the night. Silvia wanted to be long gone before Bastian presented himself. To see them locked in yet another embrace would be more than she could bear in her current unsettled state.

Rounding the corner of a watchmaker's shop, Silvia skidded to a stop on the mist-slickened brick street. A pair of courtesans who'd been behind her kept walking and passed right through her on their way into the piazza, never realizing they'd just encountered an Ephemeral. Silvia hardly noticed them either. For her attention was riveted on the extremely tall, broadshouldered gentleman who stood some fifteen feet ahead—her erstwhile employer, Lord Bastian Satyr himself!

Forgetting for a moment that he could not see her, she

ducked out of sight into the recessed doorway of the shop. And for a moment, she indulged her pathetic desire to simply observe him. The courtesans eyed him as well, and why not? Men as handsome and appealing as he were a rare sight in either world.

His head was bent, gazing at something in his hand. It flashed in the lamplight, like . . . fire. Gods! Was it one of Vesta's stones? Before she could determine anything, he slipped it into his pocket.

Thinking only of possessing it, Silvia rushed toward him and plunged a hand into the pocket that contained it. But of course she was in wraith form and her hand sailed right through both fabric and flesh. And through stone, if indeed that's what he harbored. *Damnation!* Whatever it was he had, she couldn't retrieve it while she was invisible.

Desperately, she surveyed the piazza around her. She needed a host, and now. For the first time in her life, she found herself almost wishing someone would hurry up and die! That is, if they'd been destined to, anyway. Meeting Death was never something she looked forward to. For at best the assuming of another host was a poignant experience; at worst, it was ghoulish.

As she stood there with her head cocked, Bastian surprised her by making a clumsy two-armed grab in her direction. His arms passed through her, naturally, but she leaped away from the startling sensation. When they'd briefly coalesced, she'd felt the rush of his emotions. He was thinking of color. No, not just thinking of it. Longing for it. Craving it.

"Damned colors. Won't stay. Gods, my head." He lumbered away to sit on a ledge, where he dropped his head to his hands, plowing his fingers through strands of ebony hair that glistened with the mist.

She went to stand a few feet in front of him and then craned closer, perplexed and a little worried. "What's wrong with you?" she murmured, not expecting an answer.

He heaved a disgusted sigh. "I don't know."

"What do you mean you don't—" Wait a minute! He could *hear* her? She tested him. "Bastian, can you hear me?"

No answer. She straightened. Of course he couldn't hear her. The fact that his reply fit her question had only been coincidental. Nevertheless, something *was* different between them now. Abruptly, she realized what it was. She craned her neck forward and sniffed. She could *scent* him! Although she detected only the faintest hint of alcohol on him, it was obvious from his demeanor that he'd drunk heavily before coming out tonight.

But this was neither here nor there. She looked at his pocket longingly. Unable to resist another attempt, she dipped her fingers into it. This time, the sensation of passing her flesh through fabric and flesh was akin to that of moving her hand through something viscous, as if she were swimming through pudding.

His dark head whipped up. Strong fingers wrapped around her wrist. And this time, their flesh held! "No!" she breathed. "How is this possible?" She was *invisible. Intangible.* He couldn't *grab* her! But apparently Lord Bastian Satyr no longer heeded the properties of physics, for he next proceeded to twist her arm. In a flash, her back was to him and she sat on his lap, her knees securely trapped between the vise of his own, and her bottom cushioned against his—

"Your thieving skills leave something to be desired." Warm breath tickled her nape, teasing tendrils of her hair. She shivered and ducked her head forward. Her heart pounded hard enough to leap out of her chest. What was going on? How was it that they were now interacting as solid beings? How was it that his breath could stir her hair?

She glanced back at him. "C-can you see me?" Oh Gods,

had she somehow rendered herself mortal without intending to?

He shook his head. She felt his fingers toying with her unbound hair. It felt . . . nice. Intimate. "Sunset," he murmured.

She stiffened and turned back to stare unseeing across the piazza. "I thought you couldn't see me!"

Behind her, she felt him nod. "Can't."

"Then how is it you know the color of my hair?"

"How is it you know my name?" he returned, and she realized she'd let it slip earlier. "What are you? Why don't you show yourself to me?" he coaxed in a low, velvet voice. His hands moved over her as if to determine her shape, and she smacked at them.

Thinking he was speaking to her, a comely prostitute ventured closer and sent him a rather quizzical look. It was obvious that the woman couldn't see her, and that she wondered at the odd gestures he was making. "I'll be whatever you need tonight, signor," she offered in a flirtatious voice. "Just tell me what you like." He brushed her off with a casual hand, and reluctantly she went.

Silvia peered over her shoulder at him again. "Can't you guess?" she asked in belated response to his question. "I thought the Satyr were bloodhounds."

"Something has clouded my senses at the moment," he admitted grudgingly. "But you're female. I know that much." The hand that secured her moved up the curve of her waist and across her body, covering her breast and pulling her back against him. Closing his eyes, he let his head fall back against the brick wall, and he sighed with pleasure.

Silvia exhaled harshly on a sound that was an odd blend of delight and distress, and covered his hand with her own. And they sat there a moment. Him half-lying indolently against the wall. Her sprawled over him. Their mutual attention focused on the current position of his hand. On her breast.

Then his fingers flexed in a slow caress, shaping her in a series of gentle squeezes as if testing the ripeness of a fruit. A thumb brushed her nipple through her shift, and a delicious thrill curled through her system, coursing hot, swift need to her pulse at her core. At her bottom, his cock swelled and twitched within his trousers.

"Michaela," she whispered. The name fell from her lips and tumbled between them, a wedge. Straightening, she pushed at his hand and struggled fully upright, her glance sweeping over the piazza. No Michaela. "Where is she, Bastian?"

"Esquiline. My bed. And how is it that you know of her?"

She turned sideways and his hand slipped to rest on her upper thigh. There was nothing particularly erotic about the nature of his touch now, yet she had never been more aware of contact with another being in her life. Of the heat of his thighs under hers. Of his hand.

Ignoring his question, she said, "Her note. I thought she was to meet you here?"

"Hmm?" The hand slid up her thigh.

She slapped it away. "I have to find her; have to go." She slid from his lap and he let her.

But at the last minute, he staggered to his feet and pulled her back to him. "I'd like nothing better. But you won't go." His hands hooked her hips, lifting her to stand facing him on a squat ledge that ran along the façade of the adjacent building. The stone wall at her back was cool and damp with mist. He stood with one of his forearms braced high on the wall to her left, and his other hand at her waist, his head bent close. "It was you that morning a month ago in my library, wasn't it? You, in my thoughts, night and day." He was rambling.

"You're intoxicated," she accused.

"Wrong. I don't drink." He leaned in, his silver eyes on her mouth.

She drew up, flattening herself against the wall. "You're a Satyr, yet you don't drink?"

He tapped her nose with one finger as if to say she'd hit it on the nose.

"But why not?"

Wandering his lips down the line of her throat, he told her, "Let's just say that spirits have an unfortunate effect upon me."

Her brow wrinkled over the puzzle of him, even as she succumbed to the caress of his mouth. No! She would not betray Michaela in this way. She tried to dislodge him with a hard shake of her shoulders, which availed her little. She turned her head from his lips and breathlessly pressed on, sensing a chink in his armor. "I don't understand. Your family's vineyards grow the grapes that are the lifeblood of all ElseWorld kind. You and your brothers are the descendants of Bacchus—gifted with the ability to imbibe freely without becoming inebriated."

"All true. However, I'm the exception."

She was almost glad to have this new mystery to occupy her mind. All too soon, Death would come knocking, summoning her away to gruesome tasks. She shuddered.

He gathered her close inside his coat, as if sensing her weariness of such tasks. Her fingers wandered over his pocket and he pointedly plucked them away. But not until she'd sensed what it was that he had. It was indeed a firestone! Whose she didn't know, for her contact had been too brief. Bastian must have come across it during the course of the excavations.

Damnation! Without a host, she wouldn't be able to take it from him. It might be solid to her touch while she also touched his flesh. But once she let go of him, it would fall right through her Ephemeral form to hit the pavement.

"I saw the decanter in your study," she provoked. "It stank of spirits. Who else drank from it if not you?"

"I *did* drink from it. All the Satyr must take spirits upon the approach of Moonful to initiate the Calling. But mine's a special brew, designed only for me because I cannot drink as the others do." Woozily, he straightened away from her, then put a hand to his forehead. His brow knit as a moment of clarity filled his eyes. "Hells, I do believe you're right. I *am* intox . . . intoxi . . . drunk."

She rolled her eyes. "Well, how you became so is a fascinating tale, I'm certain, but—"

His fingers cupped the back of her head and he leaned into her again. She went up on tiptoe, pushing against his chest, using words as a barrier. "You look ridiculous, you know. Speaking to thin air; your arms encircling nothing."

Those big hands linked under her bottom, lifting her against him. And when he adjusted their fit, her legs parted naturally for him. "You don't feel like nothing." He smirked. She sucked in a sharp breath, her heart pounding. This close, the effects of the impending Moonful on his body were all too evident. She'd never been held in this way by a man in all the centuries of her existence. Although her heart knew it to be wrong, her body wanted him. Lips touched hers.

"Michaela." She whispered the name against his mouth, a talisman to ward off her desire to melt against him. Angling her chin, she stared over his shoulder toward the piazza, searching the crowd for her friend. "She's here somewhere, Bastian . . . Lord Satyr. What if she sees us like this? You holding me in this . . . this inappropriate way." The prospect of discovery had her wriggling and trying to dislodge his hand, suddenly more desperate than ever to be free of his hold.

"I'd be glad to hold you far more inappropriately if you would but show yourself. I draw the line at mating a female I cannot see."

Suddenly, he didn't sound quite so inebriated. What was going on here? Catching him unawares, she managed to find her feet and duck away from him, but he caught the back of her shift. "Not s'fast. Need you," he informed her as he reeled her back in. "Gods, what's this hideous sack you're wearing?" His hands patted over it—over her—and she batted at his hands.

"A shift," she said. "And what do you mean you *need* me?" Was he in danger? She'd felt a gathering sense of trouble over the past few minutes. Something was going to happen, and soon. She glanced around them. The piazza was bustling with early evening traffic—mostly harlots, pimps, and gamblers out to begin their work with the coming of night. They looked to be a fiendish lot of ne'er-do-wells—every face cunning, hopeless, or cruel.

A horrible thought struck her. What if *Bastian* was among those destined to die tonight? Maybe it was no accident that she'd been drawn to him like this? Feeling a need to corral him and shield him from any harm that might approach, she turned her back to him and put her hands on his thighs behind her. His arms came around her and she felt the raw animal brawn of his body at her back, cloaked under a veneer of gentlemanly tailoring. She tried to imagine taking him as host—her essence filling such a masculine body in his stead. What might it be like to move about the world with such strength as he possessed? To have crowds part for you. To have women feast their eyes upon you and men respect you. Simply because you had such a powerful physical presence.

A need to exert some control over him had her clutching the arms he'd drawn around her as she suspiciously analyzed the crowd. The sausage vendor, the trio of prostitutes, the ragpicker. Did one of them have mayhem in mind for him?

"Come, I'll locate a carriage for hire and send you home to Esquiline," she said, tugging at him to follow her. "Your family is already there, and Michaela will look for you there if she doesn't find you here."

"How do you know so much about me?" he demanded as she led him, his words a bit slurred. "When I know nothing about you."

Stealthily, she slipped her hand into his pocket. He caught it before it reached its goal. "That's mine," he snarled gently. Not so drunk, after all.

"Just let me see it," she wheedled. "Please—"

"*Oh, please, no . . .*"

Silvia's head jerked back, cracking against his chest. The disembodied plea lightninged down her spine, wiping all expression from her face and freezing her blood. It seemed the near-dead were awakening. Her eyes darted wildly around the piazza, seeing nothing amiss. Swiveling, she clutched the lapels of Bastian's coat and hissed, "Did you hear that?"

His eyes searched hers, already looking far more lucid than he had when she'd first come across him, for his drunkenness seemed to come and go. "Hear what?"

"N-nothing." She let go of him, but he took her upper arm in one hand. Since he could not see her, he obviously realized he must continue to maintain a hold on her or she would escape.

It had been a terrified cry she'd heard from someone, somewhere, who was under attack. A first recognition that danger was near. All too soon it would turn into a realization that Death was imminent. And inescapable. At the moment, Silvia could detect nothing more of the situation. Although the cry had been distant, it had established that Bastian was not involved in the trouble she'd sensed brewing. That was something.

Still, it meant she could be called away at any moment. And she couldn't leave him here like this. Many others were lifting a glass or two here in Monti. He could be robbed or injured. Or murdered.

"Matters have changed and it seems I can't escort you home, after all," she informed him. "But you're an easy mark in your condition."

Red slashed over her captor's cheekbones. "I'm well able to take care of myself." At that moment, he stumbled over the uneven pavestones, then ran his free hand through his cropped dark hair, looking frustrated that she was right. "Ninety hells."

"Let's get some food in your stomach. That will help." She took his hand and led him toward one of the vendors selling food from a street cart at the bottom of the Spanish steps, then watched as he flipped a coin to the vendor. Although she could not detect the delicious smells emanating from the cart, her memory served her all too well, and she salivated as bread was grilled, cheese melted, and meat sauce poured.

"Hurry, can't you?" she begged the vendor, gazing raptly at his wares. "Before I am called away." But of course he could not hear. Yet, for some reason, Bastian could. A puzzle she would ponder at length in the hours to come.

"Called away where?" asked Bastian. "And by whom?"

"What, signor?" asked the vendor.

"Shhh, Bastian. Stop speaking to me. He'll think you mad," she scolded.

"Who else sees spirits but a madman?"

She didn't reply, not wanting to encourage him, but the sandwich seller eyed him warily, likely imagining him to be out of his wits. "Fog is theeck tonight, *sì*?" he remarked, as he handed over the food.

Bastian glanced around as if only then noticing that fog had rolled in. "Quite," he said succinctly, and put a handsome tip in the man's hand, one guaranteed to quell any misgivings he might have.

Taking the victuals, he began eating mechanically, as if he considered them an antidote to his intoxication rather than a source of enjoyment. The fog stole over him, and she watched it curl around his booted ankles, weave between his thighs . . . and caress the rather thick bulge high between them. She snatched her gaze away, hoping he could not see her distinctly enough to wonder at her pink cheeks.

He tore off part of his sandwich and held it out to her. Without thinking, she reached out for it. Then she shook her head. It was tempting, but hardly worth giving up her immortality! "I can't eat while I'm like—"

"*Stop! I beg you!*"

Gasping, she jerked around, her elbow knocking bread, cheese, and meat from his hand. Then she stared down at the ruined bounty without really seeing it. "Damnation," she gritted under her breath. "I hate when it's murder."

"Murder?" he echoed, sounding somewhat more in control than he had moments earlier. The food had gone a long way toward sobering him. "What the devil are you involved in?" He reached toward her. All the while he'd been eating, he'd still kept one hand on her, but now she'd gotten herself free.

Backing away, she stared at him, memorizing his features as he kept pace, stalking her. Her foolish heart ached to stay with him. "Find Michaela. Go home," she ordered desperately.

"Dammit all to hells—" he began, but his words were drowned out by a new shriek that only Silvia could hear.

"*Nooo!*" Torn from an unknown female's throat, the terrified cry fled through the streets as the victim herself could not. Silvia's head whipped toward the sound. It had come from an alley, only ten minutes away.

A hand brushed the back of her shift. Bastian. "Stay. Let me—"

But she didn't look back at him. Didn't wait to hear more. It was past time to go. Leaping away, she darted down one of the crazy, zigzag alleys in the maze that was Rome, leaving him behind. She'd done all she could for him. It was time to help another.

If she arrived too late, she would miss her chance. There was only a small window of time in the death cycle during which an Ephemeral could take a host. So she flew onward, through one alley after another, toward certain danger. Rounding the corner of a pawnshop that was locked tight for the night, she stumbled upon a murder in progress. A violent one, as she'd expected.

The victim was a woman, as she'd anticipated. Young, maybe twenty or so, with dark hair. But Silvia's eyes were all for her attacker, the horrific creature that was intent on wringing the life out of her. He stood seven feet tall; his body intimately pressed against hers and his long bony fingers wrapped around her vulnerable throat.

"Let her go!" Silvia commanded.

The villain's head whipped in her direction. His black eyes searched for her, but failed to find her since she was currently invisible. He was predominantly Ogre, perhaps with a hint of fey, but she couldn't tell in the twilight of the street. If the latter were the case, he'd been born of rape. No fey would ever willingly bed an Ogre, for they were the dullards of the adjacent World, and known to be cruel and selfish lovers. Even worse, they usually dined on their partner's innards when they tired of bedding them.

Over his shoulder, his victim lifted a beseeching hand toward the sound of her voice. Her eyes were wide, the color of bruised violets.

Gods, no! It was Michaela! Silvia's heart stopped in her chest, then raced on in wild, tumultuous terror. She sprinted through the fog toward the entwined couple. As if she could change destiny. As if she could save her dearest friend from Death. She, an Ephemeral currently without a host.

Michaela stood no chance against this monster. Neither did she, but her best hope lay in surprise. She rushed toward them, intending to take her true form at the last minute and slam her body into the backs of the Ogre's knees, then make off with Michaela.

But when she was still ten feet away from them, she came up against an immovable, iron wall. An invisible one. She bounced off of it and crumpled on the pavement. Leaping up again, she shrugged, not feeling any broken bones. She thrust her arms out ahead of her, pushing at the air with both palms, and felt the bespelled forcewall the attacker had erected around himself and his victim.

"I said let her go," Silvia gritted.

The Ogre's fingers loosened on Michaela, just enough to allow her a few gulping breaths. "You offering to take her place?"

"And if I am?" Silvia circled the perimeter of the forcewall, patting it down as she desperately tried to locate a chink in it. "Will you take me instead of her? I can promise you that I'd make a far tastier meal."

Greedy black eyes glinted and his nostrils flared. "Let me see you first; then I'll decide."

Michaela's eyes widened fearfully and she shook her head. Growling, he slapped her.

Don't kill her, don't kill her, Silvia pleaded silently. Michaela could not die. Could *not.* She pounded both fists on the force-wall. "Now, you know I can't do that, Ogre. Not until we strike a deal. You'd only take me captive as well." Showing herself to an ElseWorld creature would have no effect on her immortality were they on the other side of the gate. But here in this world, it was dangerous. He could lay claim to ownership of her. And stupid as they were, Ogres moved fast. He could be at her side in seconds.

His expression turned crafty. "Give me your name at least and I'll let her go."

"Rico," she lied.

Looking disappointed in her answer, he tightened his hands on his victim's throat again and Silvia's heart twisted painfully. When she'd arrived here from ElseWorld, she'd been so confident in her ability to protect Michaela from Pontifex. But here she was less than an hour later, helpless against a single one of his henchmen.

"Via," Michaela choked. She could not see Silvia in her current form, either. But she knew her voice, and in her angst, she'd revealed too much.

"Yesss." The Ogre nodded, pouncing on the revelation. He looked toward the place he'd last heard Silvia's voice, though she was several feet to the left of it now. "There'sss a nice beginning."

Turning his captive toward Silvia as if to render her a shield, he moved behind Michaela with one hand clasping her to him by the front of her throat. His clawlike thumb stroked her vulnerable larynx, drawing a trickle of blood. She whimpered, but held her tongue.

"Now, give me the rest of it and I'll release your friend here," he promised Silvia. "You know I must have it from your own lipsss."

The impulse to reveal her name and face was strong, but this would gain them nothing. He'd only have two captives then. "Let her go first, and when she is far from here, I'm yours," Silvia vowed.

His licked his lips. "Too bad I can't take you up on that offer. You sound to be a delicious morsel. Bet that skin of yours tastes sssweet." He sighed regretfully. "But you'd only trick me. And I've got my orders."

"Orders from whom?" Silvia lunged, striking the wall painfully with her shoulder. "Pontifex? Why would he want her dead?" Her mind worked furiously. Ogres were a rare breed, but Pontifex employed them as guards. One had visited Bastian's study recently and handled the decanter she'd found. And now this one. The incidents had to be related. If she could figure out how, she might be able to somehow trick Michaela's attacker.

Footfalls echoed in the distance, and the Ogre glanced toward the sound. By now, Michaela's cries had dwindled to pitiful mewls. She was fading.

"*Polizia!*" Silvia shouted, praying someone would hear.

The Ogre's face swung back toward her and he made a hissing sound, like a fire being extinguished. "Ssstupid female. Shouldn't have done that. Moonful comes tonight. Not a good time for creatures like us to be incarcerated in human jails."

Without warning, his hands tightened sharply. Michaela's eyes bulged and her fingers clawed at his. Bones snapped as he gave her neck a brisk wrench, leaving her just enough breath that she would suffer a lingering death.

"See what you made me do?" He grinned at Silvia, a horrible creasing of his face that bared double rows of small, sharp teeth. Damage done, he loped into the darkness of an alley.

Now that his clutch was gone from her throat, Michaela crumpled to the cobblestones, fog swirling violently around her. She looked like some sort of beautiful, wilted poppy as she lay there amid the crushed petals of her crimson skirts.

"Nooo!" Silvia shrieked, as if words alone could deny Death its latest victim. She beat at the wall of magic again and fell forward, finding it nonexistent. The Ogre's departure had dispelled it. She rushed to her friend's side to kneel there on the brick. Tears trickling down her face, she solidified into her true form.

Michaela's ebony curls were in lovely disarray, her head turned at an unnatural angle, and her hold on life tenuous. Wide, purple eyes gazed unseeingly toward the twilight sky. Was she already gone? But then her hand twitched and Silvia lifted it to her lap, cradling it within her own. It was already so pale, so cold.

"Don't . . . want to . . . die," Michaela whispered hoarsely.

"Gods, Kayla," Silvia said on a sob. "I'd give anything if . . ." her words trailed off. Their eyes met and the awful truth hung

146 / Elizabeth Amber

unspoken between them. There was nothing to be done. Michaela would die. They always died.

Although it wouldn't help matters, Silvia adjusted her head to a more natural angle on the brick, needing to do something. Needing to help when there was no way to help. She rubbed Michaela's soft hand and murmured comforting words as together they waited.

Cruel, cruel Death. Silvia had always hated these moments just before it arrived. Not only because it was so heartbreaking when someone's life ended, but also because of the small, shameful flicker of greed that always rose within her. The need to have someone die so that she could live. If one could truly call her existence living.

But never, never had she despised Death more than she did now. Never had she willed it away so desperately and with all her being. "Take me," she begged it. "Let me be the one to die."

Michaela spoke then, her words barely audible, but astonishing nonetheless. "I have a firestone in my possession. Aemilia's. She gave it to me that night for safekeeping as we all escaped from the burning temple. Pontifex found out somehow and sent a threatening note. I was told to bring it . . . here. That someone would meet me and . . ." She laughed, a harsh, gurgling sound.

Silvia gritted her teeth, rage against Pontifex welling up anew at this confirmation that he was behind the Ogre's attack. She tried to calm herself. To be what Michaela required of her now. There would be time for anger later. She'd listened to the last words, the longings, the regrets, and the wishes of the dying countless times over the years. But never had she imagined she would one day be engaging in this ritual with her most cherished friend in the Worlds!

"I didn't think Pontifex's minion would harm me . . ." Michaela went on. "But he planned to kill me all along. . . . Oh how stupid I was to come. You were always the smart one.

Beauty and brains. Pontifex always said that together we would have made quite a woman." She laughed, a soft, hysterical sound.

Silvia had never heard him say such a thing, but she didn't quibble. "It's all right. None of that matters."

Tears squeezed from the outer corners of Michaela's eyes and rolled into the tangle of her hair on either side of her face. "I don't want to die . . . oh, dear Gods . . . not just when I've found love." Her throat worked. "B-Bastian."

"Dear Kayla," Silvia soothed, brushing a curl of dark hair from her smooth forehead. Death was nearing. She felt it. Saw the signs.

Michaela closed her eyes, her face suddenly hopeless, seeming to accept that all was lost. "You'll take me . . . as host?"

Silvia nodded, unable to speak for the lump in her throat. *Oh, Michaela, how will I live when you are gone?* Trying to sound calm, she forced herself to say what she'd said to all the others she'd come upon in similar situations. "If there is anything you've left undone here in these worlds, just tell me, and I—" A great sob escaped her, but she forced herself to continue. "And I swear I will gladly see it done." The words slipped from her easily as if she'd said them hundreds of times before. And she had.

But this was different. This was *Michaela*. Who was dying! Fifty thousand hells! How would she bear it? She bit back another sob.

Michaela's eyes opened again and her dry lips parted. Leaning close, Silvia somberly waited to witness her Deathwish.

Then it came, in a low, shocking murmur. "I want you to . . . lie with . . . Bastian tonight in my stead . . . to let him believe you are me," Michaela rasped. "I want you to make love with him. And tell him I—you—tell him I love him."

Silvia stared dumbly at her, stunned into silence. Tonight was Moonful! Lying with Bastian during the Calling would entail far more than a single coupling. On nights such as this, it was well-known that the Satyr mated from dusk to dawn. Without realizing it, she began shaking her head.

Michaela gripped her forearm with surprising strength. "Promise me, Via," she insisted. "I want more time with him. You can give it to me. Please . . ."

A battle raged within Silvia. *No! Don't ask this of me. You'll discover that my heart has betrayed you, for I love him, too. Yes! I want him for myself. No! If I lie with him, it will only bind me further to that which I cannot have.* Although she wanted to scream a refusal, Silvia only nodded, whispering, "Yes, of course. I promise."

Seeming more at peace, Michaela lifted a hand and touched Silvia's cheek, her eyes full of compassionate affection. Silvia covered it with her own and was surprised to feel the magic in it. Michaela was bestowing a parting spell! "What are you—?"

"You must not mourn me, Via, not as long as you are with him," Michaela began gently. Silvia gazed at her, a contradiction of dismay and gratitude swirling inside her as Michaela continued. "Tonight, you will become all he requires. You will accommodate him in his pleasure just as I w—"

Michaela suddenly went deathly pale and wild fear pushed all else from Silvia's thoughts. "Oh, please, no, don't leave me. Not so soon."

But Michaela's eyes were dull now, and she didn't reply. She drew a single, shallow breath, and then another faltering one. Then her hand fell to lie on her crumpled crimson dress, limp.

A debilitating grief threatened to overwhelm Silvia, and she desperately wanted to give in to it. But she'd promised Kayla.

It was time.

Moving like an automaton, she began the familiar rite of passage. Leaning forward, she let her red-gold hair curtain around Michaela's face to create a small privacy where they might do what they must. "I love you," she whispered. And then she pressed her lips to Michaela's.

With a sharp *gasp!* she captured her beloved friend's final lifebreath. Inhaled it and took it into her own body. Then came that nebulous, infinitesimal pause as life eased into death.

A second kiss. And this time, Silvia gently exhaled and felt the familiar choke and pinch of her own life force moving outward as, slowly, she breathed life back into Michaela's body. Reanimating her. Becoming her.

And then Silvia was lying on her back, the misted brick street a damp and unforgiving bed beneath her. She blinked violet eyes, gazing up at the swiftly darkening, cloud-swollen sky. For a moment she lay there, disoriented and unsure of who she was or what had happened. Somewhere in the distance, she heard footfalls. Shouts.

Polizia. She remembered having called for them. Why?

Gingerly, she sat up and felt pain. She put her hand to her throat. Gods, it burned as if she'd worn a hangman's noose. She had once, fifty hosts ago. Or was it a hundred? Cool air found her and she glanced down, her eyes widening. Her hand went lower to cover her cleavage. She hadn't been this well endowed in quite some time. Her dress was of the sort meant to attract bees to her honey. Who was she?

Then, in a flash, everything came rushing back to her. Michaela was her host now! Which meant she'd . . . died. Oh Gods, no! This meant they had no more than a month left together. Maybe less, then . . . No, she couldn't think of losing Michaela to Death forever. Not yet. Strangely, her grief at her dearest friend's passing was at present a dull, distant pain. She recalled the warmth of Michaela's hand on her cheek moments ago. The bespelling. Michaela had apparently locked away the specific set of emotions that would have made mourning her possible. Grief would not come until later, after she'd fulfilled her friend's final wish.

You must not mourn me, Via, not as long as you are with him.

Dry-eyed, Silvia got to her knees, finding her feet. She hadn't asked Michaela for the truth about her relationship with Pontifex when she'd had the chance, for she had assumed that when she took possession of this body, she would be given its secrets. But Michaela's Will was still strong, and for reasons Silvia could not possibly guess, she was blocking that information.

She walked a few tottering steps, then stopped. Murder was always the worst, for the bodies of the victims were painful. Her throat was still on fire. After all, she'd just been choked to death. But this pain and the marks on her skin would fade within the hour.

A man passed, his eyes turning greedy as they spied her. She adjusted her bodice higher and the pleasant flowery smell of Michaela's perfume wafted to her nose. She wasn't accustomed to being so attractive. Beauty drew too much attention, much of it unwanted.

"Move along, signor!" she said sharply. Ignoring her rebuff, he took a step toward her. She faced off, preparing to defend herself if she must. Suddenly, the man looked past her, his eyes widening. Behind her, she heard footsteps and the distant clip-clop of horses. The man moved on, apparently thinking better of forcing his attentions on her.

Assuming the *polizia* had come, Silvia knew that they might assume her to be a prostitute and therefore take her into custody, since recent laws had given them license to do so. Mentally formulating a believable tale that would explain her presence here as innocent, she smiled and turned to greet . . .

Bastian!

11

At first, Bastian had no difficulty tracking the female specter he'd followed from the piazza, for it had unwittingly left a trail of color in its wake. However, the fog, the maze of crooked streets, and the effects of the impending arrival of Moonful eventually began to defeat him. He'd need a woman soon. It was past time to make his way to a safe haven, where he could begin the ritual. His belly was already rock hard, and the cramping would soon begin. The liquor he'd inadvertently drunk was going to make tonight's Calling particularly arduous for him.

Then, just as he decided to seek home, he spotted a hint of crimson two blocks ahead. A figure rose from the misted street like a corpse rising from a grave. It was a woman, a shapely one dressed in red. *Red; hearts; blood; poppies; lips,* his mind free-associated. The specter that had come this way must have lent its color to her. He shuddered, wanting her. Not her in particular. Any woman would have done for him now. He was in a sorry state. He should head for home and summon a Shimmerskin or two to attend him before it was too late. But even as these thoughts swirled in his head, he stepped in her direction.

It seemed another had similar plans to his, for as the woman straightened her clothing, a man approached her. Bastian tensed, a male animal protecting his territory—this unknown woman he wanted to fuck. He loped toward the pair, moving in and out of the halos of gaslight along the street, the striking of his boots on pavement making him known to his opponent. Seeing him as a threat, the man backed away from the female and faded into the surrounding shadows.

She was his now. Bastian prayed to the Gods that she was a whore. A willing one. Not some other man's wife or untried daughter. Judging by his body clock, the moon was easily forty-five minutes away from showing itself. Nevertheless, the desire to push this stranger against the nearest building and fuck her with everything he had already overwhelmed him. The urge shouldn't be so strong, not yet. Not so early in the night. It was the wine. When the moon did come, he wouldn't be able to trust himself not to resort to rape.

He halted abruptly a half-dozen feet from her. What the hells was he doing? The liquor was affecting his reason, as it always had. Curse whoever had tainted his decanter with it!

He had to get home before the Change came over him. With a last, lingering, lustful glance at the female, he gritted his teeth and made to go.

But then she turned. And everything changed.

"Michaela?"

Those red lips formed his name. "Bastian." Her cheeks were flushed coral; her silky black hair had blue highlights; her dress was crimson. And her eyes—they were violet as pansies. She shone with an inner light he'd never seen in her before, like a jewel in the black night, drawing him to her side.

"Beautiful," he murmured as he took her in his arms. Looking oddly nervous, she launched into some rambling explanation regarding why she was here. His suspicions were aroused, but all he could think of was getting her out of her dress. Of fucking her here in one of the alleys, or perhaps breaking into one of these buildings where he could mate with her in privacy from dusk to dawn. A desperate need swamped him to bury himself in her feminine depths, before the color leached away as it always seemed to, turning her a cadaverous gray like the rest of his world.

"So that's why I asked you to meet me here in Monti," she finished.

"Monti?" he echoed. Only then did he remember the note he'd found from her in his study. Yes, that's why he'd come here. She'd asked him to meet her in the piazza. He'd drunk from the decanter before coming out, wanting to give the elixir time to work its way through his system. It should have tamed the beast that he would become tonight, at least in some measure, but it had not. He'd thrown the decanter away the moment he'd realized it had been polluted with true liquor. Since he'd eaten in the piazza, he no longer stumbled or garbled his words. But inside, he could feel the intoxicating effects of what he'd unwittingly drunk. He was still tainted. And still dangerous. To her.

"It doesn't matter," he told her, his deep voice brushing off her words. His hand went to the small of her back, tugging her close as his fingers went to the front of her bodice, tearing open the fastenings.

She snatched the gaping sides of her dress together, looking alarmed, but he knocked her hands aside, his own hand diving inside her bodice and underthings to find and squeeze a lush breast. His thumb rubbed over her nipple, relishing the fact that it went stiff for him. His other hand went low to clutch her bottom and force her belly tight to his own. He tilted her just so and ground himself against her. His body reacted predictably.

"Gods, I want you," he gritted, his lips caressing her jaw.

"Here?" she squeaked. "B-but someone's coming."

He lifted his head, abruptly noticing the rhythmic clacking sound of horseshoes striking brick. Two of his brothers appeared out of the fog like apparitions on horseback, hailing him.

"Where the hells have you been?" Sevin demanded, his steed rearing as he pulled it to a halt. Beside him, Lucien reined in his roan as well.

"Wandering Monti, half drunk," Bastian told him succinctly. "And now if you'll excuse us . . ." Ignoring his brothers' stupefied expressions, he lifted Michaela into his arms, sweeping her toward the nearest dark alley.

And then from that very alley before them, the *polizia* suddenly descended upon them. "Gods, is this to be a convention?" he snarled, and saw Michaela smile. Red. Her lips. Berries. He bent his head and tasted them hungrily with his own, just as the officers called out to them.

"We heard reports of trouble. You gents seen anything?"

He heard Sevin make some reply, then everything else was forgotten except the mouth under his. Had Michaela always tasted like this? "You're different," he murmured against her mouth and felt her body stiffen in his arms.

A soft palm curved his cheek and the unnatural warmth of her touch jolted his sex. He growled low in his throat and released her legs, holding her body close as it slowly slid downward along his own. She couldn't help but feel his erection. "I need to fuck you," he said, his voice gone unnaturally low.

"Yes, I-I gathered as much," she said. "But, your brothers . . . the *polizia*." She gestured toward them. His hand went to her bodice again, and he grunted with displeasure when he found she'd hooked it closed again.

Somewhere behind him, he heard Sevin reassuring the constables. "All is well. We're just on our way home to Esquiline.

To the house of my brother, *Lord Bastian Satyr.*" He emphasized the name, obviously believing they would recognize it, and that his reputation would quickly have these men shoving off. It seemed he was right, for they began to take their leave.

"Are you all right, signora?" one of the officers persisted, drawing near. Bastian gnashed his teeth, fighting the urge to throttle the man.

"Very much so." Michaela smiled sweetly over one shoulder at him, and he doffed his hat in his hands, clearly besotted.

"Come on, man," called one of his partners, and the officer reluctantly took himself off. Apparently having given them all a sufficient visual once-over, the *polizia* were satisfied and moved on, searching alleys and testing doorknobs.

"The night grows dangerous," Lucien pronounced in an eerie voice, as if he knew something the rest of them didn't. Bastian's eyes snapped to him where he still sat on horseback. Their youngest sibling, Luc had been lost to the family at the tender age of five and had spent the subsequent thirteen years of his life held captive within a labyrinth beneath the Forum ruins. Somewhere in the intervening years, he had acquired some very peculiar powers. Hells, who knew what his youngest brother was thinking half the time? The doctors in Else-World had found him a complete puzzle. They'd even confided that they suspected he was toying with them in order to impede their understanding of his talents.

In a decisive move, Bastian took Michaela's arm and led her to Lucien's side. "Double with Sevin. I'll take your horse," he instructed his brother. Without argument, Lucien slid from the steed and just as lithely leaped up behind Sevin.

Swinging Michaela high, Bastian seated her sideways in the saddle; then with one boot in the stirrup, he swung up behind her. Taking the reins, he prodded with his heels, propelling their mount southwestward, toward Capitoline, one of the seven hills that ringed the Roman Forum.

"Esquiline is this way!" Sevin protested. "We were supposed to gather at your house an hour ago, remember? Dane and Eva await us there."

"Too late!" Bastian gestured toward the darkening sky. "The *Salone* is closer. And Dane will manage his wife just fine tonight without us."

"To Capitoline, then," Sevin agreed, veering to follow him. The four of them raced off toward sanctuary. Toward the *Salone di Passione,* a safe haven where the Lords of Satyr would spend this night as their ancient heritage dictated they must.

Silvia rode sidesaddle in front of Bastian, snuggled within his strong embrace, her head resting on his shoulder. Her legs were both draped over one of his, and she felt his powerful thigh muscles work as he urged their horse onward through the night. "Hold on," he rumbled. His coat was open, so she looped her arms around him inside it, hugging his solid strength. Turning her face into the hollow of his throat, she kissed him. His narrowed eyes flickered over her and his hand tightened on the reins. The horse bucked in reaction, almost throwing them. Cursing, he loosened his grip and rode on, his face grimly determined.

When she'd first seen him on the street just now, joy had bubbled up in her. The sort of effervescent inner lightness a woman feels in the company of the man she loves. A joy she shared with her host—for tonight, all of her emotions would be a heady blend of Michaela's and her own. Both were quite utterly attracted to him. But he belonged to only one of them. To Michaela, a woman not quite dead and not quite living.

Still, Silvia anticipated the coming hours with an unapologetic relish that was coupled with a tinge of wariness. After centuries of using her wits to protect her virginity, she would willingly lose it tonight, in spirit if not in fact.

Michaela's body had known many men before, and it was

her body their lover would mate under the full moon. Although Silvia would couple with him, she would nevertheless enjoy a certain impunity. This body was not truly hers, and her own virginity would still be intact when she eventually returned to her true form.

Instead of begrudging the sharing of her lover, Michaela seemed pleased with her for going with him now. She had long counseled Silvia against being so rigid in her interpretation of her vows of chastity, claiming that fornication while in the body of another host would not constitute a betrayal of them. But Silvia had always argued otherwise and had remained steadfastly pure over the centuries. Yet tonight, she would do as Michaela had long urged. She would lie with a man for the first time in her life.

A light drizzle began as they bypassed Palazzo Nuovo, and Bastian sheltered her from it with his body as best he could. Protective, as Michaela had said. His gesture, small though it was, touched Silvia's heart.

Several blocks later, they arrived at their destination: the *Salone di Passione*. The entire three-story building reeked of ElseWorld magic. Along its façade, a series of sash windows alternated with Corinthian pilasters crowned with carven olive branches. Gaslights flickered beyond its windows, and the raindrops that clung to the glass splintered their illumination into hundreds of tiny jewels. The salon catered only to an elite contingent of ElseWorld creatures and had been bespelled so that the uninitiated could not see this building or any of the comings and goings from it. To humans, it was nonexistent, appearing only as an impenetrable thicket. But to ElseWorldly beings, it was a sensual paradise.

Two enormous stone griffins watched them dismount and hand their horses off to caretakers at the bottom of the front staircase. The horses were skittish now and shied from the brothers as they dismounted. On some deeper level of the senses, they recognized that these men were devolving into something more animalistic tonight.

As they all took the steps upward, Sevin drew alongside Silvia and spoke in an aside. "Bastian's drunk. Do you know how it happened?"

"A tainted decanter in his study," she replied.

"How much did he have?" asked Lucien from behind them.

"I don't know."

"Hells, it doesn't matter. A single damned drop and he's well oiled," said Sevin.

"I'm drunk, not deaf," Bastian reminded them dryly as they reached the door. "Someone spiked my decanter with Sangiovese."

"Who?" the three of them asked at the same time.

"No idea. It was just a few drops, thank the Gods. But I still feel its effects." His gaze swept Silvia, scalding her.

At the salon's threshold, Sevin held her back, his words making it clear he assumed her to be Michaela. "This Calling will hit him harder than you've seen before," he warned *sotto voce*. "If you want to run, go now. Once all begins, it will be too late."

Her eyes widened. *Run?*

Bastian turned back in the doorway, glancing between them. His nostrils flared and his eyes narrowed with a feral suspicion that she'd never seen from him before. He extended his arm to her. "Michaela?"

Michaela. Yes. This was for her. Silvia stepped inside the *Salone* and took the arm he proffered, trying to pretend to herself that this was only to be a selfless fulfillment of another's Deathwish. That it was not merely an excuse to do precisely what she wanted. To lie with this man—her best friend's lover.

A gargantuan one-eyed sentry nodded to the four of them and took their coats as they passed through an elegant sitting room. It was dotted with small tables and couches and a throng of ElseWorld creatures—centaurs, pixies, fey, Nereid, mermen, and more. Everyone here seemed to be forming alliances and negotiating in preparation for what would happen once they entered the main salon beyond this room.

Silvia had expected the brothers to drop their guard once they arrived, since the threat of human discovery was nonexistent within these walls. However, their tension had only mounted. Their expressions went fierce and watchful as they positioned themselves on all sides of her, forming a masculine fortress around her as they navigated through the room. She soon began to realize why.

She had come here before with Michaela, while in the body of Rico. But those visits had been by daylight when the atmosphere here had been lighthearted and easy. The salon took on an entirely different mood after dark when a full moon was lurking, she discovered. Now an adversarial, carnal mood spiced the surroundings. Every male was carefully guarding his chosen mate, his eye fastened on her or him with single-minded intensity. Those who'd come alone roved, searching hungrily for a potential partner or group willing to include them in their evening's entertainment.

The brothers didn't pause in this anteroom, but instead quickly ushered her on through a red velvet curtain and into the next chamber. The central salon, where they would all pass this special night.

It was a massive, splendid room with a gilded, coffered ceiling that rose three stories high to form a dome. Encircling the vast circumference of the upper floors were rows of balconied seating boxes. Enormous candelabras forged of precious metals were positioned between the boxes, bathing strategic areas of the floor in their radiant glow, while purposely leaving others in shadow. At the salon's center, a carousel turned with mesmerizing slowness. Lacquered dragons, unicorns, and other fantastic creatures pumped up and down upon it, some bearing riders caught in erotic, undulating embraces.

The soft strains of music that emanated from the carousel were punctuated with the occasional *click* of a door opening to admit those who sought privacy in one of the smaller chambers that encircled the salon's main floor. The muffled sounds of laughter, conversation, and moans charged the air each time another door was opened.

Bastian's hand was hot on the small of Silvia's back, guiding her through the room. It was a chivalrous gesture and a territorial one. Her eyes darted around the salon. How soon would all begin? Where would he take her? Would they enter one of those chambers that ringed the expansive main floor?

At least half of them were merely alcoves, she saw; some with curtains at their entrances, and others left open to the main salon so that anyone might view the participants within. The interiors of these rooms had been designed to suit a variety of inclinations. One imitated a verdant, floral garden with a walkway, stone fountains, and wrought-iron benches. And another a hay-filled stable.

There were stark settings containing only one or more platform stages and uncomfortable furniture. Mysterious iron bolts and eyehooks were embedded at intervals in both their walls and ceiling, as well as in strategic locations upon the furnishings. Much of this hardware was threaded with lengths of leather that ended in metal buckles. In one chamber they passed, a woman was securing her own wrists in delicate shackles as her partner looked on.

In contrast, some alcoves were done up as lush boudoirs—one a frilly, girlish bedroom lit in pastel colors, and another with a bed, fainting couch, and upholstered swing, all lit in the garish, titillating scarlets and purples of a bordello.

It seemed that any fantasy one could imagine could be found here in one of these rooms. Any entertainment. She looked at Bastian and found his eyes on her bosom. She put a hand there, and their eyes caught, silver and violet.

"Where are we going?" she asked.

"The grotto," came his stark reply.

Sevin glanced at him, and reading something he did not like in his face, he clasped his arm, drawing their group to a halt. "Let me take Michaela tonight. Luc and I will see to her and return her to you well-satisfied in the morning."

"What? No!" Silvia objected violently. The shocking suggestion had her mind scrambling to reshape her image of him. She'd become fast friends with Sevin while she'd been in the form of Rico, and therefore had only seen an avuncular side of him. But he was a man, after all. One who shared the same lusty Satyr blood as Bastian. His voice had gone steely now and edgy, and he was gazing at her with his own brand of masculine hunger. And with a touch of concern.

Seeming not to hear her refusal, he took her arm and gave his brother an intractable stare. "It's for her own well-being. You know it is."

Silvia reached out to Bastian, putting a palm on his crisp white shirtfront. "Am I a toy to be passed around without my consent?" she protested. There was only one man here she craved for her own.

Though his expression was a thundercloud of conflicting emotions, his arm came around her waist and his hand squeezed her reassuringly. "She's mine."

Sevin looked ready to argue further but broke off as Luc stepped close to her. Wordlessly, he raised a hand and gently cupped her breast, touching her nowhere else. Startled, she jumped back, just as Bastian jerked her to him. A low warning issued from deep in his throat. The sound stopped everyone in their tracks. He'd actually growled, like a bear or a wolf! As if he were not a man, but rather some feral animal defending his mate.

"Not tonight." It was a somewhat obscure pronouncement to her mind, but his brothers seemed to understand his meaning. Riveted, she watched an unspoken communication flash among the trio. Michaela likely understood the nuances of whatever was going on. However, unlike other hosts Silvia had taken, she was keeping secrets, revealing only what she wanted Silvia to know when she wanted her to know it. It was a disturbing realization and left Silvia with the uneasy feeling that at any moment she might step off a cliff and tumble into some unforeseen disaster.

Lucien looked cast adrift by her rejection. His expression plainly indicated that he'd come here on the assumption that he would lie with her. But Bastian offered him no sympathy, and instead wrapped his arms around her and kissed her soundly, as if to rub his possession of her in his youngest brother's face. It was a long, deep, thrilling kiss that marked her clearly as his. Their lips clung, and their eyes.

"Yes," she murmured, answering his body's unspoken question. Yes, she wanted him. Only him.

There were other companions on offer for his brothers. At least a half-dozen ElseWorld females had already gathered nearby and were watching the brothers with feminine hunger. When other potential partners drifted near, they were turned away. These women were obviously hoping the Satyr lords might choose partners from among them for the night. One of them sent Sevin a come-hither smile. With a nod, he beckoned her over and signaled that she was to approach Luc with her favors.

But Luc took them all off guard by suddenly stepping closer to Silvia again, this time threading an arm around her in a bold move that dared his eldest brother's displeasure. She felt tension harden Bastian's muscles; then heard Sevin caution him, catching his arm as he made a threatening move toward their youngest brother. "Let him have this much, Bastian."

Then all she knew was Luc, for he pulled her close, his arm joining Bastian's at the back of her waist as his head bent to hers. His older siblings loomed over them, watching as her hands went to the hard muscles of his arms, unsure. But this youngest brother was not unfamiliar to Michaela, Silvia quickly gathered. And her body responded when he pressed his lips on hers. Luc's kiss was all solemn intensity and impassioned heat. It felt proprietary, as if he believed he had some right to her. As if they'd been lovers.

They had been, she realized suddenly. As he drew back, his eyes were knowing. Her gaze flicked to Sevin and saw a different man than the charming, urbane one she'd come to know. His silver eyes had turned molten and possessive, his body tense with carnal threat. Instinct told her that this was the male animal he would become in the dark, with a woman. In his hot gaze she read the same knowledge she'd seen in Luc's, a knowledge that told her he'd mated this body she now wore.

A full-blown vision abruptly leaped into her mind, plucked from Michaela's memories. It was a frozen tableau of four lovers—the four of *them*—all in various states of undress and locked together in a hedonistic embrace.

Wearing only an unbuttoned tailored shirt, Sevin was sprawled on a rather garish fainting couch, his feet planted wide on the carpet before him. Clad only in her stockings, Michaela knelt up between his thighs, her own legs positioned slightly apart for him, and her fingers forking the delicate folds of her pink feminine nether flesh in invitation. One of his hands was clasped at the curve of her waist, and his other guided the shaft of his immense erection. His eyes watched intently as its fat mushroom head pierced her, beginning its initial penetration.

Directly behind her, Lucien was fully dressed and on his

knees. Both of his hands were on her bottom, opening her cheeks for a prick that equaled his brother's in size and that angled from his open trousers, its head nudging at her divide.

But it was Bastian himself who dominated this scene. He stood before Michaela, alongside Sevin's thigh, with one of his hands cupped at her nape and his silver eyes glinting down at her with a lecherous sort of affection. His broad, muscled chest was bare of any shirt, and his trousers sagged open almost to his knees. Michaela's right hand was lightly braced on his hip and her other encircled his enormous, engorged cock. It rose like some erotic weapon from his dark groin and was of such girth that her fingers did not meet around it. Her lips were wet and parted, her adoring eyes on his handsome face as she prepared to draw him into her mouth, even as she welcomed both of his brothers inside her body.

Silvia glanced at Bastian and blushed at the awareness in his expression. Somehow, he'd guessed her thoughts as easily as his siblings had. Although all three of these men had apparently lain with Michaela, she had only just now confided this information to Silvia. *More warning would have been nice,* Silvia muttered silently.

"Enough," Bastian threatened, hands fisting when Lucien didn't draw back from her quickly enough to suit.

Luc's eyes flicked to him in challenge. Though his touch had been masculine and confident, it had not affected her in the same melting way Bastian's did. For she loved one man and not the other. "I'm sorry," she told him, touching her hand to his.

"Don't push matters, Luc," Sevin murmured. Turning him toward the females who had gathered nearby, he gestured to them. "Choose another." At his acknowledgment, several of their admirers surrounded him, touching his body familiarly. He owned this salon and had likely bedded many of the women here, Silvia gathered.

A fey female boldly pressed herself against Luc and pulled

his head down to hers. He kissed her deeply, but in a way that indicated his mind was elsewhere. And then, like an automaton, he put an arm around her and followed Sevin and the others off toward the wall of chambers.

Bastian's large hand came at Silvia's back, and she instantly forgot his brothers and their women as he turned her, guiding her toward his chosen destination.

12

With grim haste, Bastian directed Michaela behind the carousel and on toward the tall wrought-iron gates he sought just beyond it. Shimmerskins—servile beings that could be conjured from nothingness only by the Satyr—acted as sentries here, and they stepped aside as he approached, opening the gates. Garbed in severe, tailored black, they trained their eyes straight ahead, careful in their lack of acknowledgment of the comings and goings of their masters.

After he and Silvia passed through the gates, the servants closed and locked them. Seeing this, Silvia glanced at him. He read the question in her eyes: *What goes on here that it must be kept so secure?*

He slid a hand up her spine, under the silky fall of her hair, and guided her upward along a deliberately crude stonework path lined with lush vegetation. "Sevin warned you against me tonight," he told her. "You should have run then if you wanted to."

"I don't want to run."

He gave a hollow, mirthless laugh. She didn't know what he

would become under the influence of the grape. Not even his brothers knew the whole of it. They all looked up to him, thought him a paragon. But they would think differently if they'd seen him during the years he'd spent his days and nights fornicating, a flagon of wine always in easy reach.

His first taste of *vino* made from the crush of grapes cultivated in the ancient Satyr vineyards had come on his first Calling night. And upon that small, initial taste, he had fallen into an abyss. It had been the week of his eighteenth birthday—the same day both of his parents had died of the Sickness. Yet the moon had shown him no compassion. It had been ruthless in calling him to worship that night, requiring that he engage in the ancient carnal rituals dedicated to Bacchus.

Once all was over come dawn, he'd left Italy and his younger brothers, who'd needed him. But the wine had whispered to him that they did not, and had bade him to wander, seeking only pleasure. He'd traveled the continent, visiting ancient sites of every kind and finding his way between the thighs of hundreds of women, on a drinking binge that had lasted four years. It had ended only by accident, when he'd become trapped on a snowy mountaintop in Mongolia for a week without spirits. Thus had he been freed from the wine's spell. He had never touched a drop of liquor since. Until today.

The gentle trickle and splash of waterfalls reached his ears as he led his lamb to sybaritic slaughter along a path that took them ever upward.

"Where are we?" she asked.

He cut his eyes her way, his appetite for her rising at the sight of her slim feminine body and the knowledge that she was his for the night to come. His own body urged him to take her immediately, here in this sumptuous haven. But he must wait for the Change. Only a few minutes more until all would begin.

"It's an island of sorts, which stands remote from the rest of the salon by virtue of the ironwork grate that surrounds it," he told her. "A private domain strictly for my family's use. One devoted to our god."

The path ended at an idyllic, lush clearing, surrounded by dense plantings of ElseWorld flowers, wine grapes, and other vegetation. At its center stood a lovely grotto, which was formed in the shape of an amphitheater. Its far side rose to form a shallow cave thirty feet high and wide. Thousands upon thousands of shells had been set in its cement, forming a mosaic of erotic scenes in which the gods visited themselves upon mortals. Around its rim were carved fanciful animals and lurid beasts. This paradise was Sevin's doing and he often spent his Callings here. But tonight, Bastian had claimed it for himself, needing this walled confinement to house what he would become.

Already he felt his abdomen cramp, his skin prickle. A light down of hair would soon cover his haunches and extend lower along his legs almost to his ankles. Yet another feature of the insatiable beast he would become. He stopped beside the pool, which ironically enough was devoted to Bacchus, the Roman God of Wine. His god, who would watch over the proceedings tonight and relish in his labors here.

Bastian's eyes went to the altar set in the low wall at the front of the shallow pool, and the sight of it honed his need, twisting desire toward lecherous obsession. This was an altar the Satyr had employed since ancient times to celebrate their nuptial nights and other Callings like this one. It had been brought here from an ElseWorld temple. And it was here he would cleave his body to Michaela's, just as legions of his kind had mated their lovers over centuries past. He wasn't sure why it had seemed so crucial to him that he bring her here now, when he never had before. But something about her was different tonight, and from the moment he'd seen her rise from the street, he'd thought only of fucking her here. Of loving her here, before his family's god.

Drawn by his addiction, he glanced her way again and saw a flash of brilliant red-gold overlay her dark hair. Instantly, it was gone. What the hells?

Her brows rose. "What's wrong?"

He shook his head. "The wine . . . it's affecting me." Wine alone was enough to strengthen his sexual appetites beyond what Michaela was accustomed to. But the color that painted her now was pushing him over the edge of some ambit into new territory where carnal delights far more intense than he'd ever pursued beckoned, and where he could not trust himself to curb any lecherous impulse.

Gods, when will the moon come! He had to do something to take the edge off of his lust or he would start too early with her. Ripping open his vest, he put her hands on his shirtfront, wanting her touch. Then he watched his own hands move restlessly over her clothing, shaping her hips, ribs, breasts.

"Still?" she said in belated response to his comment, as her hands began to wander over his chest. "But I thought . . . its effects seem to have lessened."

"I meant when the Change comes. The wine I drank earlier will make things between us . . . different . . . than you're used to with me."

Her hands stilled and her gaze tilted up to his, vaguely alarmed. "Why? You and your brothers drink an elixir made from your family's wine grapes prior to every Moonful. All the Satyr do."

He took her shoulders, slipping his fingers under the fabric of her gown there. "I'm different from my brothers. I cannot tolerate spirits. Haven't you ever wondered why I only drink from the decanter in my study?"

She nodded, looking strangely furtive, as if she hadn't known this and had only just now learned it from his lips. Yet, he knew that wasn't the case.

He pushed the shoulders of her gown aside and they relaxed

down her arms, causing her bodice to gape. Her head bent and white teeth tugged at her lower lip as she watched him fondle the voluptuous curves he'd revealed. "That decanter contains a brew that substitutes for wine—one made especially for me," he went on, only half paying attention to his own words. "I never told you because it wasn't necessary. But now . . . you should know that as the night progresses, I'll become more . . ." He bent to cover the peak of a breast with his hot mouth, drawing strongly on her. Her lashes lowered and her head lolled back, her fingers fisting in his shirt.

Had she always tasted so sweet, so desirable? He pulled away, enjoying the sight of her nipples, wet and erect from his mouth. The color that tinged her had only become more intense since he'd held her. A primitive surge of ownership washed over him, and within his trousers, his cock ached for her. He gritted his teeth. Perhaps touching her like this when he couldn't yet take her under him wasn't such a good idea after all.

"Yes? You'll become more . . . ?" she prompted.

"More territorial . . . insatiable . . . even bestial," he finished roughly. He released her and ran a hand through his hair. "Hells, I don't know what else."

She put a hand on his arm and he looked at her. "I won't leave you," she promised. "No matter what happens. I—"

Now, thought Silvia. Now was the time to tell him. To grant Michaela's Deathwish. To confess her love. Now. She licked her lips, gazing at him with the hearts of two women in her eyes. "Bastian, I—"

Suddenly, she heard a rumble overhead and looked up to see a crack forming in the salon's high domed ceiling. "What's happening?"

Bastian stepped back from her and dropped his arms to his sides, then spoke in an ominous monotone. "It begins."

Above them, the domed ceiling continued to split down a

single central line, its two halves retracting to reveal a second outer dome, this one of paned glass. Bastian moved to the far side of the clearing and was staring downward. She went to him and put a hand on his back, wanting to lend comfort. From this vantage point, the grotto overlooked much of the salon below. As they watched, every door and every curtain there opened. No matter what their state of dress or undress, every creature in the salon ventured out into the central room, gazing skyward.

A collective gasp sounded as the moon finally rewarded them. Slipping from behind a cloud, it suddenly bathed them all in a glorious blue-white light. And every face lifted to it, celebrating its arrival. Arms raised and murmurs infused the air, all to welcome the coming of the moon.

Even Silvia was affected, for ancient ElseWorld blood pumped in Michaela's veins and in her own. But the Satyr were well-known to be far more affected by this event than any other being from their distant world. She watched Bastian, enthralled. His face was upturned now, and he wore a rapturous expression as he gloried in the moon's embrace. Standing there in the Calling's grip, he looked as powerfully built and as strikingly handsome as any god she'd ever beheld.

As the divine lunar light bathed him, Bastian felt the familiar cramps seize cruelly in his taut belly. Every muscle in his body contorted and twitched. An upsurge of lust filled his cock, hardening it to rock. And still he stood there, his face raised to the moon, letting it happen. Letting the ecstasy of it wash over him.

From all around him came groans of excitement, delight, pleasure, and pain. They rose in a wondrous cacophony from every corner of the salon, as every breed of ElseWorld creature changed physically in its own way—in the way the ancients had decreed it must.

His belly knotted under a sudden knife-sharp, barbaric twist. A ragged groan erupted from his throat and he went down on one knee. His face became a grimace of sublime and terrible agony. One hand fumbled at the fastenings of his trousers and his other yanked out his shirttails. All else was forgotten, as this—the last physical Change of the Calling night—occurred.

Long moments later, all was complete. He was a freakish creature now of the kind that populated humans' erotic nightmares. A bizarre anomaly they only whispered about, and that in some periods of history they had hunted and captured for their private harems and menageries. One that in this century, they brushed off as only myth and rumor.

He touched himself, drawing two fingers upward along the underside of a shaft of newly awakened flesh. Rounding the plump, glossy head of this prodigious length, he found and smeared the pearl of pre-cum at its slit. And he shuddered. Moonful had gifted him with this new shaft of bone and sinew—this second cock ripped from his own flesh. After a single ejaculation, it would be gone again, only to reappear with the next full moon. But for now, it extended high and hard from his pelvis and was of a length and girth identical to that of the cock that was rooted just an inch or so below it, in his dark thatch. Both craved the sanctuary of a female body.

Michaela. His eyes found her, and for an instant, he saw another's image imprinted over her once again. That of a woman with clear sky-blue eyes and wild, red-gold hair. His lust surged tenfold. Candles flickered around her, and the fog rising from the pool clung to her, misting her with hundreds of tiny, perfect jewels. And then it was Michaela again, with her dark, silky hair and violet pansy eyes.

He got to his feet in one lithe move. Her eyes dropped to his groin. Though his trousers hung open, his shirttails hid his erections for the moment. He stared at her, his silver gaze unwavering, predatory. The beast within him lurked dangerously close to the surface.

"Come here," he growled.

Silvia's heart pounded with a thrilling, terrifying sort of anticipation. She had no personal experience of carnal matters with men. And judging by the glint in Bastian's eye, this was not destined to be a calm introduction. Her pulse fluttered at the base of her throat and she swallowed against a tremor of fear.

Over the years, she'd taken courtesans, concubines, and wives among her hosts. Yet she had always managed to elude the wiles of their men. By now, her skills at subterfuge when it came to dodging her hosts' concupiscent obligations were well-honed. But tonight, she would not employ these wiles against Bastian.

Tonight, you will be all he requires. You will accommodate him in his pleasure. The words of her dearest friend's bespelling resounded in her head. Michaela wanted her here. Wanted this. In truth, Silvia wanted it as well.

No Moonful had ever roused her passions so strongly. Before, she'd passed all such nights in quiet contemplation as she'd been taught in the temple. What was different tonight? Was it this place? Was it the presence of Bastian and Michaela, and her love for them both that urged her to lie with him?

Her footsteps were silent as she crossed the short expanse of mossy earth and went to him. She laid a hand—Michaela's olive hand—on his chest. Her fingers found and slid inside the gap between his shirtfront buttons, finding the resilient, golden skin beneath. She brushed a taut, flat nipple and the muscle of his chest flexed under her touch. Images of him engaged with other partners during prior Moonful Callings filled her mind—images given to her by Michaela, in which his silver eyes gleamed and his body had turned more animal than human.

She snatched her hand away.

Two female Shimmerskins clad in flowing translucent silks appeared at her side, seemingly conjured from the surrounding murk. Bastian must have brought them, for the ability to summon such creatures was a talent peculiar to the Satyr. Their movements and dress were exotic, meant to titillate. When their hands came to work at the fastenings of Silvia's clothing, she automatically refused.

"Let them." At Bastian's low command, the mood in the grotto suddenly shifted and was permeated by a new sizzling tension. His gaze scorched her; owned her. By exerting his masculine Will now, he was setting the tone for how all would go between them. He would direct matters, not she. Thus was the way of the Calling. On other nights, a female might be an equal partner in the sexual dance, but on this night, masculine always dominated feminine. And it was what she craved from him. On this night.

Still, she could not help but recall other male eyes that had rested on her long ago, on a different night, when other candles had burned nearby. These had been the eyes of six men whose only goal had been to hurt her. And this memory now gave her pause.

Silently and gently, Michaela wooed her away from these painful memories by whispering of her own recollections. By filling her mind with thoughts of how this man's powerful body had brought her pleasure. Of how he could make them feel tonight if only Silvia would allow him to see her. To touch her. To do as he must.

And so her hesitation and her hands slowly fell away, and Silvia let him watch the Shimmerskins' artful unveiling of her. This was not to be an exercise in efficiency, she quickly deduced, but rather one meant to tease. As the sylphlike beings worked leisurely onward, she smiled to herself, thinking that their pace was at his instruction. Slow hands, Michaela had said.

When her bodice and corset were unfastened, her attendants gently parted the fabric to bare her for her lover's enjoyment. Their hands cupped her breasts, plumping them high and gently pinching nipples into peaks. Silvia's own hands fisted at her sides and she blushed, feeling Bastian's eyes on flesh she'd never before displayed to a man... willingly. When only stockings and pantalets remained, he finally called a halt.

"Leave the rest," he said in a voice gone dark and rough.

The Shimmerskins desisted in their ministrations and each took one of her elbows, leading her to the low stone wall that enclosed the grotto's pool. Their work done, they simply disappeared into the mist. Shedding his boots and trousers, Bastian came to her and took her in his arms before she had a chance to fully appreciate the sight of his body. When he pulled her close, she gasped at the hard shafts that strained against her belly. Though hidden beneath the hem of his shirt, their power, strength, and size were unmistakable. High between her legs, her private flesh melted, weeping for want of them.

He kissed her deeply and her curious hands ventured lower, finding twin shafts of velveted steel. His hands cuffed her wrists, taking both behind her and holding them at the base of her spine. His hard eyes glinted, fierce, and she sensed he was moving perilously close to the line that separated man from something darker and more irredeemable. His lips grazed her ear and his voice came, hot and hungry. "You know what I need."

Down, whispered a voice inside her.

Somehow understanding what was required, Silvia loosed her wrists, turned from him, and knelt at the altar of his god. And when her knees were cushioned by the springy green moss that covered the bank before the altar, he knelt behind her, his knees going between hers. His big hand pressed at her back, and she slumped forward upon the black of the natural slate altar. She gasped at the cool that met her breasts, for the altar was wet from the waterfall's mist, which had pooled upon its irregular surface.

She bent her arms, bracing herself a little higher. Twisting to look back at him, she watched as one of the Shimmerskins rematerialized at his side and tilted a carafe she held toward him. He cupped both hands loosely before him and oil was drizzled onto his palms. Finding its way through his fingers, some fell to soak the fabric of her underthings. His hands went under the tails of his shirt and began working there, slicking oil over his cocks. Silvia stared in fascination, unsure whether to feel frustrated or relieved that his shirt allowed her only random glimpses as his hands moved, readying him. For her.

Seeming to take pity on her, the Shimmerskin unbuttoned his shirt and pulled it open and back to display him to her gaze. Smiling at her gasp, the creature then disappeared once again. Silvia felt Bastian's avid eyes on her face as she watched him brazenly stroke himself with the oil he'd caught, fists moving up and down two shafts in voluptuous tandem, from roots to swollen heads, and back again. Both phalluses were engorged and enormous, their lengths embossed with knotted blue veins, and their smooth heads flushed purple with carnal hunger.

Within moments, he was going to put them inside her. Rut her with them as hard and as long as he liked, and through them he would impart his seed. Were she to somehow break free and run from him now, he would only hunt her down and drag her beneath him again, hell-bent on having his way. Although she had no intention of running, the knowledge that he craved her with such keen masculine desperation was a delicious thrill.

By now, her head was spinning slightly—a sensation similar to that she'd once experienced upon drinking a little too much wine. "The flowers," she murmured in surprise, glancing at the lush plantings at the edge of the grotto. "They're aphrodisiacs." Their fragrance was everywhere in this place, perfuming the air. Relaxing and preparing her for what would come.

Silvia's gaze shot to Bastian's. His narrowed eyes glittered at her, his expression predatory. Suddenly, everything began moving almost too quickly. Hooking her hips, he repositioned her slightly before him, a move that forced her to face away from him and toward the far grotto wall. *Rip!* With an unapologetic yank, he rent a long tear in the back of her pantalets, then tore them off and tossed them away, baring her. A knee knocked her legs wide, and his thighs pressed hers to the smooth rock wall, pinning her open for his passionate use. Big hands kneaded the cheeks of her bottom.

Transfixed, Silvia gazed breathlessly at the grotto's pool, which lapped gently at the altar on which she lay. She saw movement in its waters. The twist of iridescent bodies. Mer creatures passing through.

Sleek cockheads nudged at her entrances. Their hot, insistent smoothness parted her flesh, one pressing between the divide of her bottom and the other parting feminine folds that were already embarrassingly slick with her desire.

Gods, he was big. Wonderfully so. Yet, she felt impelled to move away from the intense pressure of his advance. And could not, for his thighs nailed hers to the front of the altar and his knees held hers wide, leaving her body no choice but to accommodate him. She cried out as her flesh was stretched beyond comfort. Bastian's hands gentled her and he murmured to her in a language of the ancients—calming words his god had likely once used to subdue mortal maidens he'd run to ground. Eventually, she relaxed just enough and took male flesh inside her own for the first time in her life.

A shallow rocking commenced, as he gave her only his heads and half of his lengths before stealing them back, time and time again. As he sawed the fullest part of his phalluses at her tender entrances, she began to grow desperate. The sensation was too arousing, too much. She whimpered and tilted for him, hoping to woo him deeper. "Please."

His hands smoothed over her flanks. "Tell me you want it."

"I do," she swore, and heard her craving to have him.

"Beg for it," he said, in a voice gone unnatural and dark.

"I want you, Bastian. Please, I beg you, come deeper."

Before she'd finished, his thighs were already tensing between hers and then came the exquisite pain-pleasure of his long, slow inward plow. In spite of Michaela's experience, this was not an easy joining. But Silvia was lulled by the beguiling aroma of flowers and the love in her heart. And so she relaxed for him, yearning, accepting, welcoming. Inch by gliding inch, soft, quivering flesh gave way to unforgiving steel, until finally, incredibly, he was home—buried deep, so deep inside her that she cried out at the tight, slick joy of their consummation.

Upon the completion of this stroke, a contented masculine sound left him, half growl, half purr. Then her lover shifted his hips, reseating himself slightly and nudging even deeper. And again. Yet again, harder this time. She moaned, hardly knowing what to do with the emotions she was experiencing at having her body so thoroughly mated to that of the man she loved. She wanted to cry out her joy, to thank him, to beg him to remain inside her like this forever, and contrarily to plead with him to move in some way that would cure her of this terrible, wonderful, painful, pleasurable, hot, aching need for release. But more than anything, she wanted to memorize the decadent sensation of holding him in this intimate way. For no matter what came tomorrow, in this precious moment, he was all hers.

Resting her forehead on the stone, she moaned again at the erotic fullness. "Thank the Gods," she whispered, and a single tear rolled down her cheek to splash upon the altar.

His hands squeezed hard on her rear as he withdrew his gifts in dual drags. Then he was thrusting forward again, setting a rigorous, powerful rhythm as he copulated now in earnest. And all the while, he spoke to her, his language slowly devolving into grunts of pleasure mixed with coarse, carnal—sometimes savage—words spoken in a blend of Latin and their ancient ElseWorld tongue. Each time he slid home, she arched for him, loving the feel of his hips slamming her bottom. His thighs were more heavily furred than before the Change, and their repeated abrasion upon his every visit was an arousal in itself. Desire escalated sharply, and her eyes closed tight as small tremors began to shiver over her nether flesh.

Resting on her forearms, Silvia gazed fixedly ahead, her face flushed with a feverish anticipation. "Yes, Bastian," she whimpered. "So . . . good."

Another of those fierce, bestial sounds of satisfaction left him in response and he covered her body with his and gathered her to him even as he continued his rut. He held her that way, her back tight to his chest as he fucked himself into her in hard, short bucks that drew him outward only a few inches before he rammed home again. She felt captured, caged—a receptive vessel designed solely to accommodate her mate's debauched pleasure.

Held as she was by the hug of his muscled arms, her breasts were bared to the altar, and they swayed and buffed against its gritty surface with his every ingress. Her nipples twisted tight under this gentle rub, and fierce need shot straight to her core. The quality and strength of his fornication grew ever more intense, dark, urgent as he drove their bodies toward fulfillment. Her breath quickened, and small moans and gasps drifted from her lips. She felt him swell inside her and sensed he was hurtling toward his finish. He whispered to her in his velvet, graveled voice, telling her how well her flesh hugged his, how much her hot welcome pleased him, how she was going to make him . . .

His hands slapped the altar on either side of her as he withdrew strongly in one long, tandem pull, almost leaving her. She made a soft keening sound of protest. "No, don't go!" Her desolate flesh rippled and trembled in the wake of his precipitous near departure. She needed him. She wanted to . . . was going to . . .

Then he fucked deep again, returning in hard, dual spears that filled her, loved her, completed her, and made her scream. His mouth came at her nape and he kissed her deeply, marking her with his white teeth, hot suction, and his ownership. Their bodies arched together as one and they turned to stone, quivering on ecstasy's precipice.

Then for the first time in her life, Silvia felt the coming of a man's seed. Her own cry entwined his masculine shout as the first searing, creamy spurt shot hard, lashing at her womb and deep inside her bottom. Her body jerked and then came a clenching wave that twisted her clit, fisted her feminine channel, and sent her tumbling into her own orgasm. And then another wave washed over her, and again, until she could scarcely draw breath between each onslaught of pleasure.

For a long endless time, he arched protectively over her, his powerful body ardently docked tight with her own. With every exquisite, zealous pump of his seed, her flesh milked at him in grateful, loving acceptance and then gasped for more.

At some point, she felt his upper phallus—the one that only came forth on the night of the full moon—slowly and regretfully disengage and then neatly retract into his abdomen.

But his lower cock, the one that was rooted in dark masculine thatch, did not depart. Did not deflate as a man's should after intercourse. Instead, he commenced rocking himself again, in short pulses, and then longer drags, plowing easily now in the mutual slickness that bathed her feminine furrow. And with every fourth or fifth push, she was made to come again, and again. One glorious sensation followed another as each throbbing of his cock fueled her orgasm so it never quite died away. Silvia wept at the fullness of her body and heart, wishing it might last forever.

Eventually, the quality of his mating altered slightly and his face nuzzled in her hair. He spoke to her again. Spoke hot, wicked, wanton words meant to arouse. "My brothers. Can you feel them fucking?"

Shocked, Silvia turned her head, catching his eyes. A devilish smile played at his lips; then he dropped his head, and his mouth fell upon the turn where her throat eased into shoulder. Satyr blood linked family members, and she knew his brothers' pleasure must be heightening his own. So it was their ecstasy that was prolonging his rut!

"Dane is with Eva, his comely new wife," he murmured in a distant voice that told her he was seeing a vision, of another room, another couple.

"Bastian . . ." she began uncertainly, but he didn't seem to hear.

"His woman is sweet . . . feisty," he went on. "He loves her, loves fucking her. They're in my bedchamber, in my bed at Esquiline. His cock is buried inside her, moving in her. Can you see them?"

Then her lover gave her the vision he saw of his brother, the one whom she had not yet met. Then he gave her still more, causing some sort of transference to occur, so that she could suddenly feel this unknown sibling inside her, just as his wife could!

"They can feel us, too. Feel us fucking," Bastian informed her, his voice thick with his arousal. "My brother now knows what it is to put his cock inside you. As I am. And his wife, she can feel what it is to have me inside her. Fucking her. As I'm fucking you."

Silvia gazed sightlessly across the pool, hanging on his every word. "I knew you all experienced one another's pleasure, but I didn't know . . ." Her voice trailed off. "Oh Gods." Her eyes went wide and she forgot to breathe, going completely still. His brother was going to—

"We're going to come," Bastian bit out. She felt a cock heat and fatten inside her, and her feminine passage shuddered in response. It was Bastian who mated her, and yet it was as though he no longer acted alone. It was as if two men lay with her at once now, both intent on wresting their pleasure from her. Her belly went taut as all four participants in this wanton activity were suddenly caught together on a tender, terrible, shared knife's edge of anticipation.

Then male groans infused the air and there came a sudden blast of molten cum that had her entire body bowing, as two brothers fountained inside her. She cried out softly, her clit throbbing and her channel milking them hard. And then she was coming as well and sharing the ecstasy of his brother's wife just as though it were her own.

"He's spending," Bastian whispered, his voice hot. That he felt his brother's enjoyment of the other unknown woman was apparent in the way his body moved on hers. "It's good for him. He's enjoying you."

"I . . . know . . ." Silvia murmured, gasping. "I can feel him."

Though the vision soon faded away, their residual passion did not for some time. But eventually Bastian sensed she was flagging and he disengaged. Lifting her, he took her into the shallow pool, where he half-lay back against a large stone, with his legs slightly cocked. And there he had her mount and ride him with her legs wrapped around his back as he raptly fondled her breasts and roved her body with his hands.

He was a tireless lover, and as the hours passed, his every orgasm inspired her own. Whenever her body began to burn from the rub and she begged for a respite, he only took her into the pool once more. The magic properties of its waters gently soothed her flesh, cleansing and repairing tissues, brushing away discomfort, and readying her to begin again.

As midnight ebbed, Bastian carried her in his arms to a narrow bank hidden behind the great waterfall that spilled from the crest of the grotto's stone arch. It was shadowy there, and secluded. He stood over her and pushed her to kneel before him in the mist that swirled and eddied just above the ground. He widened his legs, one foot on either side of her knees, and with two fingers under her chin, he tilted up her face. Gods, she was so lovely with her intelligent, sultry eyes and red-gold hair. No. Her hair was ebony. Wasn't it?

"What color is your hair?" he demanded, the beast within him angered at its confusion.

A pause. Then, "Black."

His hand curled around her throat, pushing her back against a smooth mosaic wall that depicted the exploits of the gods. Their eyes caught. "You lie," he accused her with soft menace, and she did not refute him. A primitive need surged in him to dominate her so that she might never be tempted to deceive him again. Sets of rings were embedded in the mosaic's design, disguised within the scalloped scales of a Nereid's tail. He drew her hands to a pair that were set one on either side of her head and bade her clasp them. And then he tangled the long fingers of one hand in silky hair that she claimed was black, holding her as his other hand offered up his cock. Then the raw, boorish, maddened beast in him growled. "Open for me. Tonight I own that lovely lying mouth, and I want to fuck it."

His lover's cheeks flushed and she lowered her lashes, hiding her secrets from him. His fingers tightened in her hair and he watched those cherry red lips part for him. Watched her mouth stretch around his cockhead as she took him in. And as he entered her, he gave her another vision. That of his brother Sevin, who was currently kneeling on dark satin bedcovers in the bordello alcove in the main salon below, his thighs brooking the shoulders of a Shimmerskin who lay on the mattress beneath him.

Violet eyes flashed to Bastian's, questioning. "Yes, he knows. He feels your mouth on him, too." And as Bastian braced an arm high above her on the wall, so Sevin braced his hand on a brass headboard and drove himself deeper into another feminine throat. And Bastian felt two mouths take him. Knowing that the woman who knelt before him also experienced the push and pull of his brother's cock moving in her mouth enriched Bastian's pleasure in giving himself to her this way. The beast in him wanted her to understand that she was his tonight, and that he could share her as he liked.

He contracted the muscles of thigh and hip, rocking himself out of her liquid heat and then coming back for more. Her lips bowed and pursed as he gently sawed in her wet-velvet mouth. He felt his balls draw up tight, his cock swell. Her head went back against the wall and his cock followed, relentlessly filling her. Her eyes fluttered shut and she moaned. He braced both forearms above her now, watching her take him.

"I want him to feel you," Bastian said in that softly savage tone he hardly recognized as his own. "To know that I'm fucking you like this. That my cock is in your wonderful, gifted mouth. That any minute now I'm going to come in your throat. That I own you."

And somehow this knowing only roused Silvia's passion. For in this moment, she relished her lover's treatment of her. Wanted him to dominate and command her and bend her to his will. Tomorrow, she would look back on this time and go shy again, and would likely marvel over her willingness in this. But now she suckled at him, enjoying the push of him over her tongue and the power he had over her in this act.

When he came in her, her fingers went white-knuckled on the rings they held, and she arched her throat and swallowed his passionate spill. And somewhere in the salon, the anonymous Shimmerskin took another man's spill and both shared a tandem ecstasy.

As the night continued on, Bastian seemed to further devolve, his mating and his instructions to her becoming more animalistic and carnal, sometimes brutish. Deep in his eyes, there still remained a refined intelligence, but it was completely at odds with his terrible countenance now. He was only her fornicator, her master. And she was his plaything, his slave, his mate. And though a lifetime of such handling would not have done at all, on this night, she found it to be a thrilling employment.

Later, much later, they lay together upon that soft mossy bank, and she was given yet another vision, this one of his youngest brother, Luc. Somewhere in the distant salon, he was between the legs of another woman. And as Bastian covered Silvia's body with his own, it was Luc she felt fucking her. Luc's solemn, knowing eyes watching her face as he worked himself in her . . . even as his eldest brother did.

Lying there on her back with both arms carelessly flung overhead, Silvia's impassioned gaze was drawn upward beyond her lover, toward the night. And the moon. Until dawn came, its round, unblinking eye would watch over them and fuel their ardor. Until then, Bastian would continue at the mercy of his own ruthless, lecherous appetites. And his body would make a salacious feast of hers. Her hands lifted to stroke down his back, loving the feel of his resilient, golden flesh and the flex of his muscle as he visited himself on her.

It seemed remarkable that her own virginity would remain intact when she returned to her true form one day in the future. She almost wished this were not so—wished instead that she would be physically changed by him to mark this wondrous night. For this was a precious time she would never, ever forget no matter how many centuries she lived on. A night of pure physical ecstasy. The night she'd lain with her first male lover. The man she loved.

And on that thought, she bowed from the mossy ground, caught in the stir of another orgasm. Her dark lashes drifted to her cheeks, and she gasped for him. Creamed for him. Hard. Yet again.

Scena Antica V

Silvia laid her flute in her lap, its final dulcet notes drifting away on the gentle evening breeze. "It's unfair that you have to tend fire tonight," she said as she and Michaela sat together in Vesta's temple. "Not on your eighteenth birthday."

"I'm not tending it. You've done all the work tonight."

"My small gift to you, because you shouldn't even be here. You should be celebrating."

Michaela shot her an indecipherable look. After a long moment, she spoke. "I did celebrate."

"How? I thought you spent your day in the Atrium House." Seeing that the fire was dwindling in Vesta's Hearth, Silvia set her flute aside to go rouse it.

"Not all day," said Michaela. "I went to the market, remember?"

"You call that celebrating?" Lifting her hem, Silvia took the three marble steps that led up to the tall pedestal in the center of

Vesta's temple. She bent close to the shallow golden bowl that rested upon it, feeling the low fire's warmth flush her cheeks.

"You know that dark-eyed boy at the market?"

"Which one?" Silvia asked. Cupping her hands, she blew between them toward the center of the hearth. Although there were no coals or wood or oil in the bowl to feed it, the flame leaped high and strong again, simply by dint of her magic.

"The eldest son of the spice merchant, the one who always watches me," said Michaela.

A slight smile curved Silvia's lips as she returned to her seat. "They all watch you. You're beautiful—how can they not?"

"Well, this one had me this morning. Behind his father's stall in the market. Standing upright, against a post."

Silvia gasped, all else abruptly forgotten. "No!"

Michaela's eyes sparkled. "Yes."

She looked her friend over, searching for outward signs that she'd been violated. But she looked no different. "How could you? The welfare of Rome depends upon our continued chastity."

The violet of Michaela's eyes gleamed like jewels in firelight. "Do you really believe that?"

"Yes," Silvia insisted. Then more softly, "Don't you?"

"Sometimes," came Michaela's answer. "But, oh, Silvia, you should have seen how he wanted me. Shall I tell you what happened?"

Silvia arched a brow. "Could I stop you from speaking of it even if I wanted to?"

"No." Grinning, Michaela lay on her back, her head finding a home in Silvia's lap. "Well, it began in the most exciting way. He held me like this, pinned against the post." Crossing her wrists to demonstrate, she lifted them over her head. "Then he threw my skirts high and thrust his knee between both of mine. Then he put himself in me, Via. All the way inside."

"Did it—"

"Yes, it hurt. There was no pleasure in it for me. But he assures

*me it will improve with practice. And we will try again in a few days,
when next I go to the market."*

"Kayla, no. Pontifex or Vestalis will find out."

"They won't," said Michaela. "Because I'll be gone soon. As will
you."

"What?" Eyes wide, Silvia shook her head. "No, we made vows."

Michaela sat up and grasped her arm, giving her a little shake.
"Do you want to die husbandless? Childless? In a few years, our
beauty will fade and then waste away. I'm going to run before next
Moonful comes. Before it's too late. You must come, too."

Imagining Pontifex's reaction to such an escape, Silvia shivered.
She had to convince Michaela of the foolhardiness of her plan. "I'm
told there are things that can be done. We'll get a sheep's bladder,
or something like that."

"That's not necessary. No one will think to examine me, not
until I wed," said Michaela. "But you're right that a bladder would
likely fool a new husband, so I will remember to employ one on my
wedding night. It's stupid, but men always want to be first in everything they attempt." She rolled her eyes.

In spite of her distress, Silvia smiled with her.

"That's better. I hate it when you're angry at me."

"I'm not angry. I'm frightened for you."

Michaela shrugged. "Don't be. No one will be able to tell I am
any different."

Noticing the fire had dipped again, Silvia half-rose. "Vesta
grows hungry."

Michaela stayed her. "I'll go," she said, taking the three steps for
the first time that day. Standing at the hearth, she cupped her
hands and blew between them as Silvia had done to feed the never-
ending fire.

But this time, nothing happened. The flame only continued to
sink. She tried again. Nothing. She swung around, her face pan-
icked. "The fire! I can't—I have no effect upon it."

Silvia rushed toward her. Pushing her aside, she cupped her own hands.

From behind them came a gasp. "You let the fire go out?"

They both whipped around to see Occia and Aemilia standing at the far side of the temple. They'd come to relieve them. Occia's eyes moved between them and lit with a pleased sort of malice.

Hurriedly, Silvia coaxed the fire high again.

Michaela rushed to speak. "It was my f—"

"The fault was mine," Silvia interrupted. "I should have acted sooner. Still, as you see, all is well." She pointed toward the roaring flame.

But Occia had already gone to spread the news. Aemilia just stood there, her brow knit. "Are you in trouble?"

"Try to stop her," Silvia told the girl, who immediately leaped to do her bidding.

"I will," she promised, running after Occia. Like the others, Aemilia had been chosen for the temple due to her physical perfection and the warmth of her palms. Still, although she had a kind heart, she was the despair of their tutors and could not seem to learn to read or write with any proficiency. Her mind wandered and she could not be trusted to tend fire on her own. She would never become a teacher of future initiates, and Silvia sometimes worried that Pontifex might find some excuse to ban her from their Vestal Order.

Michaela cupped her hands again and tried to stoke the fire even higher, but to no avail. Desperately, she pressed her palms to Silvia's arm, a question in her eyes.

"Your hands still hold the heat," Silvia assured her. "Nothing has changed."

And so Michaela tried a third time to stir the fire. Real fear shone in her eyes when she could not. "You're wrong. Once I could raise this fire, but now—it must be because I'm no longer pure. The sooner I go from here, the better. But I won't let the blame fall on you. I'll stay long enough to take the punishment."

As she gazed at her dearest friend, the ominous words of the philosopher Plutarch danced in Silvia's head, feeding her rising fear regarding the nature of punishments deemed fit for offences against Vesta:

For smaller offences, these virgins were punished with stripes; and sometimes Pontifex Maximus gave them the discipline naked, in some dark place and under cover of a veil; but she that broke her vow of chastity was buried alive by the Colline Gate.

"No," Silvia insisted. "If it is discovered that you've been unchaste, you could wind up buried by the gate. Is that what you want?"
"Of course not, but—"
Silvia made a slicing gesture with one hand, cutting her off. "We can't allow suspicion to turn in your direction. I will accept any scourging. That is how it must be."

13

Silvia woke late on the morning that followed Moonful. She was lying on a softly scented bed of ElseWorld moss in the grotto. Alone. Her body felt boneless, satiated, deliciously well-used. But her face was wet from crying. Michaela. Was. *Dead.* Tears leaked from violet eyes, dribbling down her cheeks. They were the tears not of one woman, but of two. Two lifelong friends who would be parted forever come next Moonful, only a month from now. When Silvia must take a new host.

Gradually, she felt her mood alter and calm under her current host's influence. Michaela wouldn't allow her to think on matters so morose. Not yet. Not while the two of them still had some time left together.

She mopped at her tears with the coverlet that Bastian had produced just after dawn when they'd snuggled here together, replete and exhausted. Below the grotto, the salon was silent this morning, save for the occasional sounds of a door opening and shutting or the clink of china as occupants desultorily breakfasted. ElseWorld males would go about their business early today, she knew. The Calling always had the effect of energizing them. But for their women, it was a different matter. They usually slept away the day following Moonful. It's no doubt what Bastian expected her to do. However, she had tasks to complete. Firestones to locate. Maybe just a few more minutes, though, before she went about things.

She stretched luxuriously and yawned, feeling sore muscles twinge. She laughed quietly, ruefully shaking her head. As usual, Michaela had gotten what she wanted. She'd maneuvered Silvia into bed with her and her lover last night, but Silvia was grateful. It had been what she wanted, and now Michaela knew, and had seemed to accept it.

It was fortunate that Bastian had departed their makeshift bed so he would not question her tears or her laughter. She should go before he returned. In the coming weeks she wouldn't leave his orbit entirely, not until she had the firestones he would unwittingly help her locate. But in the meantime, she would distance herself. Remain here at the salon instead of returning to Esquiline. Leave his bed. Her heart squeezed at the thought. But to stay and take him as her own while Michaela was her host would be an insupportable betrayal. Maybe after much time had passed and the firestones were all found . . . maybe once she'd dealt with Pontifex . . . maybe then she might return one day and see if their passion was of the lasting kind. But that day was not today. Not while Michaela was with her. Not while there were still six firestones at large.

At the thought of the stones, she groaned. She'd completely forgotten the opal in Bastian's pocket last night! After he slept, she could have stolen it from him so easily. *Fool!*

As she lay there, trying to summon the energy to move, a whisper entered her mind, like a tendril of smoke curling from a dying fire. Michaela's voice.

And what of Aemilia's stone . . . I didn't take it with me last night after all . . . not so stupid as Pontifex believes . . . No, it's hidden here. . . .

Silvia sat bolt upright, the coverlet falling to her waist. "Where?" she asked aloud. Her question died away, going unanswered. She pushed the covers aside and rose from the bed. Moving to the pool, she quickly washed under the waterfall and then cleaned her teeth in a nearby fountain, her mind racing all the while. It seemed Michaela had revealed all she planned to for the moment. But if the missing stone was in this building, it was likely she'd hidden it in her personal apartment, and Silvia was anxious to search for it.

Fresh towels had been left for her on the wall surrounding the pool, all neatly folded. Her lips curved at the thoughtful gesture. Bastian. However, his courtesy didn't extend to clothing. Michaela's dress and underthings from last night were sodden and torn, and she cringed from donning them. Instead, she wrapped the voluminous toweling around herself, and with a wistful, lingering glance at the grotto, she took the path downward.

The Shimmerskin sentries still stood guard outside the gates and when they wordlessly opened them for her, she slipped out of paradise. Feeling like a thief, which she was, she stealthily moved through the quiet of the salon. There, she passed other women, who were going about as she was, each with tousled hair and scant or rumpled clothing, and each bearing the marks of last night's lovers on their flesh. They glanced at one another with secret smiles that acknowledged the pleasurable manner in which they'd all passed the previous night.

Having visited before, Silvia knew Michaela's lodgings—her "glorified closet," as she fondly termed it—were on the third floor. When she arrived there and entered, she glanced around the room in dismay. She'd forgotten what a disastrous housekeeper Kayla was. Petticoats, dresses, corsets, gloves, ribbons, fans, hats, lace—all were strewn across the bed, flung over the chairs, or hanging haphazardly from drawers in the armoire. Michaela still refused to allow any sadness and blocked all thoughts of death, so the sight of her things caused Silvia no pain. However, she'd never find anything in here until she got dressed and cleaned this up.

She had just pulled a day gown from the armoire when she heard the door from the corridor open. Bastian! Her heart leaped with joy upon seeing him, though they'd been parted only a few hours. He joined her in the small room without invitation, and she turned toward him, pressing Michaela's dress to the front of her body like she was some sort of giant paper doll, who might wear it in that way. He was dressed in fresh clothing—black trousers and boots, a cream-colored shirt, and a black jacket—typical daywear that befitted a gentleman. A cursory glance revealed no telltale bulge of an opal in either of his pockets.

Still, she could not help but note a rather impressive bulge of another sort at the front of his trousers. Concupiscent memories of the night they'd passed together abruptly crowded her mind and flushed her cheeks. Would he remind her of it? No, last night had been just another Moonful to him. But she knew she would forever cherish that stolen time.

Bastian shut the door behind him and leaned back against it, gazing around the room. "I thought you would sleep in today," he began after a moment.

"I thought you'd be at the excavations," she said at the same time.

Pushing from the door, he came closer. He studied her face; then his eyes dropped to the dress she held like a shield. "Rico has disappeared, leaving only his dog and a cryptic note in my study. I spent the morning with the *polizia* and other contacts, sending out runners to search for him."

Silvia swallowed guiltily. She'd known he would worry, but there was nothing she could tell him without giving herself away. "I should think you'd be glad not to have him underfoot."

"I'd grown rather accustomed to him as it happens." Reaching out, he traced with masculine fingers the fragile lace at the neckline of the dress she held. "It's a beautiful gown."

She nodded, shy with him now. "Yes."

He smiled at her, having reverted to the polished gentleman once again with the coming of this morning's sun. Suddenly, their time in the grotto seemed like some distant erotic dream. Yet deep in his eyes, she saw the carnal beast of last night lurking, only temporarily held at bay. Bracing a forearm on the armoire, he bent his head and brushed his lips up the side of her throat. "A lovely gown indeed."

"Umm-hmm."

His hand came at her waist and then drew down over her bottom, gently shaping her nakedness. Her breath caught. "Very, very lovely," he added.

"However, I wish to see what further loveliness it hides." His hand fisted in the fabric between them and he slowly plucked the dress from her hands, then tossed it casually away. In a swish of satin, it plummeted to the floor somewhere behind him.

She crossed her arms over herself and arched a brow at him. "I begin to see how this room came to such disorder."

He only laughed and lifted her hands to rest flat on his crisp shirtfront, drawing her nakedness against him until she felt that impressive bulge of his at her belly. Now was the time to mention her plans to move back to the salon on a full-time basis. Before anything happened. Yet, Michaela's desire for him and her own swirled inside her, pumping renewed passion through her system. And she couldn't seem to bring herself to say the words that would send him away.

In the first twenty-four hours, a host's emotions lingered on with a persuasive strength. Silvia wanted Michaela to have what she wanted. And what Michaela wanted with a passionate urgency was what Silvia wanted—this man.

Acknowledging the hardness she felt between them, she cocked her head, slanting him a coquettish glance. "Did you want something?"

He smiled again, a flash of white teeth, and she found herself lifted and tossed upon the bed to lie among Michaela's belongings. Locating a stray petticoat by feel, she tugged it to cover her from breast to mid-thigh.

Bastian's hand went to his trousers, opening them. "Yes, I want something."

He divested himself of trousers and boots, then came down between her legs.

Silvia stared at him in amazement. "Again? After last night, I thought you'd be . . ."

"Sated?" Bastian smiled at her again, for yet a third time. Really, he was becoming quite giddy. His brothers were going to tease him for this. It was considered bad manners to mate one's partner again so soon after Moonful. But there was something about her that delighted and drew him. She'd seemed different ever since he'd found her last night, and it wasn't just the color that still clung to her and bled over into her immediate surroundings. He'd hurried through his business this morning, rushing back to find her gone from the grotto.

The guards had been instructed to inform him of her comings and goings, so he knew she had not departed the salon. Still, the relief he'd felt upon finding her here in this room was ridiculous. She was a puzzle, possibly a dangerous one. One who'd just felt up his pockets. A behavior she had in common with the presence from Monti. Yet, he wanted her. So he would keep her close and slowly work her secrets from her.

He dropped a kiss on her lips. "Thank you for last night. It was good."

"Let's not speak of it," she said, still looking charmingly shy of him.

His brows rose. Not speak of it? This from Michaela, who usually wished to wallow in conversation in the aftermath of coitus, often well beyond his endurance. And when had she grown modest? The woman under him clutched that stray petticoat to her breast like a shield.

"Are you all right? I know I was—"

She nodded, blushing, her thoughts secret.

A need rose in him to have her at her most vulnerable, in a way that she could not hide what she felt from him. He propped himself on one elbow and smiled down at her. His hand wandered over the petticoat she clasped to herself, and he drew aimless patterns with his fingertips, moving ever lower. "I'm asking because I want to lie with you again, but I don't want to hurt you."

"Oh." The tip of her tongue slipped out, moistening her lips. "You won't."

"Sevin's pool did its work, then?" he persisted.

"Yes, I'm fine. I'm—I want what you do."

His smile broadened. "What I want, my dearest Michaela, is for you to open your legs for me again." The mention of her name seemed to startle her, but she relaxed slightly for him and his hand slipped under the hem of her shield. Their eyes clung as it went between her thighs, finding her warmth.

"What I want," he informed her, "is to put my mouth on you here and to feel you come under my kiss." As his touch drew up along her feminine furrow, a full awareness of what he intended darkened her gaze. The pink of her cheeks deepened to red as she managed another nod.

"You'll let me taste you?" He watched her as his fingertip traced along her slit again, deeper this time. "Here, where I had you last night. Dear, sweet Michaela?" He punctuated the last three words with a gentle sawing motion that mimicked the carnal act.

"Gods, yes," she murmured, reaching for him.

His thigh slid between hers and his body followed. Her hands were cool on the muscles of his arms as he brushed her lips with his. "Good," he murmured.

Then he was moving lower on the mattress. Wrapping his arms under her thighs, he pushed them wide and high with his broad shoulders. Gazing upon the rosy petals of her fleshly heart and remembering the pleasure it had given him the previous night, his need for her escalated.

Turning his head, he kissed along her inner thigh and felt her body tense with anticipation. As he parted her with the pads of his thumbs, he took her with his mouth and his tongue, enjoying her moan. He hadn't shaved this morning, and she always squirmed with delight under the drag of his blue-black stubble on her flesh here. He knew what he was about in this. Knew just how to stroke and suckle a woman. Within minutes, her fingers were white-knuckled on that silken petticoat, her clit was twisting in his hot mouth, and her slick channel was rhythmically fisting on the two fingers he'd used to fuck her.

When her coming slowed, he tugged her petticoat from her and wiped his face; then she reached for him and pulled him to press her into the mattress with his body. She opened herself and let him push his cock between slick lips he'd just kissed. And let him tunnel into the reward of a nether throat rendered buttery soft by her enjoyment of that kiss. Together, they made leisurely love there in the morning sun among a jumble of ribbons and flounces and lace. And when he felt her body's passionate milking of his, he spent himself inside her, and radiant sparks in every color of the rainbow burst under his eyelids, stunning him with their brilliance. At her sweet, soft gasp, a fierce tenderness swept him.

I love you. The words formed in his mind, and he froze, shocked at the strength of the impulse that urged him to speak them aloud. It was only the color that was so new to him and the residual effects of last night's wine making him feel these foreign emotions. It had to be. After all, this was Michaela. Michaela, whom he hadn't been capable of loving for all the previous months he'd known her. It made no sense that he would suddenly love her now. Yet, he hadn't forgotten the vision he'd had of red-gold hair last night. Had it been caused by the wine? Or by the color he perceived only when she was near? Or was it something else entirely? Until he puzzled her out, he wanted to keep her close. Disengaging from her, he sat up to retrieve his trousers.

I love you. The words formed in Silvia's mouth as she watched him dress, but they refused to leave her tongue. For once she spoke them, Michaela's Deathwish would be completely fulfilled. Then there would be no more excuse to stay. And this morning, she sensed that Michaela wanted to remain with him, to enjoy him for as many days to come as she could. So the words could wait a while—at least until after he unwittingly led her to the firestones.

"I want you to move from here entirely," Bastian told her as he tugged a boot on under the leg of his trousers. "To come and live with me on Esquiline. Let Sevin have these quarters for another's use."

Her heart leaped. Their eyes met, so much left unspoken between them. She'd performed in the opera, turned out barrels as a cooper, cleaned herring, picked locks. All talents she'd absorbed from other, previous hosts. And now it seemed she was about to add another profession to her growing repertoire. That of lover. And not the lover of just any man, but that of Lord Bastian Satyr. And she could not be sorry for it.

"Yes," she told him. "Yes."

Three weeks later, Bastian's carriage groaned and lurched its way downward from Esquiline Hill, its leather seats creaking expensively as its three occupants headed to the Forum.

"We're late. Can't Luc go any faster?" Bastian demanded.

Sevin sent Silvia an amused glance, then replied to him. "You're the one who delayed us, brother." Silvia returned his smile easily, for her relationship with Bastian's brothers had returned to the friendship it had been prior to last Moonful, and no mention had been made of what had transpired between them during that decadent night. It seemed to be understood among all the siblings that she belonged to Bastian, and they would not encroach without invitation.

She and Bastian had spent this morning in bed, as Sevin had no doubt sensed. It had been a lazy coupling at dawn, then conversation, a light breakfast, more coupling. She'd been greedy and had made them late, but she'd desperately wanted those hands on her one last time. For by the end of today, she would be gone from his life.

They were now on their way to the celebratory, official opening of the Vestal Temple complex Bastian had unearthed. Dignitaries would be there, and crowds. She would find a time to slip away and examine the statue of Vesta. And retrieve the stones.

Surreptitiously, she studied her love, memorizing him. He was dressed in sartorial splendor today, the darkness of his fine tailored coat accentuating his broad shoulders. His close-cropped ebony hair had been neatly styled to perfectly frame his strong, handsome features. Love for him welled up in her breast, twisting her heart. She looked away to stare out of the window at the passing scenery.

Three weeks had seemed such an endless length of time three weeks ago. But the hours had flown too swiftly, and now the awful day had come when she must leave him. Oh, she would return at some point for the firestone he possessed. She'd searched high and low for it in his house, to no avail. But when next she came again, he would not know. He hadn't actually been able to see her in her Ephemeral form that night in Monti. So it followed that, while in that form, she might safely return to observe him until he eventually led her to the stone.

Gently, she squeezed her fingers over the handbag in her comforted to feel the solid bulk of Aemilia's firestone within. As she'd suspected, it had been among Michaela's belongings, hidden in her jewel box. One down, five to go.

Drawn by her obsession, she peeked at Bastian again, starting with his boots, intending to leisurely work her way upward. She'd chosen his clothing today, for this was a service Michaela had apparently provided for him. It was odd that he allowed it, but he almost seemed uncertain when it came to matching one fabric with another. Only this morning, he'd grabbed socks that did not match and hadn't seemed to notice when she'd selected a different, matching pair for him instead.

She'd become quite domesticated in such small ways over the last few weeks. Had found herself taking pleasure in tasks such as the folding of his trousers. In smoothing his collar, straightening his tie. The actions of a woman who knew what he liked and wanted to please him. The actions of a wife. She'd been playing a dangerous game, one that would end in heartbreak.

For she was not a wife. And yet not quite a whore either. No, he thought her to be what Michaela was—a Companion. It was a profession that lay somewhere in between the former two occupations.

When they reached their destination and departed the car riage, Bastian's hand came at the back of her jacket-bodice. She leaned back into his touch ever so slightly. That hand made her feel cherished, protected. As Michaela had said, he knew how to touch a woman. In bed and out of it. She loved the simple act of walking beside him. He and his brothers were giants, and he was built like a brute, but he was an admirable man. Intelligent and interesting, with a wry sense of humor. He found her an interesting companion as well, she knew, for she amused, intrigued, and challenged him. And they shared a passion for the excavations. But he thought she was Michaela. If he only knew what an imposter she was, he would not treat her so kindly.

Ever courteous, he guided her toward the festivities. Tables had been set under flagged awnings on the Forum grounds. They were laden with culinary delights designed by Rome's most famous *cuoco-unico*, and her stomach rumbled delicately at the delicious smells. Bastian heard and smiled down at her. "Hungry, *cara?*" How he loved teasing her about fascination with food! She studied his smile, wondering if it might be the last she ever received from him.

His expression hardened and he stepped closer, hands on her waist. "What's wrong?"

"Bastian! Sevin! . . . Michaela." The feminine voice that hailed them went infinitesimally cooler on the last name, her own at the moment. This was Dane's wife, Eva. Although her manner had been friendly on the few occasions they'd met, she was a matchmaker by trade, and it was clear that she did not consider a Companion to be a suitable life partner for Bastian. They'd never spoken of that last Moonful night when the lines between them had become so sensually blurred, and Silvia wondered if she was even aware of who Bastian's partner had been. Eva had a kind and accepting heart, and had no quibble with Michaela as a person, so Silvia excused her from malice. Nevertheless, she would no doubt be pleased when Michaela disappeared from her brother-in-law's life.

Silvia waited as long as she could, listening to Bastian's brief speech and circulating with him among the guests at his insistence. But she was only prolonging the inevitable.

A man joined them, the young minister she remembered from that first morning at the tent. She excused herself on the pretext of visiting one of the dessert tables, and Bastian didn't demur. However, she felt his speculative gaze on her. She'd noticed the way he watched her now and then as if something about her confounded him. He'd noticed differences between her and the woman he'd known as Michaela. After three weeks, Michaela's essence was fading and her own personality was showing through more and more. He'd grown suspicious. Yet another reason she must depart, before he found her out and foiled her plans to steal from him.

Casually, she glanced his way, and saw him involved in a rather heated discussion with the minister. Now was her chance, while his attention was elsewhere. She made her way to the Atrium House, her eyes on its main feature—the newly unveiled statue of Vesta.

"Tell me, do you think this ascot coordinates well with my coat?" Minister Tuchi asked Bastian.

His eyes on Michaela, who was wandering toward the food tables, Bastian was only half-listening to his banal conversation. "Ask your tailor."

"I'm asking you."

"Why?"

"So that I may dispel a rumor about you."

That drew Bastian's attention and he stared down at the young minister, a man who was steadily gaining power within Rome's Department of Culture. "What rumor? You'll have to be more specific, for so many circulate about my family. We're an intriguing lot."

"A rumor that you are color-blind." Tuchi smiled at him, reveling in his jab.

Bastian tilted his crystal goblet and took a small drink of its water, his mind racing. He'd long anticipated that someone might discover this fault in him and had wondered how he'd react. But now he only shrugged. "I assume this particular rumor was begun by the foreman you sent as spy? Tell Ilari he's out of a job. As of now."

Tuchi's gaze swept him. "So stern. But why don't we discuss the matter at more length before acting in haste? Perhaps at my gentlemen's club for a drink?"

"I don't drink."

He raised his brows at this, looking to Bastian's glass, but only said, "Very well, for a smoke, then."

"I don't smoke either."

"What a paragon you are, Lord Satyr. Tell me, what sort of vices *do* you have, so that I may better indulge them?" The man's tone bore an edge of flirtation. Had Rico been right about him? The boy had been found two weeks ago in the aqueduct, deceased—the victim of an infection. Although Bastian had seen him buried, he still privately mourned his loss.

"I assure you I have far too many vices to enumerate." Bastian thumped his glass on a passing tray, then stepped close to the man. "Are you coming on to me?"

The minister drew a sharp breath, then said carefully, "And if I were?"

"You like men?"

Tuchi eyed him, twirling his glass by its stem. "On occasion. Some more than others. You. What do you say to that?"

Bastian shrugged. "Your constituents and your wife might have a quarrel with your preferences, but I have none. However, if you breathe a word of your false accusation about me, I'll have the news of your peccadillos on the front page of the papers. So instead of fucking me, I suggest you fuck yourself, Minister. Good day." He tipped his hat.

Tuchi's smile died instantly, his cheeks flushing. "You'll regret that when we vote in Ilari as your successor next autumn," he railed to Bastian's back.

Silvia gazed at the temple as she bypassed it. Fifteen hundred years ago, it had stood glorious and had housed the eternal fire, but all that survived of it now were eight columns and a pediment. Venturing to its south side, she moved aside the barricade meant to keep crowds away and entered the Atrium House. She was unprepared for the poignant nostalgia that swamped her.

She'd lived here in this house from ages six to twenty-three.

Seventeen years. Back then, its courtyard had been tiled with white marble and surrounded by a stately two-story portico. But now, only foundation walls and several broken statues were left. An awning had been temporarily placed over the area for the celebration, and various indicators had been laid to show how things had once been arranged. She went to the place where her sleeping alcove had been, then turned away quickly, unable to deal with the emotions that surfaced.

All was gone. No, not *all.*

She moved toward the center of the courtyard. The statue of her goddess reigned there now as she'd always done, an expression of benevolence in her eyes. So many years had passed since their last meeting.

Vesta's arms were at her sides, slightly thrust outward from her body. In her left hand, she held the sacred crest of Chastity, and in her right, that of Fire. Silvia knelt before her and murmured the benediction. Then she slipped her trembling hands into those of the statue. Vesta's palms were smooth, cold. But within seconds, she felt the reassuring warmth rekindle between them. She pushed her fingers under one of the crests to locate the slight imperfection she knew would be there. Yes—there it was. She pressed it just so, finding the hollow. And the stone hidden within it. Her firestone. How good it felt to be reunited with it after centuries. Then she reached under the other crest, where Michaela's stone was secreted, and she felt Michaela's gladness when she held it as well.

Quickly, she pulled Aemilia's stone from her pocket. She would need the strength of all three if she were to attempt a firegate without ousting herself from this mortal form. She gazed at the stones filling her palms, felt their warm fire.

"Michaela?"

Clasping the stones to her breast, Silvia leaped to her feet and whipped around to see Bastian. He took a step closer, his silver gaze suspicious. "What are you hiding?"

She stared at him, memorizing his features. When next they met, she would be in a new body—a stranger to him.

Eyes narrowed, he took another step toward her. "I've had a lot of time to think over the past weeks. Since Moonful."

She stepped back. "About what?"

"About that night at the salon, when you told Sevin I'd drunk from a tainted decanter."

"And?"

He advanced another step and she fell back one, their dance fraught with tension. "I hadn't told you that. Which means that you either had a hand in spiking it with liquor, or that you were the female specter I had explained the matter to earlier that night. Which is it?"

"I didn't spike it, though I believe I know who did."

A silence. "What the hells, Michaela?" he said softly. "I'm trying not to come to a bad conclusion here." He angled his head toward her hands. "I'll ask you again. What are you hiding?"

Slowly, she revealed the stones in her palms, holding them outward as if to give them to him. But instead, she bent her head and blew gently upon them. Instantly, a wall of fire leaped between her and Bastian. She gazed at him where he stood beyond the fire, recoiling from its heat. Words unspoken bubbled up. She parted her lips to tell him what Michaela was so adamant that he know. What she felt in her own heart. "I love you."

Something changed in his face. He lunged toward her. Toward the fire. She moved toward him as well, into the fire she'd created, from its opposite side. And before his eyes, she simply disappeared, the flame winking out as well, only seconds after her departure.

Bastian stared at the spot where she'd been, stunned, his world rocked by what he'd just seen. By what she'd said. Going to the statue, he examined the crests in Vesta's palms. Found the hollows beneath them, where the stones must have been hidden. How had Michaela known they would be there? Whom did she work for?

A ruddy flush singed the bones of his cheeks, but there was little else to outwardly indicate his fury.

The firestones were gone. And her with them. *Michaela was a thief.*

Simple deductive reasoning.

Had she only stayed with him all this time in order to steal? The hot rage of betrayal rose within him. It fueled his journey homeward and saw him into his study, where he shoved aside a tremendous bookcase with the strength of his ire.

Behind it stood a steel door ten inches thick. He twirled a series of numbers in its combination lock, and when it clicked open to reveal a secret chamber, he entered. Inside was a treasure trove of the most priceless of all the ElseWorld artifacts that he and his father had found at various archaeological sites throughout Europe. At great expense and trouble, they'd been brought here for safekeeping. Each piece had been created with the use of enchantments over centuries past, and many hummed with magic.

He didn't pause to admire any of them now, but only stalked directly to the tall, glass jewel vault. Thousands of gems sparkled and winked within it, but two among them gleamed with an inner fire that burned more brightly than any other gems he'd ever seen. Twin opals. He'd found one of them three years ago and the second only last Moonful, both in the Forum digs. They exactly matched the three Michaela had held. Which meant there were five in existence. Likely six, for he believed there to be six Vestals, and that each had received one upon her initiation. Relief filled him to see that his were still here. Michaela had been in this house for months and had no doubt searched for them.

What was it that made her want these stones so badly that

she'd come here and tricked him in order to obtain them? And who the hells was she? Not the Michaela he'd first met, even if she did look like her. In these recent weeks, something about her had changed. It was as if she'd begun the month playing the role of Michaela with precision, but had slowly forgotten her part and now become someone else.

She'd claimed to love him. Ha! What sort of woman stole something so precious from a man she professed to love?

Thank the Gods he hadn't spoken of his own feelings to her. He knew his brothers thought him incapable of love, but he shunned entanglements only because he was devoted to his work. He'd never anticipated loving any woman. But over the past few weeks, all that had changed. He'd begun to care deeply for Michaela. To love her. And she'd repaid his affection with treachery.

He turned the opals in his hands, wondering at their power. How had she created fire from them and then escaped through it? Gods, what the hells was she?

The specter in Monti had sought to steal one of these opals last Moonful. And that night marked the beginning of the change in Michaela. How were the two females related? And how were they related to the presence he'd felt here in his home two months ago, and to Rico? All four shared the common theme of causing him to see color. When he'd lost the specter in Monti, he'd followed it by the trail of color it had inadvertently left behind. However, Michaela had simply disappeared, without a trace.

But he would find her another way. By dangling that which she most wanted before her. One of these opals. He would lure her with it, and she would come for it.

And then he would make her pay.

Scena Antica VI

384 A.D.
Regia, Rome, Italy

A ring of eleven glowing candles encircled the room, all lit from Vesta's flame and brought here to the Regia for this solemn occasion. Each represented one of the Vestals, who were not present here. The twelfth Vestal, Silvia, stood alone in the center of the ring, awaiting punishment. Her back was straight, her chin high. She would not cower.

The room around her was in near darkness and she could not see beyond the candles. Had all six of the pontiffs come to witness her punishment? "Why don't you show yourselves?" she challenged, and heard the rustling of their starched robes.

Vestalis Maxima stepped into the center of the ring, holding a golden chalice out to her. "Drink this. It will dull any pain."

Silvia shook her head, mutinous.

Coming close, Vestalis murmured at her ear. "They'll force you to drink if you don't take it from me. So that you will not scream."

Scream? Of course, what had she expected? That a scourging

would be painless? Silvia lifted the chalice and swallowed the entire draught, suddenly eager to have the ordeal begin, for that meant it would end all the sooner.

"I'm going to remove your gown," Vestalis said. Her voice was kind but resigned. Silvia knocked her hand away. "It's in the doctrine that matters proceed in this way," Vestalis insisted. If you fight, they'll only bind your limbs and gag you so that I may proceed."

When she reached out again, Silvia didn't stop her this time, and Vestalis began removing her infula, then unwrapping her stola. "The lash will be applied lightly. Only twelve strokes," Silvia was informed. Once she was divested of her chemise, girdle, and fascia, some final advice was offered. "Remain still, Silvia. Still as death. They won't mark you. Not unless you flinch." Vestalis gave her hand a reassuring squeeze in farewell. Then, leaving her clad only in her sheer suffibulum veil, she backstepped her way from the ring, eyes lowered in deference to the pontiffs. A door opened as she departed. The sharp click of the lock turning was loud in the room. There would be no escape now, not until her punishment was done.

A few moments passed and Silvia felt the stare of powerful men. She refused to break the silence. Refused to break. They had taken her clothing to humiliate her, but she would not give them the satisfaction of seeing her shrink from them.

Suddenly, Pontifex's voice rang out. "Virgin Silvia, you are guilty of a heinous crime against Vesta, for you allowed her fire to dwindle." He was behind her somewhere, shrouded in blackness. At his accusation, she heard the stir of robes and murmurs from the others.

"But it did not go out," she reminded them.

"A fortunate distinction, or you would not get off so easily."

Easily?

She felt his warmth at her back. Her flesh cringed, but she remained still as Vestalis had advised. Something—the braided leather handle of his flogger—lifted the curtain of her hair forward and pushed it over her shoulder so it draped her breasts and bared *her back for the forthcoming lash. The tip of the handle drew down her spine, then away.*

"Do what you will and be done with it," said Silvia. "I'll not grovel."

His voice rent the inky darkness, soft and fearsome. "And that is precisely why you appeal to me so."

Appeal to him? She shuddered, revulsion sweeping her.

"Are you cold?"

"What do you think?" she said, but her voice sounded strange to her own ears, and she felt somehow detached from it. She felt her eyes slowly dilate, her cheeks flush. The potion she'd drunk from the chalice was having its intended effect on her.

"I think, dear Virgin, that you are ready," he replied at length.

Slowly, he began to circle her. Though his eyes scalded every inch of her skin, they would not meet her own now, as if to do so might transform what he would do here into a violation rather than a sacred rite.

Then he spoke, his voice ringing with authority as it filled the room. "Virgin Silvia, for your grave offence against our most sacred goddess, you are sentenced tonight to a scourging. A dozen lashes. Each pontiff will step forward to administer two of them, so that we may equally share in the burden of your punishment. Let us begin."

Coming to a halt before her, he extended the whip over her shoulder toward something—someone—beyond her. She heard steps and the rustle of robes. Another of the pontiffs stood behind her, she assumed. Taking the whip, he stepped back, just far enough that he might strike.

Crack! The flick of the lash came unexpectedly, licking fire at her shoulder. She bowed forward, then straightened. Gods, how would she stand eleven more?

Pontiff's eyes flared and he spoke again. "One more, brother. She deserves one more by your hand."

"Brother?" Silvia echoed.

Pontifex smiled at her. "It is his right to take part in your punishment. I yield my two allotted strokes to him."

Silvia turned her head as the lash struck again, and felt its second bite cut her cheek. She lifted her fingers to her face and they came away with blood. She dropped to her knees. Through a haze of pain, she saw a dear, familiar face. "Father?"

Murmurs of distress spun around her. She glanced toward the raised voices of the other anonymous pontiffs hidden in the inky surroundings beyond the candles. When she looked back to where her father had stood, he was gone. Her searching gaze darted wildly around the room, but he was nowhere to be found.

Pontifex's face swam into view. He lifted her to her feet, and his dry hand cupped her jaw, tilting her wound to the light.

"What will everyone say when they see how you let him disfigure me?" she taunted, hoping to shame him. But he only pressed a gentle kiss to her lips, and said, "They will say that you are beautiful." Weakly, she pushed him away.

A banging came on the outside of the door. "Stop! Let me in! I'm the guilty one."

Michaela? Silvia shook her head and tried to speak, but her tongue was thick in her mouth. The potion. With a release of the lock, her dearest friend was in the room and at her side, hugging her close.

"I am responsible for what happened," Michaela announced to the room at large. "I was the one who let the fire dwindle, not she."

"Occia reports otherwise," someone countered.

"She lies. She is jealous of Silvia. Ask anyone."

Silvia managed to form words. "No, the punishment is mine. It was my fault. Ten more lashes." She swayed and put a hand to her swimming head.

Michaela left her and stepped close to Pontifex—closer than propriety allowed. Her tone lowered to a beguiling tease. "Let her go, pontiff. Punish me."

Pontifex searched her face and something changed in his own.

He gestured an attendant forward. "Take Silvia back to the house," he instructed.

"No," Silvia murmured, but she was too drugged to fight, and so was carried away and remanded to the care of Vestalis. As gentle hands tended her, the potion she'd drunk overcame her. When she woke the next morning, she found Michaela in the infirmary beside her, lying on her stomach. Silvia gasped at the sight of the ten red welts that crisscrossed her smooth back.

Vestalis was applying compresses to them. "Shhh. I've given her a medicinal philter. She'll sleep through the day and into the night. And unlike your own, her marks will fade." Silvia put a hand to her cheek, felt the fresh cut.

When Michaela woke that night, she refused to break her silence regarding all that had happened at the Regia after Silvia had gone. She made Silvia swear never to ask Pontifex about it, and she never again broached the possibility of escape from the temple. But Silvia knew something awful had happened. Never again would she trust Pontifex or her father, or any man.

And from that day on, neither of them would tend Vesta's fire without the other. For of the two of them, only Silvia's heat could thereafter stoke it. And this was something no one must find out.

14

Stones in hand, Silvia walked along the ancient street, Via Sacra. She was still in the form of Michaela, both of them uninjured by the blaze she'd created as she'd bid Bastian a hasty farewell. She had been greatly relieved to discover that Occia had been right in saying that possession of the stones would enable her to create a firegate for travel within this world. Trying it had been risky, but it had paid off. The gate had transported her from the Atrium House to this road in a quick burst. But even with the aid of the stones, she hadn't been able to travel far while in a mortal host.

And now she would take this road far from here. Since she dared not trust Michaela's fragile form to more travel by flame, she must go on foot in the human way. She passed the intersection of Vicus Eros, where the shrine of Bacchus once stood, and on the ridge above, the colossus of Nero. And still she walked on. Every step was a torture, for she longed to simply curl up and cry.

The full impact of her dearest friend's demise had largely been kept in abeyance over the past weeks, but now it came rushing at her, overwhelming her with grief. The miles passed and her eyes grew red and raw from weeping until she could hardly see the road at times. She would keep Michaela with her for as long as she could. But her mind raged at the knowledge that all too soon, she would lose her as she had every other host she'd encountered in the past.

A week after leaving Rome, Moonful came and went. Silvia didn't return to ElseWorld to Replenish, for this would have meant a permanent departure from Michaela's form. And she was not ready to face that yet. Was not ready to face Pontifex yet either, not until she had all six stones. Instead, on the night of the full moon, she found a small cavern in the hills out of sight of the main road, and there she set her three firestones out upon a rock. She worshipped Vesta and summoned flame from them, and this ritual had seemed to serve in lieu of a visit to the hearth, for it had seen her safely through the night. But she did not let her thoughts dwell on Bastian, for she did not want to ponder how—or with whom—he passed his own Moonful.

When the next morning dawned, she moved on. It was in these last days of their existence that hosts became weak. Now that Michaela was no longer strong enough to hide them, all of her secrets came flooding out. And Silvia learned things she wished she had not, for some of Michaela's whisperings were far, far too terrible: *That night of the scourging . . . after you were sent away . . . I was made to service Pontifex . . . and the other pontiffs as well . . . they threatened to hurt you if I told . . . or ran . . . so I stayed . . .*

Although Silvia shrank from the horror of these revelations, she grimly listened on as Michaela shared her past as she would, regaling her with sordid details of that awful night. There had been six of them. Grown men of religion and politics, who had used her in vile ways. None had been fool enough to defile her virginity, for they'd feared Vesta's reprisal, and Michaela had thought herself spared that violation at least.

But the following Moonful, Pontifex had been overcome with lust, and had taken her to his bed. When he discovered through his rape that she had already lain with another—the boy in the spice market—her fate had been sealed. A bargain had been struck. He would not see her buried alive for her crime—a single act of fornication with a spice merchant's son—and in return, she would become his concubine. Thereafter, when the other Vestals had taken individual prayer at Moonful, she had lain with him in secret. Even after the temple fell, she had gone to him. For centuries. To protect Silvia.

It was only once a month, Michaela told her soothingly, seeming to sense how debilitating this new information was to Silvia. *Not so awful.* But it had been, and Silvia howled with the horrible, complete knowledge of all that had transpired. Wishing she had known. Wishing they could go back to that afternoon when they were eighteen and tending fire. Wishing she had agreed to flee the temple forever, when Michaela had suggested it.

And on another day on this final walk they took together, Michaela shared yet another devastating secret with her: *Bastian did not love me.*

When this whispered thought came, Silvia stopped in the street. Had she misheard? But Michaela went on: *Dear Via— don't be angry at him. . . . He warned me he could not love me before we first lay together . . . but I thought I could change him. . . . Alas, I could not . . .*

And then on other days came better, happier memories of the joyous events in their lives. Silvia smiled and laughed and wept as Michaela brought to her mind many of the fun times they'd had as girls. First crushes on boys, pranks pulled on other Vestals, the learning of magic, the acquiring of property in their own names, the quiet times as they tended fire together, and occasional, soft summer nights of loving. A thousand silly, poignant, small, precious remembrances shared between the closest of friends.

I'm tired, Michaela whispered to her almost daily now. *Let me rest.*

But each time she heard this, panic stirred in Silvia and her steps only quickened. "Just a little farther," she would plead. "I don't want to lose you. Not yet."

And then one day as a light snow began to fall, Michaela had had enough: *I'll be with you always, Via. . . . Carry me in your heart and I'll carry you in mine . . . but my body is tired . . . let me go . . . it's time . . .*

Silvia took a deep, shuddering breath and stopped in the street, utterly exhausted. She'd paused beside an ancient mile marker. At intervals along the roads she walked, she'd passed many of these two-ton columns. Each rose five feet tall and was twenty inches in diameter. She knew this because in the Republican era, she'd been joined to a host who was part of the crew that had set the markers into the ground. The panel at eye level on this one indicated the distance to the center of ancient Rome—the Forum. She'd walked exactly one hundred miles.

Over these past days, she'd scarcely eaten, barely slept. Michaela was right. They couldn't go on. Giving in with the greatest reluctance, she veered off the main road and wandered deep into a primeval forest of cypress, pine, olive, and plane trees.

She was dry-eyed now and moved like an unfeeling automaton as she located a small hollow among the roots of an ancient, gnarled olive tree. There, she buried the three firestones for safekeeping, for she would not be able to carry them when she resumed her Ephemeral wraith form.

Next, she gathered snow-dusted boughs and heather to form a thick pallet some five and a half feet long and three feet wide. It was to be a funeral pyre, for she would not leave Michaela's body for Pontifex's minions to find.

When all was in readiness, she lay on her back upon the soft, sweet-scented pyre and gazed up at the snow drifting down from a gloomy sky. The air was fresh and cold on her cheeks. She smoothed her hair just so and arranged her limbs, folding her hands over her chest.

Then dear friends whispered one last good-bye.

Silvia closed her eyes and inhaled deeply, until her lungs were full to bursting. Then she expelled every wisp of breath they held . . . and felt her essence fleeing along with it . . .

In the next instant, she was without corporeal form—an Ephemeral once more. She stood there in the silent forest, gazing down at Michaela's beautiful, perfect, still body.

Reaching down, Silvia gathered the heather and pine boughs more neatly around her body and then sprinkled her with snowdrop petals. As she prayed to Vesta to accept her into her blessed care, she summoned a firegate, and with a fag she lit from its flames, she set the pyre ablaze. She stayed there at Michaela's side until all was done. Until her cherished friend was gone from both worlds forever. Finally at peace.

For the first time in her extraordinarily long life, Silvia felt truly alone. She had failed to protect Michaela, and now she was dead. But there were others suffering under Pontifex's rule. She worried over the fates of those Vestals, almost all of them locked away in stasis now for hundreds of years. She could save them. Would save them. This thought kept her going. And the next morning as she took invisible form and traveled on, a fierce heat burned in her. For revenge.

Her next summoning took her to a young human girl who'd become lost in the woods, tripped, and fatally struck her head. Humans were only for brief travel, not meant for a long stay. After taking her on as host, Silvia retrieved the cache of firestones, playing them in a more secure location. A day later, the girl's body was found in her bed, neatly dressed and well cared for. Her Deathwish had been to return home, and so she had.

Silvia wandered northward then, exchanging one body for another, barely living. As she ran from her loneliness, she kept searching for the remaining three stones. Only the whereabouts of two were uncertain, for she knew where the sixth resided. Back in Rome. With Bastian. She would seek it only after she had the other five in her possession. When her heart had sufficiently healed against him.

And when she had all six stones, she would visit Pontifex again. Then they would each have half the stones. Half the power. And then they would see who would win all.

A crushing pain traveled with her as she mourned Michaela's loss. She wept often and became accustomed to seeing her eyes rimmed red and her cheeks chapped from tears and frost. Winter became spring, spring became summer and then autumn, and she hardly noticed. She'd felt Pontifex's call over the Moonfuls that had passed, but she hid from him and refused to heed him. The three firestones she possessed continued to offset the moon's effects on those nights, enabling her to Replenish her Vestal fire as she must to survive.

Eventually, she heard rumors of a large opal in the city of Ravenna. This one had originally belonged to the Vestal Floronia but was currently hanging on a chain around the neck of a society matron who had no idea what it was. When one of her maids took ill and died, it was an easy matter to take her as host and make off with the opal.

After the theft, Silvia deposited the four firestones in a bank in Florence for safekeeping and continued her search for the others. During the course of her hunt, she was slowly forced to reconnect with the world around her in order to obtain information that might lead her to yet another stone. Finally, in September, she got a lead regarding a fifth. It seemed there was to be an auction in Venice soon. One that would feature an unusually sizable opal.

September 1881

A week later, Silvia was in Venice. Brushing raindrops off her cloak, she scurried inside the stately private residence just as the auction was about to commence. Behind her, the massive double doors through which she'd entered the house swung shut with a solid, expensive *thunk*. She'd only just missed having to pay the fee auction houses traditionally levied against latecomers.

Yet this was no traditional auction venue, she'd quickly realized as the majordomo took her drenched cloak. It was the grand *salone* of a stately, three-storied Renaissance-era palazzo, which fronted Venice's Grand Canal. The only access was by gondola, and since the day was stormy, passage here had been difficult and delays inevitable.

The chamber she'd been shown to was opulent, its walls painted with soft-hued frescoes. It contained little furniture aside from the three dozen straight-backed chairs set in arced rows and occupied by other attendees.

Items to be auctioned were neatly stacked in the adjacent room, which she could see through a doorway. She'd meant to arrive early in order to examine the opal and quite possibly steal it, but the storm had prevented her from doing so.

Since an auction seemed a promising occasion for finding a firestone, she'd been perusing the catalogs of auction houses for some time now, which had led her here. She was no stranger to auctions. In ancient Rome, they had been popular for the sale of war plunder and family estates, and much later, one of her hosts had been involved in the auctioneering of Tuscan wine.

A somber-faced group of men filled the bidding room, heads

bent as they examined the printed dockets they'd been given. Some were notorious treasure hunters. Each was already absorbed in calculating which purchases were most likely to bring them a profit.

As she found a seat, the gentleman next to her shot her an interested smile. Her current host was young and comely, with green eyes, brown hair, and a narrow waist. However, the man's smile withered as he noticed the bruise on her pale cheek. She read the pity in his gaze. The bruise had been worse only an hour ago when she'd taken this body as host, but it was already fading and would likely be gone soon. Her occupation of a body generally healed such wounds quickly. Unfortunately her own scar was not as easily dispatched.

When he continued staring, she leaned close to him and confided, "The worst of it is on my back, where it doesn't show. Jealous husbands can be such brutes." Her glance went pointedly to his wedding ring. Then she gave him a sweet smile, pleased that he appeared horrified, for she was not in a mood to be charitable toward husbands.

Her current host had been bludgeoned to death with a poker by her spouse this very afternoon. After his crime, he had blithely gone upstairs with his mistress. No doubt he'd been quite surprised when he'd later returned to the murder scene only to find his wife's body gone, along with his pistol and all of the savings from his safe. How she wished she could have seen the look on his face!

The auctioneer took his place at the lectern, stirring dust motes as he welcomed them and then opened the auction. First on offer was a collection of taxidermists' works. Next, an offering of antiquarian books; then a set of sculptor's tools and several busts; some jewelry. These had been the assets of debtors whose property had been confiscated and sent here to be liquidated.

The origin of the object of interest to Silvia was listed as being from an estate in Rome. She would give much to know how the previous owner might have come by the opal. His proximity to the Forum meant that he might have gone collecting before the serious excavations began there. Treasure hunting in the ruins had in previous decades been the Roman citizens' version of beachcombing. Something done as a lark during a picnic in the Forum on an idle afternoon.

Awaiting the opal, Silvia assessed her competition in the meantime, doing her best not to draw undue attention. Difficult when she was the only female present. However, that could prove to be to her benefit. Many years ago at a similar auction, she'd won an item simply because her competitors were too gentlemanly to bid against her.

Eventually, the auctioneer arrived at the opal. At the mention of it, she sensed an increased awareness ripple over the group. Her anxiety rose. Would the money in her handbag be enough to win it?

"This rare and collectible opal will be offered 'by candle,' as per the instructions of the seller," the auctioneer droned.

"And who might that be?" someone called out. Silvia craned her neck to view the man, but he looked to be nothing out of the ordinary.

"The owner prefers to go unnamed," said the auctioneer. "Now, as I said, we are to proceed 'by candle.' " He pointed upward, and Silvia saw that a flat, wide board had been anchored in a horizontal position some five feet or so below the ornate chandelier that hung well above them. As they watched, an agile lad was sent up a ladder to set a single candle upon it and light it.

"The highest bidder at the time the flame goes out will win the item," the auctioneer clarified as the boy retraced the ladder rungs downward to the floor.

Silvia's confidence escalated. Having attended numerous auctions over the course of her long life, she'd discovered the secret of winning at this sort of sale. In the instant before the candle went out, the rising smoke would reverse its course and begin to descend. That is when she would act.

The shutters on the room's trefoil windows were closed, and an eerie silence reigned in the dim room for a time. Then an agitation set in and a desultory bidding commenced. Encouraged, the auctioneer continued to extol the virtues of the opal.

Above them, the candle's glow and the smoke rising from it were visible, but the candle itself was not, being obscured by the board upon which it sat so that none might see how close it drew to its demise. After another ten minutes elapsed, everyone was sitting up straighter, watching with keen interest. Such an auction usually lasted no more than a sixth of an hour—the time it took a candle to flicker out. Silvia held her breath, eyes narrowed. Any minute now.

All around her, bids came faster and her pulse kept pace.

When she saw the smoke begin to descend, she cast her first and only bid. "One hundred and fifty lira!"

"Two hundred!" another man barked. In the same instant, the candle's light winked out.

"Sold!" The auctioneer's proclamation sent panic skittering down every knob in her spine. Silvia leaped to her feet in distress. She'd traveled all this way and then acted a split second too hastily. A man with spectacles seated across the room had won.

Others were standing now and filing past, moving through the door and beyond to the accountant's desk in the vestibule. There, they would settle their debts and make arrangements for the delivery of items they'd purchased. Anxiously, she made her way toward the man who'd bought the opal. Several other attendees had gathered around him with the same purpose. He quickly informed them he'd been bidding on behalf of another buyer whose identity he would not reveal. When both he and the auctioneer quit the room, the remaining bidders followed them like a flock of black crows intent on pecking more information out of them.

Abruptly, Silvia found herself alone. Seizing the opportunity that presented, she slipped into the adjacent storeroom. If she were quick, she might have time to pilfer the firestone. The shutters had not re-opened and it was difficult to see, but she pushed items this way and that, examining them and hurriedly working her way along the perimeter of the room.

Suddenly, something caught her attention. A flash. Riveted, she craned her neck, squinting. It was one of the opals! Whose, she could not tell until she held it. It had been placed upon a velvet cushion within a small glass case no bigger than a loaf of bread. And this, in turn, was set inside a tall glass cabinet, which stood behind a large secretary. Both case and cabinet were locked. She wedged herself behind a painted screen on one side of the cabinet and quickly picked the lock with a hairpin. Then she snatched up the small glass case from inside. Wrapping it in her skirt to dull the sound, she then knocked one of its glass sides against the desk corner, hard enough to shatter it. The force of its breaking sent the opal sliding out from the open gash onto the floor. Dropping to a crouch, Silvia set the box aside and snatched it up, feeling almost giddy at having secured it, the fifth stone.

It was warm in her hand. Now that she held it, she could intuit its original owner. Licinia. "However did you wind up here?" she murmured, wondering at the circuitous path it might have taken.

The sudden sound of boot heels striking the marble floor came like the staccato cracks of a whip. Silvia jerked around, inadvertently causing the small glass box to tip on its side with a tinkle of broken glass. Had the interloper heard?

There were thin gaps between the slats in the lower part of the painted screen that hid her. Gingerly, she peeked out. Legs were approaching. A man's legs, strong and sturdy as tree trunks, and encased in fine black wool and black boots.

The owner of those legs paused in the middle of the room, positioning himself between her and the exit. Dropping onto a straight-backed, uncomfortable-looking velvet sofa, he sat facing in her direction and crossed the ankle of one polished boot over his opposite knee.

She could see more of him now. His coat was dark and blunt-cut at the back of his thighs. A single-breasted waistcoat with three buttons and a deep V emphasized his broad shoulders. Try as she would, she could not see his face without exposing herself.

Silence reigned between them. She debated whether to remain in hiding until he left or to show herself, nod to him, and simply walk away in hopes he would not question why she'd been hiding. Then he spoke.

"Did you expect it to answer you?" The words were mildly amused. Masculine. Dear and familiar. Bastian.

Damnation. Since he obviously knew she was here, it was beyond foolish to continue hiding. Slipping the opal into her pocket, she patted the hard comfort of the pistol she'd brought with her. Then she got to her feet and stepped from behind the screen to confront him.

15

Oh, sweet Vesta! It *was* Bastian! Ridiculous joy washed over her to see him again. How many nights had she dreamed of him? Yet, in the flesh he was far more compelling than in her dreams. His jaw was strong and square, and his nose and brows straight. And his lips—the upper one had an edge of masculine steel, but the lower was cut as sensually as a Renaissance statue. Yes, he was handsome, undoubtedly so.

As her hungry eyes devoured him, his seemed to do the same to her. Well, let him look. He would not recognize her in this new host's form. Her eyes flicked to the door. She should go. If he'd guessed she'd taken the opal, he would try to stop her from leaving with it. Without speaking to him, she walked toward the door on shaking legs, expecting at any moment to be waylaid. Relief swamped her when he didn't act to detain her.

She'd drawn even with him. From here, all she could see was his aristocratic profile. She paused, questions swirling in her brain. Why was he here?

His attractive, brooding face slowly turned to contemplate

her, silver eyes tangling with the green ones of her host. "I think you have something that belongs to me."

She gazed at his mouth as he spoke, then blushed. A strange calm settled over her, releasing the tension in her neck and shoulders. Making her want to answer him. She parted her lips, then slapped her fingers over them.

"No," she whispered, shaking her head slowly, side to side.

"No?"

"Don't bother using your spells on me," she chided, revealing her knowledge of his ElseWorld origins and inadvertently admitting her own. "I only stayed behind to examine the objects on auction as I had no time to study them earlier."

In a casual, elegant movement tinged with the barely restrained strength that typified him and his brothers, he laid one arm across the back of the chair next to his own, angling his body in her direction. "They've all been purchased and are no longer available for public study," he informed her. "Or for stealing."

"And who are you to say?"

He flicked a hand to generally encompass the room. "I'm the owner of this house, as well as other holdings here in Venice and in Rome. The owner of the last lot upon which you bid. And lost. To me."

"You had a surrogate bid on your behalf?" she asked in dismay. This opal was the one he'd had with him in Monti? That meant there would be no need to return to Rome after all, and tonight might be the last she'd see of him.

He nodded.

"But why bid on your own property?"

He only shrugged, watching her in a disturbing manner, as if he knew something she didn't. Yet surely the reverse was true! He had no idea who she was.

The atmosphere between them had a dangerous edge, and she now had the fifth jewel. Best keep to her original plan and search on for the sixth. If all went well with Pontifex, perhaps . . . No, she would not think that far ahead.

"I'm leaving now. And I'm taking *this*." She pulled out her pistol so that he could see it. "And your 'property' with me. Good day, signor." She made for the door, her steps quickening as she drew ever closer to freedom. Without warning, it slammed shut before her, the force of its swing momentarily ballooning her skirt and swirling tendrils of her hair.

Silvia halted in surprise, then scurried forward to yank at the brass handle. It was locked! Though she hadn't heard him move, she suddenly felt him warm her back. Her pistol was summarily removed from her hand and tossed away to land with a clatter in some distant corner among other items on auction. And just as quickly, the opal left her pocket in his hand and was quickly dropped into the pocket of his trousers instead.

"Although my youngest brother has the greater talent, I confess that the moving of doors is something I can accomplish on my own when I wish to make the effort."

"How nice for you," she managed. Frustrated at having lost the opal, she silently plotted the best way to retrieve it.

His broad hand spread flat over her belly, and she dislodged it by whipping around within his embrace, preferring to square off against any aggression. She gazed at his mouth, then blushed. A strangely satisfied expression crossed his face, as if his touch on her had confirmed something for him.

His hands fit themselves neatly at the turns of her waist, shaping over her from rib to hip, as if he enjoyed the tactile sensation of her. His eyes traced over her cheek, then his fingers followed. "What happened to you?"

She cringed away, momentarily assuming he referred to the scar her father had given her. Remembering that he could only see the bruising of her host's face, she shrugged. "I had an abusive husband."

"Had?"

She pushed him back and he let her slip away to try the other door in the room, finding it locked as well. "Can I buy the stone from you?" she asked, looking at him over her shoulder.

He folded his arms, regarding her, and a small, weighty silence passed. Though his eyes didn't move, she sensed that he'd just evaluated and memorized her every feature. "Perhaps."

"For what price?" she asked, turning toward him hopefully.

"For the answer to some questions."

"Ask them."

"Where's Michaela?" he demanded.

His words struck her like a blow and she blanched, her stomach somersaulting. Gods! She was in the body of a woman completely unknown to him. How had he guessed she was at all acquainted with Michaela? Belatedly trying to appear guileless, she asked, "Michella, did you say? I'm sorry but I don't know—"

He was at her side before she could finish. Suddenly fierce, he nailed her to the door with one forearm across her throat. She felt hot blood suffuse her face as air was denied her.

"You know her, all right. Your face is an open book. Now, tell me where she is, or I'll make you sorry."

"Dead," she admitted, her voice a faint, desperate croak.

For a moment, the pressure on her neck strengthened and she wrapped white-knuckled fingers around his forearm, fearing he would strangle her. Just when spots began to dance before her, he relented, ramming fists on either side of her hard enough to dent the door's paneling.

"Did you kill her?" he gritted.

She put a hand to her bruised throat and coughed. "No! I saw her murdered in Monti that night you were drunk."

He gave her a single, bone-rattling shake. "Gods damn you

for a liar," he muttered. "I was with Michaela that same night. It was Moonful, and she was very much alive."

The sound of voices reached her ears from beyond the door. Someone was coming. Silvia made a pitiful attempt to call out for rescue.

But Bastian's muscular arm snaked around her waist, lifting her against him, and his free hand covered her mouth. She was quickly whisked across the room as if she weighed nothing and then taken through a series of corridors and rooms, and carried up a back staircase like a sack of flour.

Finally, they reached another door, and after Bastian took her through it, he let her go in what appeared to be a rather cozy library. He stepped inside with her, then swung the door shut behind him, effectively sequestering them inside. Turning the key in its lock, he made a show of pocketing it. Then he crossed his arms. "Now, speak."

Her mind worked furiously as she tried to decide what he knew. What she should tell. When she didn't answer swiftly enough to suit him, he took a menacing step toward her and soon had her backed up against a glass bookcase. "Your erstwhile husband may not have managed to throttle you, but I'm this close to finishing the job myself if you don't tell me what happened to Michaela."

A blend of partial truth and lies seemed her best option, for too many undiluted truths could lead to others she did not want to share. "She was murdered by an Ogre. Not that night in Monti, but another night . . ."

"What Ogre? When? Where?"

"In . . . Florence. A month ago. And I'm not friendly enough with Ogres to tell one from another."

"You're a poor liar—you should really give it up." His hand caught at her nape, and his thumb traced the bruises he'd made on her throat. His voice took on a dangerous edge. "Don't make me hurt you to learn the truth."

"I didn't kill her," she said earnestly. "I loved her."

"All right, then," he said more calmly, seeming to believe that at least. "We have all night to get at the rest of the truth. All week. All month. Take your time. And for every lie you tell, I'll add another day to your detainment."

She only laughed at his threat, surprising him. "I can leave this room whenever I wish. And when I do, you'll have a dead body on your hands."

"Do you care to explain that riddle?"

She shrugged. It had been an idle threat. She could only steal from him while in corporeal form—either her host's or her own true one. And if he saw her in true Ephemeral form, it would go a long way toward making her mortal.

His hand dropped and she scuttled away the moment he released her. "Let's make a bargain," he suggested. "You will stay until you've answered my every question. Then I'll give you this."

He pulled the opal from his pocket, showing it to her. She eyed it covetously. She would tell him almost any truth in order to have it. But could she trust him?

Bastian watched her green eyes light with interest. Her eyes were beautiful, but they were the wrong color. She was the wrong woman. Or was she? Five months ago, Michaela had departed Rome, taking three other opals and all color with her. Since then, everything around him had been bleak, an existence dressed in hues of drab gray and stark black and white.

But the moment he'd touched this woman downstairs, color had leaped to life again. Her skin was London-pale, her lips peach, her hair a lustrous chestnut, her dress striped in lavender and evergreen. The longer he was in her company, the more the color extended outward from her, even when he wasn't touching her. It had followed them through his house and now painted half of the library around her.

She was standing behind one of his upholstered reading chairs, watching him with a calculating wariness. His gaze went to her hand, where it rested on the chair's back and found the ring she wore. He only hoped she was a widow, for the arrival of color in his world was having its customary effect on his anatomy.

"Your proposition is too open-ended. Instead, I'll give you five answers to five questions," she bargained. "In exchange, I want the opal and my freedom."

"Ten questions," he countered.

"All right."

He inclined his head. "Done."

"Swear on your God."

"I swear," he told her easily. He went to sit in a chair and then gestured her to sit next to him in the one she currently used as a barrier between them. "Come, let me see your face so that I can better tell truth from lie."

She accommodated him without argument, seating herself and folding her hands in her lap. He set the opal on the small table between the arms of their chairs. Her acquisitive eyes went to it, then met his.

He sat back, his gaze direct. "What are you, and how do you know Michaela?" She looked so horrified by his opening salvo that he almost wanted to laugh. Almost.

"That's two questions," she quibbled.

"We'll count it as two, then, just as soon as I have two *truthful* answers from you."

"Very well. I'm an Ephemeral," she admitted bluntly, as if she hoped to shock him. "As was Michaela."

A short gust of laughter left him at this fantastic lie. Ephemerals were only creatures of myth. "A mythological scavenger? I don't think so."

She folded her arms. "That's an offensive term."

"Bodysnatcher, then?"

"Also offensive, as you well know. And that was your third question."

Her annoyance went a long way toward persuading him. Was it possible she didn't lie? After all, his own family could conjure Shimmerskins from mist. Was the existence of an Ephemeral really such a strange concept by comparison? "Ephemerals are created by Gods," he mused.

"Is that a question? Or—"

"I'll rephrase. Which God created you? And I expect a full answer, one that persuades me the myth is real," he said.

A pause, then she gave him her quiet admission. "Vesta." When he only eyed her skeptically, her lips tightened and she leaned toward him, willing him to believe her. "Do you think Michaela or I asked for this life? We didn't. It was thrust upon us when we were girls, centuries ago in ancient times when women had no power. You wondered at there being twelve Vestals instead of the six that the philosophers quote. Well, I can solve that riddle for you if it will help convince you. There were indeed six Virgins. But there were also six Companions. We trained side by side, taking our meals together and tending the fire together. All of us devoted to Vesta. And when her temple was violently disbanded, she transformed us all into Ephemerals."

"And how did you know that I wondered at there being twelve Vestals?" he asked softly.

She drew back. Realizing her mistake, she turned evasive. "I—"

But he already had his answer. In his mind's eye he saw himself being led to the site of Vesta's temple, where he viewed not six, but *twelve* apparitions. And then only two days later, a twelve-year-old boy ticking off facts in his work tent in the Forum: *One: Aeneas brought the eternal fire to Vesta's temple from Troy. Two: It burned there for nine hundred years. Three: Twelve Vestals kept it going.*

234 / Elizabeth Amber

"Gods, it was you who led me to the temple, wasn't it? And you're . . . *Rico.*" His eyes whipped over her, hardly able to credit that this . . . person . . . was the very same being as the girlish apparition, as well as the boy he'd known in the Forum five months ago. Suddenly, a woman who'd already intrigued him became the most fascinating creature he'd ever met. "You're actually telling the truth. You're an Ephemeral, and you took Rico as host in order to gain access to the Forum excavations."

Twin splotches formed, stark on her pale cheeks. Though she looked completely mortified that he'd guessed, all she gave him in reply was a simple, "Yes, next question."

Bastian shook his head slowly, still trying to digest the fact that this woman and Rico were one and the same. He and Rico had worked long, late hours together. Supped together, joked, argued. The boy had alternately annoyed him and amused him. They'd shared a true passion for the digs. How much of that was her? What did she look like in her true form? He lifted the opal and turned it in his palm. Her eyes trained on it. "Why don't you simply make yourself an apparition now, take this opal, and flee with it?" he asked.

"Because, as a noncorporeal form, I can't carry it. And that makes six questions."

"I'll add a seventh. Are you female?"

She nodded, looking uncomfortable at the turn in his conversation.

"One who seems to have a deleterious effect on those you come in contact with. Will you kill me as well?"

"I didn't *kill* Rico. Or Michaela!" she railed, seeming to lose the tight rein she'd thus far held on her control. "I didn't want either of them dead. I *loved* Michaela, I told you. Far more than you did. And I was fond of Rico. But he was dead when I met him. Or dying, anyway, from a rat bite. He was a stranger to me, one I lent life to for weeks beyond his natural existence. And Michaela *was* murdered that night in Monti. There was nothing I could do to stop either of them from dying. There never is!"

"You're distraught. But that has an honest ring to it at least." He stood and went to his well-stocked beverage cart, and for a moment the only sound in the room was the clink of crystal.

She eyed the contents of the bottle from which he poured. "And you are an unpleasant drunk, signor. I hope—"

Having poured two glasses, he slammed the crystal decanter on the cart. "I begin to note your resemblance to Rico more and more as time goes on. His observations often irritated as well." He took one glass to her, then tossed his own back.

After sniffing hers, she drank, obviously having realized it was only water and lemon. "Ask your last two questions so that I may go."

Silvia didn't look up as Bastian came and stood over her, his long fingers tapping his goblet. What was going through his mind? she wondered as she gazed into her drink. The concept of an Ephemeral both fascinated and repulsed others by turns. Did she disgust him?

Was he reviewing all the conversations he'd had with Rico, as she was? It had been so easy to banter with him when she'd masqueraded as a twelve-year-old. But now he suddenly knew that all those teasing remarks had actually come from her. And that the camaraderie he'd shared with Rico had, in actuality, been a closeness shared with her.

She groaned inwardly, remembering those erotic cards that morning in his tent, and their discussion about the ElseWorld Rites of Purification. Dozens more small embarrassments flitted through her mind. She straightened, telling herself they didn't matter and amounted to nothing in the overall scheme of things. She would have what she wanted from him and her freedom soon enough.

Another question came, his ninth by her count. "How old are you?"

She breathed a sigh of relief and gave him a slight smile. "Forever twenty-three," she said. But even to her own ears, her tone had a poignant edge, rather than the whimsical one she'd intended. She shifted and sat forward, pushing his legs aside and going to stand at a large bay window. Outside, the storm had worsened. Some said Venice would drown one day in the violence of such a storm. She turned to look at him where he still stood before the chair. "Next."

"Something puzzles me." He looked at her over the rim of his goblet, then set his drink aside. "If Michaela died in Monti that night I was drunk . . ." His eyes sharpened on her. "Then who lay with me that Calling night?"

Her eyes went wide. *Gods, no! Don't let him guess.*

"You," he said softly, answering his own question. "You took her as host and then spent that Moonful with me. Fucking me. On the night your dearest friend died."

She stepped back as if struck, then leaped to her own defense. "You think me callous. But you know nothing."

"Explain, then. And that's a command, not another question, just so we understand each other."

Silvia wanted him to understand; needed him not to think ill of her in this matter. So she answered. "When a host dies, they always leave some personal matter undone. I do my best to accomplish whatever final task they ask of me. To fulfill their last wish. For instance, Rico wanted a home for Sal."

A light dawned in his eyes. "And you found one for him. Mine."

She nodded. "And Michaela, she . . . she wanted to lie with you again."

"I see." He lifted the opal from the table, turning it over and over in his hand. "And so you accommodated her."

She stared at the jewel in his strong fingers and nodded again.

"You did so with gratifying enthusiasm. And for weeks."

She reddened, feeling naked before him now and vulnerable, and wishing the floor would open so she might drop through it. "You've had your ten questions. I believe we are done, signor. You owe me one opal and my freedom." She went to him and proffered a hand, palm upward.

The opal went into his pocket. "I'm afraid you miscounted. I answered that last question myself."

Her jaw dropped. "You're a cheat, signor!" she said, outraged. "Well, ask another, then, and let's be done!"

"As soon as we've eaten. Let's call respite from your counting until we mutually determine to begin again. Agreed?" He tugged at a tasseled pull, summoning servants.

When her lips tightened mutinously, he gestured toward the window. "The storm has grown furious. The canals will be impassable until it eases. Until then, stay with me. Old friends sharing a meal. Come, we have been friends in the past, have we not? And I know how you like to eat."

Silvia only glared at him and then went to stare down into the canal, seeing immediately that he was right. Not a single boat had dared brave the tremendous waves below. The rain was so impenetrable that she could barely see the row of pastel buildings across the canal from his home. She sighed. "Do you have any *cioccolato*?" And he smiled at that, knowing he'd got ten his way.

They ate together there in his library, and she regaled him with the life she'd lived in Rome from age six to twenty-three, before the temple had been destroyed. And as his servants seamlessly attended to them, he seemed determined to be entertaining, telling her stories of his boyhood. This was a side of him she hadn't seen. The urbane gentleman, with an efficient, well-trained staff he seemed to take for granted.

"How did you grow up?" she asked at length, curious about him. "You and your brothers?"

238 / Elizabeth Amber

He seemed to close off his emotions then, even as he provided the information. "In ElseWorld, until I was eleven years old. Then we all came here to Italy."

"Why here?"

He sat back from the table. "A tale for another time. Your story is the one to fascinate tonight."

"It wasn't so fascinating a life," she said. "On the day we entered the temple, we were legally emancipated from the authority of our fathers. We vowed chastity for thirty years without knowing what we said."

"A vow you broke. With me."

She only shrugged, not wanting to get into the bizarre nuances of the matter of her virginity with him. She looked toward the window. "It grows late." She pushed back her chair and he caught her wrist before she could move away.

"You feel guilty because you lay with me while in her form. Despite what you said before."

She refused to look at him. "Kayla was my best friend. And she was in love with you."

He stood before her and brought her hands to rest over his heart, his own warm atop them. "I could not love her as she wanted me to. We would have parted, even if she had not died. Even if you had not come along."

"Give me the opal," she whispered into his chest. "And let me go."

"I'm in love with you."

She laughed, a harsh, angry sound, and shoved him away. "You are *not* in love with me."

He regarded her, unfazed. "Hardly the reply I was hoping for, my beloved."

"Don't patronize me. I'm not stupid. What do you think to gain by telling me this lie? The opals? It won't work."

"There, we have that out of the way, then. I cannot possibly be telling you I love you in order to have them."

"You told Michaela you could not love," she accused, backing away as he came toward her.

"That I could not love *her*," he corrected.

She threw up her hands. "How stalwart you are! You could not love a Companion who'd slain the hearts of thousands of other men? And yet you love me, whom you have not even met? Never seen in true form?" She stopped and pushed against him. "And stop stalking me!"

His eyes burned over her. "Show me, then. Show yourself to me."

She laughed bitterly. "As Michaela did? She made herself mortal for you!"

This shocked him. "By showing herself to me in solid Ephemeral form?"

She folded her arms, nodding. "And giving you her true name. That's all it takes."

"I didn't ask it of her." He ran fingers through his hair. "Gods, she was fey—a mortal when I met her. I didn't know she'd ever been anything else."

"I've seen you work night after night to puzzle out the merest fragment of pottery. Yet you didn't take time to puzzle Michaela out. She loved you. And you hurt her."

He glared at her. "Unintentionally."

She poked a finger on his chest. "Do you know what I think? I think she was a challenge to you. You wanted to prove you were strong enough to withstand the thrill of a Companion's touch. I've never known of another man who could."

"That would indicate that *I* was the challenge to *her* rather than the reverse."

"What?"

"Michaela wanted what was unobtainable. In time, I think she would have grown bored with any man who loved her."

Silvia shook her head. "Don't speak of her that way." But a

small part of her wondered if he could be right. Impossible to know now that Michaela was gone.

A pause, then his voice came at her again. "I've been advertising the stone I possess since you disappeared. Where have you been for the last five months?"

"The auction was a trap, then?"

"Yes, and only look what I've caught." There was more than a hint of masculine satisfaction in his tone. "It seems I had only to employ the right bait."

"You've asked more than your quota of questions by now. Are you going to give me the opal? You swore on your God."

"We agreed to mutually determine when the official count would recommence."

She eyed him. "You have no intention of giving it to me, do you?"

"I'll keep to my bargain. In fact, let us agree that this next question is to be number ten: "Why is it so important that you have the opals?"

She turned the tables. "Why do *you* want them so badly?"

He answered easily. "Because I believe they're powerful. And I believe that if I can gather all six here in Rome again, they will protect all of ElseWorld kind in this world. Think of it— no more need for a constant reinforcement of the magic that hides us here. No more fear of discovery."

Silvia stared at him, appalled. He didn't know six opals had already gone to ElseWorld. But if he was right, what would happen if she took the other six there too?

"And I hope to persuade you *and* your opals to stay in Rome as well. With me. We worked well together in the Forum. And I'll be in need of a new foreman soon, once I rid myself of Ilari. You are a talented archaeologist. And I do love you."

She pinched the inside of her elbow, intentionally bringing on tears. Misty-eyed, she went to gaze up at him. "Truly?" Unfortunately his hand caught hers as it ventured into his pocket for the opal. His other hand lifted her arm, kissing the very spot she'd pinched.

"Give me that damned stone and let me go," she gritted, jerking away.

"Since I'm the optimistic sort, I'll assume you mean that only as a temporary rejection," he said. "But you didn't answer my question, yet again. And until I ask my last one—officially ask—then you must remain with me." Going to his wall safe, he spun the lock and promptly deposited the opal inside.

"Let me have it or I swear to you that I will leave you with a dead body on your couch."

"Mine?" he enquired mildly.

"My host's!" she shrieked.

"Listen to me," he said, his tone going serious. "There are other reasons for you to remain with me. Since you left, investigators from ElseWorld have been lurking around the Forum asking about Michaela's whereabouts."

Alarm filled her. More of Pontifex's henchmen. They had to be. She began pacing, winding up at the window overlooking the canal. Plopping down in the window seat, she considered her next move.

"Tell me why you want the opals. Let me protect you," he said, coming to stand before her.

"I can protect myself," she informed him.

He touched the bruise on her face, and she shrugged him away. "That happened to my host, Angelique, not to me. She was left for dead by her devoted husband."

"Gods," he said, shaking his head, as some of the reality of what her life was like began to sink in. "This form of hers; this body you inhabit. How long will you keep it?"

"She'll truly die within weeks."

"And then what?"

"Then I become Ephemeral."

"Visible?"

"I can vacillate between solid or wraith form as I choose for a twenty-four-hour duration. After that, I become weak and must take another host or perish."

"So now I know the worst," he said. "And I still want you."

He pulled her into his embrace and she let him, wanting to feel his arms around her one last time. Taking her place in the window seat, he set her on his lap and brushed her bruised face with his lips, his hands caressing her back.

"I assure you that you do not know the worst, signor." Her expression grim, she tried to drive him away with words. "You don't know me, Bastian. I don't even know myself. I never know when I wake up in the morning if I'll go to bed that night as the same person. I've exchanged hosts hundreds of times over the centuries and I'm affected by each one. I'm a jumble of their peculiarities and abilities. A certain strangeness comes with that."

But he didn't go from her, and only rubbed her back with his big hand and tucked them both more securely in their window seat. "How do you manage to stay sane?"

She shrugged. "I don't look too far ahead. So just give me the opal and accept that I have an important use for it. And don't ever again tell me that you love me just to get information."

His cheek nuzzled her hair. "I know how to get information from a woman without claiming to love her."

"I know all about the pleasure you can give a woman. I was Michaela for a time, remember?"

A tension fell between them, one spun of sensual recollections. "Yes, I well remember. And I also remember how you and she departed from me. I am reminded of how much I anticipated our reunion." His hand lifted her face.

She searched his eyes and was reminded as well. "Then let us have each other again," she whispered. "Once more, and we'll put off arguing over other things for a time."

Her mouth touched his and his arms tightened around her, his own mouth hungry. They both worked at her skirt until she was free of it; then he lifted her to kneel over his lap, facing him. His hands fumbled between them, and no sooner had he opened his trousers than he thrust himself inside her. She gasped and arched against his chest, hands clinging to his shoulders. And for a moment they did not move, but only thrilled to the sensation of their initial joining.

Her hands caressed his nape. "I've missed you," she admitted against his throat.

His arms went around her again. "And I, you." Then he was moving her over him with a masculine need and strength that spiraled her desire higher. Sheets of rain beat at the windowpane behind him as the storm raged on, matching the wild pace of her heart. They made love there in the tempestuous haven of the window seat, their mating hard and desperate and done in haste, their gasps and moans spicing the air.

He spoke, hot against her skin. "Gods, I love you. . . ." Then, "Ninety hells, what's your name?"

She shook her head, and in several more thrusts, bodies too long denied were both shuddering together in ecstasy. Moments later, she slumped over him, her breath still coming in gasps.

His head fell back against the glass, his hands holding her hips. "Anya."

She looked at him, frowning. "What?"

His eyes slitted open to view her. "Your name. I'm guessing."

She shook her head, smiling. Happy to be with him and wishing it could last.

His hands began to wander, caressing over her shape. "Maria, then? No, I have it—Esmerelda."

244 / Elizabeth Amber

She laughed. "Stop."

His hands on her back nudged her forward to sprawl over him. He was still hard in her and she pulsed on him, an echo of the orgasm he'd given her. "It's good between us, Ephemeral. Don't deny it."

She ducked her head, arms looping his back, silent.

His shoulder pushed at her, wordlessly requiring a response.

"I don't enjoy indulging in postcoital reminiscences."

A hand stroked over her hair, pushing a lock behind her ear. "I see. I'll remember that."

"What is that supposed to mean?"

"It means I plan to fuck you again in the future." He flexed his hips slightly, nudging deeper in her slickness. Her flesh pulsed around him again, harder this time.

She gazed beyond him at the rainwashed landscape outside the window. It was dark and lonely out there. He was warm, inviting. Morning would do just as well for her leave-taking. Convincing herself all too easily, she threaded her fingers into his hair and sought his kiss. "The very near future, I trust," she murmured against his lips, and felt his slow, sexy smile.

They lay together again in his library and later in his bed-chamber, coming together again and again until exhaustion set in. And toward morning, when his servants brought breakfast, she tipped a half-dozen drops of the liquor he kept for visitors into his cappuccino. A quarter hour later, she kissed him farewell and shut his bedchamber door, having left him inside, passed out. She sneaked to the library and entered the numbers she'd watched him use on the dial of his safe. And when she had the opal in her pocket, she sat and quickly wrote a note:

> *Bastian has drunk approximately one ounce of liquor from his own cabinet. I know not how it will affect him, so I have tethered him to his bed. Please come to him at once.*

She started to sign it and then stared at the sheet, her pen poised above it. A tear rolled down her cheek and plopped on the letter. She had no name to give. For doing so would be a step toward rendering her mortal. So she simply blotted away all evidence of her tear, sealed the note, and then approached one of his servants with it.

"Signor Satyr has taken ill," she told him. "Are any of his brothers here in Venice?"

"One of them—Lucien," she was informed.

"Summon him and give him this. Tell him that his brother has locked himself in his bedchamber and asks to see him." The wide-eyed servant hurried off to deliver her missive. Bastian would be angry when he woke. Best not to be here.

She slipped out into the calm morning and hailed a passing water taxi under blue skies. When she was seated inside, she felt the comfort of the stone she'd stolen from him in her pocket. She had five now, and one of them his. She had no viable reason to ever see him again. But perhaps love was reason enough for a visit to Rome one day after her work was done. That is, if Pontifex didn't kill her before she could manage it. And if her taking the opals didn't destroy everything Bastian had built here in Italy. If it didn't render this world unsafe for his family and for all of ElseWorld kind as he believed it might. Far too many ifs.

Scena Antica VII

389 A.D.
Rome, Italy

For three hours now, Silvia had sat upon the feather-stuffed cushion of the marble settee—the seat of honor, which had been specifically designated for her use tonight. Despite the raucous crowd surrounding her, she was isolated. Different. Deemed too virtuous to mingle with anyone other than elderly dignitaries.

Now that she was twenty-one—the halfway mark in her thirty-year service to Vesta—she'd been requested to officiate here tonight on the occasion of the monthly Calends. What had earlier begun as a celebration of dancing, poetry, music, and feats of magic on the parts of talented performers was now devolving into a sybaritic spectacle.

Wine bubbled merrily forth from ornate fountains as readily as rain in a summer afternoon storm. Guests' fingers were greasy from a repast of olives and venison. Wives looked on with jaded eyes as their husbands pulled nubile dancers onto their laps, so that they might writhe upon them in a slow, sensuous grind. The harlequins, who'd formerly confined their magic to the pulling of doves, hand-kerchiefs, and fruits from behind ears, now plucked them from beneath the skirts of various ladies in the crowd, eliciting cacophonous laughter from onlookers.

However, all of this jolly sport did not entertain Silvia, for she was completely excluded from it. She did not dare relax her guard and enjoy the occasion as others did. It was unheard of for one of the Vestals to participate in such debauchery.

A Nubian slave stopped to offer her a platter with a selection of honey-drizzled melon, a soufflé, fish in leeks, and an array of raisins, olives, nuts and dates. She waved him away.

In her peripheral vision, she saw the searing light of fires being tossed high overhead. She felt dark eyes on her. Had felt them repeatedly upon her all night. Sipping her wine, she sneaked a glance at he who tormented her. The principal fire juggler. His body was muscular and sculpted and bare to the waist, his hair dark, his jaw long and square, and his coloring swarthy. She had yearned to openly gaze upon him many times but had permitted her eyes to fall upon him only intermittently.

As Silvia watched, he tossed five torches high, one after the other. He had an amazing talent for eating fire and had extinguished more than one of the flames with his own mouth, only to re-ignite them again with a puff of breath. This time, he whirled and caught each torch unerringly, to the sighs and delight of his largely feminine audience. His devilish eyes caught Silvia's on him and he winked, his grin stirring something inside her. Some need. She shifted uncomfortably in her seat and looked away. Her gaze inadvertently fell on an ElseWorld Council member whose hand had wandered deep inside the clothing of a lady beside him, who was not his wife. Somewhere in the distance, she heard the sounds of copulation and she groaned under her breath. Could this get any more horrendous? A few minutes later, and to her great relief, her litter arrived and she departed for the Vestal House.

Michaela was already in their alcove when she slipped in bed beside her. "You smell of wine," she teased, her voice slumberous.

Silvia turned her way. "Thank the Gods you're still awake."

By the dim moonlight from their window, she saw Michaela yawn. "What's wrong?"

"I'm angry," Silvia fumed, punching her pillow, "that's what's wrong. Pontifex and the Council trot us out to preside over every minor occasion because they are too lazy to attend themselves. And then they set temptation before us at every turn and expect us to forgo it. It's cruel."

"Temptation?" Michaela came more awake, her eyes lighting as she curled onto her side to stare at her. "I sense a delicious story ripe for the telling."

Silvia shrugged a shoulder. "Nothing unusual. It was the typical Calends. There was a feast, dancers, magicians, licentious politicians."

"And?"

"And . . ." She smiled sheepishly. ". . . a fire juggler from Romania. A very handsome, tall fire juggler with dark hair and a golden complexion. And well-oiled muscles that gleamed in the lamplight."

Michaela drew up a little higher. "Yes. More. Continue."

"Well, he was quite . . . large. And skilled at his performance. And he seemed to watch me." Silvia turned onto her stomach, burying her scarred cheek in the pillow. "But that can't be. My face is ruined."

"It's a small scar, and you're beautiful," Michaela chided. "Men stare at you far more often than you see."

She only shrugged, not believing, and spoke into her folded arms. "I'm too restless to sleep. Perhaps I should go relieve Aemilia and tend fire in her stead."

"No, your turn doesn't come for two days. Relax. Sleep will come." Michaela touched the back of her shift, rubbing her hand there in a slow circle high between her shoulder blades.

Silvia murmured a soft sound of contentment and felt her edginess begin to ease. The circles gradually swooped lower to the small of her back and then lower still, over her bottom. At that, she glanced at Michaela over one shoulder, a question in her gaze. But Michaela's eyes were fixed on what she was doing. Her touch drifted lower from the terrain of fabric onto that of skin, the back of Silvia's thighs. Then it smoothed upward again in an unhurried sweep, dragging her shift higher until the fabric bunched at the small of her back and her bottom had been bared.

Silvia froze, staring down at her pillow now with wide eyes. Neither spoke for a long moment, and a palpable tension rose between them, fraught with possibilities. Then a fingertip came, drawing lightly upward along the crease that separated the ripe peach of Silvia's bottom.

She jerked away and rolled onto her side, facing her. "Michaela," she whispered, uncertain.

Across the pillow, Michaela's eyes were pools of dark violet. "Shhh. Don't look so scared," she whispered. Her mouth brushed Silvia's; then she drew back. "It's just touching, Via. I want you to know pleasure. It's not right that you shouldn't."

A warm palm came on her hip, and Silvia bit her lip, unsure whether she should hold it there or tear it away.

"It's wonderful with someone who knows what he's doing," Michaela promised. "When he puts himself inside you." Her hand drew down under Silvia's shift, covering her belly and gliding lower to find the nest of down at the apex of her thighs. "Here."

The hand squeezed gently, and as Michaela bestowed the gift of her preternatural warmth, a voluptuous sensation shot straight to Silvia's feminine core. Her nether lips plumped, pulsing at the surprising joy of it. She pressed her thighs tight, hugging the delicious feeling close.

She felt Michaela will her to speak, but her throat was thick with indecision, her muscles frozen. The only thing uppermost in her mind was that she absolutely did not want the glorious sensations to stop.

Silvia swallowed, hard. "I know that," she said faintly.

"No, you don't know anything, little innocent," Michaela said, sounding superior and half-amused.

Curiosity wound tight in her. "Is this what they teach you in your clandestine afternoon instruction?"

But Michaela only smiled that secretive smile that excluded Silvia from some wealth of knowledge that was an ever-growing wedge in their friendship. "It's wonderful, Via. You'll see. I want you to see, to feel, to know." She scooted closer, until their bellies met, and she smoothed Silvia's hair back, pressing a closed-mouth kiss to her damaged cheek. An arm curved over her waist and a hand came to hold the round of her bottom, squeezing and sending a pleasant tremor along already quivering tissues.

"Then show me," Silvia heard herself whisper. "I want to know what you know. I want to erase the chasm I feel widening in our experience." She rolled onto her back, and opened her heart and her body to the loving.

Michaela did nothing for a moment save gaze down at her consideringly. Then she cupped a hand at Silvia's jaw. Studying her mouth as if it were new to her, she ran a thumb over her lips. "Then close your eyes for me, dear Via," she said. "And think only of your handsome, swarthy fire juggler."

She waited until Silvia's lashes drifted lower, then murmured, "Now, imagine that his dark eyes are wandering over your body, burning over it . . . over your slender thighs, your flat belly. He likes what he sees and wants to explore. But first he wants your mouth under his again. Open for him, Via."

Soft lips angled over Silvia's, and the delicate preternatural buzz they imparted rippled over her, eventually settling in to nestle and throb within the moist cavern of her sex. Fingers tangled in her hair, holding her for the tongue that slid along hers. Silvia pulled back on a harsh inhalation, her head pressing deep into the pillow to gaze up at Michaela.

"You like his kiss." Brows raised, Michaela waited until Silvia nodded; then she moved her hand to lie upon Silvia's shift, over her breast. She squeezed gently, moving in an almost imperceptible circular motion, slow and easy, just enough so the drag of coarse fabric tantalized first one nipple and then the other. "You want to feel him here, don't you?"

Silvia thought of the fire juggler's dark, laughing eyes and roguish wink. Her "yes" came, barely perceptible.

"Then close your eyes again, Via." Silvia did. "And think of his wicked, scorching gaze on you. Of his dark watching eyes meeting yours across tonight's crowd at Calends. Think of him, dying to touch your flesh. Dying to lay his big, hot hands on you, running them up under your shift, pushing it higher." Silvia felt her shift rise, as actions were suited to words. "He exposes your plump, perfect breasts to the night air just so he can watch your pale pink nipples twist and tighten in the cool. He wants to mark you with his mouth, so you'll remember him tomorrow and know it was not a dream. So he bends closer and captures what he wants."

Silvia gasped as a hot mouth closed over the peak of her breast, suckling her gently at first, then nursing more strongly with thrilling nips of teeth, until both of her nipples stood hard and wet in the moonlight. Torturous lips blew upon them then, sending tremors of delight over her. Her moan soughed softly into the silence of the night.

"His white smile flashes, cocky. You've pleased him . . . but your Romanian . . . he's greedy. His mouth, his eyes, his body—they would all make a feast of you this night. And you want him to. It's what you longed for from the moment you set eyes upon him."

A hand slipped low, cupping her privates again. "You want his mouth here. His hot, rough breath and tongue licking fire between your thighs. You must tell him you want it. He doesn't wish to trespass where he is not wanted."

In her mind's eye, Silvia saw the fire juggler again—his sensuous lips and strong-boned, masculine face, his broad shoulders and powerful arms and thighs. "Yes, I want him," she whispered.

The warmth of a body came over her then, breast meeting breast. Lips touched the base of her throat. "Good," came a whisper. "He's glad." The body slid lower, then lower still until Silvia's legs parted for it naturally. She felt breath rustle her soft nest of curls.

"He has thought about you all this night—you with your legs pressed so primly together, sealed against him. As you sat on your virginal pedestal, he wondered about you. Wondered how you would taste. He yearned for a chance to find out if only you would look his way. If only you would let him."

The mesmerizing quality of the voice held Silvia in thrall and her fingers fisted in the sheets at her sides, every fiber of her being taut with anticipation.

A gentle fingertip came, tracing tender, blushing folds, and Silvia felt herself unfurl for it. Then came a tongue, wet and flat, licking her vulnerable, untried sex with a slow sweep of sweet fire.

Silvia sucked in a sharp breath between clenched teeth and her eyes squeezed tighter, hardly knowing what to do with the tangle of emotions that writhed in her at this new and pleasurable sensation. Her shaking hand lifted to blindly stroke over the dark head working between her thighs. Her knees rose and went wider. "A little harder," she begged. But her lover's tongue would only work over her with those slow, sensuous sweeps. The pad of a thumb found her small, sensitive nub and sluiced it with her own honey. And still that tongue lapped at her, wooing her toward pleasure with every stroke.

When it left her, Silvia made an unintelligible sound of protest. She felt warm puffs of breath against her slickness. "Why did you—he—stop?"

The mesmerizing voice lowered to an apologetic murmur. "I'm very much afraid he wants to fuck you, now that he's had a taste.

He's far, far too greedy, your Romanian. If you allow it, he will push his lovely, fat cock inside you and fuck you again and again and again, burning you with his fire until you go up in flames."

A taut silence fell.

Then a fingertip stroked once along the petals of her chaste slit and Silvia fought the impulse to agree. "My vows," she whispered.

"He won't fuck too deep. Nothing irrevocable. He likes his hot little virgin just as she is."

She wanted to believe, for at the moment nothing seemed more urgent than finding the ecstasy she sensed lay just out of reach. "Promise?"

"He knows what he's about. You'll still be virginal come morning."

"Yes, then," Silvia agreed breathlessly before she could change her mind.

Even as her words were dying away, thumbs pressed and drew upward on either side of that small, tender nub of her flesh, coaxing it from hiding and exposing it for the lash of a devilish tongue. It came at her again and again in wet, rhythmic pulses of erotic torment, laving over her. Silvia's chin rose and her back arched high from the pallet as she hung on the precipice of . . . something . . . wonderful.

Then that finger touched her again, pushing into her slick, shivering furrow until it met the fragile barrier of her maidenhead upon which it dared not trespass. It slid out again, only to return again with a partner. Two fingers, then three, four, all fucking her together in shallow, pulsing strokes. And then that sweet mouth closed over her nub, drawing on it in a single long, strong tug and with a small, ecstatic cry, Silvia gave in to the delicious fire of a very first orgasm.

16

Three weeks passed and Silvia began to fear she might never find the sixth stone. The knowledge that the other Vestals were still jailed was a cruel burden, one she'd carried for hundreds of years now. It was time to seek help. Now that Bastian knew what she was, perhaps they could work together to find the sixth stone. Perhaps she could convince him that her need for it was greater than his. If not, once he helped her find it, she would simply steal it from him.

And in truth, she missed him. And his bed. Having lain with him for a month as Michaela, she craved more. Some nights, she tossed and turned until dawn, remembering his touch and the hours they'd spent making love. For it *was* love on her part. Yet, still, she did not trust that it was love he felt for her. She wondered if he'd forgotten her, if he hated her. Or if he missed her as well.

So she traveled to Rome again, where she awaited Bastian's return for one week, passing the hours during his absence by searching his home and land yet again for the sixth firestone. She found nothing. Where was he?

Before he returned, she was sent to Naples by the needs of her host, Angelique, who had spent her girlhood there. Upon spending another few days making written arrangements for her rather glorious funeral, Angelique lay down in her mother's house and promptly passed away. Her death was put down to natural causes. As per her last wishes, she was to pass eternity in her family's cemetery plot, which included no space for her murdering husband.

Afterward, Silvia took her Ephemeral wraith form once again and returned to Rome. There, news quickly reached her that Bastian was to appear at an official government function in the heart of the city that night. Since this seemed the most expedient way to encounter him, and a venue in which he couldn't easily seek retribution for what she'd done to him when they'd last met, she went in search of a new host that might allow her easy entrance to the festivities. She'd hoped for a member of the waitstaff or the wife of a dignitary, but soon heard an even more suitable voice calling—one that drew her even as it repelled.

In the late afternoon, she found herself entering the apartments of a young, handsome gentleman who'd drunk himself into a coma and would soon die. A young politician in the Roman Ministry of Culture named Signor Tuchi.

Invisible now, she slipped into his bedchamber just as another man ran out of it. Furtively, he checked the hall, then noiselessly disappeared down the back stairs. He was only half-dressed, as if he'd come from an assignation.

Signor Tuchi was still inside, but he was not alone in his bed. She watched one of the two men remaining with him smack his face, trying to waken him. Looking terrified, the other was yanking on his own clothing as he backed away. She knew this man and searched her memory. Ah, it came to her. It was Ilari, the foreman from Bastian's excavations, who had so irritated Rico. Interesting.

"It's your fault! You bound him too tightly," Ilari accused, hopping as he tried to don trousers.

"He insisted! What was I to do?" the other man hissed.

"We can't leave him like this." The two turned to look at the minister's still figure, their gazes fearful. "To hell with the bastard," said Ilari. "He wanted it rough. He got it rough. It's not our fault. His own peculiarities are what felled him. I didn't even get my trousers off properly to get a good poke at him."

"Well, if you like fucking the dead, now's your chance," said his companion.

"He was the ticket to my fortune, dammit all!" Ilari railed. "The vote is tonight. But without him, what chance do I have at taking the job in the Forum as my own?"

Suddenly, Tuchi's body gave a hard twitch and both men jumped as if they'd seen a ghost. Then they promptly fled the room and the house, taking the same path as the first man had.

Once they were gone, Silvia loosened the tether that held Minister Tuchi's wrists fast to the headrails of his bed and she pulled the gag from his mouth. Human hosts did not last as long as those of ElseWorld origin, and this was not a man she would have chosen. But if she took him on, she could sway the vote in Bastian's favor tonight. This would be her gift to Bastian, a way of repaying him for what she'd stolen from him. And what she would steal.

A few minutes later, the minister was hers. His breath was sour from his drinking binge, but he wasn't as drunk as she'd assumed. It was the gag that had inadvertently suffocated him. After a brief, unpleasant bout of retching, she cleansed her mouth. The events of the minister's day and his life were easily read now that he was her host. He was married to a socialite who despised him because he was despicable. And he was corrupt. In her absence tonight, he'd invited three of his cronies to come here for an illicit assignation. All were *omosessuales*, who must hide what they were. In ancient Rome, things had been different, but there had still been prejudices even then.

Stumbling to the door, she threw it open to the hallway and roared to the servants in her adopted masculine voice. "Get me something for this headache, dammit!" Then, scratching her stomach, she added, "And a bath and some fucking dinner!" She felt guilty for disturbing servants in this way, but such treatment was what his household was accustomed to.

And although the thought of food turned her stomach, she had only the afternoon ahead to prepare for tonight. She and her new host had a big evening planned.

Bastian crossed the bustling Piazza del Campidoglio atop Capitoline Hill on foot, passing fine carriages that were lined up for blocks. Gaslight lanterns bobbed on their hooks in the gusty autumn wind, lighting the monumental marble staircase as he ascended and then entered the Palazzo Senatorio. *Polizia* had been stationed at every door to guard the treasures within this palatial building. As far back as ancient times, government records had been stored here, and during the Middle Ages, this was the center of civic government. And just two decades ago, the palazzo had finally been officially designated as Rome's city hall.

Tonight, everyone had gathered here to view and celebrate the spectacular finds he'd recently made in the Vestal Temple and House in the Forum. And he was to be the guest of honor.

Adjusting the cuffs of his jacket lower over white gloves, Bastian nodded to the guards and entered the palazzo, finding its interior ablaze with lights. Almost immediately, he felt the weight of expectations. Men of the highest political and social stature in Rome were gathered here. Learned men anxious to be fascinated by his tales of the Forum excavations. Greedy men who sought to build their own fortunes and careers on his discoveries. They all needed him in one way or another. Still, a few foolishly sought to unseat him.

His contract as lead archaeologist in the Forum was up for renewal, and the Parliament would vote later tonight on who would take charge of the digs. Over the past eleven years, the job had easily come his way with every vote, and all concerned had feted and wooed him, since it was obvious he was the best choice for the work. However, now the ambitious Minister Tuchi was set against him, and would rather give it to his foreman, the more biddable Ilari. He'd poisoned the minds of a small but influential set of politicians, and the vote was precarious at this point. Bastian didn't plan to let them win.

Over the months, he'd supervised the arrangement of the artifact displays in these rooms in preparation for tonight. It now appeared that flocks of giant crows had descended among them, for as the invitations had strictly defined it, every gentleman here wore black. This was fortunate for him, since it had made his dressing simple. However, his coat was the single hint of color in his wardrobe. An acquisition from his travels in the East, it was embroidered with an iridescent thread that in certain light revealed a pattern of gruesome mythical monsters. One could only hope they would keep some of the more annoying government officials at bay tonight.

The ladies here were dressed in fitted gowns, worn off the shoulders and with skirts that were beribboned and flounced and ornamented to an extreme. Fashion was of no consequence to him, but he'd despised the wide skirts of the previous era. The silhouettes were slender now and waists narrow, a look he much preferred.

"One wonders if there's a bird, bow, or ruffle left remaining in a single dressmaker shop," said a voice at his elbow. Turning his head, Bastian beheld one of his least favorite men in Rome, the youngest and newest of the Ministers in the Department of Culture—Signor Lino Tuchi.

"A joke? You surprise me, Minister."

A slight smile curved the man's lips and there was a secretly amused look in his eyes that confounded Bastian. "Expect more such surprises in the very near future." The minister nodded in parting, and as he moved past, the gazes of several ladies followed his progression. The pompous Parliament member was quite the dandy. His sleeve brushed Bastian's as he departed. And just as he was swallowed into the crowd, there was a flash of color. It was so quick that Bastian might have assumed it was his imagination if it weren't for the effect it had on his libido. He'd gone hard. As he dove into the melee after the man, he could only thank the Gods that his unusual coat hid the fact.

However, his progress was quickly impeded by the King of Italy himself, Umberto I. As he paused to speak with the man, the governor and other politicians swarmed, all eager to claim an acquaintance with him. Meanwhile the minister slipped out of sight.

"Wine, signor?"

Bastian nodded at the passing servant and accepted a goblet from his tray. Libations would be offered repeatedly unless he held a glass in his hand. The smell of the wine was enticing, but he wasn't the sort of addict who had an uncontrollable craving for the stuff—not as long as he totally abstained. So he only held the glass as a prop, as he led some of the more prestigious guests on an abbreviated tour of some of the major artifacts. All the while, a part of him was occupied with keeping track of a certain young minister. It wasn't difficult, since he continued to be the sole perceptible color in the room. When his quarry ducked down a corridor, Bastian quit a conversation mid-sentence.

A moment later, he caught up with him. "I would speak with you, Minister," he said. He took his companion's elbow and felt a disconcerting jolt of lust. Dropping it, he stepped back. He detested this man. And he was . . . a man. Gods, what the hells was happening here? He opened the nearest door at random, and finding the room beyond to be empty, extended an arm to indicate that the minister should precede him.

Instead, the minister countered, "I have an office on the upper floor where we can be private."

Bastian inclined his head. "Lead on, then." They were silent until they reached the small but elegantly furnished room upstairs. Closing the door behind them, Bastian watched the minister pour himself a glass of wine from a corner cabinet and then sit at his desk, crossing booted feet upon its surface.

The man gestured with his glass in the general direction of the festivities. "Congratulations on the exhibit. They're all wondering about you, you know. Wondering how you find treasures with such seeming ease." The minister cocked his head in a way that was oddly familiar.

Pushing from the door, Bastian redirected the conversation. "And do you know what I wonder, Signor Tuchi? I wonder what you know of Ephemerals."

The minister smiled secretively. He eyed the glass of wine he held, then took another sip. "Shouldn't you be asking me more pertinent questions? Such as how I will vote in the matter of your reinstatement?"

"You'll vote against me, of course. Because you stand to gain nothing by voting *for* me. And because you're an ass."

"True on both counts." The man smiled and, setting his wine aside, folded his arms behind his head. "Minister Tuchi is an ass. But *I* am not."

"Enough cat and mouse." Bastian went behind the desk and took him by the collar, jerking him up. Their bodies met and color exploded. His skin prickled, his cock hardening to rock. His fury rose with the attraction. "Who the fuck are you?"

"How deliciously powerful you are, signor. So masculine. But then, I am as well . . . tonight."

Silver eyes searched black. "It's you," Bastian accused in a voice gone low and intense.

Seeing the recognition in his eyes, Silvia shrugged, a movement that momentarily tautened the shoulders of the tailored jacket she wore over her slender masculine frame. She was the epitome of the handsome, stylish young gentleman tonight, garbed in stark black just as Bastian was.

He let her go, his gaze sweeping her and missing nothing. "You could have your pick of hosts, yet you choose to visit me in the form of a man? A man I despise?" A dark brow rose, speculative. "One wonders if this is some sort of test of my affections."

Her smile dipped and she sank into the chair again. "He was dying. I saw it as an opportunity to swing the vote in your favor. In spite of the fact that he wishes me to do the opposite. In fact, it was his last wish that I vote against you, and it will be the first Deathwish I've ever refused to grant. Excusable, however. Because as you say, he *is* an ass."

Folding his arms, Bastian half-sat on the desktop, looming over her. "An ass who has my opals."

"*My* opals," she countered softly. "And I'll be doing you a kindness in tonight's vote. A little thanks might be nice."

His eyes wandered over her. "Did you kill him? Not that I would mind. I'm only curious."

"You're constantly accusing me of mayhem," she said in irritation. "Ephemerals are not murderers."

"No, you only drug your lovers, leave them tethered to their beds, and steal their opals."

She stared into the wine in her glass, seeing her masculine reflection in its glossy surface. He'd said he loved her, but tonight she'd presented him with a sample of the very real difficulties that loving an Ephemeral would entail. If he was going to spurn her, let him do it now. She looked up at him through her lashes and asked quietly, "And in spite of all that, do you still profess to love me, Lord Bastian? Do you love me as I am tonight, hosted by a man—one you despise?" She reached out and ran a gloved fingertip down his shirt buttons, her eyes holding his, as she headed for his groin. Bastian grabbed her hand and knocked it away.

She smiled slightly and cocked her head. "What's wrong? Don't you want to fuck me?"

He glared at her drink, then took it from her and slammed it to the desktop with a sharp movement that told her he was angry. "You're drunk."

"No. Yes. A little." Putting a hand to her forehead, she grimaced. "I'm sorry. I told you, the personality of the host lingers in the early days, influencing my own. Don't blame me for everything I do and say here tonight. Some of the blame for any ugly temper—most of it at this point—must go to the minister."

She felt his interest pique. "Did Michaela influence you all those nights we were together?" he asked.

Slipping away from the chair, she made a slow circuit of the office and felt his hot gaze follow her. She paused at the far side. "At first. But she was there less and less every day we were together, you and I."

"Which means you were there more and more." Going to her, he planted his hands on perpendicular walls, boxing her in the corner. He studied her face, her masculine collar and tie. "Gods, how long will you be like this?"

"Male?" She smiled up at him. "I rather enjoy being male in some respects. Men have more privileges in this world. And bodily functions are certainly an easier matter. But this host will last for no more than a day or two. Humans aren't durable."

She ran her palms up his chest and tried to drive him away with the despicable truth. "I once scavenged ten human bodies in as many days, before settling into that of a fey for the entire month following."

Bastian straightened away and ran a hand through his hair.

Her hands fell to her sides. "Too horrifying? I warned you I'm difficult to love. Complicated. Run while you can, signor," she taunted in her soft male voice. "Before you are further embroiled with me."

He examined her for a long moment. Then without a word, he made for the door.

Silvia's heart thumped painfully in her chest, and she compressed her lips against the need to call him back. But it was as she'd expected. At the first true test of their fragile relationship, he'd quailed.

Snick.

She went to the desk, picked up her wine again, and took a long draught.

"Did you think I'd falter at this temporary hurdle?"

She glanced over her shoulder, startled to find him still inside the room with her. He'd only locked the door to afford them privacy. "It's not an invitation most men would accept."

Foolish hope rose in her as Bastian came to her and took her glass. Sniffing it, he frowned and set it aside. Then he lifted her to perch on the desktop before him. Nudging her thighs apart, he pushed between them and leaned close with his hands clasped on her upper arms. "I love you, Ephemeral. And I want you. No matter what shape you take, that will always be so." His mouth bussed her cheek, her temple. "If you're inviting me to hunt my physical pleasures in this body you've chosen, I accept. Gladly. With all my heart."

And with his every loving, accepting word, Silvia's doubt ebbed and she began to believe. A hesitant joy blossomed in her—sweet, new, and hopeful—and she turned her lips toward his, a flower to his sun. But he drew away, his superior height allowing him to easily keep his own lips out of reach.

She tugged off her gloves and let them fall to the desktop. "Kiss me properly," she pleaded, touching the side of his throat.

"You drank, so I cannot," he said, taking her hand and pressing a regretful kiss into its palm instead. "Not on your mouth."

"You're that sensitive to liquor? Of any kind?" Silvia pushed him back so she could read his eyes. "It's not just because I'm a man that you won't kiss me?"

"I promise you, I'll kiss you anywhere you like, except here." He pressed a finger to her mouth, then drew her hand to the buttons of his trousers, even as his own hand began unfastening hers.

"Have you made love to a man before?" she asked.

"I won't be making love to a man. I'll be making love to you—" Yanking off his gloves and tossing them away, he shot her a cross look. "What's your name, damn you?"

"You may call me Minister Tuchi," she told him archly.

He let out a snort of laughter. "I think I detect something of Rico's humor in you."

She smiled up at him, then abruptly gasped. Having opened her trousers, his big hands had gone inside to push them lower. She made a move to stop him.

"What's wrong?"

She blushed and reluctantly left him to it. "Nothing. I don't know. A man can't hide what he feels as a woman can."

"You have something to hide?" Tugging her to stand, he pushed her trousers wider, his tone teasing. "Ah. Yes, I see that you do, Minister." He wrapped a gentle fist at the root of her cock and gave her length a single, light stroke of his fist. She bit her lip and forgot to breathe. On his return trip, a soft moan escaped her.

The mood went suddenly dark between them, fraught with the anticipation of this new, forbidden act of love.

Hard hands turned her. Their bodies pressed close, his chest at her back. She felt him shove his own trousers to his knees behind her. Then the cleft of her bottom cradled his tall erection.

She licked her lips and whispered, "What if someone comes?"

"We're in your office. Simply order them away."

He reached over the desktop and took her glass of wine, and she heard him pour some of its contents in his cupped palm, then slick it over his length. "I'll hurt you if I don't use something," he murmured.

Ever the protector, even in this.

A hand clasped her hip, holding her. She felt the smooth head of him nudge between the cheeks of her rear. Felt the first pressure of his push.

Her breath caught. She turned her head slightly toward him and whispered, "He likes it . . . rough."

A pause. His hand flexed on her hip. "He? Or you?"

"Tonight we're one in the same. He cannot reach fulfillment through tenderness, which means I cannot while I am joined with him. He likes to be used. Likes it . . ."

"Rough," Bastian finished for her, his own voice gone gravely. She nodded and added in a whisper. "With little preamble."

He adjusted his stance wider and his voice came, hot against her nape. "Then that is how I shall endeavor to serve it."

She felt the subtle difference in how he held her then. His clasp was harder and more relentless; his body loomed somehow larger over hers, dominating her with the threat of his superior physical strength. He pushed his cock to angle downward between them so its head pushed at her scrotum. Then, he pulled upward, drawing his cockhead up her divide until it was well-seated at her anal opening.

His opposite arm bent over her linen-covered chest. She tasted the wine on his masculine palm as it covered her mouth. Then came a sharp push as his head pierced her. And she screamed into his hand as he took her, his thrust long, smooth, brutal. Tears formed in her eyes, trickling down her cheeks. But he only held her tighter to him with one hand on her mouth and one at her hip. And he fucked her, hard. And rough, with all of his strength, jolting her entire body with every slam of his hips at her bottom. With his every stroke, she whimpered, screamed, throbbed. Her trousers sagged lower, to her calves, then her ankles. And she moved swiftly toward release. Her own length twitched, and unable to help herself, she ran her fingertips over it.

The hand at her hip slid to palm her buttock and he squeezed hard, a sweet hurt. Then it slipped around over her belly and encircled her. Her cock jerked, bobbing upward under his touch. She gasped, never having felt such a sensation, and her hand sprang away. Her thighs quivered and blood coursed hot through her length, heating it.

"Put your hand under mine," he gritted at her ear, "and help me fuck you." When she hesitated, he slapped her haunch hard enough to make it sting. "Do it," he gritted. Her shaking hand joined his.

Together, they milked her prick with voluptuous strokes guided by the hands of men who knew how men liked to be held. The sensation of having him inside her while their hands masturbated her phallus was beyond anything she'd felt before. The sacs below her root drew up into painful fists. Semen was coursing through her cock, like passionate lava. And still the hot male at her back fucked her in long, deep thrusts that burned with sweet fire.

And then he came, deep and hot and wet inside her, and she screamed a final time into his hand. Explosions of white filled her vision like snowbursts. He shoved her knees together with his own, so he felt even bigger inside her as he spent himself. And she arched back against his chest as she spilled into her own hand. Together, they gently masturbated her length, slick now with her own seed. She shivered as cum welled up again and again with each stroke. When it became too much, she fell forward onto the desk, panting.

Eventually, he lowered over her, his chest warm along her

spine. His voice was thick and low with suppressed emotion as his lips brushed along her nape. "I miss the fall of your long hair," he told her. "If you stay a male, will you grow it for me?"

"Umm." She sighed, replete, lazy. "I won't *stay* anything. That's what you have yet to accept."

She felt him glance at the clock on the minister's desk. "Damn. Duty calls," he said. "I'm late for a speech." With a kiss at her nape and a fond caress on her bottom, he pulled out of her and went to wash himself with a pitcher of water he found in the liquor cabinet and a stock of handkerchiefs bearing the minister's monogram. She cleansed herself in the same way, and they straightened trousers and shirts, refastened buttons, found a comb in the desk and fixed their hair, and replaced their gloves.

"How will I find you again?" he asked as they made their way back to the gala.

"I'll find *you*." She glanced at him. "I actually came here hoping to discuss the opals, before we . . . got off track. I have five. And wondered if we might work together to locate the sixth."

"So that you might steal it from me as well?"

She glared at him. "My reasons for wanting the opals are not greedy, I assure you."

"Stay for the rest of the gala. Then come home with me," he urged as they neared the crowds in the palazzo. "And we'll discuss the matter. Among other things."

She shook her head. "I'll stay only long enough for the vote. This body is human. I can't remain in it." She looked away. She didn't want him to know the details of the ghoulish exercise she would undertake in order to divest herself of her current host.

"Look at me." When she did, he bent to her and kissed her on the lips, startling her and drawing shocked murmurs from those around them.

She jerked back, pushing at him. He let her go, but his eyes remained steady on hers. "Do as you must, then. And afterward, return to me."

Emotion welled up in her at his daring in making such a public claim on her while she was male, but she only shook her head and left him.

And behind her, he stood in the midst of the crowd and watched his lover go.

Scena Antica VIII

391 A.D.
Roman Forum

"*I took another lover,*" Michaela whispered one night as Silvia
was drifting off to sleep.

Silvia turned her head on the pillow, instantly alarmed. Since
the night of the scourging, Michaela hadn't admitted to any further
acts against her vows. But she disappeared now and then without
explanation, and Silvia had suspected. "Who this time?"

"Theodosius himself."

"No!" Silvia came up on one elbow. "The emperor? He's your
new lover?"

"Shhh. Not so loud." Michaela put a hand over her mouth.

Silvia tugged away. "How?" she whispered. "Where were you
that his wife didn't guess?"

"In his stable. I was veiled against the eyes of his servants. But
he knew who I was and has asked to see me again."

"Kayla, no, you'll be found out."

"I'm not asking for your approval. The only reason I tell you is to warn you of a danger I have discovered. There are rumblings of antagonism against the old gods. Talk of bringing down the temples."

Silvia stared at her. "That can't be."

"It's so, I tell you." She eyed Silvia speculatively. "Do you know what that could mean to us? If the Temple of Vesta is destroyed, we would be free. Free to marry. Have children. Be normal."

Silvia shook her head. "I made a vow."

"Under duress, when you were six."

"But since then, I've dedicated myself to Vesta. I'm bound to her now. And to the other Vestals as well. Kayla, I'm begging you. Don't see the emperor again. He has a jealous wife. She will make sure you are punished. Maybe the rest of us as well."

"In this time of political upheaval, my connection to him offers safety," Michaela argued.

"It's too dangerous, I tell you!"

But Michaela only smiled and shrugged. "What is danger to the likes of us? We play with fire every sixth night, after all."

17

"Sometimes I think sunlight might be the best antiseptic," Bastian muttered three days later.

"Are we still talking about the Council's missive?" asked Sevin.

Bastian nodded. "Look at all the effort we expend in hiding what we are from humans. If it was done with great care and diplomacy, might it not be better to reveal ourselves and negotiate the rules of our intermingling?"

"Heretical notions, brother," said Sevin.

His mood dark, Bastian only shrugged and went to gaze downward toward the main floor below from the smoked-glass window of Sevin's third-floor office in the *Salone di Passione*. He'd quit work in the Forum early today in order to meet with Sevin here on business. Another directive had arrived from the Council, this one with more dire predictions regarding the instability of enchantments that protected ElseWorld creatures from human detection in this world. And now evening was coming on, and fey courtesans were sallying forth from their chambers in the salon to mingle with patrons. His brother would invite him to stay and enjoy himself, but Bastian would make excuses. There was only one woman he desired. And she wouldn't give him her name.

As he observed the goings-on below, a comely female strolled through the main salon on her way to its front exit, her hips swaying in an exaggerated fashion that drew the masculine eye. She glanced up in his direction briefly, and Bastian's interest keened. "Who is that?"

Sevin looked up from his paperwork and supplied her name. "Christiana."

"An employee?"

Sevin nodded. "I'm surprised to see her up and about. I was told she'd taken ill. If you like, I could intro—" And then he was speaking to air, for Bastian had departed for the stairs.

Sevin's employee only just reached the sidewalk, when Bastian caught her arm, halting her. Her hair was the color of new butter and she wore a dress to match. Color. He went instantly hard.

"Where the hells have you been?" he demanded.

The woman smiled, obviously in a lighthearted frame of mind. "Good afternoon to you, too, darling." She offered no protest as he detained her, but only gave him time to examine her as he would. Her dress was high-necked and surprisingly prim, her breasts full, and her waist nicely turned. A single ringlet of blond hair hung artlessly over one shoulder, the rest gathered high. And the entire outfit was topped with a toque hat tipped with white doves' wings.

Eyeing it, he commented, "And here I thought you had an aversion to birds and ridiculous quantities of ruffle."

"You're thinking of my last host. My new host quite enjoys them. Keep up, will you?"

In spite of himself, Bastian smiled. Like Rico, she amused him. In fact, there were several pleasing qualities that threaded through all the personalities she'd thus far met him in. Wit, intelligence, and an interest in antiquities that matched his own. These, he assumed to be her own traits, rather than her hosts'.

Three days had passed since he'd seen her, and he was greedy to have her again. Wrapping an arm around her waist, he propelled her beneath a set of stairs that led up to a fashionable townhouse. There he pulled her close and pressed his lips on hers. An explosion of color assaulted him. His body reacted predictably.

"Satisfied?" she murmured when he eventually drew away. She straightened her hat, looking a bit dazed.

"Just making sure."

"Is that how you tell when it's me?" she asked, darting a look at him. "From a kiss? Or is it a touch? A glance?"

"That's information you'll have from me when I have your real name from you."

At that, she ducked under his arm and set off at a brisk pace. He fell in step. "So you're blond now," he observed.

She leaned his way and spoke to him in the manner one uses to confide to a fool who cannot comprehend the simplest matters. "It's dye, *monsieur*."

"*Et tu êtes également française?*"

Carelessly, she waved a gloved hand. "*Oui.* I am both blond and French. You are very observant."

"And you're named Christiana this time?" he asked casually. "Fey, by the scent of you."

"Right again. I am the very lovely, very vain, very flirtatious, very recently almost-dead Christiana, who spent the last two days in bed with a terrible fever. And who, to all appearances, is now recovered." She sighed blissfully. "A miracle, *n'est-ce pas?*"

"I want to be alone with you."

She nodded easily. "My host has that effect on most gentlemen who meet her. But first I have business with this lady." She paused, tapping the shoulder of a young woman they'd come upon. "For you, Sabina. With my apologies." She pressed a letter into the hands of the acquaintance, who glanced at it as if unable to believe her good fortune. Then taking Bastian's arm, Christiana moved off down the sidewalk again.

"It's a letter my host was using to blackmail her," she informed him in answer to his unspoken question.

"Ah, another Deathwish granted by the good fairy . . . um, what was your name again?"

She smiled slightly. "Christiana repented her malicious blackmail at the last moment. She's actually rather a sweet person in general."

Bastian stared down at her, imagining again how lonely her existence must be. Concern for her welled up in him. "Are there more like you? Other Ephemerals to give you counsel, now that Michaela is gone?"

Her step quickened as if to run from his compassion. Did she think accepting it would make her weak? She was always so careful, so wary. Something in the worlds threatened her, and he would damned well find out what it was if it was the last thing he did.

"Let us talk about something more interesting," she suggested. "Opals, for instance."

"Very well." Drawing her to a halt, he took her handbag from her. "Let's begin with the matter of their current hiding place." Her blue eyes watched as he squeezed her bag's softness in his fist and then returned it to her, having determined by feel that it didn't contain any of the jewels.

She slipped the slender straps of the handbag over one wrist and canted her head at a flirtatious angle. "Would you like to look under my hat now, *monsieur*?"

He brushed that long blond curl behind the shell of her ear and laid a hand on the side of her throat, his thumb stroking her high, stiff collar. "Under that and other items of your clothing," he informed her bluntly. "Tell me, exactly how many opals exist? Six? Or are there more?"

"Take me home with you to Esquiline. To your bed. And maybe I'll tell you."

"What, you've no thieving to do tonight? No foraging for carcasses?" Taking her arm, he stepped to the curb and immediately hailed a conveyance.

Although thieving was precisely what Silvia had on her mind, all she said was, "Fortunately, I have an adequate host at present, as you see. Therefore, I'm free to focus on you." She entered the closed cab he'd called and then waited for him to join her.

"And as it happens, I have a particular need of you at the moment," she admitted when he sat across from her.

He lifted a sardonic brow and pulled her to sit sideways across his lap. "I cannot wait to hear it."

She tugged at the cuffs of her gloves. "Well, it seems that Christiana has another wish, which I promised to oblige."

"Which is?" His fingers began working to open her bodice.

"That she might achieve sexual fulfillment a half-dozen times tonight."

He chuckled, one hand gliding under silk and lace to find her breast. "You're joking."

At his touch, she murmured softly and went boneless against him, resting her head on his shoulder. "I assure you I am not."

"That was one of her dying wishes?"

She nodded and peeked up at him. "But if you're not up to the task . . ." Her hand wandered between them, high on the front of his trousers. She smiled. "Oh, I see that you are. How nice for all concerned. Might I suggest that we make an agreement to reciprocate in this reaching of fulfillment? I think you'll find my current host's talents quite to your liking." Her eyes turned teasing. "Her specialty is that of school miss."

"Gods," he said, laughing.

Silvia sent him a stern look, then put a gloved hand to his chest. "However, there is one thing I must caution you about."

His brows went up again.

"Well, I'm sorry to tell you that poor Christiana has been rather naughty of late. The blackmail and all. I'm afraid you'll have to administer some discipline in order to . . . help her along with the matter of her fulfillment."

"I see," he said, intrigued. He nudged the opening of her bodice wider and his eyes darkened as he watched his hand cup the warm weight of a pale, voluptuous breast. His thumb brushed its tip, once, again, then was joined by a forefinger. They rolled her pink nipple between them until it tautened, then gently pinched. Her cheeks flushed and she shifted on his lap, aroused.

His eyes met hers. "An unseemly display for an innocent school miss," he said softly, wickedly. They shared a slow, mutual smile.

"Abundant to be sure," she agreed.

The mood between them altered then, easing toward passion. His dark head bent and he took her nipple into his mouth, drawing deeply and laving her with his sandpapery tongue.

Her head fell back on his strong shoulder, as her desire for him heated. As if some erotic sash connected parts of her body, she felt the pull of his suckle high between her legs. "Umm." Her face turned toward him so that she could kiss his throat, and her gloved hand went to his cheek.

"Tell me," he asked, as he moved to tend her other breast. "Has . . . Christiana . . . ever been with a man? Intimately?" His hand went under her skirt.

"Certainly not," she murmured, as the warmth of his touch moved over her stockinged ankle, her knee, her garters, and higher still. "She's an untried schoolgirl, *monsieur*. But very bright and interested in acquiring new skills."

"Excellent. I only work with the most promising of students." His hand slipped between her legs, and she gasped when he found her slickness. "And she does seem . . . promising."

"You'll have no complaint with her work," Silvia assured him earnestly.

His fingers left her and went to the fastenings of his trousers. "I'm afraid I can't take her word for that. I'll want to put her skills to the test before taking her on as a student."

She glanced toward the window, seeing they'd only just begun the climb uphill to Esquiline. "Is there time?"

"We'll make this first test a quick one," he assured her. Lifting her off him, they worked together to push up her skirts.

"But one with the desired result," she insisted, as he brought her to straddle him.

He nodded with arrogant confidence. "The remaining five 'fulfillments' can occur in a more leisurely fashion. In my bed—and perhaps on other furniture that might suit."

She widened her eyes, guileless. "I look forward to your furniture *and* your instruction, *monsieur.*" Then she looped her arms around his neck, pressed her mouth on his, and sank over his cock.

"My father would have liked you," Bastian told her two hours later.

Lying on her back next to him among the sumptuously rumpled covers of his bed, Silvia turned her head to look at him. "What?" she asked, thinking she must have misheard.

Bastian rolled toward her, his hand going around her to shape her buttock. She winced.

"Are you all right?" he asked, going up on one elbow to gaze down at her. His hand traced over the reddened marks his loving had left here and there on her body. To induce her sixth and final orgasm, he'd put the nearly naked Christiana over his knee and smacked her soundly before setting her on his own naked lap for "instruction."

278 / Elizabeth Amber

She nodded, smiling. "It was wonderful, Bastian. Thank you. From me *and* Christiana." She lifted her head and kissed him, then fell back to the pillow feeling rather pleasantly limp. Something scratched her leg, and she reached down to find the whipcord-thin branch he'd plucked from one of his birches on the way into his house. Her rump and the backs of her thighs bore the rapidly fading stripes it had left on her, precipitating orgasm number three. Picking it up, she tossed it to the floor. "You were saying? About your father?"

"Only that he would have liked you. And my mother would have as well."

"What happened to them—your parents?" she asked, studying him.

His expression closed against her and she thought he wouldn't answer. But after a long moment, his voice came into the quiet. "*I* happened to them. Their gifted son. The one the earth spoke to, whispering its secrets and leading me to discover treasures. It began with the lost petroglyphs in ElseWorld when I was five."

Her eyes widened. "Your father is credited with that find."

"He took credit to protect me from the Council. But they found us out when I made another discovery during his absence."

"And because of your talent, they sent you and your family here to excavate the Forum?" she guessed.

He nodded. "With orders to find and secure any artifacts that might hint at ElseWorld kind's existence."

"What happened?" she asked again.

"We'd been here for six years when both of my parents got the Sickness. If not for me, we would never have come. They might still be alive."

Silvia put a tender hand to his cheek. It broke her heart to imagine him as a grieving youth suddenly left to fend for himself in an unfamiliar world, while shouldering the responsibilities of three younger brothers and the excavations. "So you repay them for their sacrifice by carrying on their work."

He caught her hand under his. "Don't pity me, *cara*. And don't make me into some heroic figure. The night they died was a Moonful—my first Calling. During the ritual, I had my first taste of wine, and afterward, I deserted my brothers, who needed me."

"Under the wine's influence," she protested, defending him when he would not defend himself.

He shrugged. "Eventually, I escaped its pall and returned to my brothers. To the excavations. It's work I love." He kissed her palm. "Work I want to share with you."

She stiffened, wary. "What do you—?"

"These furtive visits—never knowing when or if I might see you again. It's not enough," he told her with soft determination. "I want to share my life with you."

Stunned, she slid from him and drew up to sit against the headboard, pulling the sheet over her nakedness. "You ask too much! I can't just decide to become mortal on a whim." Pontifex's captives depended upon her and she would need her Ephemeral powers in order to manage their rescue. Who knew how long it might take to free them? The kindest thing would be to leave this man and never return. Then he could find someone else to love. Her heart twisted painfully at the prospect.

Bastian's hand slipped under the sheet, caressing her ankle, her calf, the back of a knee. "I'm not asking you to become mortal. Take whatever hosts you will, whenever you must. I only ask that you bring them—and yourself—to my bed. Every night. And that you spend what days you can with me."

A poignant joy washed over her at the sincerity and raw hunger in his voice. But still she held him off. "Gods, Bastian. Do you really want that sort of life for yourself?"

"Yes."

She shook her head. There was so much he didn't know. So

much she couldn't tell him. Not yet. He wanted to keep the opals here, but she needed to take them. It put them at odds. She glanced toward the door. "I—"

"Don't run," he said, tugging her down to him. "That's all I ask for now. Sleep on it. We'll talk on the morrow."

Sliding lower, Silvia curled into him, her head on his shoulder and one smooth thigh between his. A lazy hand stroked her hair, lulling her toward slumber. She felt the strength of his heartbeat under her palm and wished they could be together like this always.

She brushed a fingertip over Christiana's smooth cheek, over the place where her own father's whip had cut her centuries ago. "I'm scarred." Her stark, whispered admission tumbled into the quiet. "Imperfect. Here, on my face."

The hand on her hair paused. Then his lips brushed the crown of her head. "It's not your face or your figure I've come to love. It's you. Whether you're mortal or Ephemeral or something in between, my feelings for you are not going to change. And I'm hardly perfect myself."

Joyful tears filled her eyes, and at that moment, she fell even deeper in love with him. Still, she shied away from furthering such an emotional discourse and sought to lighten the mood. "Yes, it's truly sad how imperfect you are," she teased gently. "Tall, handsome, intelligent, wealthy. It's a wonder any woman would have you."

She heard the smile in his voice as he replied, "Then you'll have to take pity on me, for if you won't have me, who will?"

If only she *could* have him! If only she dared reveal her name and her real form to him so that she was rendered forever mortal. The never-ending cycle of taking hosts and relieving herself of them had begun to chafe, and with all her heart, she longed to stay here and build a life with him. She now understood precisely why Michaela had made herself mortal for him. She understood that love for the right man made such a choice easy. It was a choice she would now gladly make if she could.

But first she had a duty to the others and must see it through. Tomorrow she would take possession of the sixth opal. If her plan succeeded from there, she would free the other Vestals from Pontifex's clutches.

Only then—perhaps then—she might return here. And one day truly belong to this wonderful man, and he to her.

Scena Antica IX

391 A.D.
Roman Forum

A hand shook Silvia and Michaela awake in their alcove. It was Aemilia rousting them from their shared bed. Outside their window, the inky black of night was dotted with torches in the distance.

"What's happening?" Silvia demanded in alarm.

"They're destroying our temples," the girl whispered, looking frightened.

"I warned you this day was coming!" said Michaela, as they leaped from the bed.

Floronia joined them in the alcove, wide-eyed. "They're disbanding everything. Ending all pagan worship. Turning away from the old Gods. Vesta will surely be next."

"What are we going to do?" asked Aemilia, her voice quavering.

Silvia gave her a quick hug. "All will be well, cara. Come, let's gather the others. We'll take the firestones and flee."

Moments later, all twelve Vestals had scurried from the house to the temple, dressed only in their shifts. The sound of monumental *pillars toppling and the clamor of the crowds in the distance was terrifying.*

Together, they mounted the temple steps. Each of them plucked her opal from Vesta's Hearth and clasped it tight as they solemnly watched the fire die away.

Then questions flew among them. "Where will we hide the stones? Where will we go? How will we live?"

Occia waved a hand toward the bloodthirsty mob coming their way. "Do you think they'll just let us go, you fools? We stand for all they wish to destroy. We'd be constant reminders of the past, of the pagan religion. No—they'll put us on trial and make a spectacle of us, then bury us in the Campus Sceleratus!" Several girls began to sob.

"Calm yourselves," Michaela scolded.

"Let's separate for now and agree to meet at some landmark one week from tonight," suggested Silvia.

"Or we could go to ElseWorld to join the temple there," said Aemilia.

"How?" Occia scoffed. "The gate between worlds lies in Tuscany, which is hundreds of miles from here. No, I'm leaving on my own. Now. To hells with the rest of you." But when she turned to go, they saw that it was too late. The mob had reached them, some already on the steps.

"Look! Vesta's fire has returned!" cried Floronia. As one, the Vestals looked toward the hearth and gasped to see it burning bright again.

"I don't understand. It was snuffed out by the taking of the stones," said Michaela.

"Yet it burns once more," Silvia murmured in wonder. "It's a miracle."

Then Vesta's sacred fire leaped out, surrounding the temple and enclosing them in a firewall that kept the mob and their hatred at bay. The temple began to fill with smoke. The Vestals huddled close and took it into their lungs, coughing and choking.

"Something's happening to me," whispered Licinia, sounding horrified.

Silvia glanced at her, shocked to see that her form was wavering and growing indistinct. For a moment, she was pale as a statue. Then suddenly as translucent as a wraith. Silvia glanced down at herself. Saw the same thing was beginning to happen to her own body and to those of the others.

"Run!" shouted Michaela, grabbing her hand. Before the process was complete, she and Michaela fled with their stones. In the confusion, they ran toward the Vestal House and through its front door, intending to flee out its back to elude the mob.

"My fingers are weakening. I'm going to drop my stone soon," Michaela wailed as their bodies grew ever more translucent.

"Give it to me," said Silvia. Quickly, she hid both of their firestones in the hands of Vesta's statue. "Keep them safe," she whispered to the goddess. The mob entered the house but didn't seem to notice either of them as they dashed out the door at the far end of the atrium.

As they would later discover, the other Vestals had scattered through the Forum and beyond. All twelve were phantoms now and went unseen by their pursuers. And as they made their wild escape, some lost their firestones and others hid them for safekeeping.

An hour later, Silvia and Michaela stood on the ridge overlooking the Forum, their lungs heaving from their flight. Their goddess had protected them in the only way she could. They were now invisible. Immortal. Ephemeral.

Hands clasped, they stared down at the temple, watching its destruction.

18

The following morning, Bastian's lovemaking was a tender, poignant torment, for Silvia alone knew it might be their last. Afterward, she pretended to sleep, waiting until Bastian left for the digs. She listened to the door slam behind him and heard the sound of his horse as he departed. Then she rose and donned one of his shirts, pulled a long wooden support slat from beneath his mattress, and padded down the hall with it. Entering his study, she went unerringly to the large bookcase that hid his secret vault.

Although he didn't know it, she had come here two nights ago while in her Ephemeral wraith form. Invisible, she'd patiently spied on him all evening, and had finally been rewarded when he led her here to this vault, unaware that he was doing so. She had stood silent, only a few feet away from him, and watched him dial the lock. Then she'd gone inside the vault with him and seen that he possessed the sixth opal.

And now she had come to steal it from him. Since the bookcase was too heavy to budge on her own, she'd brought his bed slat. Using it as a wedge between case and wall, she managed to send the bookcase crashing to the floor.

Then she dialed the lock's combination from memory, opened the thick steel door, and entered the vault. Crossing to the glass-fronted jewel case, she reached toward it, then froze in shock. For inside on a velvet cushion sat not one opal, but all *six!*

"Looking for something?" She whipped around to see Bastian standing in the vault's entrance. "Why didn't you simply agree to my proposal that you stay, *cara?* Then all six could have been yours."

"How did you find the opals I brought with me?" she demanded, gesturing toward them in the case.

"I assume you refer to the five you buried in my garden for safekeeping two days ago?"

She nodded grimly, as anger and wariness fizzed in her veins.

He leaned a shoulder against the doorframe, crossing his arms and studying her. "You left a trail, and I followed it."

"What kind of trail?"

He smiled slightly, infuriating her with his smugness. "One only I can perceive. I tracked it to your five opals, unearthed them, and then I waited for you to make an appearance. You made sure I would notice you in Sevin's salon yesterday morning. So I joined you on the street, and then I let things play out." His voice went soft. "And now here we are."

"Was last night some cruel trick, then? Your professions of love only lies all along?"

"No, damn you." Straightening, he made as if to come for her.

Snatching the cushion with its stones from the glass case, she held it before her with both hands supporting the cushion. She backed away as he advanced, warding him off. "These opals belong to Vesta and to those who serve her. Let me take them, Bastian. I must." Without waiting for his reply, she quickly blew across the stones and summoned a wall of flame.

At the same moment, he picked up something from the floor just inside the vault and swung it toward her. *Splash!*

Startled, she cringed away, dropping the cushion. The stones scattered at her feet. Then she just stood there, sputtering and wringing droplets of water from her hands. As his arms came around her, she blinked up at him. He'd come prepared with a bucket of *water?* He must have known all along that she would come here to steal the jewels. And now he'd extinguished the firewall!

"You . . . idiot. You don't know what you've done. You don't know anything!"

"Then tell me."

Her eyes narrowed, furious at his trickery. "I'll show you instead." Instantly, she—Christiana—went limp in his arms. Then, with a sigh, she slumped to the floor, dead. He stepped back, shocked at the sight of her divesting herself of her host.

Now in her invisible Ephemeral form, Silvia went to the door of the vault, hoping to distract him. "There, you see?" As she'd expected, he turned toward the entrance at the sound of her disembodied voice. "This is how I live—taking bodies and departing them," she told him, gazing at Christiana's limp form beyond him. "Unpleasant, is it not?"

"If it's so unpleasant for you, why not become mortal? Why not stay with me?"

"Because there's a horrible man, Pontifex, and he, he—" Frustration filled her and she bit off her explanation. He knew nothing of her situation and now was not the time to explain. Knowing she couldn't carry the stones while in wraith form, Silvia made the only decision she could. Slipping around him again, she knelt beside the opals. Keeping one eye on him as he made a visual search of the vault for her, she quickly assumed her own corporeal form and then gathered the stones low in the lap of her shift.

Slowly, she rose to face him, her long sunset-gold hair unbound and her eyes a clear blue. His gaze roved her, hungry for this first glimpse of her as her true Ephemeral self. She felt betrayed, exposed. Embarrassed at having him see her as she was, disheveled and scarred. "And so now you have what you desired," she told him, despising the betraying quaver in her voice. "The sight of my damaged corporeal form. But you'll never, ever have my name from me!"

Bastian lunged for her, then recoiled from the heat of the new firewall she created. "Stop, damn you!" he shouted.

"What, no second bucket of water?" she asked, her voice cool now and devoid of emotion. "How exceedingly careless of you not to have anticipated such a necessity, signor."

And then she stepped into the wall of fire and was gone.

Scena Antica X

391 A.D.
Roman Forum

"It's strange, this new Ephemeral existence of ours," said Silvia, gazing down at her translucent hands.

"But exciting," said Michaela. "Just think—no one can see us."

Less than a day had passed since the night of the destruction of Vesta's temple.

"And watch this." Silvia cupped her palms and blew lightly across them. A vertical wall of fire flared before her, like heat wavering in the air on a blistering summer afternoon. Something pulled her toward it. Mesmerized, she stepped into it, hardly hearing Michaela's shriek of terror at her action. And suddenly, she was through it and in ElseWorld and then back again beside Michaela.

Michaela stared, astonished. "What was that?"

"A firegate," said Silvia. And then Michaela tried it, succeeding as well.

"Only imagine what we might do with such a wondrous thing," said Silvia. "It could change the worlds."

Occia was at that precise moment discovering the same ability and showing off her talent to Pontifex.

And he was imagining far more nefarious uses for it.

19

Occia lay facedown on the desktop, grunting lazily as Pontifex's cock rocked in and out of her. They were in his private office and he stood at his desk, his thighs moving between hers, his mind on business. They'd been at it for hours, and her flesh was burning and chafed. But she loved nothing more than the feel of this powerful man mating her. As was usual in these sessions, a four-legged tray had been set over the desktop to bridge her back, so that Pontifex could stand between her thighs and still manage his paperwork atop the makeshift workstation. His wealth and power acted on her like strong aphrodisiacs. And with every scribble of his pen or rasp of paper as he turned a page, he only grew more wealthy and powerful. And her need for him rose.

"I have a task for you, Occia," he told her suddenly, jarring her from her sensual trance. "I want you to lure the eldest Satyr here to my throne room."

"Lord Bastian? Why? And by what means?"

"Because I instruct you to. Use any means." Ceasing his work, he set the tray aside.

"And what will you do," she glanced pointedly at where he was joined to her, "during my absence?"

"As I please," he said with quiet menace.

"It's the same every Moonful now," she accused. "You find an excuse to rid yourself of me on the chance that Silvia will come again. So that you can fuck *her*."

"My dear, if I wanted to be rid of you, you'd already be in the moat. And I'll fuck who I like."

To prove his point, he pulled out of her and waved another victim over from a trio of Lares seated on a floor cushion to assume her place. He thrust into his new choice as Occia watched, knowing how it wounded her when he did. Each time he'd stabbed himself in another woman over the centuries, it was like a stab in her heart.

Yet, Occia had been generous. She had let him have them all. But he could not have *her*—not Silvia. Because she feared what would happen if he ever managed it. It seemed that Silvia must be the one the Oracle had prophesied would bear his child. The one he hoped would lead an army. What place would there be in his life for Occia then? She'd given him so many centuries of love. But he didn't care. His ambitions were all that mattered to him.

Hate filled her as she watched him fuck another, even as tears filled her eyes. Still, as she turned and walked away, she yearned for him to call her back.

Silvia strode over the carpet runner toward the throne of her nemesis. Whispers followed her progress. She hadn't been in Pontifex's lair here in ElseWorld for five months.

"Well, well. Finally she comes," Pontifex called out, his tone dripping sarcasm. "What have you brought me? Better be something good."

She remained silent until she reached him. This time, she

went close, to the very edge of the moat, and glared at him across it. "I have the firestones."

Pontifex's greedy eyes searched over her. "How many? Where?"

"All six." She held her arms out toward him. And in her cupped hands were six stones.

He brushed the woman who currently serviced him away from his lap and made as if to rise. For once, it wasn't Occia, she noted in surprise.

Silvia lowered her hands toward the sizzling water. "If you or your guards come closer, I swear I'll drop them in this moat."

He searched her eyes, and seeing her determination, he sank back. "How tiresome. What do you want in exchange for them?"

Your destruction. "Information. To start. Why did you have Michaela killed?"

He flicked a hand, as if irritated by this trifling matter. "It struck me that since she'd gone and made herself mortal, you could take her as host. And that at Moonful, it seemed likely you would fall into Lord Satyr's clutches. It's widely known that the Satyrs' semen enhances the power of another man's seed."

"You planned to bed Michaela and me that night, when we were bonded together? Hoping for a child?" She shivered, repulsed.

"I even had one of my guards spike that bastard Satyr's drink, so that he would lose his mind and I would be able to steal you. But that plan came to naught when he locked you up with him in his guarded love nest in that salon of his brother's." He *tsked*. "A shame. But that's neither here nor there now. Michaela's dead. My scouts found only a trace of her ashes. You were thorough."

Rage filled her, but she tamped it down. She'd come here with a plan and would not ruin it by letting her emotions run riot. "I didn't want her decorating your throne. You'd hurt her enough, you filthy bastard."

"Careful," Pontifex warned quietly. "I took nothing she didn't offer."

"You raped her for centuries."

"Every Moonful. Like clockwork," he said, unrepentant. "She was a delicious piece of work, your Michaela. But she's dead now and I've given you your information." He leaned toward her. "Now, give me the stones."

Noting the guards creeping nearer, she extended her hands lower toward the moat. "Tell them to keep away, or—"

When he waved a hand toward the guards, they backed off. "What the hells do you want?"

"Release the other nine Vestals you hold captive. Once they are free of this place, I'll give you the stones." After a pause, he inclined his head and hope rose in her. "And once I do, you'll let me go as well," she added.

"No," he said, and her heart sank. "That I'll never do. You see, I made a vow to your father. After Vesta's temple was destroyed all those years ago, he approached me." Pontifex reached up, blindly caressing a skull lodged in his throne just above his own head. It was aged, and was one of the more garish decorations, for its eye sockets had a wistful, hungry cant, and it still bore a shank of copper-colored hair.

Silvia's breath stopped as she stared at it—really stared at it for the first time.

"Yes, I can see you've guessed that it's your father," Pontifex told her. "Over the centuries, he has watched from my throne as you came here to me each Moonful with your tithes. Just as he watched you all of your life, plotting for your future."

"Explain yourself."

"It was pathetic really, the way he would spy on you. Sometimes he crept into the Vestal House to gaze upon you in your virginal bed late at night. And he would lust for you. And hate himself for it." Pontifex winced and shifted in his chair. Obviously hurting for lack of a woman, he began stroking himself. "After the temples were destroyed and we knew what the Ephemerals could do, he came to me with a proposition. Through you and the other Vestals, we would create children, he said. An army that could produce firewalls at will, and use them to steal and plunder. We would become rich and powerful men."

"But we didn't cooperate."

He shook his head ruefully. "Your poor father, ruled by his passions." His hand stroked her father's skull again. "He wanted so desperately to fuck you himself, but feared reprisal from his Gods and his wife. Instead, he begged me to kill him so that he could finally take what he wanted through me. So I murdered him. And I ate his flesh so he would forever be part of me. And before I did so, I promised him that one day we would fuck you—together." He rose and came to stand across from her at the edge of the moat. "I think today will be that day."

She shook her head, horrified, and stepped dangerously close to the moat's edge. "I'll jump in before I'll let that happen," she warned.

"But what will happen to your little friends then?" He waved toward the Wall of Doors; then she heard a rumble as the bridge began to move toward her to link the banks between them. "Come now, be reasonable. We've been waiting so long for you, your father and I. Be a good girl and obey his last wish. Let us lie together. And through you I will create an Ephemeral army."

Seeing a glowing phenomenon suddenly appear just beyond him and guessing what it likely was, Silvia said, "What of Occia?"

"That slut?" He flicked a hand. "She's nothing to us. Nothing to me. If you want her dead, then so be it. When she returns from her errand, I'll put paid to her."

"Bastard!" Behind him, Occia appeared in a blaze of fire and flew at him across the room. "I knew it! You sent me on a fool's errand only to be rid of me, so that you could have her." In a move that took him off guard, she rushed him and hit the back of his knees. He toppled, splashing without fanfare into his own moat. Within seconds, bubbles were all that was left of him. Occia stood there, cursing him and brushing furious tears from her eyes. "Die, you thankless prick."

"I couldn't agree more," said Silvia. Cupping the stones to her chest, she began to run toward the Wall.

Occia sent her a hateful gaze and motioned to the guards to apprehend her. When they hesitated, she tossed out a firewall, incinerating one of them. The remaining guards quickly did her bidding, grabbing Silvia's arms and taking the stones from her. When they were given to Occia, she only laughed and tossed them into the moat. "You brought worthless rocks? You always were a clever girl."

Flouncing away, she flung herself onto Pontifex's throne, drawing gasps and whispers from others in the background at her audacity in usurping the place of honor.

"Did you really think I would bring him the real opals?" asked Silvia.

"You mean these?" Lifting a pouch from her pocket, Occia held it upside down and let the six firestones tumble to her lap.

Silvia gasped. "How did you—"

"Pontifex sent me after your lover just in time to witness that touching scene between the two of you in his vault. Afterward, I saw you bury the opals for safekeeping at the edge of his property before you came here, and so I took them."

"You brought them through the gate when you were in Ephemeral wraith form?"

Occia smirked, nodding. "A talent I acquired by fucking

Pontifex. He'd absorbed some interesting abilities through those he cannibalized. And he passed some of them on to me via his seed."

Silvia gave a hard jerk of her shoulders, trying to wrest away from the guards. "We were friends once, Occia. In the name of that friendship and our goddess, let us open those nine doors at last and free the others."

"Nine?" Occia made a *tsking* sound. "A clever girl like you should be able to count more precisely than that."

And it was then Silvia noticed that a new, tenth door had been added! Their eyes met, and Silvia recoiled, guessing what she had planned. "No."

"I believe Pontifex had meant me to occupy it," Occia mused. "However, I make the decisions now." She nodded to the guards. "Put her with the others."

Silvia struggled, but four guards were more than she could overpower, and without clasping her hands together, she could not create a firegate to escape. "What are you planning?"

"It occurred to me that I can make children myself, without Pontifex. Any one of these guards will accommodate me. I will make the army he longed for—an army of Ephemeral children who can move about the worlds by use of firegates. Only they'll do my bidding, not that of Pontifex or your father." Her gaze went to the moat where only a few bubbles remained as evidence that her lover had ever existed. Her voice went a little sad and wistful, for she obviously mourned him in spite of herself. "I'll be the one made rich and powerful. The only Vestal who still roams free."

Then the world went dark as Silvia was knocked unconscious.

When Silvia woke again, all was inky blackness. She reached out, and her hand bumped into an unyielding wall. Blindly, she reached in another direction. And encountered another wall.

And another and another. There were walls above and below and on all sides of her. Walls so close that she could not quite stand completely straight or lie flat. Hysteria bubbled and she squelched it, forcing herself to calm. Her knee bumped something. An oil lamp. Her hand felt around and found water and bread.

Her heart thumped in terror. Occia had buried her alive, like the others! None of these three items she'd been allotted were meant to be used. They were merely symbols to remind her that she was well and truly snared. Ancient Roman magistrates had decreed that oil, water, and bread would be supplied to any Vestal who had violated her vows and been sentenced to entombment in the Evil Fields. The Wall of Doors was encased in a form of magic, which would keep her alive without sustenance or fresh air. Forever.

She pounded the walls on all sides of her, then paused periodically to listen. She'd hoped to hear a reciprocal sound from one of the other Vestals entrapped nearby in the Wall as she was, but all was silence. As the hours passed, she considered every possible manner of escape, no matter how unlikely. Were she to create a firewall in this small space, she would only incinerate herself and possibly some of the others.

Suffocated by the dark and her own fear, she succumbed to panic. "No!" she shrieked, thrashing inside her prison. But in this she only succeeded in bruising herself.

Worst of all was the knowledge that she'd failed the others. Now no one would come to save them. And she would pass the centuries here, like the others whom she'd pitied for so long. All of them doomed to a living death.

And Bastian would never know she loved him.

Time passed slowly. Hours, days, weeks. She slept little and swam in and out of consciousness. She heard nothing, saw nothing. There was nothing to occupy her mind except hopelessness. At some point, she began to hallucinate. She saw family members, long dead. And friends. And Bastian. Always Bastian. Visions of him haunted her, making her feel when she wished to be numb.

At times, she was comforted when he whispered to her in the dark, promising to come for her. Telling her he loved her. She'd been so angry when they'd parted. So foolish and prideful. She should have trusted him with her secrets. He was a good man, one who might have helped her free the others. Now it was too late.

His phantom visits to her chamber became a torture, for each time he appeared and she tried to explain, he did not seem to hear her. Still, she would call to him, trying to make him understand. To give him the only gift she could. Her name. "Silvia," she would whisper. Then he would fade to nothingness, and she would be alone.

And so one day, when she heard his dear voice yet again, and felt the strong comfort of muscled masculine arms surround her, she didn't believe it was really he. And it wasn't.

"Bastian?" she croaked, her voice a barely discernable sound.

"No, I'm Sevin," came the terse reply, and she saw that it was indeed Bastian's brother who held her. His handsome face gazed at her with a mix of pity and anger. Turning his head, he shouted over his shoulder to someone across the room. "She's here! Safe."

Silvia turned her head to follow his shout but, unaccustomed to light, she was blinded at first and recoiled. Sevin held her close for a moment, his big hands running over her in search of broken bones or other wounds, no doubt, as he whispered soothing words to her. Beyond him, she heard the clank of swords and knives. A battle was in progress. Squinting, she managed to view the scene unfolding in Pontifex's throne room. Bastian, Dane, and Lucien were laying siege to Occia and almost two dozen of her guards.

Bastian. Silvia mouthed his name, but this time no sound

came forth. Yet, as if he'd heard, his silver eyes caught hers briefly. At the same moment, Occia's blade sliced toward him, wounding him. Silvia gasped. "Occia, no!" she croaked, and in her terror, she managed to make her voice carry. At the sound of her name, Occia darted a look toward the Wall of Doors. Taking advantage of her distraction, Bastian swung a powerful arm at her. Taken by surprise, she was flung backward and then screamed as she fell into the poisonous acidic waters of the moat. When she was gone, her soldiers desisted in their fighting and ran.

In a half-dozen long strides, Bastian was beside Silvia, taking her from Sevin's arms and lifting her in his own. "I've got her. Open the other doors and see what you find," he told his brother. Sevin nodded and left them.

"Gods!" Bastian gazed down at her, and she saw tears on his face. He folded her close, clutching her to him as if he would never let her go. She felt the rumble of his words in his chest. "I'm here now, my love. You're safe. I'm here."

Over his shoulder, she saw his brothers working at the other nine doors to pull the other Ephemerals from the Wall. Floronia was released first. Then Lucinia. They looked dazed—silent, pale zombies after having been caged for hundreds of years. And then, "Aemilia," she breathed. Struggling from Bastian's arms, she went to the others, unsteady on her feet. Dear friends who'd been apart for centuries hugged and wept. Aemilia smiled her sweet smile, and as they embraced, she whispered, "I knew you would come for us." Her eyes darted to Bastian and his brothers. "But I didn't know you would bring such handsome gentlemen with you."

Silvia laughed and then put a hand to her forehead, feeling suddenly dizzy. Bastian was there instantly and he lifted her again, his jaw grim as he carried her from the room. "Thank you," she murmured. "Thank you for freeing them."

She must have fallen unconscious, for her next lucid moment found her lying upon fresh sheets in an unfamiliar bed, still in Pontifex's lair. She'd been bathed and dressed in a soft gown, and her wild, tangled hair had been tamed with a comb. Under her ear, she heard Bastian's heartbeat, strong and reassuring. His hand smoothed desultorily up and down her side, as if he needed the contact with her.

Urgency welled in her and she pulled herself higher to gaze down at his dear face. His eyes flew open and his arms encircled her. He looked so tired, his jaw shadowed by the soft blue-black beginnings of a beard. "My name," she whispered, her voice barely audible. His entire body went still, his expression riveted. "It's Silvia."

And so it was that she was made mortal, and willingly left her Ephemeral life behind, so that she could have a life with this wonderful man. Her rescuer. Her beloved. Bastian.

"Silvia," he said, tasting the word. "It's beautiful," he breathed, pleasure stealing over his face. "You're beautiful. And mine. At last." He laughed and rolled her under him, kissing her long and deeply, and only then did she discover he was naked. And hard. "Gods, I love you. And I was so damned worried. I saw you in my nightmares every night, trapped here."

"I'm sorry," she soothed, stroking his beard and enjoying its texture. "How did you find me?"

"You mentioned Pontifex when last we met, and once I came through the Tuscan gate, this place wasn't difficult to locate. But as to how I knew where you were specifically—your door in that wall was the only one that appeared to me in color."

She canted her head, her look questioning.

He took her face in his hands and then combed his fingers through her hair, appearing mesmerized by its color and texture. "I told you I was imperfect and I am—I'm color-blind. Or I was, until you. No matter what form you take, I see you in color. It's the way I've been tracking you, for it leaves a residual trail in your wake. The hue deepens when I touch you. And it always has the effect of making me want you, physically."

"Do you want me now?" she whispered, a smile curving her lips.

He muttered a self-deprecating laugh, knowing she must feel his hard length at her belly. "Do you have to ask?"

"Then come inside me," she pleaded softly.

At his concerned look, she said, "I'm fine, and I need to feel physically close to you. It's been too long." He lifted the hem of the gown he'd procured for her to her belly and lifted her thighs around him. She gasped and arched as he pushed inside her without preliminaries. Gently, he rocked her, and lovers kept too long apart came together swiftly, their bodies reaching fulfillment in sweet harmony, their arms wrapped around one another.

His cock was still pulsing inside her, when he rose on his elbows over her. "Remember the auction?" he asked.

"Hmm?" Her eyes slitted open.

"In Venice." He toyed with a lock of her hair, brushing it over her nipple. "You owe me the answer to one last question."

She arched a brow. "Now?"

He shifted his hips, pushing deeper, and another pulse of warm seed flooded her, bringing on a strong echo of her orgasm.

Mmmm. Her eyes drifted closed and her body went boneless.

"Marry me."

She opened one eye. "Was that a question?"

His face went serious, his voice stern. "Will. You. Marry. Me?" His hips continued the lazy, rhythmic thrust, and a gentle quake of pleasure rippled inside her with his every word, with each push.

"If you're—"

"I'm sure," he told her. "My dear." A kiss on her brow. "Delectable." Another on her scarred cheek. "Silvia." And another on her mouth.

She looped her arms around his neck and spoke against his lips. "Yes, then."

"Via?" She looked beyond Bastian to see Aemilia in the doorway, watching them as she herself had once watched him with Michaela. How long had she been there?

Bastian eased his body from hers. "Privacy is at a minimum here," he said. "We return to Rome tomorrow and we'll wed the following day."

At her nod, he bestowed a parting buss on her lips and then rose from the bed, with one of its sheets wrapped low at his hips. Wide-eyed and half-besotted, Aemilia watched him saunter past. Silvia knew just how she felt.

When he was gone, the two of them joined the other Vestals for the lighting ceremony. Each time Silvia had visited the hearth here after the temple's destruction, it had only managed to produce a frail flame. Now she waited breathlessly as each Vestal placed a stone in the hearth. There were nine in all, for Michaela and Occia were dead and Silvia had made herself mortal, and therefore unable to conjure fire. But it was enough. Vesta's fire leaped to vibrant life for the first time in fifteen centuries. And it was a beautiful sight to behold.

Basking in its ethereal glow, Silvia looked on as three new initiates from among the Lares were inducted to replace the three who had been lost from the order. But unlike herself and the others, these new girls had *chosen* to serve, for no longer would Vesta's servants be brought to her by force. There would be no more scourgings, no premature burials. The Vestals would govern themselves now. But Silvia could no longer serve even if she'd wished to. For she was mortal now and wanted to be with him whom she loved.

She left the next day, promising to return often, for she still had ties to the goddess and always would. And then she traveled with Bastian and his brothers through the gate to Tuscany, and then homeward to Rome.

"Something's different," said Silvia as their coach neared the outskirts of Rome. In the eyes of every human they passed, she saw curiosity, mistrust, even fear.

Two knocks came from the front of the conveyance. Lucien and Dane were driving and were signaling a warning to them. Bastian's hand came to rest on her thigh and she felt the tension in him. Across the coach, Sevin's worry was easily read as well.

"They know what we are," Bastian gritted. "ElseWorld's existence has been discovered."

Just ahead, a dozen human men had backed a centaur into the corner of a courtyard and were trying to throw a harness over his neck. Silvia eyed the scene in horror. Farther along, several boys were chasing a fey girl and shouting insults at her.

Sevin made as if to leave the coach and render assistance, but Bastian caught his arm. "It's too dangerous. Stay inside."

"We can't just leave them to the mercy of these barbaric humans!" Sevin argued.

Bastian yanked the small window curtains closed. "Will you fight them all single-handedly? No, the best way to handle this is to bring our two worlds to the bargaining table."

"It's because of the firestones, isn't it?" asked Silvia. "Because they're gone from Rome." She hadn't taken them to ElseWorld herself—Occia had. Still, she could not help but feel somewhat responsible for their loss and its catastrophic effect.

"Do you mean to say that it was those opals that protected us all this time?" asked Sevin. "As you once told me the philosophers' texts suggested?"

"It brings me no pleasure to be right, I assure you," Bastian replied. "But I believe that when the first six stones left this world over the centuries, the magic that protected us began to fail. And when the last six left several weeks ago, it failed entirely."

"Can't you bespell all these humans? Cloud their perception? Make them forget?" Silvia asked desperately, as they passed a pixie being evicted from his home, his belongings tossed into the muddy street.

"Bespell all of Rome? All of Italy? All of Europe? All of humankind?" Bastian shook his head. "Impossible. Now that the secret is out, it cannot be bottled again."

"Then let us hope sunlight will prove to be the best antiseptic as you once posited, brother," said Sevin. "And let us work toward a better future."

Bastian nodded, his face grim. "We'll work toward harmony. But one way or another, it's a new day for our kind here in this world."

20

One month later

"Is that a new urn?"

Bastian looked up from his desk to see Silvia entering his canvas work tent where they'd first met in the Forum. By sheer force of his will, he'd managed to retain his position here as lead archaeologist, in spite of the new human suspicion toward his kind.

Since the veil of protection had fallen after the removal of Vesta's relics, he and his brothers had been at the forefront of Interworld negotiations. Between the ElseWorld Council, human politicians, and Sevin's new business enterprise, Bastian had found little time for the excavations. Or for his new wife. And he'd missed her.

As she bent to examine his newest find, his appreciative eyes moved over the line of her slim back and hips. Quickly, he tossed out a bespelling of the tent's perimeter that would repel even the most cunning of intruders.

"Come here, wife," he said. When her attention was slow to

leave the urn, he added, "I have chocolate." He rattled the confectioner's box he'd purchased for her earlier that day.

She looked at him over her shoulder, smiling that sweet half-smile of hers. Because of her, the color in his life was constant now and had spread to every corner of his world. He no longer needed the constant touch of his beloved to maintain it, though if they were apart for an entire day, the color began to deplete. Its effect on his libido was a low hum when she wasn't near. But when she entered his orbit, it rose to the same flashfire of need it had once been. As it did now.

The continued frequency of their matings remained a constant source of teasing by his brothers, but this was a small misery and he bore it well.

"I've always liked this desk," she said, smoothing a hand over its glossy surface. "It's so big." She kicked off her slippers and came around to his side of it, insinuating herself between him and his work. He pushed books, maps, and papers away, stacking them neatly, so that she might perch on its surface before him. Then he drew his chair closer so her feet were tucked on either side of his thighs.

"You shouldn't travel alone," Bastian chided, his hands finding her stockinged ankles under her skirt and roving higher. "It's not safe. Not yet."

"It's less than a mile from here to the house. Besides, humans think you and your brothers to be quite fierce and are afraid of bothering me since I'm under your protection." She leaned forward and cupped his face in her hands. "And I missed you."

"I'm covered with Forum dust," he said in an apologetic tone. But he was already pushing up her skirts and rising to stand in the lee of her thighs.

She only drew him closer. "You know I don't mind."

"Open your bodice and take down your hair," he bade her as he unfastened his trousers. Her hands moved to obey him, her clear blue eyes gazing up at him through the fans of her dark lashes. He would never tire of the sight of her full pink-tipped breasts peeking from the soft coppery gold waves of her shiny unbound hair. And when her bodice was open and her hair down, he rubbed his cockhead along her slit and opened her. "Did I remember to tell you how glad I am that you are female?" A laugh escaped her and then faded into a moan as he thrust his heat hard and long into her slick feminine welcome.

A half hour later, she lay flat on her back amid a jumble of maps and the like atop the desk's surface, her legs wrapped around his hips and her heart still pounding in the aftermath of his lovemaking. He stood before her still, but now his torso half lay over hers and his cock was buried so deep inside her that it kissed her womb. Her arms were bent high on either side of her, her eyes closed, and her bodice had been tossed to the floor at some point.

"I think you deserve a reward for that effort," he told her. Without leaving her, she felt him shift. Heard the rustle of tissue. And then came the captivating aroma of chocolate. She parted her lips and felt him place a bonbon between them. She took it into her mouth and sighed with delight.

Her arms encircled his back, her hands smoothing over his strong muscles. "Mmm. New artifacts, rapture, and now chocolate. My day is complete." She opened her eyes and smiled at him, then said softly, "Take me home, husband."

Moments later, they were walking across the Forum together, his strong arm wrapped protectively around her, his woman. Night was falling and the Forum sparkled with bobbing lights that swayed in the gentle breeze.

At the edge of the valley, they would hail a coach and head for Esquiline and his home. Their home now, though his new wife had made few changes in it, professing to enjoy its fastidious, museum-like quality. Inside the house there would be a dog named Sal to curl at his feet. There would be a warm fire burning in the hearth. And another fire in his bed as they made love again, later.

In the time since he'd met her, he had located the House of Vestals and the Temple. And within their bounds, he'd found fifteen marble tablets, eleven life-sized statues and nine more fragments, twenty-seven busts, 835 coins, jewelry, columns of breccia that ranked among the finest specimens of marble ever uncovered, as well as numerous other artifacts, which in themselves would be regarded as great treasures in a less productive dig.

But the greatest treasure he'd found in the Forum was this woman at his side. The love of his heart, his life.

And her name was Silvia.

AUTHOR'S NOTE

The House and Temple of Vesta in the Roman Forum was excavated in 1883. For the purposes of this novel, the date of discovery has been moved to 1881 and the character of Lord Bastian Satyr is credited as the archaeologist in charge of the dig.

Roman philosophers inform us that the Vestal Virgins numbered six in all. They came to the temple as girls between the ages of six and ten, to serve Vesta for thirty years, after which they could marry. (There were no Vestal Companions.)

The Vestals' first ten years were devoted to learning, the next ten with service to the goddess, and their final decade with indoctrinating new initiates to replace them. They lived lives of confinement and privilege, and were greatly revered.

However, in times of famine or defeat in war, they were sometimes used as scapegoats. Any transgression on the part of a Vestal was harshly punished. If the fire went out on her watch, Pontifex might strip her naked and flog her in a private chamber for this sin.

It was believed that the Virgins' chastity insured the good

health of all of Rome. Among the Vestals, the penalty for fornication was death. Amid great sorrowful pomp and ceremony by ancient Roman religious leaders and citizens, a convicted Virgin would be taken on a litter to a small underground room hollowed out for her in the Campus Sceleratus—the "Evil Field"—near the Colline Gate. There, she was essentially buried alive—left to die in solitude with only enough food, water, and lamp oil to last a few days.

The Virgins were specifically charged with another matter of utmost importance. They had under their jurisdiction the care and protection of a collection of mysterious relics, which were also believed to protect Rome. When Vesta's temple was destroyed during the purging of all pagan religions in the fourth century A.D., these relics disappeared. No one knows exactly what they were. They have never been found.